CASTLE EVER DARK

THE EVERLIGHT SERIES

BOOK TWO

SARA KNIGHTLY

PORTAL
PUBLISHING

Portal Publishing, LLC. Boise, ID.

Cover design Krafig Designs

Paperback ISBN: 979-8-9894891-4-5

Library of Congress Control Number: 2024906744

To learn more about the author please visit saraknightlybooks.com and join the newsletter.

*For London—
my forever sweetheart*

ONE

The carriage rolled down the dirt path, stopping by the Count's marble gates.

Jack left his seat next to mine and jumped down to push the heavy gates open. I took a moment to examine him, unobserved. Broad shoulders, blue eyes, and tousled black hair. A stranger who had shown up moments ago and was taking me from Windermere, the only home I'd ever known. My eyes moved to the two sea serpents that stood sentinel on either side of the gate. Their writhing bodies and claws stretched out, ready to maul anyone who passed beneath them and dared to enter the Count's land.

Instead of fear, a lump formed in my throat. The first time I'd seen these serpents, I'd been with York. Now I was going into the castle without him. I felt more alone than ever.

Jack and I had left Windermere without seeing a soul. I'd whispered goodbye to the empty town, wondering if this was really the last time I would see it. Next to me was my bag, containing my father's final journal, the wooden cube, and my mother's owl: the objects that had started me down this road; the clues that had opened my eyes to the strange things happening just outside of my small town.

I shivered and pulled my jacket around me. At my feet was my late father's leather satchel, packed by Mrs. Taylor—the woman who had taken me in when I'd had no one, and who I would never see again. When I'd seen it inside the carriage, I'd known it was the only goodbye I'd get. No one was coming to save me.

Everyone in Windermere would be told I had a new life across the sea and that I was happy to go. They would never know I was just down the road inside the Count's castle.

I took a deep breath, reminding myself that not everything was lost. Somehow, York had won the Count's Woodworking Tournament. My best friend had succeeded in getting away from his angry father and would open his own Carving shop. York's future was secure in Windermere. *I* was the one with no reason left to stay.

I had ruined my chance at my trade, lost my childhood home, and been disqualified from the Count's Woodworking Tournament.

Again, I puzzled over why they wanted me at the castle. Was it really to be a scientist's assistant, as Jack had told me? No one at the castle knew about the items in my bag, or that I had a burgeoning ability to perceive light differently than the average person—I didn't think.

But I did know that my father's clues had led me to this gate, and I had to uncover why.

I had to know why I saw light around certain people from the castle, what that light meant, and how York had transformed his wood to gold in the Tournament.

And I needed to pass between these sea serpents to get my answers.

The carriage shook as Jack climbed back in and whistled at the horses to continue. I held my breath, and we crossed the threshold into the Count's land.

The property was nothing like I'd imagined. Inside the gates, nothing stirred. The woods felt hollow, not bursting with life like the forests around Windermere. It was eerily still. I looked around, seeing nothing but thin trees and silver dew drops clinging to blades of grass. Mist seeped through the trees like cold fingers. I shivered again.

We followed the path as it wound through the forest. The only sound was the wheels rolling over packed dirt. Jack hadn't spoken much during our journey here, but the silence was not uncomfortable. I guessed he was giving me space to be upset, or to prepare myself for what was ahead of me.

But I didn't know how to prepare for any of this. All my life I had been told to stay away from the Count's castle, that the Count was a recluse and had no interest in our town beyond the Carving trade. But now I knew that wasn't true. Things were happening out here.

Somewhere high above, a raven shrieked. I jumped, the hair on my neck rising.

"Alright?" Jack asked. I could feel that he wanted to laugh, but didn't.

"It's colder here," I remarked, ignoring the part of me that wanted to tell him to turn back. The part that was sure I'd made a big mistake coming here. But I had no choice. I had nowhere else to go. Mr. Mallon, the Count's Regent, would never let me set foot in town again.

"I should warn you, the castle is always cold," Jack remarked.

My stomach sank as glimpses of stone grew more frequent through the trees. As we followed the path out of the tree line, the castle loomed in front of us.

It was enormous. Formidable. I felt like an ant, squinting up to the highest points that stretched into the grey sky. It was an ancient fortress made of stone towers, aged balconies, and countless windows. I wondered which window was the Count's.

Chills rolled through me as we passed through the vast, unkept lawn. The path split around a large stone fountain that reminded me of the fountain in Windermere's town square, except this one was dried up and cracked. Two stone knights on horses guarded the entrance by the door, but it looked as though their arms sagged under the weight of their swords.

Just as I wondered if the castle was actually abandoned and everyone I'd seen going into it that fated day with York had all been in my head, a person stepped out of the tall wooden door.

It was a girl dressed in dark clothes similar to Jack's. Her black hair was woven tightly into a braid that laid over one shoulder. She watched us approach, but her thin lips never lifted in greeting. The solemn expression on her small, round face did not waver. She almost looked like a child. However, when we stopped before the door and her grey eyes found mine, I took that thought back immediately. I looked away from the emptiness I saw on her face; it was too unsettling.

Jack turned to me, his warm blue eyes a welcome relief from this girl's cold grey ones. "I'm afraid this is where we part. You need to get settled, and I need to take the horses to the stable."

The mention of the stables was like a knife to my heart. I already missed my own horse, Loon, and wished she was with us right now. But Jack had promised he would see about bringing her.

Even though I'd just met him, I felt reluctant to leave his side. "You're not coming inside too?" I asked.

His lips lifted. "Not just yet."

I stood, not wanting to seem afraid to go inside without him. Jack held my arm steady as I climbed down from the carriage. As soon as my feet touched the ground, uncertainty overwhelmed me. I looked up at him, panicking. Jack handed down my bags and smiled as if he sensed how I felt.

"Chin up, Ivy. I'll see you around."

The carriage moved forward, drowning out my attempt at a parting reply. As it pulled away, the strange, silent girl and I stared at each other. I shifted uneasily, wishing I could look anywhere but her.

"Name?" The flatness of her tone matched her blank expression.

"Ivy Rune."

I searched her face for any indication that she recognized my name, or my father's, but her face remained stoic.

I swallowed. "I've come to work for Dr. Ply."

The girl nodded and turned back to the ancient wooden door. Only now I could see it was carved with strange symbols and patterns.

"Follow me." She disappeared inside without waiting for a response.

I grabbed my bags and hurried after her into the dark, narrow passage. We continued silently until the hallway opened into a stone courtyard with more dead grass. Every muscle in my body was tense and wary. I tried to brush the unease away, but it clung to me. I wanted to turn around.

"What's your name?" I asked.

"Anna."

"And what do you do here, Anna?"

She didn't respond.

We walked deeper and deeper into the castle, my apprehension and confusion growing with each step. The castle was bigger than it looked, but it felt like a ruin. The air was stiff and heavy. Even though we were the only ones walking through the hallways, I couldn't shake the feeling that we weren't alone.

In an unbelievable turn of events, I'd just learned my father had walked under these stone archways himself. Why had he worked here? What had his role been?

What was *mine*?

It had to be different from whatever his had been, that much I was sure of, because my father had been allowed to live in town, and I was not. I felt another wave of longing for Windermere and York.

As we entered a second silent courtyard, I finally saw another person, but my skin prickled at the wrongness of her.

A woman stood looking out of an arched window at a view hidden by fog.

There was an elegance to her, like she had once been magnificent, but had fallen into ruin like the stone around her. A crumbled velvet shawl hung from her thin shoulders, and the hem of her faded black dress was covered with dust.

She slowly turned in place to watch us pass. Her eyes and lips were lined with years and her hair was high on her head, encased in a black net.

My heart thudded as we passed by, but she did not smile or acknowledge us at all. I avoided her eyes, but not before I noticed one was blue. The other, violet.

I let out a breath when we turned the corner. I didn't have the courage to turn around and see if she was still watching. I wasn't even sure if she was real or a ghost, because Anna didn't slow or acknowledge the woman.

I couldn't stand the silence pressing in on me any longer.

"How long have you lived here, Anna?"

Anna stopped and turned to face me. "That's personal."

I stepped back, surprised. "It is? It's a common question to ask someone you've just met."

Her grey eyes studied me. Then she shrugged. "I'm not accustomed to conversation anymore. I've been here longer than I can remember not being here."

"What do you do?"

Anna sighed. "I was in training, but that ended. Now I'm on task."

"What does 'on task' mean?"

Anna turned on her heel. "Come. Dr. Ply doesn't appreciate being kept waiting."

My stomach dipped. Dr. Ply, the man my father had secretly worked for, and who I would now work for. We continued on and finally arrived at two doors covered in the same strange carvings and symbols as the front door.

"This wing is called the Center. The first floor is offices, where you will work. The second is living quarters, where you will stay.

You are not allowed anywhere else in the castle without permission or an escort."

"Is the castle always this empty?" Where were the people I'd seen with York that day we'd trespassed into the Count's woods? Where were the ones we saw arriving on that damaged ship on the beach—the short man who'd pulled the wreck to shore with impossible strength; the massive man built thick as a tree trunk? Where were Cora and Carl? Anyone would be a welcome addition to Anna's indifference.

She didn't respond.

I tried again. "That woman we passed…does she work here too?"

"Stop with all the questions!" Anna snapped, revealing her frustration before she concealed it. "They will not make you a single friend here."

I bit down a response and followed her quietly, feeling the somberness in the air press into me again. After another flight of stairs, Anna stopped at a door and opened it, gesturing me inside.

"This is your room."

I walked inside, and my stomach dropped.

There were two rows of ten beds, each with a small dresser beside them. The only light came from two small windows on the far back wall, but their thick glass was covered with dust. The old wooden floors and bare walls made the room feel abandoned and cold. A crumbling fireplace sat in the center of the room, but there was no fire. A stack of chopped logs was piled beside it.

"Who else stays in here?" I asked, taking in the long room.

"Just you. Take your pick of the beds," Anna said as if that somehow made this situation better.

I walked to the bed closest to the fireplace and sat down, cringing at the thin and lumpy mattress. The blanket and pillow were even thinner. I stood back up on instinct as if I could leave, but I couldn't. I was really going to have to stay here. *Sleep* here. I didn't know if I could. First, Anna; then the ghost woman; and now this dead, cold room.

I couldn't live like this.

Panic built, making my shoulders tense. I took a deep breath. I couldn't lose it in front of this strange, emotionless girl.

"Before you meet Dr. Ply, he would like you to familiarize yourself with some of his research." Anna pointed to a large stack of papers sitting on a dresser.

The pile was nearly the size of my hand. "You want me to read *all* of that?"

"Dr. Ply thought an hour would suffice."

Without another word, she left the room, leaving me all alone.

Two

I took a deep breath and picked up a folder from the stack.

The pages were filled with long, scientific words, and to my embarrassment, I couldn't tell if it was about plants or something else. I'd never heard most of these words. This had to be a mistake. I wasn't smart enough for this. I hadn't even been smart enough to be an Arborist.

I shut the folder and put it back on the table. Then I sank onto the hard bed and opened my bag, grabbing my father's journal. I needed to see his handwriting. Maybe he'd written about the castle and I'd somehow missed it. How could he have never mentioned his time here to me, or included the castle in the clues he'd left behind for me to find? If he'd wanted me to come here, why hadn't he trusted me with more information, so I'd know what I was doing?

I flipped through pages and pages, searching for anything that would make sense of this situation I was stuck in. I was here because of him, and he owed me answers.

Hedera is almost impossible to kill as it stays green even when kept in the dark.

Hedera can severely damage mortared stone, as the rootlets seek out cracks and use them to penetrate the interiors of buildings —

I shut the book, so frustrated and angry I almost threw it across the room. Why had my father been so obsessed with plants? No one cared! Especially not me.

I was the one in the dark here, not the dumb plant he'd inexplicably fixated on when he was still alive.

I pulled the bigger bag Mrs. Taylor packed for me up on the bed and opened it. To my relief, she'd included three old books bound together with twine; my father's other journals. I knew they were empty, except for one thing: Pressed flat between the pages was a wilted flower.

A white orchid.

My father had been able to move between Botanical and Arboricultural specimens with ease, but his passion was studying white orchids. They didn't grow naturally around Windermere, so every year he bought seeds from merchants during the Count's Woodworking Tournament. I still remembered these growing in pots all around his office and could recall their earthy, vanilla scent.

I put the flower back in the book and set it aside. Next, I pulled out a brown paper sack and opened it. Inside were the dozen orchid seeds I'd saved from my father's study. I'd planned to plant them around Forest and Fern when I became an Arborist, but now I would never be able to. These flowers were too delicate for someone like me, anyway. I would have killed them. I put the sack back in the bag.

There was one last item: a black velvet bag. Inside it, I knew, was my jewelry box, carved by Mr. Gable. It was so delicate, I couldn't believe Mrs. Taylor had stuffed it in this bag. Then I understood why she had.

She knew I was never coming back.

I would never visit Gable's Emporium again. Never walk Windermere's streets or eat at Wilder's Bakery again. Or see York's new Carving shop.

I stood, needing to move before I completely broke down.

I walked down the long row of beds, focusing on my

breathing and pretending I was walking through the lavender field again. But as I looked at each bed, I knew I was far from the Taylors' farm.

Each bed had a film of dust over its blankets and pillows, as if this room had long been locked up before I'd come. They hadn't even cleaned it. It was so quiet I could hear the creaks and groans in the walls, the wind whistling through its cracks. I shivered, wishing the fire was lit.

At the very end of the room was a door. I nervously pushed it open and discovered a short hallway that led to a bare and cold bathroom. Another door revealed a small closet with only one shelf, also covered in dust.

I needed to keep busy, so I grabbed a towel from the bathroom and began to wipe the shelf and closet clean so I could put my things away.

As I reached up to adjust the shelf, the whole board came loose and crashed to the ground, landing on my toes and banging against my legs. I cried out in pain and kicked the fallen board angrily.

Over and over.

Everything was all wrong.

I kicked the board violently one last time and it ricocheted against the back wall of the closet. The whole wall shuddered. I stopped. Something wasn't quite right. Hesitantly, I reached out to feel the wall, gently pushing against it. It felt almost hollow and flimsy. Around the edge was a gap. I reached my fingers inside and discovered a vast empty space. One small push and the wall suddenly swung outward. Dust swirled in the air. Coughing, I stared, shocked, into a long, dark tunnel with walls of stone.

The tunnel's ceiling was just a bit taller than I was and the stone here looked older than the rest I'd seen in the castle. I could see one unlit, rusted torch on the wall, and the shadows of others stretching away.

My heart raced. Who else knew this was here? I imagined the ghost woman with two different colored eyes creeping into my room. Terrified, I pulled the wall back in place, put the shelf up, and slammed the closet door. I whirled around, looking for anything I could use to block it.

A knock on the front door nearly made me jump out of my skin.

I hurried back into the main room, brushing the dust off my clothes. I desperately hoped it wasn't Anna, as the papers she'd told me to read still sat on the table. I hastily shoved the journals, seeds, and jewelry box back into my bag.

"Come in."

A lanky young man with green eyes and hair the color of straw opened the door. He looked around the room; when he spotted me, a shy smile lifted his lips.

"I brought you lunch." He spoke in a soft accent as he pulled a cart in after him. It rattled as he made his way over to where I stood. "I'm Vernon." His voice was so quiet that I found myself leaning in closer to hear him.

"Hello. I'm Ivy Rune."

Vernon shook my hand, gently. "It's nice to meet you, Ivy. This is for you." He spoke slowly as he removed the towel from the plate. A roll of bread, some meat, and cheese sat next to a pot of coffee.

"Oh, thank you!" I said gratefully. My mouth was already watering. I hadn't eaten since before the competition yesterday.

Vernon smiled and nodded for me to start.

I sat down at the small table and began to make a sandwich as he went over to arrange the logs in the fireplace. His movements were slow and unhurried as if he had all the time in the world. I instantly felt at ease with him. Maybe it was the food and the thought of a fire to warm me, but I felt less desperate than I had just ten minutes ago.

"Anna and Dr. Ply are now occupied. It will be a while before they come back for you."

I nodded, even more relieved. "Where do you work, Vernon?"

"The kitchen."

"How many people work there?"

"Enough to cook."

That told me nothing, but maybe Vernon was as unused to conversation as Anna. He was certainly nicer, though, so I didn't feel uneasy asking him more questions. "Where are you from?"

"Stygian. Most of us here come from Stygian."

"Stygian? I've never heard of it." I had never heard any merchants mention it either. "Do you trade with Windermere?"

A look crossed Vernon's face as he shook his head. "We are banned from all trade with Windermere, except for trade involving the Count. And even he never comes to Stygian; he just requests our ships."

"Why?"

"Others do not care for us after they hear stories about our culture."

Goosebumps dotted my arms. "What kind of stories?"

He paused. "Our island is steeped in legend and myth. Some Stygians are Dyadics, some are not. Life is not as complicated there as it is here."

"What? I'm sorry, what does Dyadic mean?"

Vernon shrugged. "In Stygian, it is as normal to have an extra ability as it is not to."

I perked up. An extra ability? "What kind of extra abilities?"

Maybe I sounded too eager because Vernon didn't answer me as quickly as he had before. He focused on the fire a moment before he finally said, "Anything. It is usually as unique as the person. No two Dyadics are ever the same."

I stared at him, thoughts and questions swirling in my head. But I noticed his expression was growing similar to Anna's when I'd asked her too much.

I had to risk one more.

"You said it's not as complicated as here . . . are you saying there are people in the castle who have extra abilities?"

Vernon stood. For a minute, I worried he would hurry away

before he lit the fire. He looked down at the iron poker in his hands.

"Perhaps I have said too much. You will learn soon that conversations here are unwelcome, and they can be dangerous."

"What's Stygian like, then?" I asked, smiling warmly. "That's not too dangerous to tell me, is it?"

He looked up and seemed surprised by my smile. Slowly, he smiled back, as if it had been a long time since he had done so. Then he turned to light the fire. I waited, trying not to press. Eventually, I was rewarded.

"Stygian is misty in the morning, but warm in the afternoon. There are rainbows that color the fog over the waterfalls and rivers." Vernon's voice turned soft, almost dreamy. "We also have mountains and green valleys, but our towns are very different than Windermere."

I leaned in. "How so?"

"They were made by Dyadic people," Vernon said simply as if it should be obvious.

I sighed. "I'd love to see it someday. Where is Stygian?"

Something passed over Vernon's face, and the openness faded. He started gathering things up into the cart. "Across the sea. It is quite a journey. That is why most only make it once."

"Can I ask just one more question?" I flashed a bright smile.

Vernon inclined his head.

"What kind of things can these Dyadic people do? Can they like, see things?"

"Anything is possible."

I wanted to know if Vernon had an extra ability, but I didn't want to push him away. "How long have you been here?" I asked instead.

"Nearly twelve years."

"But . . . you're so young!"

"There is no age restriction to live at the castle. People have come as young as five years old."

"Why would they want to?"

"Non-Dyadic Stygians are often poor. The only way off our land is to work at the castle. It is as good of a life as any."

"Is that why you came?" I asked, hoping it wasn't rude.

He smiled softly. "Yes. There is nothing special about me."

I smiled back, finding him very easy to like. "That's not true. There's something special about everyone."

Vernon looked surprised, then he ducked his head as if embarrassed. "I will come every night with your tray. I also keep the fire going and the wood filled. This block is for the end of your bed tonight." He pointed to a square rock by the fire. "Wrap it in a blanket and place it right up to your feet and you will stay warm if the fire goes out. Nights here are cold."

"Thank you," I said gratefully.

"If you have not found the bathroom yet, it is there." Vernon pointed to the bathroom door. "And I think that is all of it. It was nice to meet you, Ivy."

He slowly rolled the cart out and shut the door.

I was left alone in the room again, but I no longer felt such despair. Now that I knew I would see at least one friendly face a day, I felt better.

As I slowly finished my food, I thought of Stygian and wondered what those people were like; the Dyadics.

I tried to read through at least one file.

Time passed as I forced myself to read—and keep on reading, but nothing made sense. I picked at my lip, worried about what would happen when Dr. Ply discovered that I couldn't understand his material.

Just when I thought I couldn't read another page, there was a knock on the door and Anna stepped into the room.

"Dr. Ply is ready to meet you now."

THREE

Anna led me down another hallway of doors and dusty arched windows.

Thick wooden beams crisscrossed overhead, threaded with hundreds of silvery spider webs. Shuddering, I ran a hand over my hair and clothes as we walked. Anna looked as if she didn't even notice them.

Finally, we stopped at a door with a round window and thin iron bars. A gold nameplate read: *DR. PLY.* Anna knocked once, then pushed the door open, gesturing that I should go in first.

I stepped nervously into a medium-sized room. Overhead was a large wooden chandelier covered with globs of hardened wax and dust. Taking up most of the room was a desk covered with papers, scales, quill pens, and other instruments. The rest of the walls were lined with shelves sagging under the weight of leather books, glass decanters, ink bottles, and other strange objects. A large window overlooked a surprisingly well-kept back lawn.

The man at the desk looked up, his brows lifting when he saw me. He rose to his feet.

He was tall, with a round stomach that protruded from a white coat. His hair reminded me of sawdust, and his light blue eyes were hidden behind round silver glasses.

"Ah. You must be Ivy Rune. A pleasure to meet you." His lips pulled back to reveal wide teeth, which his lips never fully covered, even when he wasn't speaking. "I'm Dr. Ply."

He extended his hand as the sides of his blonde mustache lifted slightly.

I stepped forward to shake his hand. It felt fleshy and I kept myself from cringing away. "Nice to meet you."

So *this* was the man my father had worked for. I'd thought he'd be more intimidating, like Mr. Mallon, but he seemed almost bland, like a meal lacking salt.

"And of course you've already met Jack." Dr. Ply gestured to a pair of leather chairs facing his desk, where Jack sat with a leg casually crossed over the other.

Relief flooded through me immediately at the sight of someone familiar.

Jack untangled himself and stood. "Hello again," he said, stretching his hand toward me.

I met his blue eyes and smiled. "Hello, Jack."

Compared to Dr. Ply's, Jack's hand was warm and smooth, with small callouses on parts of his palm. He squeezed my hand just once, but his expression was more guarded than it had been earlier. I glanced back at Dr. Ply, wondering if his presence was the reason Jack was more reserved. We dropped hands and I pressed my palms together, trying to hold onto the warmth.

"Jack, we'll meet again later after I speak with Ivy," Dr. Ply said, dismissing him.

"Very well." Jack smiled easily. "Good luck settling in, Ivy. I'm sure we'll be seeing a lot more of each other in the future."

I nodded, wishing he would stay. I felt less nervous with him around. Maybe it was the ease with which he moved through tense situations. It made me think nothing bad could happen around him.

Dr. Ply looked over my head towards the door. "You're excused too, Anna."

I glanced back just in time to see Anna eye Jack with distaste before she swept out of the room. Jack followed and the door clicked shut behind them.

I turned back, feeling uneasy at being left alone with Dr. Ply. "Please, sit."

He settled back into his chair and folded his hands over his round middle. "We have a lot to get through and much less time than I anticipated. When important matters come up, I must handle them; you understand. The nature of my work is very delicate, as you'll discover shortly."

I nodded, sitting in the chair Jack had just occupied. It was still warm.

"So, you now know that your father also worked for me. For many years."

I leaned forward at the mention of my father. He had my entire attention now.

"He was a fine man. One of the smartest minds I ever had the pleasure of knowing."

I cleared my throat. "Thank you. Do you know anything about what happened to him?"

Dr. Ply frowned and averted his gaze to the window. At that moment, I was certain he *did* know something. I studied his face, but his expression relaxed to reveal nothing. After a long moment, he looked back at me, and when he spoke again, his voice had an edge to it.

"I'm sorry. I can't enlighten you any further on that matter. Your father's death was no doubt unsettling and traumatic. I myself know the pain of losing a parent . . . the loss will haunt you your entire life—*if* you let it."

I blinked, unsure what he meant by that.

"It's time for you to leave the past in the past. The only way forward is to focus on the present. Besides, people rarely like what they find when they go searching for the truth."

I pressed back in the chair, stunned. Surely he didn't mean that to sound like a threat?

Dr. Ply sucked his teeth before asking, "What do you know of your father's work here?"

I hesitated. Hadn't Jack said that Dr. Ply had brought me here to learn about my past? Why was he asking me this?

"Nothing."

"Really?" Dr. Ply studied me intently as if he doubted my answer. "You never wondered why he was always away? Or what he worked on apart from what he did in town?"

I shook my head, my confusion only growing. "I was too young to notice."

"And what do you know about your mother?"

I frowned, feeling like I was being led into admitting something I shouldn't. "Nothing beyond her leaving when I was three. No one ever spoke of her, especially not my father. Jack told me she wasn't from Windermere."

Dr. Ply nodded. His blue eyes were so light, they were almost white. Like ice.

When the silence had stretched on too long, I asked, "Do you know anything about her?" My throat tightened, and I hated how desperate my voice sounded.

Dr. Ply ran a finger along his desk. He studied his fingertip and looked pleased to find it clean. I waited, my frustration building as he took his time answering.

"You will come to learn that in this castle, information is *earned*. Maybe in time, I will divulge more. But for now, let us focus on you. The abandonment and betrayal you experienced at a young age will have hopefully developed within you a deep value for loyalty and strength—values I share. They make a person well suited to my particular line of work."

He looked at me, waiting for confirmation. But I was stuck on the words *abandonment* and *betrayal*. I could only stare back, shocked at how cruel and careless his words were.

"I understand this is a lot to take in. But know this: I believe your father would be pleased that you are here. He spoke of you often. He described your uncanny talent, even from a young age, for observation and problem solving."

I couldn't hide my surprise. My father had never encouraged my interest in anything other than the Arborist trade. He'd always dismissed my curiosity as nosiness, but maybe he had felt differently. Maybe he just hadn't wanted me to question *him*.

"This leads us to your responsibilities. I understand you've already seen your room. How did you find it?"

"Um." I struggled to find something positive to say. "It's very large."

Dr. Ply smiled, exposing even more teeth, and I found myself reevaluating my first impression of him. He reminded me of a snake suddenly squeezing you before you realized you'd been surrounded.

"Yes, it is *large*. Let me explain how life will be here: You start at the bottom. No luxuries, only necessities. When I feel that I can trust you—when you prove that you will keep *nothing* from me— you will be rewarded with more. Understand?"

Slowly, I nodded.

"Good. The job you are here to do is very important. You will be in a unique position to see not only my life's work but the Count's. Being from Windermere, you already know how fastidiously the Count guards his privacy."

I nodded again, beginning to think that was all I could do. I felt like I was drowning and Dr. Ply was standing in the boat watching me struggle.

"The Count is my patron, a patron of science. He is very invested in the results of my work. You are *not* permitted to discuss this work with anyone, under *any* circumstances." Dr. Ply's expression turned serious as he leaned over the desk toward me. "Not even others in the castle. Is that clear?"

"Yes," I said quickly, knowing he required more than a nod this time.

"Excellent. When you do earn the freedom to move around the castle on your own, you will report back to me with all that you witness. I need your word; you will come to me with any information, no matter how *small* or *unimportant* you believe it to be."

I swallowed and nodded.

"Good. Moving on. I understand you have been inside the Tree Garden."

Hope stirred within me. Just the thought of the warm glow in its trees and the lush grass filled me with longing. The cold stone around me was already a cage. "Yes? Will I be going back?"

"Perhaps. That must be earned. We have our own forest here at the castle. You will tend it when you begin to understand my work. Now, tell me about your activities inside the Tree Garden."

I answered without thinking. "I delivered packages to the tree spirits."

"Tree spirits?" His tone darkened with disapproval. "Ah, you mean the Carved faces."

I shifted uncomfortably. I was starting to dislike *his* face.

"And what was in those packages?" Dr. Ply smiled at me as if we were old friends, but his eyes lacked warmth. "Surely you looked . . . no one could blame you for being curious."

My cheeks flamed as I remembered York in the Tree Garden, touching all the golden stones. I hoped Dr. Ply wouldn't notice, but I was getting the impression that he was the sort of man who already knew everything about everyone. I decided to be honest—or at least partially so.

"I did see the contents of a package once, but it wasn't because *I* opened the package. An animal stole and unwrapped it. When I retrieved it, I saw a gold stone." Even as I spoke, I heard how unbelievable I sounded.

Dr. Ply stroked his mustache thoughtfully. "Did you touch it?"

"No. I put it right back in the tree."

"Good. I'm glad you told me. Your honesty ensures we are starting on the right foot. The material you saw was not gold, but you will learn that in due time. Now, what do you know about the Tree Garden's origin?"

"Nothing, except some legends say that the Tree Garden is a gateway to the last pure place in our world—" My voice faded at Dr. Ply's expression. "But I don't *believe* them," I added hastily.

His pause was significant; the longer it went on, the more foolish I felt for quoting a legend. His silence told me that he thought I was a fool too.

"If you had read the material I left in your room, you'd already know that the Tree Garden only serves a *scientific* purpose for us, nothing more. It is special, but only because it is unique. It has no place in legends. People who believe it does lack the ability to think critically. I do not hold with such myths—and neither should you."

I nodded, trying not to shrink back further into my chair.

"I have another question for you. It might seem irrelevant, but based on what you just said, I must ask it. Do you believe in magic? In humans having the ability to wield it?"

I licked my lips, stalling. "What?"

"Some might call it having *More*. Others call it Dyadicism."

It was the second time Dyadics had been mentioned to me today. I couldn't help but notice that when Vernon talked about them, he wasn't cynical or doubtful. And he hadn't spit the word out as if it offended him. Dr. Ply hated even saying it aloud.

My eyes drifted to the desk between us. It held all sorts of important-looking papers, brass scales, and an endless amount of books. This was the office of someone who wouldn't condone or approve of something as abstract as having extra abilities—or magic.

But Dr. Ply's work obviously related to Dyadicism somehow, or he wouldn't have brought it up.

There had been something to the light I'd seen, and to whatever York had done to his wood during the Tournament. And the strength that man on the beach showed when pulling the large ship in alone.

I wanted to know what that something was. What it *meant*.

And what my father had to do with it.

To do both, I needed to become this man's assistant.

I needed to show him that I could be the person he wanted me to be. So after a pause, which I hoped conveyed I was both serious and thoughtful, I answered, "Of course I don't. We don't entertain such ideas in Windermere and my father raised me better than that."

Dr. Ply nodded in approval. "That is very good to hear, and, I dare say, half the battle." He leaned over his desk toward me, as if sharing a secret. "I can allow that the world can be strange. There are many things that have not yet been explained. But I do believe, with my entire being, that science holds all our answers, and we will find them as long as we do the work."

His words hung in the air between us as he studied my face. After what seemed like an eternity, he said, "As long as you believe the same, we will get on just fine."

"I do," I said, pressing even more conviction into my voice.

"Wonderful. Now we can finally begin."

The rest of the afternoon flew by as I listened to how Dr. Ply liked to file and organize his research—somehow without ever getting into what that research was actually *about*. By the end, my head ached with the burden of so much minutia. I actually found myself looking forward to being alone in that horrid, cold room so I could collapse.

Finally, Dr. Ply looked up from a stack of files. "It's much later than I thought. Our time is up." He pulled on a cord that hung behind his desk and a knock sounded on the door. "Anna will escort you to your room."

I stood, relieved and surprised by how fast Anna had gotten here. I had almost reached the door when I quickly turned back around.

"Dr. Ply? Since I'm going to live here now, I wanted to ask if I could bring my horse, Loon, to the castle. Jack said you had stables here . . ."

Dr. Ply's friendly demeanor vanished. Slowly, he placed his papers down on the desk and folded his hands on top of them.

"Already a request?"

"I . . . I thought Jack spoke with you about it?"

"Yes, Jack did mention the horse was important to you. However, owning a horse here would be a great *privilege*. And here, every privilege must be *earned*."

Dr. Ply paused, staring as I shifted nervously from foot to foot.

"If you want your horse, you must give me a reason to reward you. I'd prefer that you focus on our work together, soaking up everything that I'm trying to teach you. I don't anticipate you will have time for afternoons of leisurely riding. Your future success depends on you proving yourself *now*. Can I make that any clearer?"

"No, sir."

"Anna!" Dr. Ply called out loudly, making me jump.

Anna opened the door. Her grey eyes skimmed past me. "Yes?"

"Anna, please escort Ivy back to her room. Ivy, try to rest. Tomorrow will be a long day."

FOUR

Anna led me back to my room without a word.

This time, I had nothing to say to her either. Emotions swirled inside me like a storm. I was confused by the way Dr. Ply had spoken to me, and frustrated that he'd revealed nothing about my father. Dr. Ply had promised information about my past, and had used it to lure me here. But now, he was making me earn it.

That was the most confusing part. Why not just tell me what my father's role here had been? Why was he hiding it?

I had to know.

That meant I would have to follow every rule and expectation Dr. Ply set for me. I had to mold myself into the best assistant he'd ever had, so he would trust me and eventually allow Loon to come to the castle.

Anna stopped at my door silently. I stepped inside and the door closed behind me. I was glad to be alone. I was exhausted, drained, and ready to curl up and forget where I was.

This awful room made that impossible, though.

I sighed but brightened when I saw the fire was burning steadily and the room was warmer. Vernon must have just left because a tray sat on the table by my bed. I hurried over to it, finding some sort of soup and a roll of bread. It still looked warm.

I ate slowly, ignoring that the soup was bland and needed salt badly. I tried not to remember the way Wilder's Bakery bread melted in my mouth as I ate the tasteless ball of flour from the castle's kitchen.

Dr. Ply's pile of research sat next to the tray. I picked it up, remembering that he'd said I would have understood the Tree Garden if I had read it, but after a paragraph, it was clear my mind was useless tonight. I needed sleep.

I undressed quickly in the bathroom, shivering now that I was away from the fire. But as I curled in bed, under the thin covers, I felt the warm stone Vernon had placed at the end of my bed. Grateful, I pressed my feet up against it, savoring the heat.

This was my first night away from Windermere, sleeping in the Count's castle.

It was strange to think that the Count was somewhere nearby. I wondered if he was more like Mr. Mallon or Dr. Ply. I hoped he was like neither.

Instead of those thoughts keeping me awake, I was pulled under quickly, exhausted by the day.

———

WHEN THE KNOCK SOUNDED ON MY DOOR THE NEXT morning, I had been awake for nearly an hour.

"Come in," I called, already dressed and wrapped in three thin blankets.

Vernon walked into the room, and when he saw me, he frowned. As he took in the beds around the room, many empty of their covers with mine piled high, he frowned again.

"The fire went out early this morning," I explained. "I didn't want to take all the covers, in case anyone else came, but I was so cold."

Vernon brought my breakfast tray over and then hurried to start the fire. "It's OK. You can use them all," he commented.

I nodded. No one was coming to stay in this room with me.

Why put me in a room so large, with twenty beds?

When I saw the coffee, I put those questions on the back burner. I eagerly snatched the hot cup off the tray. There was no cream, but I didn't care. I was shivering and the bitterness was just what I needed to wake up. I sipped slowly, stirring the oatmeal. A sigh escaped me.

"Do you need anything else?" Vernon asked, straightening as the flames rekindled in the fireplace.

"Depends. Is cream and sugar outlawed here?" I asked with a hopeful smile.

A smile spread across Vernon's face. "Not usually. But Dr. Ply gave the order: Nothing extra for you. He said those luxuries must be earned."

I resisted the urge to roll my eyes as I glanced at the research I had been skimming through. I hadn't learned anything about the Tree Garden, but had read a whole lot about controlling emotions and living without anything.

So Dr. Ply wanted me to feel nothing but passion for *his* research. I could fake that in front of him, but I was glad I didn't have to now. So far, Vernon was a bright spot in this castle, as unaffected by its eeriness as Anna was.

As if I had summoned her, a knock sounded at the door. I tried to suppress a groan, but didn't do very well. Vernon's eyes brightened as if he was holding in a laugh.

Anna walked in and the light winked out as Vernon straightened. Anna eyed my tray, then glanced at Vernon.

"Aren't you finished?"

"Yes."

"Then go."

I looked at Vernon, surprised. But he simply nodded and left the room without looking at either of us.

I looked back at Anna, annoyed. "That wasn't nice."

"You are not here to make friends. Or to be nice. You are here to assist Dr. Ply with his work."

I bit back every sharp reply that came to mind. I knew I couldn't risk a reaction. Anna was not someone I should cross.

She watched me, wondering if I was going to respond. When I didn't, she continued in her bored, detached tone. "You will use the morning to read. After lunch, you will report to Dr. Ply. I'll return for you then."

With that, she turned on her heel and left the room.

I debated throwing my coffee at the door, but even without cream, it wasn't something I wanted to waste.

So I choked it down and ate my lumpy oatmeal, pretending both were delicious, and read Dr. Ply's research.

I hated every second of it.

———

IT FELT LIKE YEARS BEFORE AFTERNOON ARRIVED. By then I was so ready to escape myself, the research, and my cold room that I followed Anna to Dr. Ply's office eagerly. Again, she was a silent guide, but this time, we ran into Jack in the hallway.

He was wearing all black, and his eyes brightened when he saw me.

"Hello again. How are you settling in?"

Anna swept by Jack, ignoring him entirely. I glanced after her, unsure if I was allowed to stop and talk. Especially after she'd said I was not here to make friends. Jack noticed how torn I was and he smiled, switching directions and falling in step beside me. I grinned, relieved to finally talk to someone.

"It's very different than I expected," I said.

Jack looked at me curiously. "What were you expecting?"

I thought about the wrecked ship full of people I had seen by the Count's beach. The strong man with light around his hands, and Cora, who was beautiful and also had a light around her. I shrugged, knowing I couldn't admit I'd seen any of that. "I didn't think it would be so empty. Or quiet," I added, glancing ahead at Anna.

Jack playfully nudged my shoulder. "I told you no one talked much, remember?" He said it quietly, as if he didn't want Anna to overhear.

I looked up at him, remembering when he'd said he hoped I'd come to the castle. A flush spread across my cheeks. I looked back at Anna and flinched when I saw her glaring at us.

"Our session is over, Jack," she said pointedly. "And Dr. Ply did not request you tag along after us."

I wondered what session she meant. Had they been together while I was in my room? Jack was the Count's heir, but Anna didn't seem to care. She spoke to him just like she spoke to Vernon, and to me. No one was important to her except Dr. Ply. He was the only person I'd seen her be respectful to.

Jack shrugged. "Just being polite, Anna."

"Save it for someone who matters," she snapped, spinning on her heel and walking faster.

I glanced at Jack, shrugging apologetically as I hurried after her.

His answering smile followed me all the way down the hall.

———

We reached Dr. Ply's office and again, Anna knocked and led me inside.

Dr. Ply barely looked up as he said, "Thank you, Anna. You may go finish up our morning project."

Anna nodded and left the room. Dr. Ply shuffled through a few more papers as I walked forward to stand in front of the desk. I wondered if he was still upset about my request yesterday, but I squared my shoulders, determined to fix it.

"Good afternoon, Dr. Ply."

"Hello, Ivy. I've had quite a productive morning. I hope you have too."

He meant the pile of research. I nodded. "I nearly finished what you asked me to read. I can complete it by tonight."

He folded his hands over a file he had been writing in and looked up at me. I was curious about what they had been doing this morning, but I resisted the temptation to glance down at his writing.

"Excellent. Then you may stay and work here this afternoon. I would like you to begin on my office. All the books and items on that shelf need to be dusted. Please check to make sure each book is in its correct section."

He looked back down at his papers.

Surprised, I looked at the wall of shelves behind me. It was full of books and scales and glass items that looked easily breakable. He wanted me to *dust*? Why wasn't I learning about his work? Surely he hadn't brought me to the castle to dust his office.

"There is a footstool by the wall for the top shelves," Dr. Ply said absently as he began to scratch his pencil across the paper. "The duster should be next to it."

I made myself walk calmly to the stool and move it to the shelf furthest from Dr. Ply. Then I grabbed the duster and climbed up, starting my task without complaint. I could make the most of this by taking note of what kind of books he owned and by observing his instruments. A layer of dust filled the air as I began to sweep the feather over the top of the books.

"And Ivy..."

I paused to look at him. He was staring at me with a curious expression. "Please be careful with the instruments."

I nodded, wiping all emotion from my face. "Of course."

I was relieved to look away from him and focus on something else. I wasn't sure if this was a test, but he did say I was to start at the bottom. I guessed that applied to his work too.

So I threw myself into the task, determined that eventually, I would prove myself.

FIVE

month passed, each day a mirror of the one before.

I sighed as I began my usual task of cleaning and organizing Dr. Ply's office. He'd disappeared, as he always did this time of morning. I still had no idea where he went.

So far, all my good behavior had gotten me nowhere.

I glanced out the window, alarmed to see the landscape was changing. Rich yellows and browns now painted the trees and leaves scattered across the lawn. A whole season of life was slipping away while I waited and hoped to convince Dr. Ply he could trust me.

But he didn't trust me to do anything but clean. And I wasn't allowed to go anywhere. My days were structured so strictly that I never had time for anything besides cleaning or reading his research. If I wasn't in Dr. Ply's office, I was alone in that big room—or I was being escorted between the two by Anna, who ignored me.

I picked up a glass with trembling hands. I set it back down, making myself breathe in and out deeply. I missed my old life so much it hurt.

Again, I reminded myself that I wasn't alone. Just a few miles down the road was Windermere, Loon, and York. I told myself again that someday, I would go back. But for now, I imagined that York had settled into his shop, that his mother and father were proud of him, and that he went to visit Mr. Gable every afternoon. He was probably hard at work, filling his shop so that next year it would be full when the merchants landed in the harbor again. Maybe Percy had even apologized for being so annoying, and York was spending more time with Claire at Wilder's Bakery, eating all her delicious creations. I hoped so.

I wished more than anything that I was there too.

I moved to the filing cabinet, sorting through studies and folders that Dr. Ply had used yesterday. Again, panic swelled over the thought that this was the way the rest of my life would go. Isolated. Living to repeat the same day over and over again, while learning things that meant nothing to me.

I knew Dr. Ply was hiding his real work from me. I wasn't allowed to know what it was until I somehow proved myself. But what little patience I had was wearing thin. I was beginning to feel as much like a ghost walking these halls as the woman I'd seen on my first day.

My only source of relief was when Vernon lingered in my room to talk after bringing me dinner and making a cozy fire. As the flames crackled to life and warmed my numb body, Vernon would sit for a moment and talk with me, like he could sense I desperately needed a friend. Needed someone to help make sense of this life I was brought into.

Sometimes I saw Jack in the halls too, but he was often busy elsewhere, just like everyone else. I felt like the only one excluded from whatever was really happening in this strange place. I couldn't go on like this much longer.

Lately, I had even been thinking about trying to find Cora or Carl. I imagined befriending Cora and asking her to sneak me into Windermere, just like she had Carl. Up till now, I hadn't caught so much as a glimpse of either of them. It was as if they were ghosts too.

As I sorted through the files that Dr. Ply had put out for me to read today, something caught my eye through the window. I glanced up to see a person walking along the path. The files slipped from my hands as my mouth dropped open.

It couldn't be.

I leaned closer to the window, my forehead nearly pressed against it as I stared at the person walking.

It was *Nicholas*, I was sure of it.

His silver hair was pulled behind his head, just like it had been when I'd first met him in the woods outside Windermere. But now, his clothes were different. Rather than clothes that made him seem part of the forest, he wore a sophisticated suit. In his hand was a book. He walked leisurely across the castle grounds like he belonged here. Like he was wealthy, not a recluse in the woods.

I watched him in disbelief. Nicholas was the one who'd started all this. He'd claimed my father was his friend. He'd given me the clue, hinted that my father wasn't dead. That my father had been paranoid and fearful about his research.

And, I remembered with a start, Nicholas was the reason I'd failed my Arborist test! He'd told me the plant I'd brought in for my test was wild parsnip, and dangerous. But it had only been golden Alexander, and I had failed because of it.

I'd trusted what he'd said was true, but how much of it had been a lie?

A lie designed *to bring me here*?

I watched as he disappeared around the corner of the gardens. I had no idea what was going on around me. What my father had been part of . . . what *I* was here to be a part of.

And I never would unless I started taking risks and stopped playing by Dr. Ply's rules.

Slowly, I set down the files. I had never searched Dr. Ply's office before. I was afraid he or Anna would catch me. But now I knew they were busy most of the morning. Maybe I should start using this time alone to uncover why Dr. Ply was so secretive about his work.

I would start small and do things that could easily be shrugged off as a mistake.

Files were right in front of me, stacked on a cabinet that Dr. Ply took his work from. I eased the door of the cabinet open, removed a file from the pile inside, and slipped it into my stack.

The door swung open.

My breath caught in my throat as I turned around slowly.

Dr. Ply walked into the room. "Finished cleaning, Ivy?"

"Yes, sir."

"Then let's get to work."

I nodded, taking the stack of papers and sitting in my usual chair. Dr. Ply sat at his desk, looking around to make sure it was organized with a fresh stack of papers ready for him. Satisfied, he began ruffling through files without another word.

I looked down and scanned the paper in my lap. More studies about the mind. I didn't understand why I needed to know this.

Dr. Ply began transcribing notes into this ledger. I was sure they had something to do with wherever he'd just been. I watched him stroke his mustache, knowing he was deep in thought.

I thumbed through my stack of papers until I found the file I'd taken from the cabinet, and began to read.

For a while, only the ticking of a clock and the sound of pages slowly turning sounded through the silent room.

Until I reached something interesting.

I frowned, and couldn't help looking up in surprise.

As if he could feel my gaze, Dr. Ply looked up too.

"Yes?"

"Sorry to disturb you. It's nothing."

He set his papers down. "Did you have a question?"

"Actually . . ." I scanned the folder. "Yes. This study states that if the mind performs the same task over and over, it will eventually forget anything else considered unimportant, even basic survival skills."

Now Dr. Ply put down his pencil. "And?"

"And the last part claims that such a mental state might be aided, or fixed, with electricity?"

"I fail to see the question."

"Does this mean you can . . . well, shock someone into remembering what they forgot? What was lost in their mind?"

Dr. Ply considered that. "*That* is a very advanced theory. One you are not ready for, but I'll expand briefly. Some have tested applying electrical pulses to the brain, in hopes of stimulating certain areas to function correctly. Obviously, this is considered a last-case scenario as it is very risky."

I took a deep breath. "Have *you* conducted experiments like this?"

Dr. Ply's expression hardened. "Like I said, it is a last-case scenario and very tricky. Hand me back that study. I'm not even sure how it was put in your stack; I'll have to speak to Anna about that. When I think you're ready, you might learn more about this particular theory. Thank you," he said as I handed him the file. "Ah. Here is one more suitable for you."

I scanned the new material and held in a sigh. Research on controlling emotions.

"I feel I must remind you, yet again, that the people who have made the most progress in their work here are those who hold little attachments and feel nothing. This ensures they remain the most objective and impartial. Your feelings are your enemy; remember that. This is something Anna has mastered and I hope you will learn by observing her. This is what I value in an assistant."

He held my eyes until I nodded, but inside I cringed. I didn't want to be anything like Anna.

I looked down and noticed a piece of charcoal had rolled off his desk. It was now stuck under a chair. I remembered how dirty Dr. Ply's hands had gotten yesterday when he'd used it to mark some notes on the wall.

It gave me another idea.

I looked up. Dr. Ply was engrossed in his notes again.

I quietly edged further out of my chair and nudged the charcoal free with my toe. It rolled toward me, and I hid it under my foot.

I let a few papers slide to the ground, and as I bent over to retrieve them, Dr. Ply looked up.

"What's happened now?"

"I'm sorry, I dropped these." I took another second to pick up the papers and adjust my sock before I sat up. "Sorry to bother you."

Dr. Ply frowned. "It's nearly dinner time. Finish reading in your room and we'll pick up again tomorrow."

"I will." I stood to leave, but I paused at the door. "Dr. Ply?"

He glanced up, emitting a sigh at being interrupted again. "Yes?"

"I just wanted you to know that I found that study very interesting. And when you think it's time for me to learn more, I'll be ready. I'm eager to move forward in my training."

Dr. Ply leveled me with a very long stare. Then he waved me out without another word.

As usual, Anna stood outside the door. This time, I savored the silence as she escorted me back to my room. I was considering the piece of charcoal tucked inside my sock and how it would help me find Nicholas.

And everything else Dr. Ply was keeping from me.

Six

A storm hovered over the castle.

Rain pelted the small windows at the end of my room as the wind howled and whistled through the cracks in the walls. I pulled my sweater tight as chills swept through me. I was glad for the change in weather. I hoped it would continue so no one would hear my footsteps around the castle tonight.

As my foot bounced, the piece of charcoal slid further down into my sock. As much as I couldn't wait to be free of this room, I waited patiently for Vernon to finish his duties. I didn't mind he was taking his time. I enjoyed talking with him.

When the fire was finally built and crackling, Vernon turned and eyed me suspiciously.

"Are you alright?"

I looked up from my dinner, wondering if my plans were written across my face. "Yes, why?" I said innocently.

"You seem distracted." His green eyes creased with concern. "Or upset, perhaps?"

"Oh, no. Sorry. Just another long day."

"It must have been. Usually, your questions are endless." He smiled, amused.

I grinned back. I considered sharing my plan with him but quickly decided against it. I didn't want him to get in trouble if I was caught.

"Do you know your way around the castle?" I asked.

"Nearly." Vernon perched on the edge of the bed across from me, and he also seemed to relax now that I was ready to talk.

I wondered if this was the only normal time in his day too. Sometimes it seemed like he needed to talk as much as I did.

"But there are still many wings I've never been in. Several are blocked off," he continued.

"Why?"

Vernon shrugged. "They are not in use anymore."

"Did you get lost a lot? Your first time around?"

He nodded. "Every day. The hallways all looked the same at first. That is, until I learned to spot the differences."

I sat up. "What kinds of differences?"

"Some patches of stone are different because they were added in later years. And the torches. Those in the older wings are circular and curvy. But the newer ones are straight and tall. We are in an old wing now, if you could not already tell."

"Oh, I could tell."

Vernon chuckled. He looked younger when he laughed.

"Where are the kitchens?" I asked curiously. There was so much I didn't know about him either.

"The kitchens are also situated in the old wings, like this one. But why? Do you plan on paying me a visit?" He smiled.

"No. I . . . I just wondered how far you need to walk to bring my dinner every night."

He frowned. "Is it not hot when it reaches you?"

"It's always perfect," I assured him.

He nodded, but still looked concerned. Vernon was sensitive, and I wondered if someone in the kitchen was as hard on him as Dr. Ply was on me. I felt bad for him, so I tried to steer the conversation back to the castle.

"If it's so confusing, I wonder if anyone has ever gotten lost in the castle and never been found?" I said, thinking of my father. Or of myself, if tonight didn't go as planned. What would happen if I couldn't find my way back to my room?

Vernon looked at me carefully, the way he always did when I asked something particular. "Not that I know of."

"But how *would* you know?"

"The halls are monitored at all times. No one is allowed to wander freely. Well, almost no one. There are a few exceptions."

"Like who?" I knew I was pressing my luck, but I wanted to be prepared for who I might bump into. I remembered the ghost woman and shivered, wishing I hadn't. The only person I wanted to run into tonight was Nicholas. He'd revealed a lot to me when we first met in the woods, but how much would he reveal in the castle? Would he tell me more about my father?

Vernon shook his head. "I am not allowed to talk of these things."

"I'm sorry. I don't want to make you uncomfortable. But surely it's natural to wonder about my new surroundings. Don't people in the kitchen talk about these things when they first arrive?"

"No. We don't talk about people getting lost. It would make the staff uneasy."

"I'm sure it would."

Vernon stood, almost reluctantly, as if he didn't want to go back to his room. Then he smiled. "Sleep well, Ivy."

"Goodnight, Vernon."

The door closed behind him.

I took a deep breath and ran through my plans again as I waited to make sure Vernon hadn't forgotten anything. When I was sure I was in the clear, I stood and walked down the aisle of beds to where the old torches hung on the back wall. I pried one free. It was heavier than I thought it would be, but that didn't matter when I placed it in the fire and it blazed to life.

I went to the closet, removed the single shelf, and pushed the false wall open. Again, dust swirled into the room, but not nearly as much as the last time. I held the torch out into the dark tunnel and watched the light flicker on the stone walls.

Taking the charcoal out from my sock, I drew a long line on the stone. When I saw the streak of dark grey color the walls, I sighed in relief.

After a deep breath, I stepped inside.

The light from the torch hovered in front of me, illuminating the cracked stone and making my shadow follow eerily after me. Small streams of water dripped down the walls as I shivered, holding the torch in one hand and the charcoal in the other. I continued on, eventually losing track of how long I'd been walking.

There had not been a single fork in the tunnel. That was good and bad. Good because if the torch went out, I could follow the tunnel back to my room. And bad because this tunnel was leading me to only one place. What if it was to Anna or Dr. Ply's room? Or the Count's?

At certain points, the air became colder and I wondered if I was passing the outside walls of the castle. So far, there were no doors or forks to follow.

Finally, a door appeared on the side of the tunnel.

I stopped and marked the door with a big *X*. As quietly as possible, I eased it open.

To my relief, it didn't make a sound. A sliver of light shone into the tunnel. I rested the heavy torch upright next to the door and listened for any movement on the other side. It was silent.

I pulled it open further but found the door blocked by something shiny and gold. It took me a moment to realize it was a large suit of armor. This was another bit of luck; I could stay concealed behind it as I exited the tunnel.

So far, everything was working out.

My heart raced as I stepped out of the tunnel and pushed the door shut behind me. The suit of armor was so large that my head only came up to its shoulders. As I looked around, I realized I had a problem.

I was in a hallway. On each wall, as far down as I could see, were rows of armor. How would I know which knight hid the door to my tunnel? I turned and drew another *X* on the front of the door, taking care to hide it behind the suit of armor.

I would also have to mark the suit somehow. If I marked its back, I'd have to check all the suits. I couldn't draw an obvious line because someone would notice. And of course the charcoal wouldn't even leave a mark on metal.

I squatted and reached out around the foot of the suit to shade the stone beneath it. Satisfied that the shading looked like dirt or just a shadow, I stood and took a deep breath. Then I ventured further into the hallway.

A smattering of torches lined the walls between the suits of armor. These torches looked different than those in my bedroom, which meant I must be in a newer part of the castle. I walked down the hallway, goosebumps prickling my arms. Every so often, I crept back behind the suits of armor and drew a small arrow on the wall pointing in the direction from which I'd come.

Up ahead the hallway curved left and a soft filter of light emanated along the ground as if from an open archway, so I eased back and hugged the wall close. When I reached the corner, I paused. Hearing nothing, I peeked my head around the bend and blinked in surprise.

After a month of seeing nothing but ruins, I'd assumed all of the castle was as old and forlorn as my awful bedroom. But before me was a wonder I had never seen before—never imagined—in my entire life.

Not just one, but many crystal chandeliers cast a soft glow of light on a large reception area, on the far side stood a grand staircase. Its stone steps were covered in rich hunter-green carpeting with gold threaded flowers. It looked so thick I wanted to lay on it and remember what comfort felt like.

A woman sat behind a desk made of glossy dark wood, sipping from a delicate black tea cup. It reminded me of Mr.

Gable's work. As I stared, I realized I'd seen her before. She had participated in the Count's Woodworking Tournament.

She had led York and me away when I was disqualified.

My heart began to race. She might recognize me.

Footsteps echoed through the reception area. I quickly pressed myself tightly against the stone wall just as someone walked past.

I peeked out, surprised to see Vernon pause at the desk.

The woman put down her cup. "Right on time, as usual."

She stood and disappeared through a side door. Vernon waited, staring at the rows and rows of tiny locked drawers on the wall behind the desk.

I was glad to see Vernon. Now *he* could show me around the castle. Surely he wouldn't object since I was already out of my room. I considered stepping out from my hiding place, but then the woman rematerialized.

I shrunk back toward the wall. Maybe I would just wait and follow Vernon wherever he was going next. He could show me the kitchen and all the parts of the castle he knew about. I smiled. Again, this was turning out better than I expected.

Then I heard footsteps coming down the staircase.

Anna.

My excitement evaporated.

Anna stopped when she reached Vernon. "Leave us, Margret."

Without a word, the woman left through the side door. I watched, surprised, wondering what Anna had to say to Vernon in private. Was he in trouble? Why wasn't he in the kitchen?

Only then did I notice that Vernon looked different than usual. It took me a moment to realize that he was not his kitchen clothes. He'd changed into a black shirt and pants; the same as Anna. *And Jack*, I thought with a start. My heart beat faster.

"So? What did she ask about tonight?"

"The castle, mostly. She wanted to know if anyone had ever

gotten lost in the castle and was never found," Vernon answered, quietly.

I suddenly felt very cold. Wasn't that what *I* had asked Vernon tonight?

Anna frowned. "An odd question."

"She asked how far it was for me to bring her dinner."

"What else did she say?"

My heart began to pound. I pressed my hand over my chest as if I could slow it. They were talking about *me*.

Vernon shrugged. "She wondered if the castle was always so empty."

Anna's eyes narrowed. "What seemed to be her motivation behind these questions?"

"I believe she is just curious."

"Was she reading her assigned papers?"

"Yes."

"And her temperament? Was she sulking, or reading like she was actually learning something?"

I panicked, thinking of all the times that I'd shown how miserable I was to Vernon. Had he told Anna? Did that mean Dr. Ply also knew I actually hated reading his studies?

I remembered Dr. Ply's cold stare today.

"She didn't talk to me at all while she read. I think she was interested in the material," Vernon answered.

"Anything else to add?"

I held my breath. If Vernon told her I'd asked who monitored the halls, or that I'd asked how I could tell my way around, Anna would check my room immediately. I wasn't sure I could beat her back.

When Vernon shook his head no, my knees went weak with relief.

Anna frowned. "Same time tomorrow, then."

Vernon nodded and walked down the hall away from me.

Anna watched him go for a moment, an unreadable expression on her face. Then she called loudly, "Margret!"

I jumped.

Anna didn't wait for Margret to come back to the desk. She turned and floated up the beautiful green-and-gold staircase.

Margret peered out of the side door and looked relieved to see that Anna was already gone.

I turned and hurried back down the hallway as quietly as I could, my breath ragged. I found the suit of armor that hid my tunnel and shut the door just as I heard more footsteps.

With shaking hands, I picked up the torch. Thankfully, it was still lit, but I only made it halfway down the tunnel before it flickered out. I walked the rest of the way in darkness, trembling and feeling the walls, hoping there was nothing else in the tunnel with me. Finally, I made it back to my room.

The warm fire that Vernon had made earlier still danced in the crumbling fireplace. I crouched in front of it, hugging my knees to my chest as tears slid down my cheeks. I felt betrayed and foolish. Vernon had only pretended to be my friend so he could relay information back to Anna. I'd thought he was a lost person, just like me, who needed a friend.

But none of it had been real.

I swept the tears away with the back of my hand as I combed through everything I'd ever said to him. Everything that I now knew Anna and Dr. Ply knew.

The yellow light of the flames reminded me of the light I'd seen before I came to the castle. I was glad I'd never mentioned that to him.

I stood and put the torch back on the wall and fixed the closet so no one would know I'd left my room tonight. After I changed, I took my father's journal and hugged it as I got in bed.

The tears started again. I'd never felt so deceived or so alone. I'd trusted Vernon too easily . . . because I hadn't known how much I needed to protect myself. Now I knew.

I could no longer be naive.

I had to be someone who survived.

SEVEN

I was leaving the bathroom when a knock sounded at my door.

My stomach twisted. It was still early, so it had to be Vernon. I wanted to hide in the bathroom until he left, but I knew I couldn't avoid him forever. Vernon would continue to bring me meals and report whatever I did to Anna and Dr. Ply.

But now I had the upper hand because none of them knew that *I* knew this. I could use it to my advantage.

I took a deep breath. "Come in."

Vernon stepped into the room, rolling his cart in after him. He was back in his grey kitchen clothes, but now that I had seen him dressed in black like Anna, it was hard to see him any other way.

He smiled his usual smile at me. "Good morning, Ivy. Did you sleep well?"

I stared back at him, surprised at how good he was at pretending. I knew now that everything he said to me was a lie.

I took a deep breath, knowing I needed to pretend everything was fine too, but his betrayal stung deeply. I'd thought Vernon was harmless. I'd thought he was my friend.

He was neither.

I forced myself to smile back at him. "I did sleep well, but not nearly long enough. I read pretty late into the night."

Vernon set my tray down and went to restart the fire. "Is the research starting to interest you?"

That was something he usually asked me, but I had only thought it was from friendly concern. Now I knew what a pointed question it was.

I swallowed some coffee before I said, "It's fascinating. I only wish Dr. Ply would show me more about what he does."

"I'm sure that will come soon enough."

I looked at him curiously. "Why do you say that?"

Vernon wiped his hands on a towel and put the rest of his things back under the cart. I thought I caught a flash of panic make its way across his face; he'd revealed more than he should. "Only because it's bound to happen. Have a good day, Ivy. I'll see you later tonight."

"Mm-hmm," I said, pretending I was eating so I wouldn't have to continue being nice.

The door shut and I breathed out a sigh of relief. Then I ate as quickly as I could before Anna arrived to walk me to Dr. Ply's office.

When I opened Dr. Ply's door, I was surprised to find him already at his desk with a steaming cup of coffee and a large raspberry croissant.

My mouth watered. I hadn't tasted anything freshly baked since leaving Windermere. I thought wistfully of the sweet rolls at Wilder's Bakery. The food in the castle was not all bland and simple, just the food they served *me*.

I tried to push the growing irritation I felt aside so Dr. Ply would not sense anything but loyalty.

Dr. Ply looked up at me with flakes from the pastry stuck in his mustache and falling onto his shirt.

"Ivy. Have a seat."

I sank into the leather chair, worried by his stern tone. Did he already know I'd snuck out last night? I kept my breathing normal. In and out.

"Yes?"

"I've considered your last request carefully. And I've decided that this morning and every morning hereafter, you will now join me in the lab."

I had not been caught. The relief I felt must have shown as excitement because Dr. Ply looked pleased at my reaction. When he continued, his tone was nearly friendly.

"This past month you've done everything I've asked of you. I know it has not been easy or enjoyable. However, it was necessary for me to see if you could do what was required. Now that I feel we've established a solid foundation, and you have vocalized your interest in my work, I am moving your training to the next step."

I nodded and sat up. Maybe if I did even better, Dr. Ply would bring Loon here too.

"Your new schedule is as follows: You will now join me in the lab each morning. In the afternoon, we will record our findings. You will continue to accumulate tasks as you prove yourself trustworthy. Your assigned reading will also be reduced, as long as you continue to show progress."

"Thank you."

Dr. Ply set his coffee down. "Do you remember the first time we met? I asked if you believed that certain people could have extra abilities?"

A shiver slid down my spine. "Yes."

"And what was your answer?"

"I told you I don't."

He nodded, pinning me with another icy stare. "Please remember that inside the lab, for you will see things you won't understand. Things that might make you question everything. But you must never discuss them with anyone except me."

"I won't."

Dr. Ply held up a hand. "There is one more thing. You must *never* question my methods. Ever."

I felt a stab of fear, wondering why he needed to add that. "Yes, sir."

"My life is dedicated to discovering how science affects our world. Most people are quick to assume wrongly when confronted with strangeness, simply because they don't understand science. My job—and now your job too—is to rise above common thought to reach scientific reason. Reason above nonsense. Do you understand?"

"Yes."

"Good. Now please follow me."

We only made it a few steps out of his office before Dr. Ply opened another door on the right. I followed him, assuming we were walking into another office. Instead, a long narrow hallway stretched out in front of us. It was lined with several black doors, each bearing a silver padlock. The hallway seemed to go on forever.

What did Dr. Ply need to keep inside this secret hallway, behind locked doors? The castle was always empty. Or so I thought.

We kept walking, and I wondered if my father had ever been in this hallway too. His part in this was still unclear. Maybe something about him was hidden behind one of these doors. Maybe whatever I saw in the lab would finally give me a clue to follow.

I thought about the light I'd seen. Perhaps I would finally discover the reason for it . . . although I hadn't seen it again since I'd arrived at the castle. That was an interesting realization.

In Windermere, I'd only seen the light around people or objects near the castle. But since I'd been here, I'd seen nothing remotely special or unusual.

Dr. Ply finally stopped in front of a door with a small sign that read *Private: Study Use Only.*

He pulled a key from his white coat and unlocked the door. The room was empty except for a long table, chairs, and a large cabinet. Dr. Ply walked over and unlocked the cabinet as I looked around the room.

"This is our observing area. The double-sided mirror allows us to see everything undetected. Take a seat."

The chairs were placed on one side of the table, so when I sat I faced a large window on the opposite wall. Not a window, but a double-sided mirror that looked into another large room on the other side of the glass.

The room I found myself looking into was sterile and quiet. There were five tables with tools hanging down the sides, like workstations. A single desk sat at the front of the room next to another locked cabinet. Two chairs were placed next to the door. I wondered why we were watching this particular room and who was going to come in.

"Darn. Excuse me for one moment, Ivy. The files I need are in another room."

Dr. Ply walked out, leaving me to look around alone.

I sank back into my chair, and a light on the other side of the glass flickered on.

Through the double-sided mirror, I could see Jack walk in.

I sat up, uneasy about being in here without him knowing. I watched him open the desk's drawer and take out a key. Then he unlocked the large cabinet beside him. Its door swung open, but his body blocked its contents from my view. He pulled out a stack of files and placed them on the desk.

I glanced at the door, wondering when Dr. Ply would return. I felt uneasy spying on Jack, but I also knew I had to take every advantage to learn more about what Dr. Ply was doing.

Jack walked closer to the double-sided mirror. A hidden door I hadn't noticed—just beside the mirror—opened, and suddenly he was standing in the same room as me.

For once Jack looked surprised. "Oh! Hello, Ivy."

I flushed, feeling like I just got caught spying. "Dr. Ply was just here. He left."

His brow raised. "And how long have you been watching me?"

"I didn't come here to watch you! I'm waiting for Dr. Ply. He went to get something."

"So . . . you *weren't* watching me?" Jack's blue eyes narrowed, but I saw a hint of teasing in them.

"I wasn't trying to," I said, exasperated. "But if you're worried about it, maybe you should make sure you're alone before you unlock a secret cabinet. Or maybe hide the key in a better place than the top drawer where anyone can find it."

Jack laughed. "I take it today's your first day in the lab?"

"Yes."

"Nervous?"

"Should I be?"

"Well, I did tell you that Dr. Ply is very particular and demanding. His previous assistant lasted just one day."

I glared up at him, making him chuckle again. Jack's laugh was one of the happiest and truest sounds I'd heard since I'd been here. I couldn't help but smile back at him.

A throat cleared loudly from the doorway. I flushed when I saw Dr. Ply standing there, watching us with a disapproving expression.

"Jack," he said gruffly. "Where are the Transposers?"

Jack was instantly all business. "Good morning, Dr. Ply. Flex and Anna are bringing them down now."

"Good. If you're finished here" —he raised an eyebrow at me — "I'd like to get started."

"Of course."

Jack walked back into the adjoining room and shut the door firmly behind him. This room was suddenly too small for the two of us.

Dr. Ply placed a few tattered files, along with a crisp new file, on the table and sat down with a huff next to me. I leaned away slightly, wishing we could sit across the table from each other instead.

Dr. Ply shifted in his seat to look at me. "Ivy?"

I shrank away from him, avoiding his eyes. "Yes?"

"Is Jack going to be a problem for you?"

I reddened, understanding his meaning. "No. No, of course not!"

Dr. Ply gave me an incredulous look. "I require a serious assistant. Not a lovestruck, silly girl."

"I'm not!" I stuttered, embarrassed.

"Please remember why you are here. I can't possibly stress that enough."

"Yes, sir. I'm sorry." I wanted to crawl under the table. Why had I let my guard down? I was finally doing well and now he thought I was an idiot.

Then I saw the names on the files and the ground dropped out beneath my feet.

My breath wheezed from my chest, causing a sound to escape my lips before I could stop it.

The worn file read: *Carl Knight*.

And the crisp new file read: *York Pembroke*.

EIGHT

Every part of my body turned cold and numb as I stared down at York's name on the file.

My mind raced through the possibilities of why Dr. Ply would have a file with York's name on it. He also had a file on Carl, and Carl was in the castle. Was it possible that York was here too?

Had my best friend been in the castle with me this entire time?

York had not won the Count's Woodworking Tournament. He was not in Windermere running his own Carving shop. He must have been brought to the castle when I was.

My hands began to shake, but I willed them still. I could feel Dr. Ply's eyes on me. Everything he had told me in his office took on a terrifying new meaning.

The room swam. I felt sick.

"Ah. I see you recognize these names. Of course you would; I believe you went to school with both of these boys?"

Even my lips were numb. "Yes, sir."

"And were you close?" Dr. Ply asked, sounding much too casual now.

I was aware that he was watching me, waiting for any hint of how I truly felt. I couldn't react how I wanted, or allow myself to speculate over York. Instead, I slipped into survival mode. Everything refocused.

I wiped my face clean of any expression and I looked up at Dr. Ply, determined to play this role perfectly.

Now, I was playing for myself and for York.

And I didn't know the rules.

I made my voice sound detached. "I'm the same age as York. Windermere is a small town, so of course we knew each other. The last time I saw him was at the Count's Woodworking Tournament. I assumed he was still in Windermere."

"Yes. York came here shortly after the tournament." Dr. Ply's tone remained as impassive as mine and his smooth brow gave nothing away. "He, too, shows a lot of promise."

He paused. When I didn't respond, he continued.

"Well, it doesn't sound as if observing him will be a problem for you, and I'm relieved. This is a very rare predicament, having one person from Windermere here, much less *three* of you. But Carl and York pose no conflict, as they were never friends. And you won't be interacting with York at all."

"I won't? He won't be in the lab?"

Dr. Ply looked at me sharply. "He will, but you will be here behind the glass, observing. He will never know you are here, just as you didn't know he was here this last month. Remember: you have just earned this position. It is not in your best interest to allow him to know you are observing him. The Transposers only know their part of the lab: Carving. They do not know they are being studied."

Dr. Ply turned back to the files without another word. He took York's file and slid Carl's over to me. I took it, hoping I could manage whatever came next.

The door in the next room opened. An icy feeling crept through me as Anna stepped inside. She was not alone. People dressed in black, wearing heavy gloves, filed in after her. The first two men had darker skin; the next was a boy. He reminded me, somehow, of the strong man I'd seen pull in the ship. Then Carl walked in. He looked just as he had when I'd seen him last in Windermere. Tall, brown hair, and a swagger in his gait. He looked like trouble.

My stomach clenched as York entered the room next.

He looked thinner and somber, wearing all black and heavy gloves like the others. The enormous bald man, who I'd seen last with Carl in Windermere, trailed after them and shut the door.

Carl and the bald man *were* in the castle after all. That likely meant Cora was somewhere here too. But I couldn't think about all that now.

This was the strangest experience of my life. York was in another room, separated from me by a single sheet of glass, and he didn't know it.

He and the other gloved people were Dr. Ply's "Transposers," and I was here to *study* them, whatever that meant.

My heart began to pound as each man sat down at a work station and Jack placed a bag on each table. Anna and the bald man—I assumed this was the Flex Dr. Ply had referred to earlier— followed him, opening each bag and laying out several tools that I recognized as Carving instruments. Anna and Flex then removed the black gloves from each person's hands. When the gloves came off, the transposers stretched and curled their fingers, as if the gloves had been heavy and restricting.

Jack filled his arms with something else from the cabinet and placed a white block of wood on each table. The five transposers seemed to come alive as they picked up their blocks and held them. It almost looked like they'd missed the wooden blocks, and were relieved to hold them again.

It was the strangest reaction I had ever seen a person have to wood. I had never seen even a Carver in Windermere approach their Carving work with such desperate reverence, especially not York. But now, he seemed just as excited as the others.

Dr. Ply began explaining what behaviors he wanted me to watch for and note: the intensity of work, the transposer's level of focus, and the state of the wood at the end of the session. I was to focus on Carl today. I nodded as if I understood, desperate to win his trust and uncover what York was doing here. But it felt like I was out of my body, watching through someone else's eyes.

The session started without another word. There didn't appear to be any instructions or rules; transposers seemed free to Carve whatever they liked, and at whatever pace they wanted. Wood shavings accumulated on the desks and floor, and I thought it strange to witness Carving in such a sterile environment. I was used to being surrounded by the scent of wood, hearing the tools scrape across the grain, and even peeling the wood shavings apart with my fingers. I'd never realized how comforting Carving could be until Dr. Ply stripped it of everything I loved.

Carl worked quietly and slowly, so there wasn't much for me to record. But the more I glanced at York, the more I was filled with dread. The York I had known was carefree and happy, but this York—with his head bent over his white block—was intense.

Beside me, Dr. Ply scribbled notes and cleared his throat pointedly at my lack of note-taking. I quickly jotted down observations about Carl: He had seemed focused in the beginning, but his interest was fading.

I began to notice other odd things. The transposers did not touch anything but the wood and the tools on their desk. Anything else they needed, Anna and Flex brought them.

Carl set his tools down and removed the straw from the glass of water on his desk. He picked up the glass with two hands, like a child scared to spill, and began to drink.

Flex shot out of his seat so fast that I jumped. He grabbed the glass out of Carl's hands and put the straw back in it, holding it up to Carl's lips himself, but Carl refused to drink.

Flex set the water down so forcefully it still rippled as he stalked back to his chair.

Anna even broke her distant, calm exterior to look disapprovingly at Carl.

Jack, too, flashed him a look of warning.

Carl began to Carve again, his lips upturned in a small smirk.

"Did you make a note of that, Ivy?"

"Yes," I said as I quickly scrawled a note. "Why did Flex react like that? What did Carl do wrong?"

Dr. Ply set his pen down and spoke carefully. "Both fair questions, as I have not yet explained to you what a Transposer is or the rules they must follow. For now, all you need to know is that they are not allowed to use their hands for any common, meaningless tasks. Their hands are critical to the work they do in the lab." He paused, surveying the room.

"In this room, it's Flex and Anna's jobs to act as the 'hands.' The gloves serve as physical protection, but also as a reminder to the Transposers that when they are not in this room, they should not be handling or touching anything, or compromising their hands in any way. If a transposer breaks these rules, I must be alerted immediately. Therefore, you are to document everything that happens here, even if it seems trivial."

"Carl can't drink water by himself?" I asked, startled.

"No, he shouldn't hold the glass without gloves. He should only hold wood to Carve, or his tools. What he just did was not the greatest offense, but Carl has grown difficult. Anna and Flex are trying to do their jobs, but Carl makes it challenging. We aren't sure why he is being so hard to manage. I may have to intervene soon if the situation doesn't correct itself. He's our first transposer from Windermere and we have had the most problems with him."

Dr. Ply turned his attention back to the transposers.

I couldn't help but feel a shiver of dread as I wondered what it would mean for Dr. Ply to intervene. Somehow I knew that whatever it entailed, it wouldn't be pleasant.

I scribbled notes in Carl's file and continued to watch him, but there were no more episodes.

As the morning wore on, my eyes continued to drift over to York whenever I knew Dr. Ply wouldn't see. York stayed bent over his desk, intently Carving the white wood. I tried to guess what he was working on. I hoped it was a horse. I hoped that York remembered me and Windermere and how much he loved to Carve. But he was too far away for me to see what he was making.

When I looked over a little bit later, I noticed a change in York's hands. My breath caught as I watched a thin band of light outline his fingers and spread over each knuckle, over his palm, and stop abruptly at each wrist. It was the same shimmer of light I had seen around Cora, like shards of a rainbow. I watched in disbelief as the light began to spread into York's hands and they too began to fill up with light until they glowed.

Then the wood changed, too.

The white color of the wood seemed to peel back and melt away. A golden color began to spread over the entire piece of wood, and then suddenly the light drained from York's hands. The halo of light disappeared, leaving behind tiny shimmers of light that burst in the air, and then faded. Just like the shimmers I'd seen on the wrecked ship.

York's block of wood was now a transparent golden color . . . just like his ship at the Woodworking Tournament.

I looked around, my heart racing, but no one else seemed to react. How had York done that? Was I the only one who had seen it happen? Was he a Dyadic?

Dr. Ply stiffened next to me, and I knew he'd finally seen. Almost immediately, Jack was out of his seat and over at York's table.

"That's great work, York!" Jack clapped him on the back in a friendly way. "You've earned an early break. Anna will take you back to the South Wing."

But York didn't move.

He just stared down at the block. Then he pushed his finger into the material and I watched it fold into itself, like a very soft metal.

I thought he must be in shock, but then he smiled, and my heart sank.

That was not York's smile. That was something proud and harsh.

Anna put York's black gloves back on his hands. Then Flex quickly walked him out the door, but not before I noticed York's smug expression. I had never seen that look on his face before.

Jack covered York's work with a cloth and placed it inside the cabinet. "Keep working, everyone," he called out as he took his seat again.

The other transposers looked around, their expressions unreadable. Carl looked annoyed. He began gouging holes into his block in a disturbing way. Anna scowled at him.

I turned to Dr. Ply. "How did he do that? Did it turn to *gold*—"

"Ivy," Dr. Ply interrupted, his voice cold and even. "Do you remember what I told you before we came into the lab?"

Only now was I aware of how loudly I had spoken. At once I smoothed my face to match his. "Yes," I said, calmer.

"That was *not* gold. What you just saw was *not* what it appeared. Yes, York's wood was transformed—but there is a scientific reason as to how it happened. I understand seeing it for the first time can be jarring, so I'll let this reaction of yours go. Just this once."

I stiffened immediately at his warning.

"I admit, we are still not sure how it happens," Dr. Ply continued, looking into the lab. "A transposer has a fascinating genetic makeup and the longer I study them, the more questions I have."

He paused, as if he considered sharing more, but decided against it.

"Can you handle your work discreetly, objectively, and in a calm manner?"

I nodded, not trusting my voice.

"Good. That's all for now. Have lunch. Be in my office in one hour."

I stood, still shaking, and made my way to the door.
"And Ivy?"
I turned.
His face was set like stone. "*Never* react like that again."

59

NINE

The Count

Dark clouds rolled ominously above the castle.

The wind tore at everything in its path, bending trees and beating weak branches to the ground.

High above it all, in his tower, stood the Count, staring through the windowpane. His breath fogged up the glass as raindrops splattered and bled down it. Another black mood consumed him.

It was the kind of day where he hated even his closest allies.

Windermere sat below him, just out of reach of the rough sea. Waves, speckled with white caps, crashed mercilessly onto the shore as ships swayed back and forth over the inky water. The town square was empty; no one dared to venture out.

The Count hated the town today. He despised the tiny shops and the simple people who worked in them. He hated their small lives—how could they not wonder what was beyond the sea? Why did they not wonder what was up in the mountains, as the Count had wondered when he was young?

Perhaps they were wise not to wonder about anything beyond their small existence. They were spared the torture the Count's curiosity had caused him. Now that he *knew* what was hidden high in the mountains, he could never return to a normal life.

Not that his life had ever been normal.

He closed his eyes and allowed himself to recall the woman in the white lace dress. He saw her beautiful blue eyes staring at him from among the white trees. As she reached her hand out towards him, a familiar pain tightened in his chest. Over the years, the pain had hollowed and dulled so that it no longer took his breath away. However, some days it still affected him deeply.

He *longed* for her.

He *hated* her.

She had ruined him. Consumed him. Some say she'd even driven him to madness.

How much of his life was still wasted on *her*?

A knock on the door shattered the silence and pulled the Count from his dark daydream. He shuddered, reorienting himself to his library.

He pitied the person on the other side of that door.

The door swung open and Jack walked into the library. He searched the room and smiled when he found the Count by the window. He stepped inside, unaffected—as always—by the dark cloud hanging over the room.

"Sir. May I join you?"

"If you must."

Jack shut the door behind him but remained near it as if reevaluating the situation.

"What is it?" the Count asked pointedly.

"I thought you would like to know the status of your newest Transposer."

"Why would I care—unless he is costing me more resources? I do not need to be informed of every little thing. Isn't that part of *your* new position, as my prospective heir?"

Jack did not respond.

The Count finally moved from the window. He sank into his leather chair and opened an ornate box on the table. Inside was a glossy black pipe and his favorite tobacco. He picked up the pipe and began to stuff it with rare leaves, hoping this familiar ritual would restore his mood.

Still, Jack said nothing. He slowly moved away from the door and sat in the chair opposite the Count, waiting.

Staring into the red glow of the fireplace, the Count blew out the first few puffs of smoke. The smell was hearty and heavy and it filled the room with its unusual deep scent.

The Count's shoulders relaxed. He took a few more puffs from the pipe and blew out four perfect rings of smoke. Then he looked at Jack.

"Well, what else do you have to say to me? Out with it."

"Mr. Mallon was right. Our new Transposer is special."

The Count blew out another smoke ring. He refused to ask for information—it was beneath him—so he waited for Jack to continue.

When the Count didn't press him, Jack said, "This morning, the Transposer turned a six-inch wooden block into laun."

The Count's brows rose a fraction. That *was* significant.

"It seems highly unlikely that a young transposer could do such a thing."

"I thought the same. He was only working a few hours when I noticed the change begin. After a few minutes, the whole block was transposed."

Slowly puffing and lost in his thoughts, the Count mumbled. "In his second month, too . . ." He said this more to himself than to Jack. If a transposer could do that in two months, what could he accomplish in a year?

For the first time in decades, there was a sliver of hope.

This feeling was completely foreign to the Count, and he didn't care for it. Hope made people weak. It kept them focused on the future, which was not guaranteed.

"What did you say to him? How did he react to the transformation?" the Count asked.

"I complimented his work and removed it. But later, he did ask if it was gold."

"Gold?" the Count repeated, exasperated. "That town reproduces the same common mind. Do they even know what gold looks like? Gold isn't *transparent*, for God's sake. Utterly ridiculous."

Jack shifted in his chair. "Well, at times laun can resemble gold."

The Count watched him, hiding his amusement. He knew that Jack had thought the same as the young Transposer when he'd first seen laun.

"What did you tell him?"

"About the transformation? I told him it was not gold, that he'd done very well, and would be rewarded. Then I sent him back to Cora in the South Wing."

"Good." The Count laid the finished pipe on a silver plate to be cleaned by the staff. He stood, so Jack stood too. "You were right to come tell me."

"I would have been here earlier, but I stopped at the stable. It took longer than I expected."

"What was wrong?" the Count asked, instantly concerned about his most prized possessions.

"Nothing sir; everything is fine. A mare had a foal. He is strong and doing well."

"Very well. I'll be by in the next few days," the Count said, dismissing Jack as he walked back over to the window. The day did not feel as dreary anymore, and even the wind seemed to give up on its mission of misery.

He heard the door open behind him.

"Jack?" the Count called without looking back.

"Yes?"

"I would like regular updates on this new Transposer from now on."

"Yes, sir."

The door clicked shut and the Count was alone again.

He looked down on Windermere once more and thought about all his past Transposers. None of them had accomplished so much in such a short time. His breath crept across the window, blurring the little town from view.

It was time for him to visit the lab.

TEN

My breath floated away from me in tiny puffs of white vapor.

Dewdrops clung to blades of grass, covering the lawn in a frosty sheen. To my surprise, we hadn't gone to the lab this morning when I reported to Dr. Ply's office. Instead, we headed outside, to the furthest courtyard from the castle.

"It's just up ahead," Dr. Ply called over his shoulder.

Shivering, I pulled my coat tighter and higher around my neck, thinking it was strange to see Dr. Ply anywhere but in his office surrounded by books. In the natural light, he looked quite different. His skin reminded me of a plant withering in the sun.

We walked along a stone path lined with green hedges cut into perfect squares. I was surprised to see bushes neatly trimmed into animal shapes toward the middle of the garden. The back lawn was well kept, and I wondered if the Count allowed the front lawn to remain run down so people assumed nothing was going on here.

The path stopped abruptly at a stone wall. A thick canopy of vines dropped over a partially hidden wooden door. Dr. Ply tried to push the vines away, but they grew thick, and were difficult to move.

"Can I help you?" I asked, watching him struggle.

"Damn *Hedera*," he huffed, tearing at the leafy green vines. "It will probably pull down this whole wall eventually."

That word made my world stop.

Hedera.

The plant my father had obsessively written about in his last journal. The plant he had written about like it was something more.

"But those are just vines of ivy," I stammered.

Dr. Ply turned, his mouth pulled down in disapproval at my correction. "*Hedera* is the scientific word for the plant ivy. Shouldn't you know that from your Arborist training? Or at least from your father? My goodness, it was his idea to plant it here to hide the door. What a mistake that was. This blasted plant takes over everything."

Hedera.

Ivy.

My father had been studying *vines* before he disappeared.

I suddenly felt so foolish for thinking it had been a rare plant or that somehow his journal meant something more.

"I probably should have known that," I said quietly. "But I wasn't a very good Arborist."

"Let's hope you make a better scientist."

He took a large rusty key out of his pocket and disappeared under the vines for a moment. I heard the jiggle of a lock and then a heavy click. The wooden door swung open.

I followed him under the ivy-choked archway and stepped into a solemn, dreary world.

It was a forest of abnormal trees. Each one looked as if it had been charred by fire. Rough bark, black as tar, grew up into snarls of branches. I wondered if they were all dead. Even in my Arborist training, diseased trees looked better than this.

This place was vastly different from the perfect manicured lawn we had just walked through. There were no birds singing in these trees. It was utterly dead, depressed, and silent. I noticed dark patches of upturned dirt around the ground as if more trees were being planted. But who would want to plant such ugly, dead things? Each tree had at least one branch sawed off. The inside of the tree was just as black as the outside.

"What is this place?" I asked, trying to keep the unease out of my voice.

"The Dark Woods. You can see where it got its name. These trees are part of another experiment I'm working on, and moving forward, they will be added to your responsibilities."

A large cloud passed over the sun, turning the sky grey and making the forest seem even more barren. I shivered, longing for the Tree Garden, where the trees soaked up sunlight and grew tall into the sky—living and thriving.

This wood was the Tree Garden's opposite. Its shadow.

"What kind of trees are they?" I asked carefully. "They don't look anything like those in the Tree Garden."

Dr. Ply stared at the black woods, as if deep in thought. "No, you're quite right. The Tree Garden was not made by us; however, we think we have discovered how to maintain it. These woods" — he gestured around— "are something the Count and I have been working on for years. We are trying to replicate a forest the Count came across in one of his many travels up the mountain. So far, no luck. We successfully grow these trees to a certain point, but then without fail, they die. Even how their bark changes is a mystery."

"Does transposing have something to do with it?" I asked, shivering.

"Yes, at least now we believe so. Do you remember yesterday when you asked if the Transposer's block turned into gold?"

I nodded. He was referring to York. It was strange Dr. Ply didn't use his name.

"It is not gold, but laun, which is another material entirely. We believe that the Tree Garden is sustained—and thrives— because those trees are fueled by the energy found in laun. And laun is the product of the wood that is transformed by the Trans- posers. Whoever Carved open mouths into the Tree Garden trees obviously intended for something to be placed inside. Laun was the obvious choice and seems to work there. However, these trees" —Dr. Ply frowned at the warped shapes around us— "are the result of planting the laun supplied by the Transposers directly into the ground. After a few weeks of being planted, trees sprout up. Even if they are initially promising, after a while, they all turn to this."

Disappointment colored his words. I looked around, mystified.

One tree looked different from the rest. It was the only one that looked most like a normal tree, growing straighter and taller, with a healthy trunk. It was not as black as the others; its branches still grew in awkward directions, but in a subtler way.

I pointed to it. "Why does that tree look healthier than the others?"

"Interesting you picked this tree out, Ivy. It was planted using the laun York transposed during the Count's Woodworking Tournament. So far, it seems to be holding up better than the others. But before York arrived here, Carl produced the best trees." Dr. Ply pointed to another corner of the woods and continued, "But even they aren't as good as York's first tree . . . and they seem to be getting worse."

"How are they getting worse?"

Dr. Ply took out his pocket watch. "That will be covered in another lesson. I am out of time. I have a meeting before the lab begins. You know the way back; you can lock up today."

I looked up in surprise. I was never allowed to go anywhere without Anna.

Dr. Ply held out his hand and dropped the large key into my palm. "Surprised to be without an escort?"

My fingers closed around the heavy, iron key. "Yes. But glad if this means I've earned your trust?"

Dr. Ply studied me. There was no warmth in his eyes, only cold calculation. "Your father helped with the Dark Woods."

That was not what I'd expected him to say. My heart skipped at the revelation, but I remembered to keep my face neutral.

"He claimed an Arborist needed to work alone, so I am giving you the same courtesy. You may stay behind for a few moments to get acquainted with this place, then you will meet me in the lab. I do not need to tell you to keep this place a secret, do I?"

I shook my head. "Of course not."

With a curt nod, Dr. Ply left.

I glanced around, half dreading being in here alone, but half intrigued that my father had worked here. This was the first facet of the castle that I now knew he'd had a definite part in. But why this place? My father had never grown anything less than perfection. This made no sense. Still, there might be a clue here.

I walked through the dead trees, my heart thumping with each step. I searched everywhere for something unusual but saw nothing but damaged trees. Some trees were tall and skinny, but many were short—not even as tall as me, like they lacked the strength to grow any higher. When I was sure I'd missed nothing, I made my way to the door, aching to leave.

It wasn't until I stepped back through the green archway that I felt like I could take in a full breath. I had to work to lock the door. Dr. Ply had done it so easily, but the lock was rusty and I had to refit the key and jiggle it several times. Finally, it clicked shut.

As I stepped out from the archway, I paused to look at the vines of ivy my father had planted. I brushed my hands across them, realizing that he'd probably stood in this very spot. He had planted them to hide the Dark Woods, but why? Why was he involved in any of this? I wondered if I would ever know.

I sighed and turned back towards the castle. From here, it was larger and more grand than I realized. I scanned the balconies and windows; there were so many ornate details in the stone I'd never noticed before.

This was my first moment of freedom from Dr. Ply since arriving at the castle. I hoped it meant I was making progress and that soon, he would reveal even more to me. If he didn't, how long could I stay here? What would my future become?

I shivered, thinking of York. As long as he was here, I would be here, too, figuring out what the purpose of all of this was. I would only leave when York could leave with me.

Something caught my eye—a dark silhouette standing in a window.

The hair on the back of my neck rose. Whoever it was was watching me. Was it Nicholas? Anna? Or Cora?

I shielded my eyes for a better look, but the figure had already disappeared. They'd left the moment I'd spotted them.

Spooked, I hurried back to the castle. Only when I touched the rough stone and pushed open the door did I breathe easier.

That is, until I realized that although Dr. Ply might have given me some freedom, it was as much a lie as Vernon's friendship.

In the castle, there would always be someone watching.

ELEVEN

I spent the afternoon in the lab watching York when Dr. Ply wasn't looking, waiting for something to happen with his wood.

But by the end of the day, no transposer had created laun.

"This is why we record every session, Ivy," Dr. Ply explained. "To note the environment in which laun is created—if it is created. Then we can compare the days when a transformation occurs to the days it doesn't. Eventually, we will uncover why."

I nodded. "Can I read through the existing notes?"

Dr. Ply looked at me, surprised. "I would prefer you rested, to have fresh eyes for tomorrow."

"I'll go to bed early. I promise."

"Alright, then. You may start with these," Dr. Ply agreed, handing over a stack of files.

He seemed pleased, which had been my primary goal. But I also wanted to uncover why the Transposers were in the lab, and what Dr. Ply planned to do with them.

Since seeing the ivy my father had planted in the Dark Woods, I had the strangest feeling that my father and York were somehow connected—or, at least, their purposes at the castle were. If I could solve one mystery, perhaps it would unravel the other.

Back in my room, I sat on the bed and scanned a file about materials being altered by unseen chemicals in the air. Was this how Dr. Ply thought transposing worked?

I tried to come up with my own scientific theories of Transposing, in case Dr. Ply asked for my thoughts, but couldn't think of a single one.

Because I knew what had happened to York. And I knew it was my fault.

If the golden stones I'd put in the trees in the Tree Garden were made of laun, then touching them was what had made York a transposer.

But if touching them had changed York . . . then what had happened to change *me*? What was to blame for the sudden ethereal light I could now see around certain people, and certain things? I reached for my father's journal and opened it, flipping through the pages. I reread his notes, now knowing that they referred to vines. I felt deflated.

Hedera ruins the walls it clings to . . .

A sigh escaped me. I didn't understand why he'd thought ivy important enough to study in such detail before he'd disappeared, but it must have meant something. My father had known about the castle and the transposers.

I snapped the journal shut, frustrated, until I had a thought. If my father had planted the ivy at the entrance to the Dark Woods, maybe he had planted it in other places around the castle too. If I could follow his trail of vines, maybe I could discover what he had been doing during his last days in the castle.

There was a knock on the door and Vernon entered the room with my dinner tray.

I forced myself to smile.

"Hello," he said in his quiet way.

"Hello." *Traitor.* I returned to my reading.

Vernon must have sensed I didn't want to talk, so he set my tray on the table and went to stoke the flames in the fireplace. The silence went on until Vernon finally said, "You have been preoccupied lately. I miss our talks."

I looked up, not so easily fooled. "Yes. Dr. Ply has increased my responsibilities."

He nodded and began sweeping. "Are you happy about that?"

"Of course. It's what I wanted. It's why I'm here."

I continued to read so I wouldn't have to make small talk with him until I had a thought. "Hey, Vernon?"

He turned. "Yes?"

I chose my words very carefully, knowing this would all get back to Anna. "Remember my first day in the castle? You mentioned people in Stygian with extra abilities. The Dyadics?"

Vernon frowned. "Yes, but I should not have told you that."

"Well, you did." I took a deep breath and tried to sound nicer. "I'm wondering what you meant by that. I mean, what can they *do*?"

Vernon hesitated. "Why do you ask?"

"Something in these papers." I tapped the study I was reading. "I hoped I could impress Dr. Ply with knowledge about Dyadics . . . but never mind. You don't have to tell me if you don't want to."

Vernon turned and finished arranging the burning logs. Then he swept the remaining ashes into a bucket. He glanced back at me like he was glad I was asking questions again. He looked like he wanted to talk, but knew he shouldn't. I almost felt sorry for him, until I remembered he would be meeting with Anna later tonight to relay everything I said.

"Dyadics can do all sorts of things," he finally answered.

I looked up. "Like what? Fly?" I laughed to show I was joking.

"I have not seen anyone fly," Vernon answered, seriously. "But their abilities vary. The simplest way to explain it is like this: If a person has a talent for something, being a Dyadic will enhance that talent. Instead of being just good at it, they are the *greatest*."

"Oh." That didn't sound anything like York's transposing

abilities, but could it have something to do with me? Did I have a talent for seeing what others couldn't?

"Well, you should know that isn't actually possible." I looked back down at my papers, but I could feel his surprise.

"Oh?"

"I'm not saying you're making it up. I'm sure you believe in these sorts of legends because you weren't educated properly. Enlightened people believe there is a scientific reason behind what others, like yourself, perceive as magic." I looked up to see his reaction.

Vernon's eyes narrowed. "Goodnight, Ivy," he said quietly.

"Night."

He walked out of the room, shoulders tight.

I sighed. I hadn't wanted to offend him. It was cruel but necessary. I wanted what I'd said to get to Anna. Maybe if Anna told Dr. Ply that I believed everything he said, I would continue to earn more freedom.

I placed the studies back on the table and quickly ate my dinner. Choking down bland food was now my specialty.

When I was sure enough time had passed since Vernon left, I slipped off my shoes and silently crossed the room in my socks.

I pulled open the door. The hallway was now dark; only flickers of weak light lit the walls. The door shut quietly behind me as I hurried down to the lab before I could change my mind. Knowing someone might be watching wouldn't stop me from trying to uncover the truth about this place.

My feet made no noise. Hugging the walls, I constantly scanned ahead for places to hide in case someone appeared. Thankfully, my luck held, and I saw no one.

Finally, I opened the door to the lab's hallway. I wasn't sure where the South Wing was, but I guessed if I passed the lab and continued, I might end up there, because that was the direction from which the Transposers always came.

I jiggled each doorknob gently as I passed, but each was locked. These rooms were probably where Dr. Ply conducted his other experiments. I wondered where he kept the keys. In the last month cleaning his office, I'd never come across them.

I jiggled the knob to the door of the lab as I passed, but it was also locked. I continued walking, now in unfamiliar territory. My heart thudded as the hallway seemed to snake and wind endlessly.

From up around the corner, I heard a faint noise. I crept forward and tucked myself into an archway cut into the wall. It was shallow, but it hid me well enough.

I leaned out and looked into the next hallway. There were more doors, but there was also a woman I had never seen before. And she wasn't wearing black; instead, she was dressed in light blue. I wondered if that meant she didn't work for Dr. Ply, given the outfits I'd seen Anna, Vernon, Flex, and Jack wear. Who was this woman, and why was she here?

She leaned against the wall casually, but kept sighing loudly as if she was waiting for someone to arrive or something to happen. That wasn't good. I started to turn away when the door across from her suddenly opened and light flooded the hall.

Anna stepped out of the doorway.

I shrank back, alarm filling me. I had been counting on Anna meeting with Vernon right now. I needed to leave, but couldn't help but stay to watch when I saw Anna turn to help a man out of the room. He was either exhausted or very ill. He looked to be around fifty years old. He was dressed in all-white clothing that hung from his thin frame.

"We're finished for tonight," Anna said in her bored voice.

"Come on, Glen." The other woman gently took his weight from Anna. Her voice was soothing. "Let's get you to bed."

Glen's eyes were only halfway open, and he seemed disoriented. He swayed and the woman staggered under his weight.

Anna watched the woman struggle to hold Glen up without a trace of compassion. Finally, she asked, "Lane, do you need help?"

"No. You've already done enough."

"I'd watch that tone if I were you. I'm sure both Dr. Ply and

Cora would frown on such rudeness. Especially when I was offering help."

"Please don't speak on my behalf, Anna."

My heart leaped as I recognized Cora's voice. She stood at the far end of the hallway, her dark hair braided and wound on top of her head like the first day I'd seen her in Windermere. Her crimson gown shimmered in the light and her skin glowed. She wasn't just beautiful, she was magnificent—even without the light I'd seen around her that day.

A scowl crossed Anna's face before her features smoothed.

"Come along, Lane. I'll help you walk him back," Cora said.

But when Cora looked at Glen's face, she paled with anger. Without another look at Anna, Cora turned and walked slowly down the hallway—away from me, thankfully—with Lane. Glen's legs dragged between them.

Anna watched them leave before she turned and walked back into the room. I caught a glimpse of black cables scattered on the floor as she shut the door.

My stomach flipped uneasily. Was this another lab? Had York ever been in it?

After waiting to make sure Anna wasn't coming back out, I crept past the door quietly. I continued down the hallway, trying to catch up with Cora so I could find where she was taking Glen. I prayed it wasn't to the South Wing where York was. I didn't want him connected to this.

After passing countless locked doors and flickering torches, I stopped, confused. I should have caught up to them by now, but somehow, they had disappeared. I turned and backtracked, checking every door I passed in case they'd gone down one. Each was locked.

I pulled my sweater tighter around me, knowing if I stayed in this hallway any longer, I was bound to run into Anna. There was no choice but to go back to my room and try again tomorrow night.

I hurried back down the hallway, consumed by thoughts of

where Cora had gone, and what had happened to Glen in that room. When I noticed footsteps behind me, I couldn't be certain of how long they'd been there.

My heart crashed into my chest as I whirled around. I swallowed a scream when I nearly crashed into the person.

It was Carl.

I stumbled backward, looking up at him. "Oh my goodness! You scared me!"

Carl didn't react the way I thought he would. He held a red apple and watched me as he took a big bite. My heart raced as he crunched for at least a minute, saying nothing. He looked much paler tonight than he had earlier in the lab.

"Do you remember me, Carl? I'm Ivy Rune. We went to school together in Windermere."

If he recognized me, he didn't show it. "Oh. Yeah. Hey."

"Hey," I echoed, warily. "What are you doing? Shouldn't you be in the South Wing?"

"I'm going for a walk."

"Are you allowed to?"

"No." He shrugged. "But what are they going to do? Strap me to that chair again? It doesn't work on me anymore. I'm no good, so it doesn't matter. Pretty soon they'll realize it too."

A chill ran through me. "Who will? Anna?"

Carl took another bite out of his apple. I remembered how healthy and proud Carl had looked that day in Windermere, but now . . . he was beginning to look like a shell of his former self. There were purple circles under his eyes and a simpleness about him that reminded me of a child. What was happening to him?

"Are you friends with Anna?" he asked casually.

"No!" I spit out. "Not even a little bit!"

Carl looked surprised, then his brown eyes turned serious. "She's not so bad. Sometimes she's really nice. She even gives me apples."

"She shouldn't be strapping you to anything! It's wrong—"

My eyes darted to the apple in Carl's hand. Did he mean Anna had just given him *this* apple?

The blood drained from my face, imagining Anna finding me here. I needed to leave but I didn't want Carl to follow me—or worse, make a scene. I began backing up slowly.

"It's not her fault she's mean. She sees everything. The castle changes all of us," Carl said.

"It is too her fault. People always have a choice."

Carl suddenly peered closer at me, as if he was seeing me for the first time. "Hey—Rune. *Rune.* Mr. Rune—didn't your father disappear?"

I froze mid-step, the shock hitting me like a punch to the gut. "What?"

"He stole something too. That wasn't nice. He made everyone mad for a while."

"Who was, Carl?" I forgot my fear of getting caught and marched up to him. "*Who was mad?*"

Carl backed up, startled by my intensity. Sudden awareness crossed his face, as if he'd realized that he was in the hallway, and not where he should be. Panic overtook him.

"I have to go! If I'm caught again, it's over."

Then he turned and sprinted down the hall.

"No! Wait!"

But Carl was already gone.

I ran after him, slipping as I went, desperate for him to tell me more about my father, but just like Cora, Carl had also disappeared.

TWELVE

The next morning, Dr. Ply handed Carl's file to me.

As the transposers filed in, I watched Carl closely. He looked better than he had last night. The paleness had left his face and his eyes were no longer glazed. How could he change so rapidly?

My eyes cut to Anna. She sat at her normal spot by the door, disinterested as always, as she scanned the room.

Last night, I'd felt like she and Cora repelled each other like magnets—people on opposite sides of something. It was clear they only tolerated each other. But why? And who was Glen? If he was a transposer, then why wasn't he in the lab? Maybe he was too sick to work.

I glanced at Jack. He sat at his desk, watching the room and also writing in his own file. I liked Jack and I wanted to believe the best about him, even if he was the Count's heir. Still, I wondered what he knew, or how much he knew. I was deeply unsettled by the room with the cables and the way Glen had stumbled out of it. It reminded me of the study of electricity and memories that Dr. Ply hadn't wanted me to read. In fact, he'd been downright strange about it. Surely he wasn't conducting experiments like that?

My eyes darted to York. I couldn't handle the thought of him being hurt. But he looked the same as he had the first day I'd seen him here: Still intently focused on his white wood, still unnaturally excited about seeing it. There were no changes in his demeanor like there were in Carl's.

Carl had said that my father had stolen something. That people were upset.

Next to me, Dr. Ply's pencil scratched his paper. Did *he* have something to do with my father's disappearance? Was I sitting next to the person responsible? Goosebumps broke out on my arms.

After last night, I was more worried about York than ever. He was in danger. I needed to find a moment with him away from the lab. I had to make it to the South Wing.

I yawned, wishing I had gotten more sleep last night.

"Tired, Ivy?" Dr. Ply asked casually.

I snapped my mouth shut. "I'm sorry. I'm afraid I didn't sleep well."

"Were you reading late? I asked that you be well rested for our lab work."

"No, I wasn't. I mean, I did read a little, but I just couldn't get comfortable."

Dr. Ply cleared his throat and continued scribbling in his notebook. I picked up my pencil and began writing too.

The rest of the morning passed uneventfully. I was relieved when Jack dismissed everyone for lunch. Carl was last to stand and leave. He glanced at York's table as he passed and inspected York's Carving, but I didn't understand the expression on his face. It looked like relief.

The lab emptied, and Jack entered the room as Dr. Ply was collecting my file. He looked handsome as always, his dark shirt crisp and his hair neat, like he'd just had it trimmed. I had no idea if there were people in the castle who cut hair or pressed shirts, but I realized there must be.

There was so much going on that I was being kept from.

"Hello, Dr. Ply. Ivy," Jack said.

I smiled politely, making sure not to look at him too long in front of Dr. Ply. "Hello."

"Jack, did Carl's schedule change last night?"

I froze.

Jack frowned, as he always did when Carl's name came up. "Not that I know of. Why?"

"Anna reported that Carl was acting difficult today, particularly towards her. Usually, she's the only one who can reason with him."

I tried to breathe normally. Surely my words about Anna hadn't affected Carl? What if Carl told them he'd seen me in the hallway?

"I'll talk to Cora," Jack said. "I don't think anything changed, but you never know with Carl."

"Let me know when you do," Dr. Ply said, before turning to me. "That's all, Ivy. I'll see you in my office later for research."

———

THE REST OF THE DAY PASSED IN A BLUR OF WORRY, BUT I made it through my work with Dr. Ply without raising his suspicions. Vernon asked his usual questions, but he was more cautious after what I'd said to him about being uneducated. I fed him the information I wanted Anna to hear, and then he finally left for the night.

I yawned as I walked to my closet. These late nights were becoming exhausting, but I was determined to find the South Wing and York.

I walked into the cold tunnel, thinking about Carl's claims that the castle changed everyone. I believed him. All I wanted now was to get myself and York out of here before it was too late.

I wondered if it had been too late for my father.

What and who had he stolen from? Dr. Ply was the obvious choice since my father had worked for him, but I shouldn't just assume that. If I ran into Carl again, I would make him tell me more.

I shivered, wanting to leave this tunnel quickly. I had just passed the door that led to the extravagant staircase when I saw another door on the wall opposite. Again, I left the torch in the tunnel and pulled the door open slowly. I stepped into another empty hallway.

The stone looked older, the torches barely lit, but it felt the same—cold and eerily silent.

I marked the wall with my charcoal and wandered for a few minutes before I saw a fork up ahead. I drew another line on the wall as I veered left. Suddenly, I was outside.

I walked slowly out into a large courtyard of pillars and stone archways draped with jasmine. The middle of the courtyard was only a flat piece of grass, but it smelled heavenly. The sky glittered overhead like a dark jewel and a cool breeze ruffled my hair. In the distance, owls hooted from high in the trees. Under the glow of the moon and twinkling stars, I took in a deep, steadying breath as tears prickled my eyes.

It seemed like it had been years—not months—since I had been outside at night. Only now did I realize just how caged I was inside the gloomy castle. I had forgotten how wonderful a dark, crisp night could feel. It reminded me of home.

Then the sound of neighing drifted up to where I stood. A light danced on the stone pillar at the far end of the courtyard. Curious, I walked over and peered into the darkness. A dirt path wound down toward a large grey stable tucked into the edge of the woods.

A fire blazed next to it, circled by a dozen men, eating and drinking. In the orange light, their distinct features made me gasp.

I recognized them from the ship York and I had seen near the Count's beach. They had come here after all. I looked for the short, strong man, but didn't see him.

Footsteps sounded behind me. Whoever it was was coming

swiftly. Panicked, I looked around for a place to hide, but before I could move, Jack appeared.

Instead of what he normally wore, he was dressed in outdoor clothes, and the first button on his collar was undone. He stopped mid-stride and his blue eyes widened.

"Ivy? What are you doing out here?"

"I'm lost," I lied quickly. "I was walking back to my room and I made a wrong turn."

Jack's brow raised. "Yes. That was quite a *long* wrong turn. You are completely on the other side of the castle. Didn't you realize it after walking a mile?"

He smiled, and I sagged in relief.

"I thought I could figure it out, but then it was too late. I just kept making wrong turns. Everything looks the same."

"Ah. You'll get used to it, eventually. I got lost a lot too when I first arrived."

"When was that?" I asked, wondering if he would give me a truthful answer.

Jack stared at me for a moment and something flickered across his face. "About a million years ago. Another lifetime."

"Oh. I didn't realize you were so old."

A grin spread across his face. "Yes, I'm ancient."

I smiled back, letting myself look at him openly now that no one was here to watch us. Jack always seemed at ease to me, but away from Dr. Ply, he was even more relaxed.

He tilted his head. "Where's Anna? I thought she escorts you around?"

"Not anymore. But she probably will now, after she hears about this."

"*If* she hears."

I narrowed my eyes. "You're not going to tell?"

"Why would I do that? Like I said, I like having you here. Perhaps after meeting Anna, you understand why."

I couldn't help but laugh. "Where are you going?"

"I was about to check on the Count's horses. I usually visit the stables in the afternoon, but this is the first chance I've had today."

My throat tightened, thinking about Loon. "How many horses does the Count have?"

"Hundreds. He collects a rare breed from across the sea. Very few people have even laid eyes on them. Maybe someday I'll show you."

My hopes lifted. "I'd like that."

"Would you?" Jack looked pleased. "Of course, we'd have to clear it with Dr. Ply. Unauthorized visits are not allowed in the stables. I showed his last assistant and they disappeared the very next day."

I looked at him, startled. My smile dropped.

"Did I say something wrong?" Concern flashed across his face. "You look like your whole world just fell apart."

Tears began to leak from my eyes. Horrified, I spun around and squeezed my eyes shut to stop them. I wiped my cheeks, embarrassed by my unexpected breakdown. But why had he said that? He knew my mother had vanished on a ship and my father had disappeared in the forest before being declared dead.

There was a gentle touch at my elbow. I looked down to see Jack offering me a handkerchief. I took it and patted my eyes, trying to compose myself before I faced him again.

"I'm sorry for saying that." He spoke softly. "I didn't realize how you would take it. I'm sorry."

I sniffed. "It's OK. It just took me by surprise."

"I understand. You're under a lot of stress. I've forgotten what it feels like to be new here. Life at the castle can be a hard adjustment."

"Yes." My breathing was now under control, so I turned and handed him back the handkerchief. He tucked it into his pocket.

"It is a lot," I admitted. "I miss home, but I *really* miss my horse. I asked Dr. Ply months ago if I could bring her here and he said no . . . She's more than just a horse to me. She's all I have left of my father."

For a moment, there was nothing but the sound of crickets. Jack broke the silence and said, "Come on, I'll show you the stable."

"Really?" I looked up at him hopefully. "Won't we get in trouble?"

"We might." Jack smiled, revealing white teeth. "But only if someone tells. And I won't say anything."

"I won't either," I vowed, smiling.

He gestured to the path leading toward the grey stable.

We started down the path, and then I felt Jack take my elbow. I looked up, surprised. But he held a finger to his lips and nodded toward the group of men by the fire.

"They trust me, barely. But you, they won't."

The men looked up and watched us walking toward them, their expressions unreadable in the firelight. No one smiled, but several eyes flickered to the hold Jack had on my arm. My heart began to race. Up close, I could tell their grey clothes were thick and sturdy, with neat stitches. Gold studs glinted in their ears, noses, and lips. And they looked similar; each had the same broad forehead, wide nose, and light green eyes.

Jack greeted them flawlessly in their language. I looked at him, startled, as more unfamiliar words were exchanged. Clapping the man closest to him on the back, Jack uttered something that sounded like a command.

The men nodded, then turned back to the fire and their drinks.

Jack dropped my arm as he slid open the tall stable door. I wanted to ask him what he'd said, but the question faded from my lips as I followed him into the most elegant stable I had ever seen.

Stall after stall stretched down, each formed from looping black iron bars and each door with a nameplate. Not a piece of hay was out of place. The sound of neighs and hoofs brought waves of emotion over me. I felt right at home.

I had never seen such spectacular horses. I doubted anyone had. These horses had coats of rich grey velvet and manes and tails like wet ink. Each horse had angled, sharp features and large coal eyes. When they saw Jack, they came forward eagerly, pushing their faces out of the stalls to be greeted. Jack petted each horse fondly.

"They're beautiful," I breathed.

"A perfect blend of genetics and breeding."

"Are they all this color?" I asked, stroking each soft face that let me.

"Most are. It's the Count's signature. But there are a few black horses here too. What does your horse look like?"

"Oh, Loon's beautiful too," I said, reaching up to scratch a velvety nose. "But she's tan but her mane and tail are white."

"Loon? That's a unique name."

"I named her after the birds around Windermere. When I was little, I used to love listening to them out on the water. There is something so heartbreaking and beautiful about their call."

A horse nudged my shoulder, nearly knocking me over. Jack reached out to steady me, and our eyes met. I blushed at how close we were, but then an enormous black horse charged into the stable.

Thirteen

The black horse reared and landed, stomping its hoofs. Its mane was braided into tight loops, and its tail flicked side to side. I couldn't tell if the rider was a man or a woman. A black cloak covered their head and body. All I saw was gleaming brown boots.

I took a startled step backward.

"Whoa!" Jack stepped in front of me and threw up his hands.

When he'd finally calmed the horse enough to grab the bridle, the rider swung gracefully to the ground. The cloak's hood fell back to reveal Cora's flushed face. Her dark hair rippled loosely around her shoulders and down her back. Under the cloak, she wore elegant riding clothes.

"Cora!" Jack snorted. "I should have known. Where have you been?"

"Hello, Jack." Cora smiled. When she caught sight of me, her eyes widened in disbelief.

I shifted awkwardly, wondering why Cora seemed so shocked. Did she remember me from that day in town?

"This is Ivy Rune from Windermere," Jack said. "She's Dr. Ply's new assistant."

Cora's expression quickly smoothed into a friendly smile. "A pleasure to meet you, Ivy. You must know York."

York's name hit me like a bucket of cold water. For a wonderful moment, I'd lost myself in the stable. Now everything came rushing back.

I nodded. "I do. How do you know York?"

"We work together."

I frowned, thinking of Glen.

"Dr. Ply must be hiding you, since our paths have never crossed," Cora said lightly. "How long have you been here?"

"Only a few months. I'm not really allowed out, but I got lost tonight walking back to my room."

Cora's brow raised. "Dr. Ply doesn't know you're here right now?"

"No." I glanced at Jack. But he didn't seem worried that Cora would tell on us.

Cora must have sensed my discomfort, because she quickly said, "Don't worry. Your secrets are always safe with me."

I smiled, hoping that was true.

The black horse stamped its feet impatiently and Cora took a moment to steady him. Then she asked, "So, tell me. How did you come to be at the castle? Did you want to work here?"

"No. It happened after the Count's Tournament. I was, um, disqualified, and then Jack came and told me that Dr. Ply wanted me to be his assistant."

"Is that so?" A look passed between Cora and Jack.

"I was following orders," Jack said lightly.

She turned back to me. "Are you a Carver, then?"

"No, I was training to be an Arborist."

Cora's brow creased. "Then why were you in the Count's Woodworking Tournament?"

"Mr. Mallon gave me the extra spot."

"Why would he do that, if you were going to be an Arborist?"

"I didn't pass the test." I reddened, now having to admit two of my failings to Cora. She looked like she had never failed at anything in her life.

She frowned again, but then a young groom appeared at her side.

"Thank you, Geoff." Cora handed him the reins. "Well, it was very nice to meet you. Hopefully we'll see much more of each other now that I know you are here. If you ever need anything, you can find me in the South Wing—I'm always happy to help. We'll talk later, Jack. And remember, the two of you never saw me here either."

Jack smiled. "I never do."

Cora nodded, pulling her dark cloak back over her head as she hurried out the side door. Her groom swiftly led the black horse away and the stable was quiet again.

Jack turned to me. "We should get you back to your room before anyone else discovers you're somewhere you're not supposed to be."

I sighed. "OK."

Jack chuckled. "I see you're enjoying your accommodations as much as I did when I arrived at the castle. Really, those rooms are hard to live in."

"It's not just that. I forgot how much I love being outside. Sometimes it feels like I'm living in a cage."

Jack looked thoughtful. "I guess I don't appreciate how much I get to be outside. If I were stuck indoors, I'd be miserable too."

"Do you ride a lot?" I looked at the horses, imagining flying over the castle grounds just like Cora had.

"Yes, but never as much as I'd like."

We continued back through the stable, and Jack said goodbye to each horse that came up to him again.

"Do they love the Count like this too?" I asked, then flushed at my choice of words.

Jack looked surprised but then grinned. "I guess you'd have to ask them."

I laughed. "You know, I can't picture *you* in a room like the one I'm staying in at all. Or Cora."

"It took me almost two years to work my way up to a better room. But you're right about one thing—Cora didn't start there like we did. She's one of the few that came to the castle already in her position."

"She works with the transposers?"

"Yes."

When he didn't expound on it, I knew that Jack didn't want to share anymore. But I had never been that easily deterred. I tried again.

"What did you have to do to earn a better room?"

Jack looked at me, his eyes twinkling, and shrugged.

"It must have been a lot of work, if you are in such a high position now. Especially as the Count's prospective heir. What does that even mean, by the way?"

"That everyone here loves me and hangs on my every word."

Now I snorted. "Except Anna, you mean. She doesn't seem to like you very much."

Jack frowned as we reached the doors. Outside, he took my elbow again and steered me past the men by the fire. The night air now had a bite to it and I noticed the fire was higher. Jack gave the men a parting nod as he led me back up the path to the courtyard.

"No, she doesn't does she?" Jack said, finally responding to my last question.

"Why not? Did something happen between you two?"

Jack looked at me quickly. "No. Why would you think that?"

I shrugged, hiding my smile. "I don't know, maybe because Anna acts like a woman scorned?"

Jack snickered. "You know, you're very funny when you're not crying."

I swatted his shoulder. "You're never going to let me forget that, are you?"

"Definitely not."

"Great."

We reached the courtyard, but instead of going back inside the castle, Jack paused to look up at the night sky. I wondered if he was as reluctant to end the night as I was.

I leaned against the pillar to look at the stars. A comfortable silence fell over us. The stone was cold against my back, but I wasn't ready to go inside just yet. This was such a welcome relief after the past few months. It felt like both time and my problems had paused, but once I stepped back into the castle, my new life would be real again.

"Are you from across the sea too?" I asked.

"I'm from a place called Stygian. And yes, it's far across the sea."

"That's where Vernon's from! He said people in Stygian have extra abilities."

Jack frowned. "Vernon talks too much. You should forget he said that. And never let Dr. Ply hear you sound so happy about it."

"Why not?"

"Dyadics are a *very* touchy subject with him. If you haven't already, you'll find that out soon enough. I'm assuming Vernon's been assigned to your room?"

I looked at Jack, wondering if he knew Vernon was spying on me. "Yes," I answered, carefully. "And you're right, Vernon talks *a lot.*"

Jack glanced at me. "I didn't mean that as an insult. It's just . . . people from Stygian are not supposed to share that kind of information with anyone. But some people find it harder not to talk than others."

"Is that why Anna doesn't talk to anyone else?"

"Ah, Anna." Jack sighed. "She's in a class all her own. No one's good enough to talk to her, although it hasn't always been that way."

"That shouldn't make me feel better, but it does."

"When it comes to Anna, you'll find it's rarely you." Jack looked like he wanted to say more, but decided against it.

"Is Anna from Stygian too?"

"Yes. But—now I have a question for you. Why did you assume I was from across the sea? I could have come from somewhere in the mountains."

"There's nothing up there. Everybody knows that."

Jack looked amused. "Are you sure?"

"That's what everyone in Windermere says. The mountains are just snow and ice and barren land. Completely uninhabitable." I quoted everything I had ever heard about the mountains.

"I wouldn't believe everything you hear."

"Have you been up there?"

"Many times."

"With who?"

Jack hesitated. "The Count."

My stomach dropped. I knew how close he must be to the Count. I had begun to hope that Jack's involvement in whatever Dr. Ply was doing didn't run that deep, that he didn't know everything that went on at the castle. But as the Count's heir, he must. I wanted to believe that Jack only took care of the horses, but I had seen him in the lab too.

I found solace in one thing: Cora liked him, and she didn't like Anna.

"What's the Count like?" I asked. "I've only heard stories."

He shook his head, smiling. "I've already said too much. You have a way of making people talk, do you know that? That's dangerous around here. Ever hear the saying *curiosity killed the cat*?"

"Lots of times, from my father."

"Well, listen, then. It's good advice."

I felt Jack's gaze on me. When I glanced over, he was staring at me intently. I straightened, my stomach dipping. I pulled at my hair, twirling it around my finger to give my hands something to do.

"I like the color of your hair," Jack said quietly. "It's like honey."

"Oh . . . um, thanks." I brushed it from my shoulder, suddenly very aware that we were alone.

For a moment, neither of us made a move to leave. Then I shivered.

"It's cold. I wouldn't be surprised if we got an early snowfall soon. Let's get you inside before you freeze."

The temperature had been dropping steadily. I quickly followed him into the castle. We walked down the stone hallways, but this time, our footsteps echoed quietly together.

"Didn't you need to check on the horses?" I asked a moment later. "I'd hate to keep you."

"That can wait a little longer—*rescuing* you was more important. And I wouldn't want you to get lost again."

"I guess I'm lucky it was you who found me," I said, keeping up the charade. "Anna or Dr. Ply probably wouldn't have been as nice about it."

"You're right about that. This better stay our little secret."

"Fine." I smiled at the thought of keeping two secrets with Jack. Seeing the horses, and seeing Cora. If he wasn't telling on me, then he couldn't be all bad.

When we reached my door, disappointment filled me. For a brief moment, life had felt simple.

"I'll see you tomorrow in the lab, then," Jack said.

"See you tomorrow," I echoed.

He smiled and walked back down the hallway, whistling as he went. When he disappeared around the corner, I stepped back into my big, cold room.

The fire was still lit and the room looked exactly the same, but I felt different. More hopeful about my future, maybe. I washed my face, taking more care than I usually did. I changed my clothes and walked back into the big room, and it was only then that I noticed something lying on my bed.

A chill snaked its way through me. It was difficult to breathe.

Out of all the beds in the room, only the one I slept in had something on it.

Someone had been in here.

I walked closer to see what was on my pillow.

A white orchid.

It had been over ten years since I'd seen a fresh one. The only one I had was pressed in my father's journal. I picked up the white flower and carefully touched the velvety petals. As I breathed in its vanilla scent, I considered the message.

Someone in the castle knew about my father.

And they wanted me to know it.

Fourteen

After breakfast, I made my way to Dr. Ply's office, yawning and shaking the drowsiness from my head.

I reached into the pocket of my dress and felt the velvety petals of the white orchid, relieved that someone had finally shown they knew my father. But the thought that someone had been in my room unsettled me. I supposed they could have used Vernon to put it there, but I couldn't ask him without Anna knowing about it.

What if they had come to talk, but found me gone? I wondered if they would try again. I hoped so.

I knocked on Dr. Ply's office door and went inside.

He was behind his desk, enjoying his usual coffee and scone. I didn't even look down today to see what kind it was. My plain oatmeal sat like a lump in my stomach.

"Good morning, Ivy. Have a seat."

I sat and smoothed my dress, taking care not to crush the orchid in my pocket. Dr. Ply looked at me expectantly. This was the part of the morning where I was given the opportunity to ask a question about our training.

"Where is the white wood that the Transposers use from? I

assume it's rare and directly influences the outcome of transposing."

He nodded. "It does, and it is. We have a small supply, but the source is unfortunately extinct. One of our goals is to create more. Remember the Dark Woods?"

I frowned. "That wood is black."

"Exactly. But it shouldn't be. We aim to change that."

"Is white wood the only wood that will turn into laun?"

"Yes."

I took a deep breath, aware that I had gone well over my one allotted question. "And what is laun?"

Dr. Ply sipped his coffee, considering his words. "It is a material more valuable than any precious metal or gemstone you can think of."

I leaned forward, my curiosity getting the better of me.

Dr. Ply noticed. "Have you ever heard of the Isles of Gelid?"

"No."

"It was an ancient city surrounded by islands. The ruling class bought and settled debts with laun coins. Only the elite handled them. It was so rare that no one else knew it existed. Even now it is considered only folklore."

"Did Transposers who made laun from white wood exist in the Isles of Gelid?"

"If they did, their existence was not recorded. The Count is the only one who keeps Transposers now—at least, that we know of."

"How do the Transposers . . . Transpose? Scientifically, I mean."

"I'm still working on my theory, but I've tested both the white wood and many transposers themselves over the years. I don't understand the exact details of *how* it happens, only that it *can*."

I thought of the room with the cables. Was that how he *tested transposers*? I tried my luck with one more question. "How did you first discover the white wood could turn into laun?"

Dr. Ply held up a hand. "That's enough questions for today.

In due time, you will learn more if you continue to prove yourself trustworthy. Now, today will be different than usual."

"Oh?" I hoped I would still get to see York in the lab. Even if he didn't know I was there, it was still comforting to be near him.

"You have an opportunity to prove your loyalty."

A tingle went down my spine. I wondered what I would have to do.

"Your father was also able to enter the Tree Garden. Soon thereafter, he began to work with me on our experiments with laun in the Tree Garden. I know he passed the key onto you and that is how you were able to get inside as well."

I nodded, surprised. I didn't add that I could get into the Tree Garden on my own now—no key necessary.

Dr. Ply opened a drawer and took out a small package wrapped in brown paper. It was identical to the packages I'd found in the basket at the Tree Garden.

"Unwrap it. It's time you understood what's inside."

I picked up the package and carefully unwrapped the paper. A small block of laun shone up at me. A magnetism seemed to float up from it, compelling my hand to touch it. I leaned back ever so slightly to stop myself.

"Very peculiar, the attraction it gives off," Dr. Ply said, watching me. "Somehow you know not to touch it, but I don't believe I ever told you not to."

I swallowed, keeping my face calm even though my heart was racing. Dr. Ply might know about my father's wooden owl, but he didn't know about my father's clues leading me to the Tree Garden.

I wondered if he was going to ask me how I'd found it.

What would I say if he did?

It was possible that there would be no harm in admitting the clues. They had only led me to the Tree Garden and the castle. And, of course, the clues had stopped. I was stuck on the last remaining one: *Hedera*.

"Another legend warned that laun coins made the noble class

vicious because the coins gifted those who owned them powerful abilities; that the noble class hoarded laun and refused to part with it lest they lose their gifts. Much blood was shed by those trying to accumulate the most laun." Dr. Ply sat back in his chair and rested his hands over his round stomach. "Eventually, laun was hunted and destroyed by those who disapproved of the power it gave."

The clock ticked on the shelf. I pulled my eyes away from the shining laun and looked at Dr. Ply.

"In my decades of research, I've found that once a person touches laun, they only want it more. And once a transposer has handled it, they become fixated. Obsessed. Once laun is created in the lab, we take it away quickly and always keep it covered. So, let this be your warning never to touch it. For once you do, you will never be able to undo the change. Understand?"

I stared down at the laun, in awe of how it seemed to grab onto rays of light and pull them inside itself. It was so beautiful. I swallowed. "If I touched it, would I become a Transposer too?"

Maybe if I were a Transposer, I could talk with York. I could work with him in the lab and live in the South Wing with Cora.

Dr. Ply watched me carefully. "I can't predict how you would change. Only that you most certainly would."

Despite his warning, I got the sense that Dr. Ply would not physically stop me from touching it. Then he could use me in his experiments too.

I shuddered, coming back to my senses. I rewrapped the package, but not without effort, and looked up at him. He didn't reveal if he was disappointed or not.

"Dr. Ply, how would you describe the color of laun?"

"I have recorded it as a dull, muted gold. With a transparent quality."

I nodded. So Dr. Ply couldn't see the light around it.

"Normally, I would go with you, but today I have a meeting with the Count. I am trusting you to go alone. Take this to the Tree Garden and place it within the oldest tree, then return to the castle immediately. Ensure that you are not seen by anyone from Windermere. As you know, we don't like raising any curiosity from town."

I nodded, surprised he was allowing me to leave the castle. This was progress.

"Do you know the way from here?"

I thought through the route in my head and nodded. I was so happy to be going, I didn't even mind how far a walk it would be.

"Very good. And I have something else for you. A reward."

My brows rose in shock. There was more?

"I appreciate that you've accepted my rule to abstain from friendships or relationships with such grace."

I forced the guilt from my face. Just last night I had snuck out to find York and had spent the night talking with Jack. And secretly, I was looking forward to seeing Jack again.

"I've arranged a surprise. Jack is waiting outside to escort you to it."

"Thank you." I knew I should be more wary, but I was just too happy thinking about going to the Tree Garden.

"You're welcome. Let this serve as motivation to continue to build my trust."

———

JACK WAS WAITING IN THE HALLWAY, LEANING AGAINST an arched window, a heavy coat slung over his forearm. When he saw me, his face relaxed into a smile.

I smiled back as my stomach dipped. "Hello."

"Hello, yourself. It's been a while."

I glanced back at Dr. Ply's closed door. "Yes, it has."

Part of me wished we could go back to the stables. Last night had been my brightest moment in the castle so far.

Jack's blue eyes twinkled. "Are you ready for your surprise? I think you're going to be happy."

"Where are we going?"

"I'm keeping it a secret. But first, we'll stop by your room and get your coat. It just started to snow." Jack shrugged on his heavy coat as we started walking.

It made such a difference, walking the halls with Jack rather than with Anna. There was a lightness to him, like the gloominess of the castle couldn't touch him. And when I was with him, the gloom didn't touch me either. He was the sun, and I eagerly soaked up his warmth and excitement as he went on and on about the snow falling outside.

"It's like you've never seen winter before!" I chuckled, amused.

"I haven't. Well, not until I came here. In Stygian, it's summer all the time."

"Is your family still there?"

He nodded. "My parents, brother, and two younger sisters."

How strange it must be to have so many family members, but not to be near them. I had no one left, but if I did, I would want to be with them. "I bet you miss them."

"I do."

"Why are you here without them, then?" I asked, hoping I wasn't prying too much.

Jack hesitated. "My father was a watchmaker. He began to lose his sight, so my older brother took over the business. I was supposed to help too, but I had no talent or patience for sitting indoors and tinkering with metal. I decided to help in a way that allowed me to feel like I wasn't wasting my life doing something that was not for me. So I came to take care of the Count's horses. I can send more money home from here than I would have been able to earn in Stygian."

I looked up at him, thinking that was really honorable. "And now you're the Count's heir."

"*Prospective* heir," Jack corrected.

"What does that mean?" I asked again. I was still confused by his role here.

His eyes cut to mine. "That at any moment, it could be taken away."

"Oh." I mulled that over as we walked. It sounded like Jack needed to watch his step as much as I did.

I lowered my voice. "Are you happy here?"

Jack made a sound like he was holding in a laugh, and he glanced around us to make sure the hall was empty. "I'm happy my family is taken care of."

"But what about *you*?"

Jack glanced at me, curious. He shrugged. "I get to ride the most legendary horses that ever existed. And someday, they may be mine."

"And that's enough?" I pressed, without knowing why. I guessed I just wanted to know if what he did here—whatever he was involved in—was something he would be happy doing forever.

Jack looked thoughtful. "Till now, it has been enough. But that's the beauty of life; things change." He nodded ahead; we'd reached my room. "Better hurry."

He leaned against the wall as I slipped inside.

I glanced at my bed first, but nothing was there. I went down the aisle toward the closet, stopping to look out the small window. A blanket of white already covered the ground. I shivered and pulled on thicker socks, boots, and my warmest coat. I doubted it would be enough, but it would have to do. I would endure any weather just to get out of the castle for a while.

I met Jack back in the hall. "Lead the way!"

He grinned in response.

Ice crept up the windows of the corridor and our breath filled the hallway in front of us. The halls didn't look familiar to me until we turned the corner and were hit with a blast of frosty air. Then I saw pillars and archways. Only then did I realize we were heading toward the stable. Excitement swelled in my chest—

"Ivy, Jack. *Stop*."

Anna stepped out from behind a pillar.

FIFTEEN

Snowflakes fell around Anna, melting on her black braid. Her grey eyes matched the lifeless stone around her. She was carrying a large bundle of fabric.

My heart dropped. Dr. Ply must have discovered I snuck out last night after all and sent Anna here to stop me. Or maybe they'd heard Jack and I laughing and had come to put a stop to it.

"Anna." Jack's voice had an edge to it. "Fancy meeting you here."

Anna ignored him and looked at me. "Dr. Ply retrieved your horse and is allowing you to ride it on your errand given the terrible weather."

I huffed out a relieved breath, turning the air white in front of me. That was not what I'd expected her to say. My happiness faded as I saw the contempt on her face. Anna had always been cold and detached, but now she actually looked hateful.

"Way to ruin the surprise!" Jack exclaimed. "You knew she hadn't seen Loon yet."

Anna's eyes flickered to Jack. "Dr. Ply also asked me to make sure *you* do not leave the castle grounds. He wants you to report back to him immediately."

"I wasn't leaving," Jack said.

She turned her attention back to me. "This is for you. Another reward from Dr. Ply." Her eyes shot daggers as she stepped forward and held out the bundle of fabric.

I took it and quickly put space between us again. It was a dark-green wool cloak, its hood trimmed with spotted white fur. It had to be the finest thing I had ever touched.

"This is from Dr. Ply?" I asked, my voice colored with awe. It reminded me of the rich carpet on the grand staircase I'd seen the first night I'd traversed the castle through the door in my closet.

"He wants you to wear it today. I'm supposed to trade it with your other coat."

Jack took the cloak as I slipped out of my coat and handed it to Anna. Then he dropped the heavy green cloak around my shoulders, flooding me with warmth. I tied it with shaking hands, almost embarrassed by how much I loved the color. It felt like coming home somehow. I felt as sophisticated as Cora.

But then I looked back at Anna, who was standing in the cold without anything to keep her warm.

"Do you want to use my coat?" I asked, feeling guilty. Had Dr. Ply ever given her something this nice?

Anna looked disgusted by my pity. "I don't feel the cold anymore."

I stared at her in surprise. She turned and walked back into the castle.

"Sorry she ruined the surprise." Jack sounded frustrated.

I shrugged, the warmth—and the fact that I hadn't gotten caught—a relief. I turned to look up at him. "Is Loon really here?"

A smile lit his face. "Yes, she's really here. And she's beautiful, just like you said. She can hold her own even with the Count's horses."

"Come on, then! I can't wait to see her!" I took off down the slippery path toward the stable.

Jack followed, laughing.

The scent of evergreen drifted through the fresh, crisp air.

Snow had a way of wiping everything clean and making it new. Even the stable looked cozy and inviting, covered in white fluff and tucked under the trees.

Inside was full of hay and the heat of horses.

"This way."

Jack led me past the stalls of stormy-colored horses until we reached the stall that held Loon. When Loon saw me, she whinnied and stomped her feet. I flung open the door and threw my arms around her neck. I didn't even stop the tears that filled my eyes.

"I missed you so much!" I whispered, stroking her white mane and rubbing her velvety neck. Something in me eased, feeling Loon's strength beside me now.

"When did she arrive?" I asked, remembering Jack, who leaned against the stall door, smiling.

"Early this morning. I had her groomed for you too."

"Will she stay here?"

"Yes. There are other stables on the property, but this one is the best. I moved her here so I could watch her, just in case you can't see her as much as you want. At least you'll know she is being well cared for."

Our eyes met across the stall. My voice sounded thick when I said, "Thank you. That's more than I ever expected."

He nodded. "You know, that color matches your green eyes perfectly."

Heat rushed to my cheeks. "I can't believe Dr. Ply gave it to me."

Just hearing Dr. Ply's name seemed to instantly sober Jack. He reached to take a lead rope off a hook on the wall. "Do you know where you're going?"

"I think so."

"There's a path. I'll show you." Jack led Loon out of the stall to saddle her. I stayed close, petting her and feeding her carrots from a basket on the ground.

"Is it hard for you to be here, away from Windermere?" Jack

asked, nudging me over a bit so he could fit the bridle on Loon's head.

"It's harder than I thought it would be. I miss everything; even little things."

"Like what?"

"Like . . . the scent of lavender. Walking across the lavender fields on the farm. I walked through them every day and never appreciated how beautiful they were." I took a deep breath. "Why are you asking me this? Are you trying to make me cry *again*?"

He chuckled, pulling a strap tighter. "Maybe that was my goal."

I pretended to glare at him. "What about you? Have you been back to Stygian since you came here?"

"No."

"Do you think you'll ever go back?" I asked, thinking about his family.

"I hope so."

"Really?" I bit my lip. "So you don't see yourself here forever, then?"

He paused to look at me. "Do you?"

"No!" The word came out faster than I intended.

Jack gazed at me, his expression thoughtful. Then he turned and began walking Loon outside.

I stared at his back, realizing that I had begun to trust him. When had that happened? How had we fallen into this ease with each other? And why did it feel so honest?

I followed slowly, hoping it wasn't another mistake, like Vernon. This would hurt much more.

When I caught up to him, Jack began describing the path that went through the castle grounds and led directly to the Tree Garden.

"You've been there before?" I asked.

"Yes." He looked down at me, as if he was deciding something. "Who do you think delivered the packages inside the tree stump?"

"*You*?" I asked.

He nodded.

"Did you know *I* was the one collecting them?"

Jack paused, as if he was considering how much to say. Finally, he nodded. "Of course."

I didn't know what to say. This meant Jack had known me *before* he'd come to get me from the Tournament. Had he watched me, too? Did everyone in this castle spy on each other? I had to know.

"Did you ever see me?"

"Yes. I had to make sure you found the packages and took them inside. We can't get in, you know. I would have left once I saw you enter—that was all I was tasked with—but then I saw your face light up . . . and you laughed." He smiled, remembering. "I might have stayed a little longer."

"When you came to get me in Windermere, I thought you seemed like you knew me."

Jack nodded. "I did a bad job of hiding it. Does that upset you?"

"That you spied on me? Not at all. It's only fair." I arched my brow. "I saw you before we met too."

He looked surprised. "When?"

"At the beach. I was behind a boulder and saw you greeting that wrecked ship. You were riding that amazing black horse. I hoped I'd meet you again."

I flushed, admitting that out loud. We stared at each other, both of us at a loss, not knowing what to say next. The snow came down harder around us.

Finally, Jack stirred and reluctantly looked out into the trees. "You need to go. But if it starts coming down any harder, turn around and come back."

"OK."

Jack frowned and pointed out over the castle lawn. "The path begins just past that big clump of trees. You can't miss it. Stay on it and you shouldn't see anyone from Windermere."

"I will."

Loon stamped her feet and snorted, pushing her head into my shoulder. She was excited to ride too.

Then he looked back at me, his blue eyes piercing mine. "If you're not back in an hour, I'll come after you."

I nodded and turned to mount Loon, but Jack caught my elbow and gently turned me back toward him.

For a moment, I forgot where we were and only saw his blue eyes, parted lips, and the smallest trace of stubble along his jaw. My breath caught.

"Don't go anywhere you're not supposed to. Dr. Ply will know. I'd hate to see you lose Loon."

A chill spread through me that had nothing to do with the weather. I gripped Loon's reins tighter, as if I could protect her. "What do you mean?"

Jack hesitated. "I just meant—be careful. You really *don't* have any idea how it works here yet. You've shown that Loon is price-less to you and now they will use her to keep you in line. Honestly, it's probably the only reason she's here."

"Dr. Ply said it was a reward." But I twisted the reins in my hands, realizing how naive I was to believe that. I had let my guard down. And now Loon was vulnerable.

"You'll keep her safe, won't you? If anyone tries to take her?" I looked up at him, the tears threatening again. It was too much to ask of him, but I couldn't help it.

Jack frowned at my expression. "I'll do my best, Ivy. Just be careful. It's dangerous to show that you care about something here." Jack held my eyes like he was trying to communicate some-thing else with those words.

Then he took a step backward.

I must have looked scared because his face relaxed and he smiled at me. "Sorry if I worried you. That wasn't my intention."

Then he leaned down, gripped my boot, and hoisted me up in the saddle. Before I could say anything else, he slapped Loon's rear, and we took off across the castle lawn.

Sixteen

My fears melted away in the steady pounding of Loon's hoofs across the ground.

The cold air stung my lungs, but I didn't care. I had missed this feeling of flying through the trees. Loon ran as if she knew I needed to put the castle far behind me. I could almost pretend we were free.

We made it down the path and approached the Tree Garden faster than I expected. Loon slowed as I looked around, amazed.

We walked through a silent world. Snow fell through the dark trees and piled high upon branches. As we got closer to the Tree Garden, I saw the tall archway stretch before me, now completely white. The green glow I'd hoped to see was masked by snow, but I still felt that same sense of wonder. It was so peaceful here. I found myself wishing I could stay. Wishing York was with me again and not trapped back at the castle.

I swung down and looped Loon's reins around a low branch just outside the arch. Just as I was about to step beneath it, I froze.

A dark figure was inside the Tree Garden.

A girl about my age lay on her side facing me. I had never seen her before; I didn't think she was from Windermere.

Her eyes were closed, her black hair draped over her arm. A

thin layer of snow had already accumulated on her. She wore no coat. Her chest rose and fell slowly. Was she sleeping . . . or hurt?

I watched her, unsure of what to do. Before I'd been taken to the castle, I would have rushed over to make sure she was alright. But now, I hung back, cautious, thinking there was more to this than what I saw. Why was she here? *How* was she here? No one was supposed to know about this place, and no one should be able to get inside unless they had a key like my mother's owl.

Could there be more keys . . . or did she not need a key? Was she like me?

The hairs on my neck prickled. Suddenly, I was sure it wasn't just us here. I quickly scanned the trees and found a pair of black eyes watching me.

My breath whooshed out of me. Instinctively, I reached back for Loon. Through the swirling snow, I slowly recognized the silhouette of a deer.

It was the most beautiful, most intelligent-looking deer I had ever seen.

Except for its black eyes and nose, it was completely white, almost blending into the snowy trees around it.

The white deer continued to stare at me, unmoving. I didn't dare move or look away. It didn't look dangerous, but I was glad to have Loon standing beside me.

The deer slowly stretched out its neck and sniffed the wintery air. An instant later, it leaped back into the trees.

I remained frozen, listening for any movement, but every sound in the forest seemed to be muffled by the snowfall.

A white deer. I had only heard of them in legends. I couldn't believe I had actually just seen one.

I glanced back at the girl, whose eyes were still closed. I was suddenly certain that the deer had been watching her long before it had seen me. But that couldn't be right.

A shiver racked my body. If I was cold in my warm cloak, this girl had to be freezing. I hurried beneath the arch and walked closer.

She was beautiful, in an otherworldly way. She reminded me of one of Mr. Gable's delicate bone statues. Her skin was as white as the snow falling on her; her facial features were small but pronounced. She wore a deep, shimmering dress and I felt better when I saw how heavy it looked. And expensive. She didn't have anything else with her.

Then without warning, her eyes sprang open.

I shrieked and slipped backward into the snow, the hood of my new cloak falling over my face. I pushed it back quickly, but the girl didn't say anything, or move to get up.

It took me a minute to speak. "Hello?"

No response.

Brushing the cold snow from my hands, I sat up so I could see her face. She was looking around with large violet eyes. As she took in the Tree Garden, her brow creased.

"Hey, over there. Are you OK?" I asked.

Her violet eyes finally rested on me.

The hair on my arms rose. The only other person I had ever seen with eyes like hers was the ghost woman in the castle, who I wasn't even sure had been real.

After a long moment, the girl spoke. "Who are you?"

Her voice was softer than I expected, and that made me feel brave. "Ivy Rune. Who are you?"

She hesitated, and then a lost look crossed her face. "Ember?"

I frowned. "Why do you sound so unsure?"

She didn't respond.

"Do you have a last name?"

"I can't remember."

"Oh," I said, at a loss.

Ember struggled to sit up and I automatically reached out to help her. I took her elbow and noticed the veins on the back of her wrist were illuminated ever so faintly, almost yellow. Her skin seemed to be lit and shimmering from within. I dropped her elbow, and she slipped in the snow.

"Sorry!" I steadied her again and tried not to stare as my heart began to pound. This girl was not *normal*.

Was I seeing light again, but *within* her? I'd only seen it *around* people, not *inside* them.

Ember brushed the snow off her long dark hair and dress. That simple movement caused her to sway again and I grabbed her elbow, surprised by how fragile and light she felt.

"Why am I so tired?" she asked.

"I don't know. I just found you. Were you asleep?"

"I must have been."

The snow continued to fall around us. I sensed something in her that I couldn't explain or put into words. The air seemed to crackle with electricity.

"Where did you come from?" I asked curiously.

"I don't know . . ." For a moment, Ember looked confused. "Where am I?"

"The Tree Garden." I wondered what she thought of the holes Carved into each tree around the clearing. But she didn't seem to notice them.

"How do you know *this* isn't my home?" Ember finally said.

"What?" I was certain I heard her wrong. "The *forest*?"

She nodded, looking around at the trees. Her brow creased again, as if she was trying very hard to remember something, but couldn't.

"You don't live here. You're not even supposed to be here."

"Why not?"

Her challenging tone surprised me.

"Oh. Well, no one is. Not unless they are . . . Never mind. Well, I know you're not from Windermere. Did you come from across the sea? Are you a merchant's daughter?" Even as I said it, I knew it wasn't possible. How would she have gotten all the way out here if she were a merchant's daughter? How did she get in?

Ember frowned. "No. The sea doesn't call to me. But this place does." Ember lifted her face to the sky, which was quickly darkening with more snow. The way she breathed in deeply reminded me of the deer. "This place is different. It's a place where legends come true."

I drew in a breath. "What do you know about legends?"

"Nothing. Perhaps everything."

She looked so solemn that I found myself believing that Ember *did* know more about this place than I did. Besides the color of her veins and her strangeness there was something familiar about her. For some reason, I was drawn to Ember in the same way I had been drawn to Iaun.

"Are you from Stygian? Are you a Dyadic?"

Again, her brow furrowed. "Where?"

"Stygian? It's across the sea. There, it's always summer, so that would explain why you don't have a coat . . ." I faltered.

"No, I don't think so. That doesn't feel quite right either."

"You don't know anything about yourself, but you know about legends?"

"Yes," she said simply.

"Would you tell me?" I asked, curious.

Her violet eyes found mine again, and she studied me as if considering. "That's probably not the most important thing right now."

"Oh. I guess not. I'm sure you're very cold."

She looked down at her dress as if it could tell her who she was. "This is very warm," she murmured thoughtfully.

"Good. So, what are you going to do now?" I stamped my feet. The cold was creeping into my boots.

"I'm not sure."

Even my hair was beginning to feel wet. The snowflakes fell heavier, clinging to the bark of the trees and lining the branches. Soon, everything would be thickly hidden. We couldn't stay here talking much longer. And I had a job to do.

I thought about taking Ember to the Taylor's farm, but Jack warned me not to stray from the instructions I was given. Plus, it was snowing so hard that I'd risk getting stuck there overnight, and then what would Dr. Ply do to me? This was my first outing. I couldn't mess this up.

I huffed, watching my breath turn white. "Well, I can't just leave you here. Why don't you come back with me? If you stay here, you'll freeze before dark."

Ember looked unsure, but it was clear she had nowhere else to go. She nodded. "Thank you."

But first, I had to deliver the package. "Hold on a second."

I trudged through the snow towards the oldest tree. Its wise, Carved face looked out at me from inside the hole. I slipped the package of laun inside its mouth. When I turned around, Ember was watching.

"What did you just do?"

I hesitated, then smiled. "That's probably not the most important thing right now, is it?"

A smile tugged at her lips. "I guess not."

"Maybe I'll tell you when you tell me about the legends."

Ember smiled wider. "Fine."

"Let's hurry." I walked back toward Loon, who was neighing impatiently. I quickly brushed off the layer of snow on her.

"What a beauty," Ember said, patting Loon's neck.

Loon nuzzled her back.

"Can you ride?" I asked.

"Yes." Ember shivered. It was the only human reaction she'd had this entire time.

"Don't worry, it's not far."

When we were both up, I guided Loon back down the snowy path toward the castle. In the blinding whiteness, I almost swore I saw the white deer watching from a distance.

But I blinked and it was gone.

Seventeen

The Count

The Count cracked his knuckles impatiently. It was a disgusting habit, but he could not help it. He only did this when he was alone; he craved the feeling of relief in each joint.

When he'd cracked each knuckle, he stared into the fire and waited.

Thick dust lined nearly every inch of the room—the tops of his books, the papers on the desk, the curtains. Only the glass decanter on the table next to him, handled often these days, shone clear.

He hated waiting.

Thoughts that the Count had buried long ago slowly bubbled to the surface in quiet moments such as these. Images flickered through his mind—white hair, a ruby smile, piercing blue eyes—before he slammed them shut. They were too painful. So far removed, yet so near to him.

A sharp knock rattled his door.

As it opened, Dr. Ply stepped into the room, but he was not alone. He was shadowed by a pretty, young girl. Even before being introduced, the Count knew her.

Smoke-jade eyes and honey hair. But an unexpectedly open expression. Her face showed everything she felt; her eyes roamed the room as if she were searching for and collecting clues.

She had not gotten that openness from Mr. Rune, though she did have his eyes.

The Count fixed his eyes on the girl intently, like a lion on prey. He prided himself on reading people, a skill that kept him in control in every situation. She appeared more excited than nervous. Her hands smoothed her long hair back into place as she looked curiously around the room. He watched her face light up in recognition of Mr. Gable's work when her gaze landed on his elaborately Carved chess board. Then her eyes met his, and she drew in a sharp breath, her step faltering slightly.

The Count was well aware of his reputation in Windermere, of the stories about him; few true, many embellished. If this girl knew just half of the truth about him, she probably wouldn't seem so *pleased* to be in his study. However, that spark in her eye interested him, and he rather liked that she wasn't timid like her father. The Count approved of boldness in people—so long as *he* could direct it any way that suited him.

He gestured that his guests should sit. "Dr. Ply," he said by way of greeting. "And this is?"

"Good afternoon," Dr. Ply answered. "This is Ivy Rune, my new assistant."

"Hello, sir."

Her voice was strong and she greeted him almost eagerly. The Count didn't care for that, so he stared at her until she dropped her eyes.

Ivy Rune. Mr. Rune's only child. The Count had always wondered what she would be like. She seemed bolder than her father had been, and her father had caused the Count plenty of trouble. This also interested him.

"Something's happened that I thought you should be made aware of immediately. I'd like Ivy to tell you herself since she was the only one involved."

Dr. Ply sounded casual, but the Count had known him for many years and could spot the undercurrent of excitement running beneath his calm demeanor. His suspicion was confirmed by the look Dr. Ply pointed at him.

The Count slowly picked up his crystal glass and swirled the glittering black liquid. He gestured to the decanter and to Dr. Ply. When Dr. Ply finished pouring his own glass, the Count fixed his gaze on Ivy. She sat quietly with her hands folded in her lap. He gestured to her next and watched her eyes widen.

A swallow, then a nod.

He filled her glass generously and handed it to her. Then, he tipped his glass toward her, waiting to see what she was made of.

She echoed his movement and took a determined sip.

He smiled inwardly as she coughed and sputtered. Dr. Ply shot the Count an exasperated look and poured her some water.

The Count took a long sip from his own glass, savoring the delicious burn in his throat and the warmth that pooled in his stomach.

"Well, Ivy *Rune*?" the Count drew her last name out. He was ready to hear the news. He *was* rather curious, but had spent a lifetime perfecting control over his emotions, so coming across as disinterested—bored, even—came naturally to him.

Ivy coughed once more and cleared her throat. Her eyes were now red-rimmed and she'd finally lost some of that confidence, which had been the Count's goal.

"Dr. Ply sent me to the Tree Garden this afternoon and I found a girl inside. At first, I thought she was asleep—or passed out . . . I'm not sure which. Anyway, she woke up, and she couldn't remember who she was or how she got there. I brought her back to the castle with me."

"What made you think that Dr. Ply would want that?"

"Because she needed help."

"The castle is not here to take in strays or lost people."

Something like anger flashed in her eyes, but she was quick to control it. "Because she was able to get *inside* the Tree Garden, even though it's supposed to be . . . closed."

"So?" The Count looked away, as if bored. He sensed this would bother her, and he was right.

"And because she talked about *legends*."

The Count's hand stilled. After a moment, he resumed swirling his glass. "What about them?"

"She said the Garden seemed like a place where legends come true."

The Count felt his heart skip a beat. He nearly cursed at its weakness. "How old is she?"

"My age, I assume."

The Count fixed her with a withering stare until she stammered, "I'm seventeen, sir."

"What does she look like?"

"Pale skin. Her hair is long and black. Her clothes were dark and made of a material I've never seen before."

The Count looked toward the fire, unsure if he felt relief or not that she hadn't said white hair. "Anything else?"

"She seems like she is from somewhere far away, like another world."

The Count inhaled. "Why do you say that?"

Ivy shrugged. "She just has this way about her. And her eyes are nearly purple."

The Count tapped his fingers together and stared into the fire, aware that Dr. Ply and Ivy were both watching him. He needed to think alone.

"Thank you." The Count waved her away. "Now go."

Ivy looked at Dr. Ply as if she was surprised to be dismissed so quickly.

"Wait for me outside, Ivy," he said.

She nodded and rose. "It was nice to meet you, sir," she said to him.

The Count continued to look into the fire.

When the door closed behind her, the Count looked at Dr. Ply. "She has spirit."

Dr. Ply relaxed in his chair. "She's smart, but headstrong and guided by her emotions. However, she has also expressed a desire to move up in her position at the castle."

"Is she loyal?"

"To me, yes."

"How much does she know?"

"Very little. I only give her information as needed," Dr. Ply said.

"This girl in the Tree Garden, what is her name?"

"Ember."

"Unusual."

"Yes."

"Could she be . . ." His voice drifted as images flashed through his mind—white lace, tall trees, hummingbirds . . . and the violet eyes; they reminded him of another place entirely.

It was silent for a moment before Dr. Ply answered the Count's unspoken question. "I'm not sure, but she will be monitored closely, just in case."

"Well, you were right to come. But perhaps I should see this girl for myself."

"I assumed you would want to."

"She should be put in the lab."

"I agree. Though not at first. Let me have a few days to see what we can uncover."

"Fine. Do not let her leave until we know for sure who she is."

"Of course not."

Both men sipped their drinks in silence.

Dr. Ply finished his first and placed his empty glass on the table next to him. "Just let me know when you would like to visit her. I will arrange everything else."

The Count continued gazing at the burning logs and glowing embers, swirling his drink absently.

When Dr. Ply reached the door to leave, the Count said quietly, "Cora must be left out of this."

"Yes," Dr. Ply agreed. "But she has an irritating way of inserting herself into situations, even when I do my best to exclude her."

"Then you must do better." The Count looked up from the fire. "I want you to keep her out of this as much as you can without raising suspicion or alienating her. The less she knows, the better."

"I'll do my best."

"In the meantime, grant *all* her requests, even if you deem them unnecessary. We need to pacify her."

Dr. Ply frowned. "Of course."

The door closed behind him and the Count was alone once more. He poured himself another drink.

If he was going to handle this properly, he wanted—no, he *needed*—to remember absolutely everything.

He leaned back into his chair and recalled the White Forest again, but this time, he opened his mind and allowed the memories to wash over him.

EIGHTEEN

I paced outside the Count's study, thinking he was nothing like the frail, old man I had imagined.

He was as intense and powerful as the burn of his awful drink, which still lingered in my throat. Just his presence and that unwavering, piercing stare nearly unraveled me. His black suit reminded me of inky waves glittering under moonlight.

The heady scent of his pipe lingered even in the hallway. I rubbed my throat as I passed the suits of armor lining the hallway for the tenth time. Each suit was duller than the last, matching the state of the threadbare navy-and-gold carpet. I'd expected the Count to live in extravagance. But now that I'd met him, I thought this eerie wing suited him perfectly.

I passed the door again, and then sank down onto the bench outside it, worrying about Ember. I brought her to the castle to help her, never once thinking that Dr. Ply would notify the Count. What could they possibly want with her? When she was just some girl I'd rescued, they didn't care. But now that she was someone who knew about legends, they were interested.

I jumped up as the door opened.

Dr. Ply emerged, waving for me to follow as he began walking briskly back down the hallway.

"Well, you have now met the Count. Do you know how rare that is? Most people never even lay eyes on him, let alone enter his personal library. It's quite an honor."

"Yes, it was. But . . . why is Ember so important? I mean, why did the Count need to know about her?"

Dr. Ply stroked his blonde mustache as he walked. "She's a mystery. Who is she? How did she come to be in the Tree Garden? Who else is involved? I believe there is more to the story. We must proceed carefully. It was very wise of you to bring her to me. If you had left her in the Tree Garden, she might have been gone when we went back for her."

I looked up, startled. My first thought flickered to Jack, wondering if he would have been sent out for her, just like he had been sent for me. That bothered me.

"Today you proved that I can trust your instincts and loyalty. This has earned you another reward. Quite a feat for a single day. Today, you will be moving to the Top Floor, to accommodations that are much more agreeable."

"Oh!" I said, taken aback.

Dr. Ply looked at me sharply.

"I mean—thank you!" I quickly infused my words with gratitude.

"You're welcome."

It wasn't that I didn't want a better room—I did. That was all I'd wanted since my first night in the castle. But I didn't want to lose the tunnel. How would I find York or the South Wing now? And what about the person who'd left the white orchid in my room? Would they know where to find me?

"You will not be alone," Dr. Ply continued. "Ember will be sharing a room with you."

"Oh?"

"Yes. We must persuade her to stay here as our guest. If she is comfortable, I hope she will trust us with who she really is. And I think she will share more with you than me. I want you to befriend her and learn anything you can about her."

My step faltered. He wanted me to spy on Ember—just like Vernon spied on me.

"Do you think she has something to hide?" I asked carefully.

"She might. Either way, I want to be sure we know exactly who she is. We'll start by making her comfortable. If that doesn't work, we will move forward with another plan."

I was too upset to respond. It was my fault Ember was here, and I was overwhelmed with guilt that I had just doomed her with Dr. Ply's attention. Even though I didn't want to spy on her, I felt like I had no choice. Too much was at stake now.

I couldn't help but think maybe Vernon had felt this way too. I felt another stab of guilt.

"You should know, I considered giving this responsibility to Anna. She has proven herself to me and I know that she can handle a delicate task such as this. But I feel you are a better fit. Anna is excellent at controlling her emotions. However, this also makes her less friendly and approachable. So, it falls to you. Do not fail me."

"I'll try not to," I said uneasily.

"Good. I want to know where Ember is from, how she got into the Tree Garden, and what she thinks about *everything*. Notify me immediately if she mentions legends again. Do you understand?"

I nodded, miserable.

"This time, it is not just me counting on you, but the Count as well. He will be monitoring this situation closely and expecting updates." Dr. Ply rubbed his hands together. "What a development. I must say, when you came into my office in such a hurry, I thought it was to thank me for the horse. I thought you would be overjoyed to be reunited with it."

"Oh, I am! I'm sorry," I said, feeling Dr. Ply's sharp gaze. "I meant to thank you properly, but I got distracted by everything else."

"Yes, well. This has been quite the afternoon."

"It has. Thank you again for the warm cloak, and for Loon."

"Loon?"

"My horse."

"Ah. You're welcome. Any visit to the stable must be cleared by me. No unauthorized rides, or your access to Loon will be revoked. Prove yourself loyal, and I will shower you with rewards."

We reached Dr. Ply's office; he stopped at the door that hid the hallway to the lab. He seemed agitated.

"Ember is inside waiting. Don't worry about your things; Anna will move them up to your new room."

My stomach turned at the thought of Anna touching my father's journal and Mr. Gable's delicate box. "I don't mind packing. I can be quick."

Dr. Ply looked at me disapprovingly. "Your priority is now Ember. Wait with her until Anna arrives to escort you both up to the Top Floor. From now on, if Anna is not with Ember, I want you to be."

"Yes, sir."

Dr. Ply nodded as he opened the door to the lab and disappeared down the winding hallway.

I watched him, suddenly feeling the imbalance of all that he had given me today. And how I now felt even more pressure to comply.

Jack was right; this had been Dr. Ply's true intention the whole time.

———

I PUSHED THE DOOR TO THE OFFICE OPEN. EMBER AND Jack were sitting at Dr. Ply's desk before the most impressive plate of food I had ever seen. Not once during my time at the castle had I been served food like this. Even the china was exquisite. Ember had changed into a blue dress that set off her violet eyes even more. The simple cut flattered her slender figure and I was struck again by how pretty she was.

But my stomach dipped uneasily seeing Jack next to her, drinking coffee. They looked good together. Their dark hair, their crisp clothing . . . It was like I'd walked upon a pretty picture and did not belong. Waves of uncertainty washed over me, unraveling all my feelings about Jack.

They both looked up at me.

My gut tightened; even their movements were in sync.

"Hello." I hesitated by the door, feeling like I was interrupting something.

"There you are." Jack set his cup on the table and smiled at me. The plate in front of him was now littered with crumbs. They had eaten a delicious lunch together. I was starving.

"I'm relieved you made it back in one piece. And you saved Ember from freezing to death!"

I nodded, my eyes flickering between them. I wished I didn't feel so awkward. I wished I could turn around and leave. "I left Loon at the entrance. Was she taken back to the stable?"

Jack's eyes creased at the strain in my voice. "Yes. I passed the groom on his way in with her. I'll check in on her later. Don't worry, she'll be taken care of."

I nodded, then looked at Ember. "How are you feeling?"

She smiled. "I'm thawing out, thanks to you."

Seeing her in the castle somehow muted the differences I'd noticed about her in the Tree Garden. The veins at her wrist were now a normal blue.

"I'm glad Ivy found you, especially in this snow." Jack casually lounged in his chair and looked at Ember. "I doubt you would have been able to make it far especially without knowing where to go."

Ember frowned. "I'm sure you're right, but that's a dreadful thought."

I needed to leave the room now. I stepped forward, avoiding Jack's eye. "Ember, Dr. Ply has invited you to stay here until you recover your memory. Then we'll help you get home. He's offered us a big room on the Top Floor to share so you'll be comfortable."

Jack let out a low whistle. "Well done, Ivy. I guess we'll be running into each other more often now. My room is up there too."

This morning, that would have made me happy, but now all I could think was that Ember would also be near him.

"Will you stay?" I asked Ember, feeling Jack search my face.

"Of course she'll stay here. Where else would she go?" Jack answered, turning back to Ember. "You'll be taken care of here. We will do everything in our power to help you remember where your home is. Won't we, Ivy?"

I nodded, pulling at a thread on my sleeve so I wouldn't have to look at him. He was laying it on thick. No one in the castle was that nice or helpful. Why was he making it seem like they were? And why did *he* want Ember to stay so badly?

"Well, I don't seem to have another choice, so your kindness is appreciated," Ember said.

"Good." Jack stood, slowly. "Now that's settled, I must go. There's a horse that needs me."

I still didn't look at him, even though I could tell he wanted me to.

"It was nice to meet you, Jack. Thank you for the delicious food," Ember said.

"You're welcome." Jack paused as if waiting for me to say something. "Ivy?"

"Bye," I said, flashing him a quick look before I took his seat.

He hesitated, then walked out of the room. The door clicked behind him and I felt his absence more than ever. I took a deep breath and shook my head to clear it.

Anna stepped into the room. She walked right up to Ember and smiled warmly as she extended her hand. "Hello. You must be Ember. I'm Anna."

My mouth dropped open.

"Hello." Ember shook her hand.

"I've heard all about you," Anna continued, still smiling. "Dr. Ply informed me that you will be staying as our guest until your memory returns. We will do everything we can to help you. Dr. Ply is investigating your situation as we speak, hoping to gain some insight."

I snapped my mouth shut, narrowing my eyes at her. Anna wasn't warm—or *nice*. Was everyone in on Dr. Ply's plan? Apparently, no one could be trusted here. Just that thought made my heart heavy.

"Thank you." Ember smiled. "Everyone has been so welcoming. If Ivy hadn't found me, I don't know what I would have done."

"You're certainly welcome to stay as long as you'd like. It's our pleasure to host you. Now, let's get you settled," Anna said. "Ivy, are you ready?"

I wanted to challenge her kindness and see how easily she would snap, but I resisted. "Sure."

I trailed behind them down the hallway as Anna continued to make small talk with Ember. Ember's introduction to the castle was much different than mine. Why was everyone trying so hard with her?

I thought of Jack's confusion over my behavior in the office. I hated the unease I felt now about us.

We turned a corner and suddenly the grand staircase with the beautiful carpet stretched in front of us.

So this was the way to the Top Floor.

If Ember was impressed with the grandeur and the chandelier's twinkling above, I couldn't tell. Maybe she was from an equally beautiful place. Or didn't place a high value on material things. Or really just didn't remember.

A different woman from the one I'd seen my first night exploring sat at the front desk. When Anna's friendliness extended even to her, the woman looked back at her, confused.

"Are you feeling alright?" She peered at Anna, clearly unnerved by the change in her demeanor.

"Fine," Anna said through her teeth.

As Anna explained we were both to be allowed access to the

Top Floor, the woman stared at Ember, fascinated. Then she interrupted Anna.

"Excuse me dear, but are your eyes *violet*?"

Ember looked startled. Didn't she know that violet eyes were not common? Maybe everyone had violet eyes where she came from.

"For God's sake, have some tact!" Anna snapped, dropping her polite pretense. Ember jumped, and I bit my lip to hide a smile. Anna couldn't even fake it for ten minutes.

The woman at the desk lowered her head and quickly wrote our names in a ledger. Then she waved us upstairs without another word.

The grandeur was overwhelming. Everywhere I looked, I was dazzled by something more beautiful or interesting than the last. The first room off the staircase was a large library. It was filled with plush couches, shelves filled with books, and a long table covered in cakes, pastries, and coffee. The table was big enough for a large group of people, though of course all the seats were empty.

We continued down the long, spectacular hallway—if hallways could be spectacular. A beautiful ivory-and-silver carpet muted our footsteps. We passed several wooden doors that were so well polished my reflection shone through clearly. Gilded mirrors hung between every door, glowing from the illuminated crystals of the chandeliers above.

Anna stopped at a door with a gold nameplate. I was surprised to see it had already been engraved with elegant cursive letters: *Ivy Rune & Ember*.

"This is your room." Anna opened the door. "Mine is next door."

I drew in a startled breath. The room was beautiful. Two enormous four-poster beds, with plump pillows and thick covers . . . carpet so deep my feet sank down to my ankles. Two large wing-back chairs sat in front of a fireplace, which glowed with a blazing fire. At the far end of the room were double glass doors, leading to a balcony. Velvet curtains draped each window.

I looked at Ember. "What do you think?"

"It's very nice. Which bed do you want?"

Anna answered for me. "Ivy will take the bed closest to the door. Ember, I understand you don't have any personal belongings. You will find everything you need in your closet. Ivy, your closet is also stocked with dinner dresses, outdoor clothes, and everyday clothes. Everything should be your size but if something is not, please tell the steward assigned to your room. Your appearance is very important here. You must be dressed appropriately for every occasion and maintain your grooming. You are representing the Top Floor now and must look the part."

I stared at her, confused. *Who* were we representing ourselves *to*? There was barely anyone in the castle. This was almost as strange as my first room, where I had twenty beds all to myself.

Anna ignored my look and continued. "Settle in and feel free to use the common area as much as you'd like. It is always stocked with refreshments."

Anna gestured to a pink cord with gold tassels hanging on the wall near the fireplace. "That cord rings a bell to your steward. Use it if you need anything. I'll be back in three hours to escort you both to dinner."

Nineteen

My bag was deep in my closet, and I wondered if Anna hid it on purpose.

I was relieved to find everything inside and nothing broken. I took it out to our room, where Ember was still exploring. At first, I watched her carefully, in case she found a hidden tunnel. But she was more interested in looking at the pictures, not looking under them, so I stopped watching. I'd investigate later.

I opened my bag and took out the three bound books and brown bag full of orchid seeds. I took the now-crushed white orchid petal from my pocket and put it inside my jewelry box. Eventually, I'd press it, but not yet. I didn't want it to lose its scent just yet.

Ember wandered over. "What's in there?" She pointed to the brown bag.

"Seeds."

She looked interested. "What kind?"

"White orchids."

"Why do you have orchid seeds?"

"They were given to me."

Ember held out her hand. "Can I see them?"

I hesitated.

"Oh. Never mind." She quickly pulled her hand back. "I don't have to."

"No, it's OK." I handed it to her.

Ember opened it gently as if she knew it was special to me. Then she looked up. "These seeds are rare. Are you going to plant them?"

"Maybe someday. I don't have the green thumb my father did. I'm scared I'll kill them if I try."

"I could plant one for you."

"Really? Are you good with plants?"

Ember nodded. "I feel like this is something I've done before. It will be nice to know if that's true."

"Alright. I guess we'll need a pot and dirt."

Perhaps if we grew an orchid, I could use it as a sign to whoever had left one on my bed. Maybe they would feel more comfortable approaching me.

"Maybe we can call for supplies, and request some tea, too," Ember said.

I remembered the spread Ember had in Dr. Ply's office with Jack. Suddenly, I was ravenous for good food too.

Ember tugged the cord by the fireplace. Then we both sank into the chairs to wait.

It was hard to believe how drastically my life had changed since this morning. I'd woken up thinking about white orchids and Jack. Now, I felt a pang in my heart whenever I thought of him and I had moved into a new room with a stranger. My new job was to spy on her. It was enough to make my head spin.

"You seem to be handling this very well," I said.

Ember shrugged. "You can handle anything when there is no other choice."

"I hope your memory comes back soon. I'm so curious to know where you're from. I can't imagine what it's like not to know anything about yourself."

"It is strange. But I have to tell you that *this*," Ember gestured between us and to the fire, "feels like déjà vu."

"The fire?"

"*Sitting* by the fire—and something about tea." Ember wrinkled her forehead. "I feel like I'm supposed to be doing something, but I'm not sure what."

"I'm sure it will come to you soon."

"Maybe. Can you tell me about the castle? Is it your home?"

"No. I'm from Windermere." Just saying the name made my heart ache. "It's the only town nearby."

"Windermere? I feel like I've heard that before."

"Technically, we're *in* Windermere, but the castle has always been separate, like its own world."

I did my best to explain my life to her, quickly glossing over my parents. When I mentioned Carving, Ember sat up, fascinated. I showed her Mr. Gable's jewelry box, and she finally looked impressed.

"Beautiful," she murmured, carefully turning it over in her hands. "It's so delicate. I wish I could see his shop."

A knock sounded on the door, and I rose to answer it.

"Oh, hello, Vernon," I said, opening the door. "Have you moved up here too?"

He nodded. "Dr. Ply wanted me close by." His eyes grew wide as he looked around the room. "I've never been allowed up here."

"Really? Well, come in." A thought occurred to me. Vernon was from Stygian, a land steeped in legend, where Dyadics existed. Maybe he knew people like Ember or would recognize her as different.

"Vernon, this is Ember." I watched him closely.

Ember stood and held out her hand. "Hello, Vernon. It's nice to meet you."

"Hello." Vernon crossed the room to shake her hand. "I know all about *you* already. You're all anyone is talking about. They've nicknamed you Violet."

"Why is everyone talking about her?" I asked.

Vernon smiled. "There is not much to do here, and people love a story. Cora was front page news for months. You too, Ivy."

"Me?" I asked, surprised.

"Yes," Vernon said frankly. "Constant talk of your shocking arrival after your father disappeared from these woods."

I wasn't prepared to hear that, and I couldn't hide how much it affected me. "He disappeared while leaving *these* woods?"

Vernon nodded. "These very ones."

I tried to breathe normally. Why was Vernon telling me this now? Was it even true, or was he doing Anna's bidding? So far, Vernon hadn't lied to me about anything . . . but he was still a spy and a traitor—wasn't he?

Weren't he and I the same now?

Ember looked at me, puzzled. I quickly smoothed my expression.

"What can I get you?" Vernon asked, changing the subject. "I'm at your service."

"What's on the menu?" I asked.

Vernon listed so many dishes that my mouth dropped open. The castle had all this to offer, meanwhile I had been fed nothing but cold meals for months. Ember and I decided on tea and a small tray of sandwiches.

"Don't forget, we need a pot with dirt. We have a seed to plant," Ember reminded me.

I turned to Vernon. "Can you get us that too?"

"Of course."

When he left, I sank into a chair by the fire.

No one had ever told me that my father disappeared from the *castle's* woods. All this time, I'd thought he'd been in the forest around Windermere. This must have been why my father's body was never found, because his disappearance occurred on the Count's land—and no one from town knew he'd worked here.

My thoughts drifted back to when I met Nicholas in the woods. He hadn't believed that my father was dead. I'd seen Nicholas walking across the castle lawn months ago. If he worked here, he must know my father had worked here too. Had Nicholas left me the white orchid?

"Are you alright?" Ember asked.

"Fine." But my thoughts continued to spiral. I twisted my hands as I stared into the fire.

Did *Jack* know the truth about my father's disappearance? The possibility that I couldn't even trust Jack bothered me more than I wanted to admit. I realized now just how much I *wanted* to trust him, to trust these feelings that were starting to bud between us—

"Are you upset about what Vernon said about your father?"

I rubbed my eyes. I needed to pull it together. I wished Vernon hadn't said anything in front of Ember. "Yes."

"You don't have to talk about it if you don't want to," she said quickly. "I know we just met. But if you want to talk, I'll listen."

"Thanks. I'm OK . . . It just caught me off guard. My father has been gone for a long time. There's not much to say anymore."

Carl had said my father had stolen something. Now I knew he'd disappeared from the castle.

Something had happened to him here.

I thought back to the vines of ivy that grew over the gate to the Dark Woods and my father's obsessive notes on *Hedera*. I needed to find more ivy, follow its trail—

A knock pulled me from my thoughts, and I looked up to see Vernon wheeling an ornate silver cart into the room. He held up an elaborate gold pot, already filled with dirt.

"Will this do for your plant?"

Ember jumped up and took it. "It's perfect. Thank you."

Vernon nodded, pleased. Then he began filling our table with crystal tea cups and saucers, a jeweled sugar bowl, milk, and a blue-and-green teapot. Last was a plate of fancy tea sandwiches.

Then Vernon pulled a bouquet of fresh lavender from the bottom of the cart and handed it to me.

My breath caught as I took the bouquet and pressed it to my nose. I drank in the calming, familiar scent of Windermere and my eyes welled up. Who knew I liked lavender? I remembered my conversation with Jack in the stable this morning. I'd told him about missing the lavender fields.

"Where did you get this?"

Vernon smiled. "It was meant to welcome you to the Top Floor."

I blushed but hid it by sniffing the lavender again. I knew Jack could tell I was upset in the office. Was this his way of telling me I could trust him? And if Jack trusted Vernon with delivering this, could I trust Vernon too?

Maybe we were all trapped here, doing things we didn't want to.

Maybe we could all help each other out.

"Did you know that someone put a flower in my old room? A white orchid?" I asked Vernon.

"It was pushed under your door when I came to check your fire. I put it on your bed so you wouldn't step on it when you got back."

That was the night I snuck out and went to the stables with Jack. Which meant I hadn't been in my room when Vernon put the flower on my bed. But he hadn't told Anna. If he had, I would have already been in trouble.

Perhaps he wasn't such a traitor after all.

I looked up, meeting his eyes. "Did you tell anyone?"

"No. I try not to disclose what I deem to be private matters with others. At least, not if I can help it." He looked sad. "Sometimes, though, it cannot be helped."

I nodded, understanding. I was in the same position with Ember now. And I felt horrible about it.

"Thanks, Vernon." For the first time in a long time, I gave him a sincere smile.

Vernon returned my smile, easing something in my chest, and left the room.

I decided to do right by Ember, just as Vernon was trying to do with me. If I didn't absolutely have to tell Dr. Ply something, I wouldn't. I already regretted telling him and the Count what Ember said about legends.

I would have to be careful. I couldn't risk losing Loon or my place at the castle. My first loyalty was to York. I was determined to uncover what happened to my father.

Ember set the pot on the table between our beds and came back over to the fire. "You like lavender?"

"It's my favorite. There were lavender fields at the farm where I used to live and I miss it. Would you like me to pour you some tea?"

"What kind is it?"

"It looks like black tea." I filled the two cups with hot water. "Would you like sugar or milk?"

"None, thanks." Ember took a small knife and cut her tea bag open, then poured its contents into her napkin.

I was about to explain that the tea bag was meant to go inside her cup when Ember made a face.

"What's wrong?"

"May I have a few of your lavender buds instead?"

"Um, sure. Why?"

"Because something is coming back to me: A big garden, with lots of flowers, specifically grown for tea rituals. I'm going to try to make a cup of tea. Would you like to try it?"

"Sure."

I watched as Ember stripped the tiny buds from the lavender stalk, gently crushed them, and dropped them into the hot water in both cups.

"Now we wait a few minutes for the flavor to come out."

The buds softened and swelled as the tea turned the water a light shade of purple.

"I've never drank flowers before," I said.

"This is the only way we have tea at home. I remember that now. We also use dried herbs, but never bags." Ember wrinkled her nose at the torn tea bag. "Mmm. This just feels strange . . ."

"Are you remembering something else?"

"No, just a feeling that I *should* be remembering something. It's very frustrating. I can remember things like how I take my tea and that I like plants, but if I think specifically about home, my mind hits a wall. Like the memory is there, but *blocked*. Could someone have blocked it?"

I leaned in, fascinated. "How?"

"Where I'm from, people can do all sorts of things." She gasped. "See? I hit a wall again—I know that people can manipulate memory, but I don't know how . . ."

Ember looked so frustrated that I felt bad for her.

"I'm sure you'll remember soon."

She smiled. "I hope so. The tea should be ready now."

The water in the cups had turned a pretty shade of purple, just like Ember's eyes. I picked mine up and took a tentative sip. Lavender tea was delicious.

TWENTY

After tea, Ember and I went to our closets to dress for dinner.

My side of the closet was vastly different from Ember's. Mine had five outfits consisting of fitted jackets with rows of silver buttons, full skirts that ended at my knee, and a pair of black boots with silver buckles. My hand brushed over the thick fabric that looked like black sand. The Count's color; the same material that Jack and Anna wore.

Hopefully, this meant I was getting closer to my goal.

I just hoped I wouldn't have to do anything worse than spy on Ember.

There were also two beautiful dresses in my closet. One was a glittering black with silver threaded leaves on the shoulders and a long cape. The other was a fitted hunter-green dress with gold flowers decorating the sleeves and waist. The color reminded me of my father's Arborist vest. I chose that one to wear to dinner.

Ember's clothes were the same style as mine, but colored were navy and rich purple. I could tell they were meant to highlight the feature that marked her as different: her violet eyes.

I wove my hair into a long, loose braid, and remembered that night at the stable, under the stars when Jack said my hair looked like honey. I smiled at my reflection in the mirror, hoping I would see him tonight.

"You look magnificent," Ember called from across the room. Her navy dress shimmered a deep blue when the light hit it just right, like the feathers of a peacock.

"Wow. You do too," I said honestly.

Anna arrived wearing a black dress that at first seemed very plain. But when she moved, I saw a subtle flash of silver. She gave us a critical once-over, and I suddenly worried that I had chosen the wrong dress. If I wanted to show I was loyal to Dr. Ply and the Count, should I have chosen the black dress like hers?

My mind eased when Anna nodded her approval, and we followed her down a different set of stairs. I wondered what awaited us at dinner, and why we needed to dress like this, until we walked into the ballroom.

The grandness of the room took my breath away. The vaulted ceiling showcased a large mural that glowed above the row of chandeliers. Paintings in gilded frames and flickering candelabras lined the walls. A long table was set with glimmering crystal candles, stacks of china, and huge vases of silver-and-black roses sprinkled with green sprigs.

But the room was empty.

Anna led us to the middle of the table. "Take a seat on either side of me. The others will be along shortly."

We sat next to Anna in the center of the long table. There were at least fifty chairs and place settings. I frowned, doubting there were even this many people in the castle.

"What's wrong with you?" Anna whispered.

"Nothing."

"Then wipe that look off your face and act happy for our guest's sake. Dr. Ply wants you to make a good impression."

My eyes widened. Did Anna want me to pretend that I thought all these seats were going to be filled? I nearly laughed at how ridiculous it was.

Anna raised a brow. "I mean it, Ivy. One word from me and it's right back to your old room."

I sobered instantly.

Then, to my surprise, people began to enter the room. People I'd never seen before. Real people, dressed in glittering blacks and deep silvers, the men in elaborate dress coats, and the women in swishing gowns. They casually plucked sparkling glasses from trays as they mingled with each other. Some took a seat at the table and stared at us. I tried not to stare back in disbelief.

Had this whole world existed in the castle all along? I hadn't realized how isolated I'd been until this moment. I couldn't wrap my head around what it at all meant . . . or why my extreme isolation had been necessary.

I thought of York behind the glass. He didn't know *I* was here, but did he know about all these people? Panic filled me. What if the transposers came to dinner? What if York saw me? For both our safety, I would have to pretend I didn't care about him. Would he have the sense to act the same? My heart dropped.

I scanned the crowd and my stomach dipped as Jack wandered in. He looked amazing. His dress coat was of the deepest black, embroidered with silver vines and leaves all down the lapels and the cuffs of his sleeves. His black vest beneath was decorated to match. The waves of his hair were neatly combed back. He glanced around the room and his blue eyes paused on me. I flushed and quickly looked away; he'd caught me staring.

When I peeked up again, I saw he had stopped to talk to a few people and now held a glass casually in his hand. I glanced back at Anna and Ember. Anna looked bored, but Ember seemed interested. No one spoke to either of us. I wondered if that was because of Anna.

Someone set a glass on the table. I looked up to see Jack take the seat directly across from me. I glanced away, scared to acknowledge him, scared that everything I felt showed on my face, and most of all, scared that Anna was watching. I wanted to tell him I wasn't mad. When I looked up again, I noticed he was twirling a single sprig of lavender between his fingers. When he saw me watching, he leaned forward and tucked it into the centerpiece so it was sticking out between us.

My heart hammered, thinking of the bouquet of lavender in my room.

He took a casual sip from his glass. "Hello, Anna. Ember, Ivy. You all look lovely tonight."

Anna looked away, ignoring him.

Ember smiled. "Thank you, Jack. So do you."

"How are you adjusting so far?" Jack said, still not looking at me.

"Everyone has been so kind, and our room is beautiful. It's hard not to feel welcome."

"I'm glad." Jack smiled at her, and then briefly glanced at me. His blue eyes quickly scanned my face, as if he was trying to see if I was still upset. I gave him a small smile.

He lifted a brow. "I like your dress."

I didn't trust myself to speak. I was painfully aware that Anna was right next to me. I wished she would switch places with Ember so I could talk to Jack more easily.

Cora swept into the room in a bold crimson gown. Like moths drawn to a flame, everyone in the room turned to look at her.

Her dark hair was braided intricately on top of her head like the first day I'd seen her in Windermere. Her skin glowed like polished porcelain against scarlet lips, and her green eyes were lined with long dark lashes. She smiled at everyone she passed. Now that she was here, everyone made their way to their seats, as if they all had been waiting for her. But I noticed a few empty seats remained near the end of the table.

Jack stood and greeted Cora with a kiss on each cheek. I blushed and pressed my hands together in my lap as I watched Jack pull out the chair next to him for Cora to sit. Cora sank down in one graceful movement that I would never be able to mimic. As Jack pushed in her chair, he caught me staring at them.

For that brief second, our eyes locked, and my heart began to race. I squeezed my sweaty palms together as his head tilted, and something like a question flashed across his face.

Cora arched backward toward Jack and he pulled his eyes away from mine. Down to hers. Jealousy erupted like a wildfire in my chest as I watched Jack sink next to her and lean in closer to listen. Their shoulders brushed.

I stared down at my plate, trying to compose myself. How would I make it through dinner like this? It suddenly felt like I would combust if I didn't know how Jack felt about me right this second.

I knew I was being irrational. Dr. Ply had warned me not to let my emotions get the best of me. I hated to admit he was right about something. I made myself breathe in and out, focusing on what was important. Finding York. Following the trail of ivy. And leaving the castle.

Leaving. That was still what I wanted, wasn't it?

Cora stood and clinked her fork against her glass with a flourish. The table fell silent. I lifted my eyes to look at her, ignoring the magnetic pull from Jack across the table.

"Good evening." Cora's voice floated over the room like music. "Let me introduce two new faces at our table. First is Ivy, Dr. Ply's new assistant." Cora gestured for me to stand.

The blood rushed to my face as I slowly rose to my feet. I stared at Cora, realizing she hadn't used my last name.

"I have high hopes for you, Ivy. And we are happy to have you join us. To Ivy!" Cora's eyes glittered at me as she held up her glass to toast.

"To Ivy!" the table echoed, and everyone drank. I quickly sipped my glass so I could sink back into my chair. I wondered what Cora meant by having high hopes for me. Was she trying to tell me something?

Cora turned to Ember, who, in the glow of the candlelight, looked almost ethereal.

"And this is someone you all have heard about already. Ember, your situation is most unfortunate, but we hope you feel right at home here and come to think of us all as friends. Anything I can personally do to make you feel more comfortable, just ask. It's my honor to help you," Cora said sincerely.

Ember stood, and Cora raised her glass again. "To Ember."

"To Ember!" We all drank again.

A stream of butlers in black coats began serving food from silver trays. Ember and I were served first, then Cora, Jack, Anna, and then the rest of the table. I took a bite of my candied pecan and goat cheese salad and sighed at how delicious this food was compared to what I had been eating.

The courses of food continued as quiet conversations were sprinkled with the clinking of silverware and glasses. After Cora's speech, everyone was sneaking peeks at Ember, clearly enamored of her. I tried to decipher if people were only interested in her because of her beauty and strange story, or because they noticed she was different—could anyone see, in Ember, what I had seen in her in the Tree Garden?

Occasionally, I glanced over at Jack, but he was talking with Cora. I looked down at my plate, and all the uncertainty I felt earlier came rushing back. The sprig of lavender in the centerpiece caught my eye, and I stared at it, wondering what it meant.

I knew what *I* wanted it to mean.

Then I felt something brush against my foot. I jumped, and it was gone. I peeked up. Jack was still talking with Cora, but the slightest smile tugged at the corner of his lips. Another gentle brush against my slipper and my heart began to hammer in my chest.

After a moment, the foot moved away, and I felt the absence sharply. Before I thought about what I was doing, I reached my foot out further, and found him there, waiting. Jack's shoe slid by mine. My breath caught in my chest as his foot hooked around the back of my leg. We stayed like that, no one the wiser.

His conversation with Cora hadn't missed a beat, but my food lost all taste. I tried to eat and respond normally when people spoke to me, but it was hard to focus on anything else. All I could feel was our feet pressed together beneath the table.

Jack and Cora's serious conversation lasted throughout the entire five-course dinner. I didn't care; what was happening beneath the table was better than talking to him. Sometimes, I wondered if I was imagining it, but then Jack's shoe would trace a circle on my calf, and shatter whatever focus I'd managed.

When two other people entered the ballroom, I stifled a gasp. It was the ghost I'd thought I'd seen my first day in the castle.

And *Nicholas*.

The man who had given me my father's wooden cube in the forest.

Who'd told me the owl was the key to the Tree Garden.

Who'd told me he lived in the woods, but now here he was, wearing an elegant black suit and plucking two fluted glasses from a tray. He handed one to the woman I'd taken to be a ghost.

She wore the same black faded gown I'd initially seen her in, her dark hair was still tangled in what looked like a fishing net, and a black crystal starfish was stuck in her hair. She sipped from her glass and looked around the room with her two different-colored eyes.

Nicholas's silver hair was still pulled back at his neck, but he didn't look like he belonged in the woods anymore. He looked like he owned the castle. I felt the blood drain from my face as his eyes found me sitting at the table.

Nicholas didn't falter, but I found it difficult to breathe.

I swallowed. I didn't know what to do. Was he on my side or not? Should I admit to knowing him before the castle?

No one acknowledged the two of them as they walked to the remaining empty chairs and sat. Their plates were quickly filled, as if the staff were scared of them. All I could think was that they looked like they belonged on a wild sea island.

"Who are they?" I asked Anna quietly.

Jack's foot stilled.

"They aren't important," she responded, surprising me by answering at all.

"Why not?"

"Dinners like this are for those in the castle who've earned it. Those two haven't earned anything their whole lives. They just leech off the Count."

I leaned in closer. "How? Are they related?"

Anna leaned away and ignored me.

I couldn't help looking back at Nicholas. He was staring at me.

"Hello, Ivy Rune." His deep voice carried down the table. My heart began to beat frantically, like a hummingbird.

Jack's foot pressed into mine, but I didn't know if it was a warning or for support. He didn't turn away from Cora.

Anna's head turned in his direction. "*Sebastian.*"

I flinched. Sebastian? That wasn't his name. It was Nicholas.

"Yes?" He stared Anna down without a trace of fear. "Am I not allowed to even speak?"

"We used to be able to speak to anyone," the woman beside him said, lifting her glass to her lips.

"You two are only here to *eat*. Not to bother Dr. Ply's staff." Anna's voice sent shivers down my arms. Jack and Cora's conversation paused. Jack's foot stayed pressed against mine.

"Dr. Ply's staff?" Nicholas—*Sebastian*— looked at me, amused.

I felt incredibly foolish without knowing why. He had lost that slow way he spoke to me in the woods. I could see now that it had all been an act . . . so I wouldn't question his motives.

I glared at him, suddenly furious.

"We're not bothering her. We were just going to introduce ourselves since no one else at this table was raised with manners." The woman looked pointedly at Anna.

Anna looked away as if she were bored by them. I was surprised she didn't say anything back.

"I'm Velora." The woman looked at me with her strange-colored eyes. "This is Sebastian."

"Nice to meet you, *Sebastian.*" I stared him down. "And how long have *you* worked here?"

Sebastian frowned, but before he answered, Velora said, "How insulting. No one even knows who we are anymore . . ."

A hush fell over the table. Forks suspended midair.

"That's because no one lasts long enough to," Sebastian responded, looking directly at me.

Chills went down my arms as I thought about my father.

Then someone far down the table called out, "How have you two lasted so long then? Shouldn't *we* be the ones worried?"

People laughed, and the conversation around the table resumed again, but it felt like everyone was trying to erase that moment. Velora and Sebastian turned inward toward each other and began eating and talking too low for anyone to hear. It was clear Sebastian wasn't going to address me again.

I looked down at my plate and noticed Anna's fist clenched tightly in her lap. Ember was talking to a woman on her right, unconcerned.

I peered up at Jack from beneath my lashes to see what he thought of all this.

He looked frustrated, but then I realized it was from something Cora was saying. She had begun talking intently again.

Finally, the plates were cleared away, and Cora flashed an apologetic smile down the table and gracefully slipped from the room.

Jack stirred his coffee absently, politely listening to the man on his left who immediately claimed his attention. Throughout dessert, I noticed his brow never completely unfurrowed. Our feet were still tangled together, my pulse fluttered whenever his shoe grazed my calf.

That was the only thing that kept me from falling apart at finally seeing Nicholas, and realizing he wasn't who he said he was at all. I felt foolish; I should have been immune, by now, to the feeling of betrayal.

Soon, the dessert plates were swept away with the empty glasses and coffee cups. Sebastian and Velora left the room next and I finally felt like I could breathe. Slowly, others began to trickle out too.

I didn't want the contact between me and Jack to end when one of us would have to move away.

But who would be first?

The ballroom grew emptier, and then Jack's shoe gently nudged mine. I looked up, meeting his serious blue gaze. He slowly untangled himself as he stood, his foot leaving mine cold.

I watched him walk down the table and talk to the people he passed. Everyone had a smile for him. A somber-looking man called to Anna, and she stood, leaving the seat between Ember and me empty.

Jack was suddenly there, leaning down by my chair. Our eyes were nearly level, and I blushed as my heart pounded.

"How was your first dinner?" His voice would sound distant to anyone listening, but his eyes roamed my face, twinkling with mischief.

My heart fluttered against my rib cage. "*Interesting*."

"Interesting as in pleasant?" he murmured, looking away.

"Very."

"Then you're not still upset with me for whatever happened earlier?"

"No," I whispered.

"Good." He reached out his hand and for a moment, I thought he was going to touch my cheek, but his hand passed by me, closely, and plucked the stem of lavender out of the centerpiece. He straightened, twirling it between his fingers.

"Well, I'm off to the stables. If you ask nicely, I'll check on Loon too."

I raised a brow. "I thought you already do."

"I do. I just like it when you're nice." His lips twitched as if he was fighting a smile. "Although jealousy certainly keeps things interesting."

My face burned, but before I could form a response, he turned away, saying goodnight to Ember as he passed.

I watched him leave the room, fighting a smile.

When I looked away from the door, Anna was across the room, frowning at me.

TWENTY-ONE

Rays of sunlight shone through the window, gently waking me.

Before I opened my eyes, I savored the softness of my new bed and being tucked beneath a mountain of warm covers. Even after a week, I still wasn't used to it.

I heard Ember shifting across the room and sat up. She was in a chair by the fire, already dressed and reading.

"Good morning." I pushed back the covers and stretched.

She looked up from her book and smiled. "Morning."

"Did I oversleep?"

"No, I just wanted to read a little before Anna came to get me."

I yawned. "What will it be today? Painting? Music? More gardening?"

Ember smiled. "Hopefully something in the garden, although Anna doesn't like being outside. I doubt I'll be able to convince her to take me there again."

"Because it didn't trigger any memories?"

"Yes. She only wants to do things that show I'm making progress."

"What book are you reading?"

"Diverse Forests." She flipped through the pages. "It's very scientific. Maybe you'd like it?"

I snorted but jumped off the bed and waded through the soft carpet to her.

The page was opened to an image of a forest of birch trees with thin trunks and layers of peeling and flaking white bark.

"Those are interesting trees."

"I've seen a forest like that, except the trees don't shed."

"Is it where you're from?"

"I'm not sure." Ember sighed. "I wish I knew."

"Have you remembered anything else?"

Ember hesitated. "Sometimes when I'm in the garden, I get flashes. Like I'm supposed to be doing something . . . like I have a purpose, but I can't figure out what."

"Do you think you have a family?"

"Actually . . . sometimes I feel like someone *sent* me here."

I looked down at Ember's hands and remembered the illuminated veins I saw under her skin. "Why would you be sent here?"

"I don't know." Ember shrugged. "It doesn't make any sense."

"Have you told Anna?"

"No."

"Does she ask?"

"Every day." Ember frowned. "It's strange she would care so much. And she's getting impatient."

I straightened, uneasy. I knew why Anna cared so much, and I hated keeping it a secret. Ember was caring and kind, and our friendship felt as natural and easy as my friendship with York had. Having her around eased the pain of not being able to see him, and I was selfishly glad she was here.

"So, you remember white trees and you think you were sent from there by someone, but not sure why?"

"I said I might have seen *something* like these trees once. It doesn't mean that's where I'm from."

I narrowed my eyes. Ember was backtracking. I thought about the Tree Garden and the Dark Woods. Both places had distinctly different trees. I would know each place by color alone. If Ember said she remembered white trees, surely such a place could be found. How many forests grew only white trees?

There was a knock on the door, and Anna stepped into the room. She took in my nightgown and tumbled hair next to Ember's neat appearance, and leveled me with a look of disapproval.

"Are you ready, Ember?"

"Yes." Ember snapped the book shut. "See you later, Ivy."

I nodded. "Have fun."

Anna studied me coldly. "Is this how you wish to present yourself? That's surprising."

I knew she was hinting at Jack. She hadn't stopped since our first dinner. "I'm getting ready now."

I quickly went to the bathroom, washed my face, and hastily brushed my hair. As I pulled on my new dark clothes, I began to worry that I hadn't done anything in the last week to further my search for ivy or York's living quarters. I'd been adjusting to my new role with Ember, but I needed to refocus.

Life was starting to get complicated.

My first week on the Top Floor had passed quickly. It was as if I'd crossed behind an invisible curtain and was now on the inside with others who worked in the castle. I frequently saw others on the Top Floor, but they were secretive about what they did and careful with their words.

I grabbed a large croissant from the table in the library and inhaled it as I hurried down the corridor. I brushed the crumbs from my dress as I pushed Dr. Ply's door open.

"Ah, Ivy. Good morning." He continued ruffling through a pile of folders.

"Good morning." I crossed the room and sat.

"Today is a rest day for the transposers, so we will not be

going into the lab. Cora insists on their rest when she feels they need it. So they are in their quarters enjoying a leisurely morning."

"Are they going on another outing?" I asked, thinking of the day I saw her in Windermere with Carl.

Dr. Ply set his papers down and looked at me intently. "What do you mean?"

I froze, realizing what I just admitted. There was no way around it. "I—I saw Cora once. In Windermere."

"Tell me about it."

Something warned me to tread carefully. "It was right before the Count's Woodworking Tournament. Before I worked here. I didn't think it was relevant."

"I see. All information is important, Ivy, no matter how much time has passed."

I swallowed, feeling like a bird caught in a cat's paws.

"Was she alone?" he prompted.

"No. Carl and Flex were with her."

"And what were they doing?"

"They stopped at Wilder's Bakery. But they quickly left and headed back to the castle. Obviously, I didn't know Carl was a transposer then, so it didn't seem significant at the time."

"I see. Nothing out of the ordinary happened?"

I remembered the light around Cora but shook my head firmly. "No. Carl looked restless and Flex seemed frustrated with him, like always." I tried to lighten the story so Dr. Ply would forget about it. But he frowned.

"I'll have to speak with the Count about this. Cora is forbidden from taking transposers into town. I'm disappointed she didn't mention it to me. Remember to make a note of that in Carl's folder. It could be what's affecting him now."

I nodded, hoping I hadn't gotten Cora into trouble. "Yes, sir."

Dr. Ply resumed organizing his papers. "Cora's job is to ensure the transposers are well cared for. Sometimes, she becomes overly invested and creates many inconveniences for me. I do my best to accommodate her recommendations, but she somehow still feels I don't do enough. But no more of that. Today we're in a predicament. I must meet with the Count. I have nothing pressing for you to do at the moment—not even research, if you can believe it."

I smiled weakly.

"So, you have an afternoon of freedom. How would you like to use it?"

I realized this was a test. "I'd like to read more about your research on electricity if you wouldn't mind."

I had no idea why I'd thought of that file. Even Dr. Ply looked surprised.

"I know you said that was beyond the scope of my training, but now that I have seen the transposers more, I think I'm ready for it."

Dr. Ply stroked his mustache. "Very well. I'll allow you to read it. However, this research is not for the faint of heart. These experiments are difficult to comprehend, even for the strongest of us."

"I feel ready, sir."

"Do you?" He lifted a brow, but he turned and unlocked his cabinet. After searching through the papers, he handed me the thick file.

"Thank you. Would you mind if I read outside today? I also wanted to study the trees in the Dark Woods, if I have time."

Dr. Ply looked pleased. "Very well, Ivy. And might I add, I'm impressed. I thought for sure you were going to ask to ride that horse."

I smiled as I left the room. I did want to ride Loon, but there were other things I had to do first.

———

I threw the file on the bed and quickly seized my chance to comb the entire room for a secret tunnel; I hadn't been alone here since moving in with Ember a week ago. I knocked on walls, moved tables, and even checked out the balcony, but I didn't find anything. Defeated, I grabbed the files and my father's journal and started to leave when the vase of lavender caught my eye.

I leaned in to smell the flowers, remembering how Jack twirled it in his fingers and the feeling of his foot against mine. I smiled and pulled a sprig out and tucked it into my book, hoping I might run into him today. Maybe I would wander towards the stables after all.

The sun was shining. All the snow from last week's strange blizzard had melted, leaving the air fresh. Today, the warm breeze reminded me of an early spring day, full of life and possibilities.

I circled the gardens, pretending to read on a few benches as I wandered further out in directions I had never been. I passed the Dark Woods, but couldn't make myself go inside by those gloomy trees. The thick ivy vines swayed in the breeze as I passed, but I continued further, searching everywhere in the gardens for another trail of ivy, but there was none.

I sighed and settled on a bench in a far garden I had never been in. As I flipped open my father's journal, the stalk of lavender fell out. I picked it up, studying it, as a realization hit me.

The pollen in my father's journal had made me sneeze when I first inhaled it. Mr. Everett had said that when researching and writing about a certain species of plant, my father liked to put its pollen within the pages, to be near its essence as he wrote. I cracked open the spine of the journal, looking for more yellow pollen. I couldn't remember if ivy vines flowered or even had pollen. I should know this.

Frustrated, I began reading his notes again, looking for anything about pollen. Then I heard voices on the other side of the hedge.

Curious, I gathered my things and walked to where the thick green hedge met an old stone wall. I peeked over it, surprised to see yet another part of the castle. Glass windows overlooked a wide terrace filled with plants and tables. Another long hedge separated it from a sprawling green lawn that turned into fields. Cora sat at a table on the lawn under a large white umbrella. She looked impeccable as always, in a turquoise dress.

Sitting next to her was *York*.

My heart leaped as I scanned his face, taking in his green eyes, freckles, and light brown hair that was windblown as if he had been outside all morning. He wasn't dressed in black or wearing the dark gloves I'd seen him in for months. Today, he wore a loose white shirt and pants that matched those I had seen Glen wearing outside that room with cables. That made me nervous, but York looked relaxed, and I was glad Cora had asked for a day off.

But I also had a sinking feeling that there was something different about him; I couldn't put my finger on it. I wished we could just talk to each other.

I heard a familiar whinny in the distance and looked up to see someone riding in the field beyond the garden.

Jack was riding Loon.

Loon looked stunning in a gleaming black bridle and saddle. Her white mane streamed behind her, her caramel coat shining in the sun. I felt breathless at the sight of Jack's unbuttoned collared shirt and his sleeves rolled up his arms. His dark hair ruffled in the wind, and I realized that I had never seen anyone else on Loon before, but he looked so natural.

Another movement caught my attention. I pulled my eyes from Jack to see York now standing. His face was red with fury. He charged down the lawn, yelling and waving his arms.

"Jack! Get off that horse *right now*! Hey!"

Cora jumped up, startled, and began hurrying after York.

York was halfway down the lawn now, still yelling. I saw Jack pull on the reins, looking confused. Then Loon began sidestepping nervously in response to being charged.

She was deciding whether to rear or bolt.

Loon was either going to throw Jack, kick York, or hurt

herself. I panicked, unable to stomach the idea of any of them getting hurt. They were the three most important things to me in the world. I dropped my father's journal and Dr. Ply's file and raced after them.

"York! Stop!" I screamed, dashing around the stone wall and sprinting across the garden after him.

Cora turned, then startled when I sped past her.

York was still yelling at Jack, and he had almost reached Loon now. Jack was pulling on Loon's reins and working to steady her.

"Get back! What's wrong with you?" Jack yelled, frustrated. "Stop charging us!" He looked shocked that York was so angry, and then he saw me running up behind York. Concern flashed across his face.

"Ivy!" Jack called.

"That's right! She's Ivy's! She's not your horse! Where did you get her? Ivy would never sell her!" York's face was red and it looked like he was thinking about pulling Jack down. "I said get *off*!"

"York, stop!" I grabbed his arm. "Stop it! You're going to hurt someone!"

"Ivy?" York swung around and looked at me in disbelief. "Ivy!" He smashed into me, crushing me in a hug.

My arms instantly went around him too. He felt taller and thinner. I looked over his shoulder at Jack. His brow was creased with tension.

"Sorry about that. He's like my brother," I said, as an explanation of why York was so angry and protective.

York pulled back, surprised by my words. He studied my face, then looked up at Jack.

"What were you thinking?" I pushed his shoulder. "You could have hurt Loon!"

York shook his head as if gathering his composure. I heard Jack say quietly to Cora, "I'm sorry. I didn't even think about him recognizing the horse . . ."

"I know," Cora said. "This is new for all of us."

York looked at Jack sheepishly. "I'm sorry. All I saw was Loon and I snapped, thinking something had happened to Ivy. Or someone had taken Loon from her." He turned back to me. "What are you doing here?"

I nearly answered, but I glanced at Cora first, wondering if she knew I wasn't supposed to talk to him.

"York, would you please wait at the table for us? I'd like to talk to Ivy for a moment alone, if you don't mind."

York looked like he was about to protest, but Cora said, "You can talk after, I promise."

York nodded and looked at me one last time before heading back down the lawn to the table.

Loon pushed her head into me and I took a moment to hug her as Jack got down.

"Are you alright?" I asked him.

"I'm fine." But he sounded conflicted. He squinted into the sun and brushed the dark hair from his forehead, making the corded muscles in his arm flex.

"Ivy . . ." he glanced at Cora, who shielded her eyes as she watched York walk back to the table.

"I didn't realize until now. I should have . . ."

"What?"

"I should have realized that York was the friend you were worried about the day I brought you here. He didn't arrive at the castle until later; for all I knew, you could have been talking about anyone."

"What would you have done?" I said lightly, searching his face.

Again, he looked torn.

"Jack, if you're finished with your ride, I could use some help locating Carl," Cora said. I got the feeling that meant something more because Jack quickly responded.

"Of course." He smiled as he waited for me to pet Loon again, then walked her away.

I looked back at Cora, my heart still racing.

Her eyes sparkled, and her cheeks were pink as if she was happy about this turn of events. "What are you doing way out here? I thought Dr. Ply likes to keep you stuck inside?"

"There's no lab today, so I asked to do my research outside."

"Ah. Yes, that lab is so sterile. I can't imagine being in it as long as you are. That's why I insist the Transposers have days off."

I cleared my throat. "Dr. Ply has forbid me from talking to York. He says it will make it harder for me to be objective in his research."

"I'm aware of that." Cora looked in York's direction. "But now he has seen you and I think it would be much more harmful not to speak with you. I have to do what's best for York."

My heart leaped. "And that is talking with me?"

Cora smiled. "Do you know what I do here, Ivy?"

"You work with the transposers like Dr. Ply?"

She shook her head firmly. "*No.* Not like Dr. Ply. I'm the opposite of Dr. Ply. There's nothing I care about more than making sure the transposers are taken care of. Dr. Ply's research—rather, his *experiments*—come first. But I want you to know that the only reason I am here is to help *them.* I manage their lives when they are not being *used* by Dr. Ply. I monitor their stress levels and physical abilities, ensuring they are not overworked. Transposing is very taxing and I am most concerned with its long-term effects. I make sure Dr. Ply is balanced and fair in his treatment of them." Cora smiled. "You see, my job makes his job much more difficult. Usually, we are at odds with each other."

She said it cheerfully as if it didn't bother her in the slightest to make Dr. Ply upset. I bit back a smile, thinking I liked her.

"Is this the South Wing?" I gestured to the terrace and wall of windows behind us, thinking I'd finally found it.

"Yes. But no one is allowed here except my staff, and occasionally, Jack. However, I will make an exception for you today."

"Why is Jack allowed? He works for Dr. Ply."

"No, Jack is first and foremost the Count's heir. He only just started in the lab because he has a way of making people feel comfortable. People naturally listen to him, as I'm sure you've noticed."

I nodded. Something in me eased, realizing that Jack might not know as much about Dr. Ply's experiments as I thought he did. I hoped that was true.

Cora looked thoughtful. "You've observed York. Does he seem different to you?"

"Yes. That's why I really want to talk to him."

"And you should. York could use some human interaction outside of the other transposers. His adjustment to life here isn't going as smoothly as I hoped."

"Really? Maybe he feels suffocated like Carl did that day in Windermere."

Cora's brow wrinkled. "What?"

"That day you came to Windermere with Carl? I heard him complain of being suffocated and you calmed him down. Do you remember seeing me?"

"Ivy, did Dr. Ply ask you about this?"

My heart dropped. "Yes. This morning, I had to tell him the truth. I'm sorry. I hope I didn't get you in trouble."

"You didn't. But it's always nice to stay one step ahead of Dr. Ply and what he knows."

"He said you weren't supposed to take a Transposer into town."

"He's right, I'm not. But I never could have known that someone from Windermere would come to the castle and tell him."

"Oh, right."

Cora looked back at York. "Never has a person in the castle known a transposer *before* they came here, so this situation is truly rare. I'll make you a deal. Talk to York and I won't say a word to Dr. Ply. In return, just tell me honestly how you think he's changed. Emotionally, physically, his attitude. Deal?"

"Yes," I breathed. I was finally getting to talk to York, instead of observing him silently from behind a glass window. Who cared that I had to also analyze him? I would be doing that anyway to make sure he was OK. And then we would both figure out how to get out of here.

"Marvelous. Let's go get him. Afterwards, you and I will talk."

Twenty-Two

York broke into a huge smile as I walked back over with Cora.

He stood and wrapped me in a hug again.

"Have a nice talk. I'll be back soon," Cora said, disappearing inside the doors off the terrace.

I pulled away, sank down into the chair beside him, and took in his every detail. His brown eyes studied me back. The freckles on his nose were fading and his face was longer.

"I just can't believe you're here!" He shook his head in disbelief. "When I saw Jack on Loon, I assumed the worst."

I felt a pang of worry; did he know something about Jack that I didn't? "Why?"

"I don't know. Just seeing him ride Loon like she was his, and knowing how much she means to you. I snapped."

"Oh." I breathed out in relief. "Jack's taking care of her for me when I can't see her."

York looked surprised. "You're friends?"

I blushed. "Yes. Why? Don't you like him?"

"Sure, everyone likes Jack. But I wouldn't say he's my friend. He's in charge of us."

"The Transposers?"

He froze. "You know about us?"

I nodded.

"You knew I was here?"

"Yes. I'll explain, but first, tell me what happened to you after the Count's Tournament. When I left Windermere, they told me you won! I didn't know you were brought here too. How did it happen?"

"That was all kinda a blur. Mr. Mallon said the Count needed someone with my skill set, that I'd earn more at the castle. They even send money to my parents when I do well in the lab. *A lot* of money."

I paused, the realization setting in. "Oh my gosh . . . you like it here." All this time, I naively thought York was aware that he was being used. But he wasn't.

York looked at me strangely. "Of course! You know I couldn't wait to get away from my father. Right after I got pulled out of the Tournament, Mr. Mallon arranged it all with the castle. It was the best day of my life."

I clamped my lips shut. How was York not aware of how he was being used? Even I wasn't completely sure, but I knew whatever Dr. Ply was doing to him and the other transposers was harmful.

"Why did your father agree? He hates the castle."

"My mom insisted. I've never seen her so determined. I think she thought she was doing me a favor by getting me away from my father. He was really angry, but no matter what he said, she wouldn't back down. Then it was done, they said goodbye, and I went with Mr. Mallon."

I felt sick. If York's mother knew what she gave York over to . . . something so much worse than her husband . . . it would destroy her.

"I just figured you went back to the Taylors and were fine. Why *are* you here?" He sounded confused.

"Dr. Ply needed an assistant. He chose me because of my father."

"What?"

I leaned in, even though no one was in the garden. "My father secretly worked for Dr. Ply and the Count. I'm still trying to uncover what happened to him. And I just found out that it was *these* woods he disappeared from. He also stole something."

York stared at me, then he shook his head. "You're still following clues?"

I tried not to show how much that comment hurt. I thought seeing the castle would make York realize I'd been right to follow the clues the way I had. Didn't he feel the darkness here too? Or was he already changed so much that he couldn't tell that something was wrong?

"You like being a transposer," I said in disbelief.

"It's incredible! Now you tell me how you know about it."

Dr. Ply would never forgive me for telling York things he was not supposed to know—like how we watched him behind the mirror. But what if York said something and it compromised us both? I chose my next words carefully. "Dr. Ply told me because I take notes for him."

York relaxed back into his chair. "What else do you do?"

"Just the notes. Sometimes I clean his office and file research. Do you see him often?"

"Just when he interviews us. He also does tests, but mostly on Carl because he's so difficult."

My stomach sank. York didn't think he was in danger because he was following orders and doing well in the lab. He thought he was above Dr. Ply's tests.

I felt the urge to spill everything to make him understand. Seeing light around him when he Carved. My fears regarding Dr. Ply and the transposers. How the castle broke people, like Anna. And how we needed to get out.

But I stopped. York wasn't a person I could confide in anymore. Maybe he never was. Because even back in Windermere, every time I'd seen something unusual with the Count, he told me to stop investigating.

York didn't *want* to know the truth. It wouldn't make things better by telling him; it might make them much worse.

He was in trouble, and *I* was the only one who could help.

"Do you miss Windermere?" I asked softly. What I really wanted to ask was, didn't he miss me like I had missed him?

"No, I don't miss it at all."

Tears sprung to my eyes. I missed Windermere so much I ached, but a lot of those feelings had to do with York and our friendship there.

"Is that because you're so good at being a transposer?" I asked, swallowing.

"Yeah, that part is great. But also, I fit in here more than I ever did in Windermere."

I didn't know how to respond to that. My heart was splintering. Cora had said York *wasn't* fitting in. He was so blind. To all of it.

"Do you get along with the other transposers?"

"Sure. Although most of them get upset that I'm new and doing better than they ever have. But it's not like I can help it; it just happens."

"What happens?"

For a split second, York looked like he was going to say something, but his expression changed. "I don't want to talk about it."

"We've never kept things from each other before," I said, knowing how much I was withholding too.

"Even if I could tell you, I doubt you'd believe me."

"Try me."

He shook his head. "I better not."

I felt like a chasm had opened between us, one too deep for this conversation to fix. I worried I might never get York to leave the castle now. But if I did, could he ever be who he was before?

"Are you alright?" York asked.

"No. And neither are you," I snapped.

His eyes widened. "What's that supposed to mean?"

"You've changed, York. I'm really worried about you. About us. About what will happen if we stay here. It scares me."

He frowned.

"Carl's not the same either, is he?" I pushed. "He was *never* difficult in school. It's the castle. It's *transposing*. You need to open your eyes and believe me for once!"

We stared at each other, the thread connecting us ready to snap. Then York looked away and I feared I would never be able to reach him again.

Then he spoke, his voice soft. "I do think about the Tree Garden sometimes."

I frowned. "But you were only there once?"

"I feel connected to it. I think it changed me—my hands."

"When you touched the packages . . ." I whispered.

He nodded.

"I went back," I said slowly. "I thought about you too. And . . . I found someone in there." I don't know what made me say it. I just wanted to connect with him again.

"Really?" York looked interested. "Who?"

I explained finding Ember in the Tree Garden, and how she didn't remember anything.

"So where is she from, then?" York asked. "Not Windermere . . . the ships, maybe?"

"She didn't think so. Oh, and I got to tell the Count about her."

"You saw the Count? " York leaned forward in his chair. "Is he as scary as everyone said?"

I leaned in too. "He is so intense . . . and yes, really scary."

"Even I find him a little intimidating." Cora suddenly appeared at the table.

We both jumped.

"Oh, I'm sorry! I didn't mean to startle you both. York, it's time to go now. Please say goodbye."

I stood, disappointed that our time was over just when we were getting back to normal.

"Bye, Ivy," York said, studying me like he was memorizing my face.

I hugged him, wondering when I would see him next. "Think about what I said."

I watched him leave, then turned back to Cora.

She sat at the table and gestured for me to join her. "My, I certainly didn't expect this to happen today. No one saw the incident with Jack, so don't worry. Dr. Ply will never know you were here."

A waiter appeared at the table holding a tray with fresh coffee and an assortment of little cakes, fruit, and croissants.

"This looks delicious," Cora said as he placed everything on the table.

He poured steaming coffee into my cup, then Cora's, and left.

Cora picked up a spoon and stirred in sugar and cream. "Please, help yourself."

I was about to say thank you, but the words died on my lips.

The light I'd seen around Cora for a brief moment in Windermere was back. Her hand holding the spoon glowed just like York's hands had when he changed the wood, except the light didn't stop at her wrist. The iridescent light came down her arm, engulfed her palm, and flowed down into the spoon.

The spoon wilted, then completely *melted*. The round part hung limply down toward the table, dull and ruined.

Cora didn't notice anything amiss until she saw my wide eyes. She looked down. "Oh my."

Then the waiter was back, taking the mangled spoon from her hand and immediately replacing it with another.

"I apologize, Cora," he said smoothly. "I should have checked the silverware more carefully before I gave you a ruined one." Then he was gone.

Cora smiled at me as if nothing happened. "How's the coffee?"

I snapped my mouth shut. "Very good."

The new wooden spoon didn't match any of the other silverware on the table. I'd just seen Cora do something similar to what the transposers did. It was the same light. I wondered why both she and the waiter acted like the spoon had been ruined before it got to the table. I *saw* it change.

Was it possible that they didn't know there was light around the spoon? Was I the only one seeing light around objects *before* they changed? Even in the lab, I saw the change in the wood before anyone else did. They only saw it after the change was complete.

Cora sipped her coffee. "Did you have a nice visit with York?"

I shook my head, trying to focus. "I wish it had gone better."

Her brow raised. "Then York *has* changed these last few months."

"Yes. He's rash, proud, and insensitive. And he never was before."

"Anything else?"

"He thinks he fits in here."

"How interesting. Did he fit in at Windermere?"

"No." My voice cracked. "Neither of us did."

"Is there anything else bothering you?" Cora asked gently.

"Everything's bothering me!" I exploded, unexpectedly. "I don't understand any of this! I don't know who I can trust! There's something off here, and all I have is a stupid book full of research on vines my father left me, instead of just telling me things about himself that I should know! And now my best friend is *broken*!"

If Cora was startled by my outburst, she didn't show it. "You can trust me, Ivy. I want to help you, just like I want to help York."

"How do you know anything about me?" I remembered the strange way Cora had stared at me in Windermere, like she had known me. It was the same knowing look she'd given me in the stable, like she'd known I shouldn't have been there.

"Because your father was a close friend of mine."

I sucked in a breath, startled. "Can I ask you a question about him?"

"Of course."

"Could he do anything out of the ordinary?"

Cora looked at me sharply. "What do you mean?"

I flushed. "Was anything different about him? Something no one else knew? He's such a mystery to me, still. I feel like I never really knew him."

Cora paused. "To my knowledge, your father didn't have any talent that was out of the ordinary, although he was a gifted Arborist. However, he was fascinated by those who did possess extraordinary talents. He argued a lot with Dr. Ply, who, as you know, is opposed to the theory of people having extra abilities. There was a great deal of tension between them. It was something your father and I bonded over."

"The theory that people could do extraordinary things?"

"Yes."

"Do you know what happened to him?"

Cora hesitated, and for a moment, I thought she was going to tell me something important. Then she said, "I'm sorry, I don't."

I let out my breath, disappointed. "It doesn't seem like anyone does. I fear I'll never find out."

"You've survived losing both parents, a fate most people can't imagine. *Your* worst fears have already come true, and you learned you *can* live through it. This should give you strength to draw on in these uncertain times."

"It should," I said wearily. "But it doesn't."

"Then remember this: Fear plagues us all, and there will always be people who try to use your fears to control you . . . but there is *power* in fearing nothing. Over time, hopefully, you will learn to become fearless, as I have."

"Does that mean you don't care about things anymore?"

"No, it means I've learned that nothing *belongs* to me anymore. And because nothing belongs to me, I can't really lose anything. Do you understand?"

"Not really."

Cora smiled. "Perhaps tomorrow you will. Now it's time you got back, but I hope we meet again soon."

Then she handed me my father's journal. I had dropped it when I chased after York, but now Jack's lavender sprig was tucked neatly into the pages. Along with the electricity study.

I looked up at her, wondering if she'd seen the file, but her face gave away nothing.

"I meant what I said about having high hopes for you. And if I were you, Ivy, I'd examine your father's journal again. I've never known him to write even a single line that didn't matter."

TWENTY-THREE

I checked the library for Ember, but it was empty.

I poured another cup of coffee, thinking maybe York just needed to be reminded of our life back in Windermere to return to who he was. When I saw him again, maybe I could bring my jewelry box from Mr. Gable. It was the only thing I had from Windermere with me—

"What are you doing?"

I nearly dropped my cup. "Anna! Why are you sneaking up on me?" I hoped the guilt of this afternoon wasn't written on my face. Or in my shaking hands.

Anna crossed her arms. "Where were you? I knocked on your door several times and you didn't answer."

"I was reading outside." I sipped my coffee, trying to act normal. "Now if you'll excuse me, I need to get back to it."

"How much of the study have you read?"

"I'm nearly finished," I lied.

"Then follow me. Your free time is over."

"Can't I finish my coffee?"

"No. I've already wasted enough time looking for you."

Worry clenched my stomach as I set my cup down and followed Anna down the stairs. I thought we were headed to Dr.

Ply's office, but Anna continued past it and opened the door to the hallway leading to the lab.

Our footsteps echoed on the stone floor. We passed the lab, and the longer we walked, the more worried I became that someone had discovered I had been with York. Or that I had been sneaking out at night. Had Carl finally told on me?

I panicked, thinking through how I could escape, but I didn't know what to do except run through this maze of hallways.

Then Anna stopped and opened the door I'd seen Glen stumble out of. The room with the cables.

I followed her inside, dreading what I would find.

The circular room was dimly lit by lanterns and candles. A small desk with a chair on either side was in the center of the room. Dr. Ply sat in one chair, the other was empty. He continued writing in a notebook and didn't stop to acknowledge us. Anna pointed to another set of chairs near the door. We both sat quietly.

To the side of Dr. Ply sat a strange-looking machine with black cables stretching across the floor to the empty chair. My heart began to race as I looked at the machine's faded knobs and levers. What did it do?

Finally, Dr. Ply looked up. "Welcome to the Dome room."

Nervously, I looked around. Along the walls were rows upon rows of shelves, and on them were at least a hundred sealed glass domes. There was nothing inside them that I could see.

He watched me inspect the room. "How did your reading this afternoon go?"

I swallowed. "I'm intrigued with the study, but I haven't finished it. I wanted to take my time and not miss any important details."

He nodded. "What do you think of the experiment so far? Has it satisfied your curiosity, or do you find yourself feeling differently? This is the time to be honest."

I hesitated, not sure how to answer. On one hand, I was terrified to know what Dr. Ply was doing, but on the other hand, I needed to know for York's sake. I wiped my sweaty hands on my skirt.

"You were right, it is a very difficult subject. I didn't understand most of it if I'm being honest."

Dr. Ply leaned back in his chair, studying me. "Yes. This one is not for the faint of heart. I debated allowing you here, but this morning, when you said you'd been thinking about this particular experiment, it got me thinking about a theory I have yet to test. Since you've been doing well, I believe you can be trusted with these more delicate subjects. Anna has many other responsibilities now, so sometimes, I will require you to assist me here as well as in the lab."

I nodded, trying to hide the panic rising in my chest. Whatever Dr. Ply was going to do, I didn't want to see it. I could only hope that he wouldn't experiment on York or Ember. She still hadn't remembered anything, but why wasn't Anna with her now? Where was she?

"Anna, you may go get the Transposer."

My heart dropped. I tried to control my breathing, praying it wouldn't be York. What would he do if he saw me in here?

Anna left the room, and Dr. Ply set an empty glass dome on the table. There was a fist-sized hole in either side of the glass; he placed a piece of white wood inside the dome through one of the holes. Then he began to arrange the cables carefully around the chair.

"I thought today was a rest day?" I asked nervously.

"It is, but Carl was found wandering around the halls earlier, and so I doubt Cora will miss him. This should only take half an hour or so."

"What are you looking to measure?" Panic tightened my chest, making my voice too high. But Dr. Ply didn't notice.

He sat down in a huff. "This machine is useful for many of my experiments, including memory. In the lab, we monitor social interaction and Carving. We are looking for certain patterns in behaviors, shared mannerisms, and general concentration issues.

But in this room, my goal is to capture the energy in the transforming moment. The captured energy—those charged molecules—is later studied and compared to see if there is anything consistent I can use to form a theory."

I looked around at all the empty glass domes, filled with what Dr. Ply thought were charged air molecules. My stomach sank as I realized that each one represented a transposer sitting in this room, attached to this machine. I felt sick.

"Of course, the study you read has all the specific details. You may refer to it later if you have more questions."

The door opened. Carl walked in with Anna.

I shrank in my chair as if I could make myself invisible. Carl had already seen me in the hallway. He could blurt it out now to save himself, and I wouldn't blame him. If he told, I couldn't deny it—not if it would save him. I looked up, meeting his eyes, hoping my pleading look wasn't caught by Anna or Dr. Ply.

But when I saw Carl's face, guilt washed over me. Here I was, hoping Carl didn't put me in danger when Carl was the one walking right into something awful. My stomach turned at my own selfishness.

If Carl saw me, he didn't seem to notice. He walked right past me and sat down in the chair across from Dr. Ply. His eyes were glazed and his body seemed unnaturally relaxed. They had already given him something.

Then he looked up and his eyes caught mine.

I held my breath, staring back, hoping I could support Carl through whatever he was about to endure. At least I could be here for him.

Anna walked around Carl's chair and began preparing the black cables. She stuck grey tabs along his arms and head. Then she placed both his hands inside the glass dome through the two holes so they were in to just above each wrist. I watched his fingers curl over the white wood instinctively.

Anna sealed the perimeter of each hole and Carl's arms with a thick band of black rubber, so that no air was able to travel in or out. Then she looked at Dr. Ply.

"Carl," he said.

Carl's eyes left mine and he looked over at Dr. Ply. The muscles in his arms tensed.

"The white wood is in your hands. I would like you to turn it to laun, just as you have several times before. Concentrate, just like you do in the lab. We are going to assist you today with your focus, and perhaps it will also help you in the future."

I gripped the edge of my chair. There were no tools. How did they expect Carl to Carve? What kind of cruel joke was this?

Dr. Ply nodded at Anna, and she turned up the first knob. A whirling sound filled the room. Carl didn't seem affected yet. His hands cupped the wood, turning it over and over.

Anna pressed a few more buttons and turned the level up higher. This time, Carl straightened. His chest and arms flexed, and he squeezed the wood, breathing rapidly.

"Hold it there, Anna."

I shifted in my chair. Watching Carl react to the electricity pulsing through his body was difficult. It took everything inside me not to jump up and yell at them to stop.

"Don't fight it, Carl. Work through it and change your wood," Dr. Ply coached. His voice sounded gentle, and I hated him for it.

Carl breathed deeper now, but his wood remained unchanged.

Tears pricked my eyes and I willed myself not to break down.

Dr. Ply fished a syringe out of his white lab coat. He removed the cap and flicked the air bubbles out. I winced as it plunged deep into Carl's arm.

Carl relaxed immediately, his body slumped backward, and he closed his eyes. But his hands never let go of the white wood. In fact, they gripped it tighter, until his hands and wrists turned white. His thumbs pressed into it and his fingers began to knead it. Almost like he thought he was Carving.

For several minutes, they held the machine steady, and Dr. Ply took notes. Then, when I thought I couldn't take much more, I saw Dr. Ply give Anna a signal to increase the level on the machine.

Tiny bubbles formed in Carl's mouth. The veins in his arms began to rise. I gripped my chair harder and clamped my mouth shut. I knew *I* was just moments away from breaking; how could Carl take any more? His shoulders were shaking—

"Hold it there, Anna," Dr. Ply said calmly, still writing in his file.

I glared at Anna as she watched Carl, detached and emotionless. How many of these experiments had she seen over the years? How could she stomach it? I was about to be sick.

Then I noticed faint particles of light inside the glass dome. I leaned forward. Anna's eyes flickered to me immediately. The light Carl created wasn't nearly as strong as the light I saw when York transposed, or when Cora bent that spoon today. It was much weaker. Then I noticed it wasn't just in the glass dome . . . it was seeping out of Carl's entire body and onto the floor.

The glimmering dust fell gently to the ground. The more that fell, the greyer Carl became.

His lips were white, foam was forming in the corners of his mouth, and his hands were shaking. Whatever it was, the fact that it was leaving Carl was bad—very bad.

I stood up, about to rip the cords off him, but Dr. Ply waved at Anna.

"There! Cut it off, Anna. Now!"

Immediately, the whirling stopped and Carl slumped forward onto the table. His head rested on his arm. I wasn't sure if he was breathing anymore.

"Is he alive?" I whispered, trying to keep my emotions hidden when all I wanted to do was scream at them and cry. They were monsters.

"Of course. He'll recover shortly," Dr. Ply said, distracted.

"Anna, please record the exact dosage you used. It cut his best time down by ten minutes. Anna, did you hear me?"

"She saw something." Anna pointed a finger at me. "Ivy knew before the block changed."

I froze. I looked up from the dust on the floor into Anna's accusing face.

"What?"

"I saw you react to something before the block changed to laun, like you *knew* it was going to happen."

"That's ridiculous." I forced my voice to sound cold. "How could I know that? I've never even seen an experiment like this before."

"I don't know, but you did. You knew!" Anna insisted.

Dr. Ply looked at her angry face and immediately dismissed her accusations. "Anna, control yourself. Take Carl out of here. Get him ready to go back to the South Wing."

"But she knew! I know she saw something!" She was getting more emotional than I'd ever seen her, and that was what saved me.

"That's enough," Dr. Ply said sharply.

Anna glared at me as she struggled with Carl. Soon he was conscious enough to walk and Anna led him from the room. I hoped Cora could help him.

Dr. Ply worked quickly to seal up the dome. Only then did I notice the wood inside had turned to laun, but it was a weak golden color. I had been too busy looking at the dust to notice Carl had managed to change it.

The dust was still lying on the ground under the chair. Dr. Ply and Anna didn't seem to see it. But whatever it was, it was important. There was little, if any, in the glass dome.

Just as Dr. Ply stood to leave, with the dome under his arm, an idea struck.

"Would you like me to put these away?" I asked, gesturing to the black cables.

"Yes, do that. I'll send Anna back to help you if she hasn't dissolved into hysterics. I must go compare these notes with those from Carl's previous session."

He left, eager to study his new findings, and I was alone with the dust. I quickly kicked the cords in the corner, then I rummaged through the drawers for something to use to collect the dust. I found a small box and a piece of paper.

I used the paper to gather all the dust up and scoop it into the box. All I could think was that I had to hurry and get it all inside before Anna came back.

Then something strange happened. The dust seemed to gather itself together and it suddenly was easier for me to get it in the box. It was as if it *listened* to me. But there was no time to think about that.

I finished tidying the room and left quickly. My hands shook holding the box the entire way back as I tried to process what just happened. I'd known something was not quite right in the castle, but this was more awful—more dark— than I could have imagined. It was difficult to breathe. How would I stop this from happening again?

I turned the corner and saw Anna waiting by my door. My steps faltered.

Immediately, she zeroed in on the box. "What did you steal? Show me now!"

I hid the box behind my back. "I don't steal. And it's none of your business."

Anna's eyes narrowed and she stepped closer. "I know you saw something in that room, just like I know you have something you're not supposed to behind your back. Show me right now before I force you to."

She meant it.

I held the box out. "It's just this."

Anna snatched it and opened it. She looked inside and slammed it shut. "It's empty," she said, tossing it to the ground.

"No!" I cried, lunging for it before anything spilled out.

Anna looked at me like I'd lost my mind. "Open it again," she said, spitting every word out.

Slowly, I opened the box back up.

Anna looked in and then looked back up at me. Her face was full of hatred.

"I don't know what kind of game you're playing with me, Ivy Rune. But I'm going to make sure you regret it."

Twenty-Four

That night, I dreamed black ravens chased me through the castle.

Their wings flapped as I ran down a hallway of locked doors. They squawked and dove at me as I covered my head in my hands. I couldn't escape them. But then another bird appeared, shimmering in light. It tried to lead me toward an open door. I desperately followed as the ravens continued to dive at me. But it didn't matter how fast I was, I couldn't reach the door. Somehow it kept moving further away—

I jolted awake, shivering and covered in sweat. I sat up and looked around the room. It was morning.

Ember was gone.

My nerves felt raw as I quickly got ready. I grabbed a pastry as I walked to Dr. Ply's office, trying to shake off the dark dream, but anxiety covered me like a heavy cloak.

I tossed the pastry out an open window, too uneasy to eat.

I dreaded seeing Dr. Ply. I never wanted to witness that experiment again.

I closed my eyes, remembering the shimmering dust seeping out of Carl and falling to the ground. I put the box with the dust, along with my father's journal, in my bag. I didn't trust leaving either in the room with Anna so determined to ruin me.

Anna would stop at nothing to prove what she claimed was true, that I'd seen something in the experiment that they hadn't. If Dr. Ply ever found out what I could see, he would experiment on me too.

If I didn't get York out of the castle soon, our futures would be the same as Anna's and Carl's. How could York not see this? Or didn't he care? Was it possible that being a Transposer blinded him to everything else?

I shook my head as if I could shake the fears out of it.

But every rule I'd broken: sneaking out, falling for Jack, seeing York . . . those secrets were piling up and threatening to bury me. It was just a matter of time until Dr. Ply or Anna uncovered them.

And now I knew what they were capable of.

When I reached the lab, Dr. Ply was waiting outside the door for me.

"Ah, there you are."

I slowed, my body flooding with anxiety at the sight of him. "Good morning, Dr. Ply."

He nodded. "Anything new to report with Ember?"

"No, she seems to be adjusting well."

"She still doesn't remember anything?"

I hesitated, knowing I had to say something to ease his impatience, but I hated the feeling of betraying her. "She said she hits a wall in her mind whenever she tries to remember specific details."

I cringed; that was the wrong thing to say.

"How curious. I wonder what it will take for her to start remembering. There must be something I could do."

My stomach dropped. "Like what?"

"I've conducted a few experiments regarding memory. You haven't learned that part of my research yet and it would be very educational for you. A bit tricky, but I have had a lot of practice over the years to learn the right way to go about it."

Alarm bells sounded in my head, but before I could say anything, Dr. Ply changed the subject.

"Now, this is an unpleasant topic for us both, but I've heard you're spending a lot of time talking with Jack. Is that true?"

My heart began to pound so loudly that I wondered if he could hear it. "Not at all. If we speak, it's to discuss the Transposers. He's been a big resource for me, explaining things about the lab so I don't have to bother you with all my questions. I did try to ask Anna first, but she wasn't very helpful," I added.

"Ah. Well, see to it that you don't become distracted by interpersonal relationships. You have a bright future here. Any type of friendship, or relationship, would absolutely derail that. Have I made myself clear?"

"Yes."

"Anything else you need to tell me before we go inside?"

My stomach tangled in knots as I shook my head.

Dr. Ply nodded. "Good, let's get started then."

He opened the door and gestured for me to go first. I stepped inside the lab and another wave of shock slammed into me.

Sitting at the table was the Count.

His presence filled the room, making it feel too small. His hands were folded in his lap as he stared through the double-sided mirror. When he heard the door open, his sharp blue eyes cut to mine.

"Hello, sir," I said uneasily, still stuck by the door.

The Count nodded, dismissed me almost instantly as he looked over my head at Dr. Ply, and then looked back into the lab.

"Good morning," Dr. Ply said. "Have a seat, Ivy."

The only chair available was on the Count's right side. My heart hammered as I perched on it, leaning slightly away. I was scared to move or breathe.

I tried to calm myself down as I waited for one of them to say something.

"Ivy." I jumped at Dr. Ply's voice. "I want you to take notes as usual today, but please watch extra carefully this morning to make sure we don't miss anything. Our lab will be different this morning, which is why the Count is here."

I nodded as the door in the lab opened and the Transposers filed in, taking their usual seats. Anna and Flex followed and went around removing the gloves as usual. When that was finished, they took their seats by the door. Only Jack was missing.

I peeked at the Count. He looked uninterested, but I was beginning to think that his placid demeanor might just be an act. The Count seemed too alert to truly be indifferent. He watched York intently.

I took a second to compose myself as I opened the file Dr. Ply gave me. For the first time, I had York's file. I was free to watch him openly today. And study him.

Was this another test, or did Dr. Ply really trust me to study York now?

My stomach was in knots. What would happen if York acted strangely after our talk yesterday? Or if Carl finally blurted out he saw me in the hallway by the lab? There was so much that could go wrong with the Count here.

The door opened again.

Jack walked in with Ember. A feeling of dread flooded me as Ember looked around the room, curious. Her brow wrinkled in confusion.

I tried to mirror the calm, remote posture of both men beside me, but inside I felt pure turmoil. Why had the Count come to watch Ember in the lab? What did he and Dr. Ply think would happen? It didn't make sense.

Unless . . .

Unless they *had* known all along that Ember was different.

My pencil froze midair. They had hidden their interest in Ember from me this whole time.

But what did they think she could do?

I glanced at the Count as he watched Ember with the same sedate expression . . . but his eyes seemed brighter.

Jack led Ember to York's table. I realized I was tapping my

pencil against the table and forced myself to stop. To my relief, when Jack introduced them, York didn't act like he knew Ember at all.

I slowly let out the breath I'd been holding, grateful that York had the sense not to give away that he heard about Ember from me yesterday.

Jack walked away to open the cabinet to pass out tools and wood. I watched him too, wishing I could just talk to him.

Everyone began Carving.

Ember watched with interest as York selected his tools. Wood chips fell to the floor as York made the first few scrapes across his block. He seemed to be Carving a bit more intently than usual, probably showing off now that he had a spectator.

If he only knew who was watching behind the mirror.

The morning continued uneventfully, so I was able to relax a little. Dr. Ply and the Count spoke sparingly to each other, but when they did, their comments were strange, almost like a code.

I watched and scribbled down meaningless notes. York's grandstanding had stopped an hour ago and now he was really working.

Ember feigned polite interest, but I could tell even she was getting bored. Her foot swayed side to side as she glanced discreetly around the room. She studied the mirror for a moment before her eyes flickered back to York.

Carl suddenly became irritated with something on his desk. Jack stood and went over to help. Anna and Flex sat up, waiting to see if they were needed. Jack was patient with Carl, but Carl seemed determined to be upset. It was hard to watch his outburst now without imagining him during that experiment. Today, Carl looked like he'd deteriorated.

Dr. Ply began explaining to the Count how difficult Carl had become lately; I could hear the frustration in his voice. The Count's eyes narrowed as he studied Carl.

Carl was on very thin ice.

I hid my scowl, knowing it wasn't his fault.

While everyone watched Jack try to reason with Carl, I glanced back to York and Ember.

Just then, York accidentally knocked his wood off the table. It slipped through his hands and before it hit the ground, Ember caught it.

As soon as Ember's hands closed around it, I saw a burst of light and the wood instantly turned to laun.

York looked down at her hands. His eyes widened.

Ember looked horrified.

Quick as a whip, she shoved the shining block into York's hands and sat back in her seat, still as a statue. York looked down at the golden block, speechless.

Jack heard the commotion a second too late and when he looked over, he saw York holding the laun. He immediately signaled for Anna to take over with Carl and walked over to York's table.

Dr. Ply's, and the Count's, eyes followed Jack.

"Great work, York! This must be the fastest record ever. May I?" Jack picked up the wood with a cloth to inspect it. He looked genuinely impressed. "How unusual; you didn't even finish Carving it this time."

York glanced at Ember, who was silently pleading with him not to say anything. York frowned, but he remained quiet and let Jack continue to praise him over the transformed piece of wood.

Ember closed her eyes briefly, relief washing over her face.

I watched frozen behind the mirror, amazed and shocked. Ember had turned the entire piece of wood into laun just by *touching* it. It didn't take her hours of intense Carving. And there wasn't even an outline of light around her hands like I usually saw. It had been an explosion. Then it was gone.

Besides York, I was the only one who knew what happened. Everyone else had missed it.

My heart pounded in my ears, knowing I had to make a decision.

Write it down in the file, or keep it quiet.

Jack called for lunch and everyone filed out of the lab. A few transposers looked upset that York had once again performed better than them. Carl had the worst expression of all on his face.

My pen hovered over York's file as I quickly debated my options.

Jack stepped into the room. He slowed slightly when he saw the Count, but completely composed himself as he handed the laun to Dr. Ply.

When the Count and Dr. Ply leaned over the black cloth to examine it, I felt Jack's eyes flicker towards me.

All my resolve nearly melted away.

I wanted to look back so badly, but I kept my eyes on the file. I couldn't risk Dr. Ply catching me staring at him now—not after his warning this morning.

I remembered something Jack had said in the stables; that they would use Loon against me because they knew how much I cared. At the time, I'd felt as though Jack was trying to tell me something more . . . that he wouldn't show how much he cared about me because they would use it against him.

I wanted to lift my eyes and show him I understood, but I knew just a look would undo me. I had to keep control.

And I still needed to decide what I was going to do.

Dr. Ply commented on York's quick work and how solid the laun was. The Count listened, looking faintly impressed.

"Ivy," Dr. Ply called, making me jump. "After lunch, I want you to take the measurements of this block and then plant exactly half of it in the Dark Woods. Study the protocol to ensure you do it correctly. You may go."

I hesitated. My jaw ached from how tightly it was clenched shut. I was the only one in the room who knew the truth about Ember and York.

Dr. Ply looked up, noticing I hadn't moved. "What is it?"

The Count looked at me too. His cold eyes searched my face as if he was looking for my weakness—or secret. For a moment, I thought I saw something—a look of sheer hunger that made me want to run. It was the look of a man who would stop at nothing to get what he wanted, no matter who suffered.

I slowly put my pencil down and closed York's file. I would not condemn anyone to further experiments.

I stood, trembling, and quickly left the room.

I walked down the hallway, my head swimming, but I breathed easier. I still couldn't believe what Ember had done. All I could think about was the explosion of light.

Brighter than any light I had seen so far.

I had just withheld perhaps the most important information yet from Dr. Ply *and* the Count.

It was just a matter of time before I was caught.

TWENTY-FIVE

The wooden door creaked open and I passed under the archway choked by vines.

I shuddered as I took in the Dark Woods. Branches sagged as if they struggled to hold themselves up. Again, it was eerily silent, as if anything living avoided this place. I wanted to leave too.

This place screamed of desolation and death.

Yet, my father had convinced Dr. Ply to plant ivy at the door. Was it a clue, or just a practicality, to hide this place from prying eyes? I needed to learn the reason the Dark Woods existed if I was going to learn more about my father.

I picked up the shovel and walked quickly so I could finish planting and leave before sunset. I couldn't help but frown as I passed small wooden signs with Transposers' names crudely carved into them.

In Windermere, Carving was meant to showcase the Carver's talent. But in the castle, what the Carving looked like wasn't important—only the outcome was.

I passed Carl's section and noticed more consistency within the trees. Carl hadn't transposed since I'd been in the lab, yet these trees proved he had, once. Most of his black trunks were equal in thickness, and their leaves were all nearly the same size. All of his worst looking trees were freshly planted . . . meaning these trees were the result of the laun he made during Dr. Ply's private experiments.

Chills went down my arms as I counted the scrawny trees. There were over ten.

I hurried to York's section, populated with by far the best-looking trees. It was strange to see York be the best at something. I couldn't blame him for liking the way it felt.

I took out the bundle of black cloth and unwrapped it.

Ember's laun.

Outside the lab, it looked completely different. This laun pulled the natural light deep inside itself, glowing and shimmering like a tiny sun in my hand. It took my breath away and I wondered how Ember was able to create this—and what it meant about her.

The laun practically hummed with energy, and I covered it quickly before I was compelled to touch it. It was hard to believe that no one else had seen the explosion of light. Was I a Dyadic now? Were York, Ember, and Cora?

If Dr. Ply ever discovered that I was something he was actively trying to disprove existed—I shivered. He could never find out.

I picked up the shovel and quickly began digging a hole in the black dirt. I could only hope this tree would grow to look like York's other trees. If not, Dr. Ply would wonder about the difference, and maybe even think York was becoming inconsistent like Carl.

I took all my frustration out on the dirt. When Dr. Ply discovered what I withheld . . . just the thought made me sick with fear. In my efforts to protect York and Ember, I was failing to protect myself.

Dr. Ply would accuse me of putting friends above his work. From the beginning, he'd warned me that relationships were distractions. I'd just proved him right, but what else could I have done? I couldn't harm others just to keep myself safe.

I paused, breathing hard. The hole was bigger than it needed to be. The longer I withheld the truth from Dr. Ply, the more deceitful I would look. He might even send me away—maybe on the wrecked ship I'd seen, if it'd been repaired by now—and no one would know where I disappeared to.

If that happened, I wouldn't be able to protect York, or Ember, or anyone else from Dr. Ply's experiments. And I would never uncover the truth about my father, or why I saw light . . . or what the dust was that had fallen from Carl.

My stomach dropped at the thought of never seeing Jack again.

I dropped the shovel, my energy depleted. I let the laun slip from my hand down into the hole. I covered it over with dirt.

Maybe I could find a way to confess, make Dr. Ply believe it was just a mistake. Then I wouldn't lose everything that mattered to me.

The problem with that was, York and Ember were keeping the same secret. If I confessed, both of them would be in danger. York went along with it because he wanted to protect Ember. But why did Ember want to keep it a secret? Why did she think she needed to hide it?

Did she think something bad would happen to her?

When the hole was filled, I wiped the dirt from my hands, breathing hard.

I only had a few days to figure out how to spin this story with the least amount of damage to everyone—myself included.

———

Our room was empty when I returned. I assumed Ember was at dinner with Anna so I changed and ate by the fire alone, glad for more time to think. But no solution came to me.

After eating, I walked out onto the balcony and stared at the dark patch of woods beyond the stone wall. Even from up here, it looked dreary and ominous. I wondered if Ember's laun was already growing beneath the dirt. My stomach churned anxiously, imagining what it might look like.

I wandered back inside, suddenly missing my old room. At least that room was real—this room was nothing but a pretty facade hiding dark things. This room—these *rewards*—were bribes, a payoff to keep the secret that something terrible was happening to the Transposers. It made me sick.

I noticed the orchid on my bedside table. I had forgotten all about it, but now, I stared at it, confused. Ember had planted it the first day she arrived, just over a week ago.

Surely it shouldn't be as tall as it was now?

I walked over to the table. I didn't know white orchids could grow this fast, and those my father had grown looked nothing like this. Instead of a single stalk, a double stalk braided around itself to form something like a tree trunk. Tiny green leaves were sprouting.

I found Ember sitting by herself in the library.

"Where's Anna? I didn't think she ever left you alone?" I sat next to her, nodding to the tray of tea on the table. "What's it today?"

"Jasmine." Ember gestured for me to help myself. "Where have you been?"

"Outside on an errand. So where's Anna?"

"She got called away, but she said she'd meet me here later."

"Great."

Ember suppressed a smile.

"Have you seen the orchid today? It's so tall!" I remarked.

"Is it?" She continued staring at her book.

"Yes. What did you do to it? My father's never grew this fast."

"I think it's showing normal growth for an orchid."

"No, I think you have a *special* touch."

Ember shrugged but didn't respond.

I decided to cut to the chase. "What did you think about the lab today?"

She looked up, startled. "How did you know about that?"

"Dr. Ply mentioned something about you being there. Did you see York?"

Ember nodded, looking uncomfortable.

"We were best friends in Windermere. But we haven't talked to each other since being here." I left out my last visit with him; no one could know about that.

"I'm sorry. He seemed really nice."

"I'm worried about him."

Her eyes flickered to my face. "Why?"

She looked concerned, so I decided to be honest. "I feel like he's changed since being here. And not in a good way."

"Have you talked to Dr. Ply about him?"

I snorted. "Like he'd care. He forbids me from seeing him. It was Cora who let me talk to him." I froze. I hadn't meant to admit that.

"Is that another secret?"

"What?"

"That you talked with York? You just said Dr. Ply won't let you, but Cora did. And then you looked like you wished you could take it back." Ember's lips turned up in a small smile.

I lowered my voice. "Dr. Ply doesn't know I saw him. Please don't say anything. Especially to Anna."

"I won't," Ember promised. "I'll just add it to the list of all the other secrets here."

Ember was clearly paying attention. "What other secrets?"

"Well, the transposers in the lab, for one. What's their real purpose? And what do they do with the laun they get from the wood?"

"How did you know it was called laun?"

The pink in Ember's cheeks faded into two white spots. "Um, Jack called it that."

I frowned. I'd never heard anyone refer to it as laun besides Dr. Ply. "Have you heard of transposing? Before the lab?"

Ember flipped a page in her book as if disinterested. "No, is it common in Windermere?"

"No. No one knows about it outside the castle."

"As I said, this place has lots of secrets."

"It sure does," I said, studying Ember.

I wanted to ask her more but I couldn't figure out how to phrase anything without hinting that I knew *her* secret. Should I just tell her? I was dying to talk with someone, and she was also suspicious of the castle. Together, maybe we could figure everything out.

Then Jack walked into the room.

When he saw me, his eyes brightened, and I felt my entire body respond. Every emotion coursed through me: relief, excitement, and the desire to spill everything I had been through and demand he tell me what it all meant.

I remained still, but my composure chipped away with each step he took closer.

Jack sat on the couch across from us, holding a crystal glass of dark liquid. It reminded me of the drink the Count had offered me.

"It's nice to find you both here." Jack looked at me, his eyes twinkling.

And suddenly, I didn't want anything anymore, except to forget I was in the castle like I had that night in the stable.

Ember stood. "Hello, Jack. I'm sorry, but I'm very tired. If you both don't mind, I'm going to bed."

"Night," I called as she left us.

Jack eyed me over his glass, before taking a sip. "Was it something I said?"

My stomach dipped at being alone with him again. He was wearing all black tonight, and his hair looked like he had just been outside.

"No, not you. I think she feels confused about why she was in the lab."

He nodded. "She's hardly spoken to me at all since then. Maybe it was too much for her, seeing York transpose that block. I don't know why Dr. Ply wanted her in there. Even Cora doesn't come in, and she's in charge of the Transposers."

We were the only ones in the room, but I lowered my voice anyway. "Did you tell Ember it was called laun?"

Jack paused over his drink and frowned. "No. I don't think so. Why?"

"Just wondering. I don't think I've heard anyone call it that besides Dr. Ply."

"We don't mention it at all, in case of being overheard. The existence of laun is a closely guarded secret. Truthfully, I'm not even sure the Transposers know about it fully."

I leaned in. "Jack, how would you describe laun?"

"What do you mean? You've seen it."

I shrugged. "I know. I just want your take on it."

He swirled the glass in his hand. "Well, I would say it's translucent. It can look similar to gold, although I would be able to tell the difference if they were side by side."

"Really? How?"

"Laun is dull. Real gold shines."

I sat back. If laun were placed next to gold, the gold might shine, but the laun would glow and radiate with light.

Jack smiled at me. "I saw Loon today. I can tell she misses you. When are you going to come ride her?"

Longing pierced my chest. I sighed. "Between us, I don't think Dr. Ply will ever let me."

"He is keeping you rather busy. Maybe I can say something to him. I'd like to go riding too."

My cheeks flushed, imagining riding Loon with Jack beside me.

"Would you like that?" He studied my face, a small smile danced on his lips.

"Yes," I confessed before I fell sharply back into reality. "But you'd better not."

"Why not?"

"Dr. Ply doesn't want me being distracted by anything or

anyone. Actually . . ." I felt my face turning red. "He already warned me about you."

"Me?"

I blushed redder. "I think Anna told him that we talk. I'm not allowed to have a relationship. I mean, not that *we* have one . . ."

Jack's brow raised as he crossed his ankle over his knee. He studied me as he took a sip of his drink. "I hadn't realized Anna was watching so closely."

I nodded, my eyes lowering to his black shoe. I remembered when it had been pressed against my slipper, and how I'd felt so sure of his feelings. I looked up to find a teasing smile hovering on his lips.

"No table to hide under tonight . . . unfortunately."

I raised a brow as my heart skipped a beat. "Is that all this is? Stolen moments and hidden feelings?"

His blue eyes bore into mine, suddenly serious. "Are we here so soon?"

My heart pounded. I was about to discover if this was real. And maybe even how deep his involvement here was. He must know more about the experiments—how could he not? But how much more? Did he know what the Count and Dr. Ply were really after? Would he tell me?

"I want to trust this . . . *you*. But can I? I don't really even know you . . ." I whispered. "And everyone here lies."

Jack swirled his drink, his eyes never leaving mine. Every second of silence made my stomach tighten and fill with dread that I had just ruined everything.

"I'm someone who loses chess games to the Count."

"What?" I looked at him, speechless. "What does that even mean—"

"I'm someone who loses chess games to the Count . . . when I could win."

I narrowed my eyes, confused.

He scooted forward in his seat so our knees grazed each other. Heat shot through me where we touched, and my heart began to race. Jack put his drink down on the table and leaned in further, staring into my eyes. I couldn't breathe as I stared back and waited for him to make sense of his words.

"Each week, I play chess with the Count. I learned very early that if I won, I would lose something in life that really mattered. The Count is a very proud man and doesn't like to be bested by anyone. So I lose. Over and over, despite there being, in every game, a moment when I see a piece I can move to begin to win. I see every single move after that one, and how it will all play out in my favor . . . But I *never* move that piece. Because if I do, I know that I'll lose something that matters much more."

He reached out slowly and tucked a loose strand of hair behind my ear, his fingers brushed my jaw and my skin burned in the trail of his touch.

"I lose because I know that one day, I'll care about something so much that I will not allow it to be lost. And when that happens, I'll make sure that every move of mine is planned out so carefully that *I* will be the winner when it matters."

My head felt light. "Have you found something you want yet?" I whispered. I held my breath, painfully awaiting his answer.

His eyes scanned my face. "Don't you know?"

I shook my head, unable to speak or look away. Suddenly, I didn't care about anything anymore except making the space between us disappear.

"I wish I could be more clear . . ." he murmured.

"Then be more clear," I breathed.

A smile touched his lips. He leaned in closer. "If you insist . . ."

Footsteps sounded in the hallway outside the door and I shot up and off the couch.

Startled, Jack stood too, and knocked over his drink.

He looked down at the mess as Anna walked through the doorway. Her eyes narrowed as she saw us together.

Jack started to say something, but I didn't wait to hear it. I hastily said goodbye and fled down the hallway with my heart lodged in my throat. I didn't stop until I was back in my room.

I leaned against the door and closed my eyes. That had been too close.

Then I groaned.

I had just made us seem even more guilty. If I'd just sat back and acted normal, it wouldn't have looked as bad as it did. I could only imagine what my face had looked like when she walked in. I'd never been good at hiding my feelings.

I'd made another foolish mistake.

One I certainly couldn't afford.

TWENTY-SIX

A week had passed since that night in the library with Jack.

A week of replaying that moment over and over, wishing we hadn't been interrupted.

And a week spent on pins and needles waiting for Anna to reveal she'd found me and Jack together.

But surprisingly, Anna said nothing. However, a smugness rolled off her, warning me that it was just a matter of time before she did. She was either waiting for something or she was enjoying torturing me.

It had also been a week since I'd planted Ember's laun in the Dark Woods.

I pulled the fresh air into my lungs, glad to be outside even if I had to spend it in the Dark Woods. Spring had a way of making everything seem better. Even the castle had lost some of its staleness as a new breeze blew through the hallways.

I brushed the vines away from the wooden door and fit the key inside the lock. It creaked open, revealing the dark, mangled trees inside. I passed them without looking; they didn't matter. It was Ember's tree I'd come to see.

The past week, I'd watched in wonder as the orchid seed

Ember had planted grew taller and taller, spiraling and twisting, blooming new leaves. Ember insisted there was nothing unusual happening, but I knew even *she* didn't believe that. Soon it would need to be repotted on the floor. And when the orchids bloomed, how large would they become? At the rate it was growing, I wouldn't have to wait much longer to see the biggest white orchid known to man.

I hurried through the trees, thinking if Ember could do that with a normal seed, what would her laun do?

Finally, I reached York's section of the woods and stopped, my mouth dropping open. The place where I'd planted Ember's laun was no longer just dirt.

A tall white sapling now sprouted up, already as tall as me.

It was beautiful. And it looked nothing like York's trees.

I walked around it slowly, staring in wonder and disbelief. Its white bark was velvety soft and tiny green leaves had already sprouted on the branches.

How was growth like this possible in just one week?

I searched for any sort of light around the tree, but there was nothing. Not even a shimmer. Could it be a real tree? It felt real.

Then I heard rattling and the creak of the wooden door. Startled, I sprinted as fast as I could and dove against it, slamming it shut with a thud.

"Hey!" someone yelped from the other side.

"Who's there?" I asked breathlessly.

A boy answered. "I was sent by Dr. Ply to help Ivy with the trees?"

I frowned. Dr. Ply hadn't mentioned sending someone to help me. Was he checking up on me?

"I don't need you today after all. You can go."

There was a pause. "Are you sure?"

"Yes," I said as firmly as I could.

"Well, I'm going to tell Dr. Ply that I came out here, just like he told me to, but you wouldn't let me in," he threatened.

"Go ahead. He'll understand."

"Fine."

I sagged against the door in relief. After a minute, I opened the door a crack and peeked out into the garden. The boy was already almost back to the castle. Clearly, I was not the only one who visited here, as I thought.

Now I had no choice but to confess to Dr. Ply about Ember's laun.

If I didn't, someone else would.

And no one could see this tree before I told Dr. Ply.

If I said nothing and planted another piece of York's laun and it didn't produce another tree like this, Dr. Ply would question York's ability. Carl was in trouble because of his inconsistencies. If Dr. Ply thought York was starting to become like Carl, he might even start experimenting on him.

I had to tell him.

Now.

I stepped back into the garden and locked the door to the Dark Woods behind me. I rattled it a few times, making sure it was locked. The vines brushed my head and I reached up, wishing my father could save me from what was to come.

My feet were heavy as I walked back to the castle. I spun one confession after another, trying to frame them so I wouldn't hurt anyone. Or lose Dr. Ply's trust.

But when I reached the castle, I knew it wasn't possible.

———

We were surrounded by dark, charred trees, staring at the single white tree in front of us.

Dr. Ply was ominously silent.

I shifted nervously. The tree already looked taller to me than it had this morning.

He finally spoke, but his tone was unreadable. "You're telling me this is *not* York's tree? It's *Ember's?*"

I lowered my eyes to the ground, wincing at the sharp edge in his voice. "Yes."

"Why didn't you speak up when it happened?"

"I wasn't sure what I'd seen. I didn't want to be wrong. So I decided to find out more before I said anything."

"*Find out more?* Your job is to inform *me* of everything you see—not withhold information until *you* think the time is right. What were you hoping to find out that could be bigger than Ember being a natural Transposer?"

"Natural?"

Dr. Ply looked at me sharply. "Ember changed the block and York took the credit. Why?"

I hesitated. "She asked him to."

"*She asked him to?*" Dr. Ply echoed in a nasty tone. "Ivy, you'd better start speaking freely and stop making me drag things out of you. I'm already beginning to question your use."

Panic flooded me. What would he do with me if he decided I was no longer useful to him? No one returned to Windermere after leaving for the castle. Loon, York, Ember, and Jack flickered through my mind. I had to salvage this.

Before I could think through what I was doing, the words began pouring out. "Ember didn't ask him with words, but after the wood changed, I saw her face. She looked scared, so she gave it to York. Her face begged him not to tell."

"And besides York, who else knows about Ember?"

"No one. It happened so fast."

Dr. Ply looked down at me with cold eyes. "Then how did you see it?"

I hesitated. "I was looking at them. You gave me York's file that day."

"I will not ask this again. Is there anything else you haven't told me? *Anything?*"

I cringed, thinking about all the times I'd snuck out. When I'd talked with York. The dust seeping out of Carl. Cora melting the spoon. And . . . Jack. But I couldn't confess any of that. What could I say that would do the least amount of harm, but make Dr. Ply see my value, so he wouldn't get rid of me?

I hated my next words. "I did find out more about Ember."

Dr. Ply glared at me, waiting for me to speak.

"She said she remembers white trees. She thinks she was sent here by someone, but doesn't know why."

"Anything else?" he asked quietly.

Fear snaked through me. "She knew it was called laun. When I asked her how she knew, she said Jack told her. But then I asked Jack and he said he didn't. I swear, that's all of it."

Dr. Ply didn't respond. He stared at Ember's tree, frowning. I could feel fury rolling off him. Whatever he was thinking—whatever he was planning—terrified me.

I wrung my hands. "Dr. Ply?"

"Yes?" His voice could cut glass.

"I'm so sorry I didn't tell you right away. The Count was there and he was so intimidating. I just panicked and didn't want to be wrong. I didn't want to reflect badly on you. I'm sorry."

"And yet you had an entire week to tell me without the Count around." Dr. Ply turned on me. "You were wrong to keep this information to yourself. The Count has been waiting for something like this to happen for years, and when he finds out that he could have known about it a *week* ago . . . and that someone I trusted *kept it from us*, well, I don't know what he will do. Let's just say I wouldn't want to be you."

I shrank away from the rage in his eyes.

"I should make you tell the Count yourself. He won't be pleased. You had an opportunity to impress us both and you failed." Venom dripped from his words. It unnerved me more than if he'd yelled.

I stared at the ground. What a mess. I'd betrayed both Ember and York. I'd angered and disappointed both Dr. Ply and the Count, and I was *still* holding onto secrets. On top of everything,

I was a spineless coward for spilling Ember's secrets to spare myself.

I didn't think it could get worse.

But Dr. Ply wasn't finished. "I'm also surprised at the *amount* of information you kept from me. I placed you in charge of Ember with my full trust. I expected you to keep me informed about her. Now it appears to me that you have decided to put your feelings for her above your duty to me and the work I am doing."

"No, I'm not. I just wasn't sure what to do," I protested weakly.

"You were also protecting York. It seems your friendship back in Windermere was stronger than you claimed."

"No. I'm loyal to you."

"That's thrilling to hear, Ivy," Dr. Ply responded drily. "Forgive me if that doesn't make me feel any better about this situation. I should never have brought someone else from Windermere here. That was my mistake—a mistake I also made with your father."

My head whipped up.

"Yes, your father was weak, too." Dr. Ply stared out into the woods. "He couldn't be objective when he needed to be and he also didn't understand what it meant to be loyal. I thought you would be different since you were only raised by him a handful of years."

Red-hot rage boiled in me hearing how Dr. Ply spoke about my father.

But now I knew that my father had gone against Dr. Ply. He'd been *against* the experiments, not helping with them. My father had done the right thing, just like I was trying to do.

Carl's words replayed in my mind. My father had stolen something, and people were angry. Dr. Ply seemed capable of almost anything when he was angry.

Dr. Ply continued, unaware of how his words were affecting me. "I was kind to give you a chance. And look at how you repay me. This castle does not treat people who are disloyal and untrustworthy well."

If I was going to fix this mess, I had to minimize the damage. Quickly. Everything rested on me playing a part now. I hung my head like I was ashamed.

"My intention wasn't to be disloyal," I whispered.

Dr. Ply continued as though I hadn't spoken. "As punishment, I should sell that horse and put you back in the room you started in. And, of course, let the Count punish you."

I fought to keep my hands from shaking. So much was on the line now.

"However, because of Ember, I won't do that. *Yet*. She clearly trusts you."

Surely he was not going to let me off without punishment? I didn't allow myself to relax just yet.

"I'll ask again. Is there anything else you need to tell me?"

I looked up, straight into his eyes. "No. That's all of it. I promise."

"Well, you say that, but obviously I can't tell if you're lying. Only time will tell the truth." He paused, thinking. "Perhaps I gave you too much responsibility too soon. I trusted you with the Dark Woods and you made a mess of your very first assignment. That speaks volumes to me. If you are already so careless with your responsibilities, how will you behave down the road, knowing much more?"

I stared at the ground, knowing he didn't expect an answer. The more he talked, the more I was beginning to hate him.

"Since this is your first offense"—Dr. Ply's tone became less hostile— "I'll note it as a 'misunderstanding' between us. But be warned, I will not overlook disloyalty from you again. I expect nothing but immediate honesty from now on."

I looked up at him.

He nodded as if to show he was putting the matter behind us, but I sensed it wasn't sincere. Something significant had changed between us. Was he pretending now, just as I was?

"I understand," I said, careful to sound humble. "Thank you for giving me another chance."

"Do not make me regret it. I do not forgive a second time."

I shivered, thinking about everything he still did not know about me.

He could never find out.

TWENTY-SEVEN

The Count

The Count stared out the window, his pointer finger tapping slowly against his elbow.

Spring had crept into his dusty library and once again, the mountains whispered to him. There were serious matters on his mind, but perhaps a distraction was in order. On second thought, a visit to his stables would suffice.

The thick file from Cora sat on his desk, unopened. He'd neglected it for nearly a week now, for he knew that when he read it, he would be displeased, as he always was when she gave him her reports.

For such a beautiful woman, she really was quite a nuisance.

Her files brought out a mixture of feelings in the Count that he was unaccustomed to dealing with. In the past, anger, regret, and guilt could nearly overpower him. He had since stopped allowing that to happen.

But anger was an excellent emotion to focus on, as it kept his attention outward. He'd similarly discovered that guilt was the most worthless emotion one could feel. Guilt weakened people and the Count was anything but weak. Anger gave strength and focused him, helping him direct the blame—and the blame for this particular situation rested squarely on Dr. Ply.

The South Wing was an enormous sore spot for the Count.

He hated even thinking about it. If it were not for Cora's monthly files, which *she* insisted on delivering, the Count would never give the South Wing another thought. After all, he already did his part—and then some—to ensure the retired transposers were well taken care of. No one was more nurturing than Cora, and if anyone could cure them, or at least make their worthless lives more bearable, it would be her. Of course, their lives would never be the same, but that was not his fault. It was Dr. Ply's.

A knock shook the door, disturbing the silence in the library. In a rare moment, he welcomed the interruption. Perhaps it was Jack, coming to lose yet again at chess. For such a bright young man, he was really quite stupid.

Dr. Ply stepped through the open door. "I have news. And you're going to be pleased."

The Count turned. He could count the number of times he had actually been pleased on just one hand—and nearly all had been in the mountains.

Just seeing Dr. Ply made the Count feel even less agreeable, but he promised good news, so the Count walked over to his chair.

A drink sat on the table next to him and he picked it up and sipped, savoring the fire in his throat. He waited for Dr. Ply to fix his own drink and settle into the chair opposite him.

"It has to do with the girl, Ember. Last week, when you visited the lab and saw York change that block into laun so quickly? Well, it turns out it wasn't him at all. It was *Ember*."

The Count inclined his head slightly and gestured for Dr. Ply to continue. The doctor had a flair for dramatics, but he would not get a reaction out of him so easily.

Dr. Ply continued. "That's not all. The laun was planted in

the Dark Woods, and already, a light grey tree has grown. It's nearly as tall as I am."

The Count dropped all pretenses and leaned forward, setting his glass back on the table. "You're serious?"

Dr. Ply seemed pleased to finally get a reaction, no matter how small it was. He took a moment to sip from his glass before he continued. "Apparently Ember also knew it was called laun without being told, and thinks she might have been 'sent' here by someone."

"You are serious," repeated the Count.

But he was not listening anymore. His drink, Dr. Ply, the fire, and the smell of dusty books all faded and suddenly, he was pulled swiftly into the memory he'd worked so hard to suppress.

He saw the White Forest in his mind as clearly as the first day he stood in it. This particular memory was of his last time there.

Even after all these years, he forgot nothing: not the blinding light of the sun as it hit the white trees, not the thick carpet of sage grass below them. Not the woman silently standing in front of him.

To this day, no one the Count had ever met rivaled her beauty. Still as a statue, she almost blended into the forest around her. He drank in the sight of her face, the fragile lace on her dress, and her long white hair like a parched man who had wandered through the desert far too long. As her ice-blue eyes found his, her lips upturned into a lovely smile.

"You're here." Her voice was light and sweet like the mountain air.

"Because of you."

He wasn't sure how he'd made it back into these woods, or how it was possible he was standing in front of her now. Since the first time they met, he'd thought of nothing else but seeing her again. He'd tried over and over to find his way back into this forest, but at every turn, he was lost. The only reason he stood here now was because *she* had brought him back.

"Yes. But not for long. I had to see you again."

The Count slowly stepped forward, afraid any movement might make her disappear. "Why was I chased from this place? And why couldn't I find it again when I tried?"

Her brow creased at his questions but she remained silent. He waited for her to speak, even though he was concerned that time was running out, and at any moment he would be chased off again.

She seemed to understand. "Don't worry, you're protected. Only I can see you."

"How?"

"I can't answer your questions. But I can give you this."

She walked toward him and opened her hand. Inside was a golden acorn.

"Why? What does it do?"

"You cannot enter the forest again unless I call for you. And I cannot call for you unless it is necessary. But I would not leave you unprotected. If you need help, use this. The acorn is tied to the forest, and recognized as part of it. If it is in your possession, the White Forest will be revealed to you. Without it, the forest could be right in front of you, but you will never see it."

The Count looked down at the gleaming acorn in his hand, for once, his attention drawn away from the woman in white. It was a moment he still regretted deeply.

"Only use it if you must," she warned, her voice suddenly sounding farther away. "There is not another like it . . ."

"Ahem," Dr. Ply coughed, pulling the Count out of his precious memory.

The scene faded from his mind like mist.

The dark wood paneling of his study walls was a stark contrast from the light trees in his mind. He stared into the flickering fire, avoiding Dr. Ply's questioning gaze until he had gotten ahold of himself again.

When he finally looked up, his gaze was unforgiving.

Dr. Ply shrank away. "Forgive me. I was wondering if there's anything else I should know about . . . *that place*?"

"What exactly are you referring to?" The Count's voice was sharp as a blade.

Dr. Ply spoke quickly. "Ember is a natural transposer. I've done nothing to 'manipulate' her ability. With the exception of Carl and York, all the other transposers have come from across the sea, and I have, ah, interfered. Ember is an anomaly. As is York, since we can't be sure where he was affected by the change. It is strange, though," Dr. Ply continued, "we have been working this whole time to recreate this mysterious forest—which only *you* have seen—and suddenly, a girl shows up and can produce a white tree quite naturally. She also says she has been *sent* here. I find that very peculiar . . ."

The Count tapped the tips of his fingers together silently.

"Were you, ah. Did you . . . expect this to happen?"

The question hung in the air between them. Again, the Count did not reply. He merely stared at the logs in front of him, watching them swell scarlet as the wind whistled down the fireplace.

Dr. Ply emptied his glass with a long drink.

"I don't do well with things I can't control," Dr. Ply said, placing the empty glass back on the table. The condensation made a wet ring and it slid toward the edge of the table.

The Count stopped it before it fell. When he spoke again, his voice was cold.

"I know you become very nervous when you are faced with things you can't understand. However, I assure you, I have seen things that no matter of science could ever explain."

"Please do not speak of that again," Dr. Ply said wearily.

"No? Yet, you have spent several years and resources to find another explanation without results."

"How *do* you explain Ember?"

"She is an unexpected development," the Count said frankly.

That confession seemed to relax Dr. Ply. "One we can handle, I'm sure of it. As of now, she doesn't know anyone saw her transpose the laun, and she doesn't know Ivy informed me."

"Ivy has proven useful."

"I thought so too, until she confessed that she waited an entire week to inform me about seeing Ember transpose the wood. It took her seeing the new tree growing to admit it, along with a variety of other things she's been holding back. If she hadn't found the tree, I don't know when, or if, she would have told me. I still can't place her motive or understand what she could possibly gain by keeping the information to herself."

The Count frowned. "Has she been dealt with?"

"I severely scolded her. Then I led her to believe I forgave her and we would continue on as usual. But she is finished here. I simply cannot trust her."

"And?"

"She is being watched carefully until she is no longer of use to us."

"Has she grown fond of Ember?"

"I think she must be. At first, I thought Ivy was jealous of her."

"Perhaps we should start feeding that jealousy. Do you have any idea how?"

"In a word, I do," Dr. Ply said. "Jack."

"Of course," the Count responded grimly. "If that doesn't work, it may be wise to motivate her with a growing position here. Promise her whatever she wants."

"I will."

"And what about Cora?"

"She knows nothing."

"Good. Keep it that way. Now, I must see this tree."

Twenty-Eight

Tension lingered in the air.

"Ivy, I think we should talk before lab begins."

I raised my eyes from the folder to where Dr. Ply sat at the table next to me. We were waiting for the transposers to be brought in, and so far, we had managed to avoid speaking to each other.

"Yes?"

"I've thought more about what has transpired and I feel you may have been put in an impossible situation. You and York were childhood friends and working so closely with him must have been hard. I underestimated just how difficult it would be, especially after losing both your parents. It's only natural that you feel attached to him. The blame for this is with me, not you."

My eyes widened. I slowly nodded.

"Then, I asked you to room with Ember, after you'd been alone since arriving here. My intention was not to isolate you, but to give you time to adjust to the work without distractions. I see now that you needed more social interaction with peers. I should have realized that you two would grow close once I moved you in with Ember. Again, it was only natural."

I was unsure of what to say. He looked sincere, and he was

saying all the right things. Yet I sensed an undercurrent of impassivity in his voice, like when Anna tried to be nice to Ember. It felt hollow.

And what about the cruel things he'd said about my father? I hadn't forgotten.

Still, I cast my eyes down to the floor as if I was still ashamed of my behavior. "Thank you, but I was the one who made a mistake by not telling you everything at once. I'm so sorry."

"I accept your apology. I would like to put this completely behind us. But before we do, there is one thing I must ask: Will you be able to resume your responsibilities from this point forward? Can you put your friendships second to the work? You're important to the process now, and I need to know I have your complete loyalty."

This was my chance to redeem myself. "Yes, I can."

"Wonderful." Dr. Ply's voice became even friendlier. "I've also reconsidered Loon. I will allow you to ride her once a week from now on, assuming you have completed all your tasks."

Maybe he *was* serious. "Thank you," I said, surprised.

He nodded. "This is an act of good faith. To show that I will continue to trust you. In return, I would also like you to trust me."

I nodded quickly. "I'll come to you first with everything from now on."

"Good. Just see to it that Loon does not become a distraction. Oh, and there is something else, I'm afraid. Have you and Jack grown attached to each other?"

The shock must have shown on my face because Dr. Ply said, "Something was mentioned to me about the library?"

Instead of a blush coloring my cheeks, anger flared in my stomach. "I'm afraid Anna misunderstood what she saw. As I already told you, I asked Jack about Ember knowing about laun and she walked in, startling us. We were speaking low so no one would overhear us. But again, Anna jumped to her own conclusion. I am committed to your work and nothing will come before it."

"I'm glad to hear that."

I nodded and stared back through the window into the lab.

"I must say, I'm glad that we seem to be in agreement now. I feel much better knowing I don't have to worry about you and Jack. He's a fickle young man who's left several hearts broken around the castle. And now he seems to have taken an interest in Ember."

My jaw tightened. What game was Dr. Ply playing? I was saved from responding when the door to the lab opened and Jack walked in. I looked down at my file. This was the first time I'd seen him since the library, and my heart thudded. I hated this.

I gritted my teeth harder and reminded myself how much was at stake now.

The transposers filed in, Anna and Flex behind them. Gloves were removed and white wood was placed on the tables. Like always, the transposers looked relieved when they touched the wood.

The morning began.

I opened the file in front of me, trying not to think about Jack's trail of broken hearts, when Dr. Ply handed me York's file again. I uncapped my pen, planning on proving just how objective I could be.

But instead of Carving as he normally did, York just stared at the white wood in his hands, turning it over and over. I wondered what was wrong.

Dr. Ply and Jack noticed too.

Then York turned and looked directly into the mirror.

I froze. Even though I knew he couldn't see me, it seemed like he was looking right through it at *me*. My palms began to sweat. What was he doing?

Dr. Ply echoed my thoughts. "What is he doing?"

York continued to stare at us.

Dr. Ply turned in his chair to face me. "Does he know you're in here?"

"Of course not! I haven't spoken to him." I cringed at the lie.

"Then why is he staring at the mirror?" Dr. Ply said slowly, all pretense of friendliness gone.

"I don't know!" I stared back at York, flustered. Why wouldn't he start Carving?

Jack stood and quickly walked over to York, placing himself in front of the mirror. All we were able to see was Jack's back, not York or what he said. But whatever Jack said worked, because York began to Carve. Jack walked back to his desk without a glance in our direction.

I sagged in relief.

The rest of the morning, I scribbled notes furiously. My hand ached, but I never slowed once. I had to demonstrate my loyalty. I could feel Dr. Ply's suspicion in his silence.

If I ever saw York again, I was going to punch him for being so careless.

Finally, it was time for lunch. Everyone cleared the lab, and Jack stepped into the room.

Dr. Ply wasted no time. "What was the problem with York this morning?"

Jack looked startled. "You mean because he took a while to get started? He was just distracted."

"He focused on the mirror. Does he know he is being observed now?"

"I don't think so," Jack said calmly. "Why would you think that? Did something happen?"

Dr. Ply turned to me. "I wouldn't know."

Jack's eyes flickered between us, but his face was a mask of calm. I dropped my eyes to the table.

Just as the tension reached a breaking point, there was a knock on the door.

Cora waltzed into the room. Her perfume drifted over to us, light and sweet. I felt like I could breathe again.

"Good morning!" she said as if she didn't notice Dr. Ply's frown.

"Hello, Cora." Jack gave her a quick kiss on the cheek. "You look lovely today."

"Thank you, Jack."

Dr. Ply nodded stiffly.

I offered her the smallest smile, not wanting to make Dr. Ply angrier by showing how relieved I was to see her.

"Dr. Ply, now that your session is over, would you mind terribly if I borrowed your new assistant? I could use some extra help with a garden project I'm working on and I heard she once trained as an Arborist."

"Of course." Dr. Ply snapped his file shut and stood. "You may have her tomorrow as well."

Cora's brow raised slightly. "How generous. Thank you. Well, come along then. It's Ivy, isn't it?"

I nodded, my legs wobbling as I stood.

Dr. Ply walked to the cabinet and began arranging papers with his back toward me. When it was clear he had no intention of speaking to me again, Jack and Cora exchanged a worried look.

Which made *me* worry even more.

"Dr. Ply, please let me know if you need me and I'll come right back," I said meekly.

He didn't turn. "Goodbye, Ivy."

"Goodbye, Dr. Ply," Cora called cheerfully.

I followed her from the room. As I passed Jack, he glanced over to make sure Dr. Ply was still turned around and brushed his fingers against mine. "*Chess.*" He mouthed to me.

I nodded, wishing we could walk out together and never look back.

Only when we were farther down the hall did Cora turn to me and ask, "Now what was *that* all about?"

I jumped, wondering if she saw what happened between Jack and me. "What?"

"Dr. Ply was quite put out."

"I know. He found out I kept things from him, but he forgave me and gave me another chance. Until York stared into the mirror like he knew I was behind it. Now Dr. Ply suspects I told York about the mirror—that I lied again."

Cora frowned. "He couldn't know you spoke to him. I made sure no one saw."

I sighed. "Do you really need help planting today? I should warn you, I really wasn't a good Arborist."

Cora laughed. "Maybe not, then. I thought you'd like to see York again."

"I sure do," I said, planning to tackle him before I asked how he'd found out I was behind the mirror.

Cora looked surprised at my tone. "You don't sound excited."

"I'm already on such thin ice."

"I see." Cora frowned. "Ivy, if someone in Windermere told you that you couldn't speak to York ever again, what would you have done?"

"I would have ignored them."

"I thought as much." Cora started walking again. "Now where has *that* Ivy gone?"

THE SOUTH WING WAS A VAST BALLROOM OF CRYSTAL chandeliers and checkered marble floors. A wall of windows overlooked the terrace and garden. Around the room were gold picture frames, gleaming suits of armor, marble pillars, and a grand double staircase.

Cora led me through a room scattered with cream furniture shielded by potted trees. A harpist played softly while waiters glided around tables and couches. Two men played chess, and everyone wore light colors, making the room feel peaceful and elegant.

She led me to the far corner, away from everyone, to a large dome made of gilded and cracked smoked glass—it was another room. It was impossible to see inside, but when we walked in, there was a private table.

Cora left me as soon as I sat. I stared up and around the dome in awe. Soft light from candelabras lit the space. The table had a bouquet of lavender and wildflowers. I could see the black shoes of a waiter just outside, ready to bring in whatever was needed. This was amazing.

Then Cora brought in York from another entrance and left us to enjoy the most delicious meal I'd eaten since I'd been at the castle: A tender roast on a bed of vegetables sculpted into flowers. The meat melted under my fork, and I sighed after each bite.

For the first time, I could understand why the Transposers thought life was so good here. Now that I understood they were addicted to the laun, I knew they actually liked Carving in the lab. It was the only time they could hold the wood. And when they weren't in the lab, they were here.

I pressed the white linen napkin to my lips. "You're so lucky Cora's in charge of you."

York nodded. "I heard the Top Floor is pretty nice too."

"It's nice but completely fake. It's nothing like this."

"What do you mean fake? Are the walls not walls?" York smiled.

I shook my head, wanting to explain it was like the Tree Garden compared to the Dark Woods. The Tree Garden was alive and lovely, while the Dark Woods was a dead place trying desperately to look alive.

"They're trying to make us believe we've been given something wonderful when really all it is is an empty floor with nice furniture. But here, you have Cora, who really cares about you. *She's* what makes this place feel cozy and safe."

"Dr. Ply isn't safe?"

I hesitated. York already proved he could be careless. "No, he's OK."

He laughed. "You're such a bad liar."

York placed his napkin on his plate, and stretched out his arms, satisfied. I was glad he looked so content today.

So far, our conversation had been pleasant. York hadn't mentioned looking in the mirror this morning, or anything about Ember and the laun. I was thinking about how to bring both up, but I didn't want to ruin our time yet.

Coffee arrived in delicate cups decorated with pink flowers circled with green vines, and a white cake with sugar flowers, almost too beautiful to eat.

"I've been thinking about something you said last time we talked," York said, setting his coffee down.

Everything I'd said about Carl and transposing flashed through my mind. "What?"

"Something you said to Jack when I was yelling at him for riding Loon."

That was not what I expected. "What did I say?"

"That I'm like your brother."

"So?"

"I just wondered why you told him that?"

For a second, I thought York was asking because he'd forgotten how close we'd been. Panic coiled in my chest. He had to remember our relationship back in Windermere. I refused to believe he'd forgotten.

I leaned in. "Because you *are*. You've always protected me like that. And I protect you, too."

York shook his head. "I know that. But why did you tell *him* that?"

I stared at him, confused.

"Because he's *not* like your brother?" York pressed. A smile touched his lips.

Oh. I felt my face burn, remembering Jack leaning in towards me in the library.

York laughed. "I think you just answered the question. But isn't he a little old for you?"

I glared at him, blushing, but then I was smiling too. And just like that, the tension unfurled between us and we finally felt normal again.

Under this cream-and-gold dome, we found our way back to our friendship.

"You two look like you're enjoying lunch," Cora said, stepping into our little hidden world.

But she wasn't alone.

"Ember!" I said, pleased. "You've already met York."

York was suddenly preoccupied with his coffee.

"Yes. Hello." Ember smiled, but she didn't look at him.

"I offered to give Ember a tour of the South Wing this afternoon, but I'm needed for a moment. How about she join you for dessert? That cake looks divine." Cora snapped her fingers to a nearby waiter and gestured for another place to be set.

"Yes! Sit down," I said.

A waiter held out a chair for Ember, and she sat, looking uneasy.

"Ember, I just ordered you tea," Cora said. "I'll be back soon."

Cora left, and the three of us looked at each other. This was probably the first time they had seen each other since the lab. And neither of them knew that I knew their secret, or that Ember's laun had grown a white tree.

Cora had just provided me with the perfect opportunity to tell them everything.

After what had happened with Dr. Ply today, this might be my last chance to warn them.

TWENTY-NINE

The waiter refilled our coffee while another one carried in a tray with dried herbs and a teapot. Ember thanked him and chose flowers that matched her violet eyes.

"What are those?" I asked, fascinated.

"Lavender roses." Ember placed tiny buds in the hot water. "It takes a while for them to soften up."

"Are they good?"

"They're delicious. I'll make you some if you want?"

"Sure."

"Would you like some?" Ember asked York, finally making eye contact.

"Nope." York sipped his coffee as if suddenly fascinated with it.

The silence stretched on as Ember and York looked anywhere but at each other. If I didn't stop this now, it would ruin the rest of our time together. I set down my cup.

"You both are acting very strange. Almost like you have something to hide."

They both looked at me, surprised. York's eyes flickered to Ember, but it was clear neither was going to say anything.

"Fine. I'll talk. I know Ember turned the wood into laun, not you, York."

Ember's eyes widened. "How?"

At the same time, York said, "I knew you were behind the mirror!"

I glared at him. "Yes, and thanks to you Dr. Ply is angry at me because he suspects I told you somehow. I was on thin ice already, and now I don't know what's going to happen when I go back to him. He's not a good person."

"I'm sorry," York said, suddenly serious. "I didn't want to get you in trouble."

"Why are you on thin ice?" Ember asked.

I sighed. "Because I hid the information about you changing the laun from him for as long as I did. I'm so sorry—to you both, really, I am—but I had to confess to what I'd seen yesterday. I planted Ember's laun in the Dark Woods and a white tree grew, unlike any other there."

York sat up. "That's what they do with it? Make *trees*?" He looked disappointed.

I snorted. "*Trees* is a generous word. They grow dead, black, and mangled. Except Ember's. When her white tree grew, I had to tell Dr. Ply, so he wouldn't think you were becoming a problem like Carl. He would start experimenting on you." I locked eyes with York so he would understand how serious this was.

York frowned.

"Dr. Ply is doing horrible experiments. I saw him conduct one once." I shuddered. "On Carl."

York's expression turned grave. "What was it like?"

I remembered Carl's tense, uncontrollable shaking, and the dust leaving his body. I thought of Anna's blank expression as she watched Carl struggle. I clenched my hands together and said quietly, "It was the most horrible, barbaric thing I have ever seen."

"You helped with that?" York said, stunned.

"Not helped, just watched. And hopefully, I'll never have to again. I want to stop them."

York took in a deep breath. "What do you do in the lab?"

"I record what happens with the Transposers and the wood. To be honest, it's kind of boring unless one of you transposes the wood. The Count was in the room the day that Ember transposed the wood, but he didn't see because everyone was looking at Carl."

York's eyes widened. Ember didn't know much about the Count, so I explained as much as I could.

"Why are they so interested in me?" Ember asked.

"I don't know. Maybe because you were found in the Tree Garden—"

"But no one can get in there except you," York interrupted.

"No one is supposed to be able to," I clarified. "You can see why they are intrigued."

"But why do I matter so much?" Ember asked.

"I don't know. I've worked here for months and I still haven't figured out what the purpose of all this is. And there's more."

Ember looked wary. "What else?"

It all came pouring out. I explained how Dr. Ply had asked me to spy on Ember since her first day in the castle, just like Vernon had spied on me. How Dr. Ply and the Count had known she was different from the beginning. How anxious they were to get her to remember where she was from. The Dark Woods, the experiments, and Iaun.

I drew in a deep breath. "Dr. Ply also mentioned helping you remember. And I don't mean the pleasant activities you've been doing, like gardening and painting. He's considering conducting an experiment on you if you don't remember something soon."

"Wow." Ember stared into her cup.

"I'm sorry. I know it's a lot, but I had to tell you. Dr. Ply is really upset with me, but I think you both might be in danger."

"No, I'm glad I know," Ember said.

York nodded.

Silence filled the small space until York leaned in.

"Why didn't you want anyone to know you transposed the

wood?" York looked like he had wanted to ask Ember this forever. "Everyone would be impressed. I've never seen a piece of wood be transposed like that."

I looked at Ember too. "How did you do it?"

"I honestly don't know. When the wood was transposed, I was just as surprised as you were. I have no memory of being able to do anything like that. I don't know why the plant in our room is growing so fast either," Ember said, turning to me. "That's why I changed the subject whenever you brought it up, Ivy. I didn't want anyone else to know about me until I could figure out what my extra abilities are."

"Extra abilities?" That was exactly how Vernon described Dyadics.

"I don't know," Ember looked down at her plate, shaking her head. "I don't know why I said that."

"I've never thought about transposing like that—like having an *extra ability*." York smiled. "That's even more impressive."

I rolled my eyes. "Careful, York. You're starting to sound like Percy."

York leveled me with a deadpan stare, making me laugh.

"How do you think you transpose the wood?" I asked York.

"I guess I'm not completely sure either. The first time it happened was at the Count's Woodworking Tournament. I lost all track of time and where I was. Honestly, I don't even remember it happening. I was so focused that everything sort of blurred away. When I looked down, my wood had changed."

I noticed he said nothing about light. "Is it like that every time?"

"Usually. I have to concentrate really hard and block everything out for so long. And even then, sometimes it doesn't happen." He looked at Ember. "But it wasn't like that for you. You just touched it and it changed."

Ember shrugged.

"York," I said, changing the subject. "I know you don't think I should be following my father's clues anymore—"

"I didn't mean that, Ivy. I'm sorry," York interrupted. "I don't know why I said that."

"Clues?" Ember asked.

I explained my father's death and the trail of clues I'd been following since coming to the castle. "When Dr. Ply was really angry at me, he said horrible things about my father. He sounded so bitter, like he hated him."

York sat up. "Do you think Dr. Ply had something to do with your father's death?"

"If you saw what he did to people, people who have never harmed him . . . he's capable of anything. Especially, I imagine, if he thinks someone has wronged him."

Ember looked thoughtful. "Anna told me something about your father once."

I sat up, surprised. "*Anna* did?"

"When I first got here. Anna said that she worked with your father a long time ago, that he didn't do his job properly and she got blamed for it. She didn't like him at all. And she said you're just like him."

I bit my lip. That was a lot of information coming from Anna. "Why would she tell you that?"

"I think she was trying to confide in me so I would confide in her. It was really strange. I think she regretted saying it later."

"That must be why she's always been cold to me. She'll never tell me what he did."

"We'll uncover it," York said. "Together."

"Yes." Ember nodded. "Tell us everything else you know, and we'll figure it out."

I smiled, feeling like I could breathe again. We were allies now.

After many more pieces of cake and cups of tea, I told them everything. We made a plan to act normal but try to uncover what we could. I would pretend to be loyal to Dr. Ply, Ember would try to get more information out of Anna, and York would watch and learn more about the experiments. It wasn't a perfect plan, but I wasn't alone anymore, and that felt better than anything.

When Cora interrupted us later, we were all laughing at a story York was telling.

"You three look like you're having a marvelous time." Cora looked pleased. "But it's time to go. Don't worry, I'll try to arrange this again soon."

"Can I come back tomorrow?" I asked, dreading the thought of seeing Dr. Ply again so soon.

"Assuming he was serious about giving me two days with you. I'll ask him, but you should stay out of sight. He needs some time to calm down," Cora said.

"OK." I didn't even mind that he was upset with me; the way the day had turned out was worth it.

As I walked back to my room, I thought about how everyone I saw with light around them had one thing in common: they could all do unusual things.

York and his wood.

Ember and her golden veins in the Tree Garden.

Cora and the bent spoon.

If Dr. Ply knew any of us had these abilities, he would be after us all.

We were all in danger . . . until we could figure out what he and the Count were really up to.

THIRTY

The Count

The tree had grown.

It was now significantly taller than the other trees in the Dark Woods. The Count considered its color to be grey—not quite white, as it had been described to him by Dr. Ply. However, someone who had never seen the whiteness of the White Forest could undoubtedly mistake the color for white. Especially compared to the sooty trees around it.

"Well?" Dr. Ply asked.

The Count studied the tree. He couldn't believe what he had been working toward for so long had finally happened. "Remarkable."

"What are we going to do with it?" Dr. Ply asked. "I wonder if it can replace our other wood? We are nearly out."

The Count's eyes wandered over to the flat piece of earth where the original tree had grown. He had made the foolish mistake of cutting the whole thing down at once. He would not make that mistake again. "How much is left?"

Dr. Ply's eyes followed where the Count was looking. "That tree lasted us a long time. We still have a few weeks of supply left."

"I don't want to ruin this tree. We will wait until a branch is thick enough to be cut and tested. From how fast it's growing, it appears we won't have long to wait."

Though many years had passed, the Count could still recall that day perfectly, when he first realized that tree was special. It had been years since his last visit to the White Forest when he was given the acorn by Airlend Frost. He had waited months for her to bring him back, but when she didn't, he grew restless and set out to find the White Forest with the golden acorn.

But no matter where he looked, he couldn't find it. It was as if it didn't exist.

He spent years searching, always convinced it was just over the next ridge. His men thought he was chasing a ghost. The Count began to lose track of how many times he brought them up the mountain only to return to the castle disappointed. It took him years to accept that he would never see the White Forest or Airlend Frost again. Finally, he gave up looking.

In his disappointment, he shut himself in his library, alone. Over time, his obsession began to shift from Airlend to the golden acorn. He held it, day after day—and his paranoia grew into madness. He worried the acorn would be taken from him or that he would lose it. He became obsessed with why it would not reveal the White Forest to him. Day and night, it consumed him. It haunted his dreams until he forgot the feeling of peace. His hair turned white, his face grew serious, his cheeks sallow, until he was only a shell of the man he had once been.

Resentment festered in his mind and he blamed Airlend for his ruined life. Resentment turned to hate as he convinced himself that she had toyed with him, taunted him by revealing paradise and then shutting him out of it forever.

Until one day, as he sat alone in his dark library, the wind blew the curtains away from the window and sunlight flooded the room. And with that bright light came an idea.

The golden acorn had to be planted.

He could make his own paradise—his own White Forest. Instead of using the acorn to find *her*, he would plant it and take control of his life.

So he planted it just beyond the garden at the edge of the castle grounds. The minute the acorn was in the ground and covered with dirt, the Count's mind was restored and he returned to his old self.

Then, something remarkable happened. A white tree sprouted up from the dirt where the acorn was planted. It was beautiful and majestic. It reminded him of Airlend and the White Forest.

As he stared at the perfect tree, his heart dropped because he now realized that Airlend *had* given him a piece of the forest. She must have cared for him too, but in his fit of madness, he had wasted her gift. The Count stood there, drowning in despair as he realized he would never be able to find her again.

Unless . . . Unless *this* tree produced another acorn he could use.

Clinging desperately to this new hope, the Count took every precaution to protect the tree. He watered it, cared for it, and even sheltered it from the strong winds that swept down the mountain. He watched over it tirelessly.

But the white tree never produced any golden acorns. It just continued to grow taller and taller, its trunk massive.

One day, the Count came to check on the tree and he saw a gardener whittling a branch. As he got closer, he noticed it was a branch from his white tree.

"Stop!" the Count thundered, startling the man. "Who gave you permission to cut from that tree?"

The man dropped the wood and his knife.

"I'm sorry, sir! I didn't mean to do anything wrong. It's just, this wood . . . it's so different than anything I've ever Carved before. I couldn't help it."

"You fool. This tree is priceless to me. Get out! And hope I never look upon your face again."

"I'm sorry!" the man stammered. "Please, I've worked in these gardens since I was a boy."

"Get out!" The Count shook with rage. "And if you tell a soul about this tree, you will pay for it with your life."

The gardener turned and ran, leaving the wood and his knife still on the lawn.

Something glinted in the light.

Curious, the Count went over to examine it. When he saw what it was, he dropped to his knees.

He was not looking at the white wood from the tree anymore.

The branch had *changed*.

It looked exactly like the golden acorn. It, too, was now slightly soft and translucent.

As the Count turned it over in his hands, an idea formed. He would plant this material and grow more trees. He would create his own White Forest. It would make Airlend reveal herself again —or bring him back to her. Surely she would feel the pull, as he had with the acorn that drove him mad. Or perhaps another tree would produce acorns and he could use one to find her.

The golden branch was planted. But it did not grow another white tree. The Count tried everything to make more wood from the white tree change into laun. It was only after he'd cut the whole tree down that he realized his mistake. Not just *anyone* could Carve the wood and change it into laun.

The *person* Carving it mattered most.

At a loss as to how to proceed, the Count traveled to Stygian, a place where people were rumored to do special things. He confided in Dr. Ply about the White Forest and what the wood could become with the right person Carving it. Dr. Ply had needed convincing, and in the end, he had only agreed to help because the Count paid him handsomely.

It was Dr. Ply who found the gardener and brought him back

to the castle. After seeing the man change the wood into laun with his own eyes, Dr. Ply became fascinated with transposing—but for an entirely different reason than the Count.

Dr. Ply was determined to know exactly how the wood was transposed and unearth a scientific reason as to how it was possible. Dr. Ply became convinced this was his life's mission.

He became as invested as the Count.

It had been Dr. Ply who forced the gardener to Carve over and over, sometimes with no break. The gardener transposed constantly, and his laun was planted. His trees were the first in the Dark Woods. At first, they grew straight and grey, not quite white. Until suddenly one day, the gardener's ability stopped. Frustrated, Dr. Ply performed experiment after experiment on the man, until eventually, he was too ill to continue. Then, each of his grey trees turned black and died.

The Count shook himself out of those unpleasant thoughts. Those memories were too dark. He did not want to think any more about that first transposer.

The Count looked over at Dr. Ply. "You're sure no one else knows about this tree?"

"Just Ivy, yourself, and me."

"You are certain that neither Jack nor Cora knows?"

"Not as far as I know."

"That's enough."

The Count spun on his heel and walked out of the Dark Woods. He kept his eyes on the ground, not wanting to even look in the direction of those first trees, which had started with such promise. He was glad when they stepped back out into the garden. He faced the castle, his hands folded behind his back, and waited for Dr. Ply to lock the door behind them.

The two men walked back to the castle together.

"You need to watch Ivy even more carefully now. You said she is fond of both Jack and Ember. And now you have let her visit Cora, where she probably saw York. How do you know she hasn't told them all she knows already? After all, she did wait quite a while before confessing to you."

"I have someone watching her closely—day and night. I am certain she has not divulged a word."

"I'd also like someone to watch Cora. We can't take any chances now."

"Of course."

"Don't touch the tree just yet; I'd like it to grow more, then we will reevaluate. This time, we will do things right."

Thirty-One

The next morning, I sat by the fire with my father's journal. On the table beside me was the box of dust I'd collected from Carl.

Ember walked out of the bathroom just as something slipped beneath our door. She went over and picked up a thick cream envelope.

"It's from Cora. You're to meet her in the South Wing this morning, and I in the afternoon."

"Dr. Ply is still angry with me, then."

Ember sat down next to me. "Find anything new?"

I shook my head.

"Can I take a look? Maybe something will stand out to me," Ember said.

"It couldn't hurt." I handed it over while I opened the container of dust. It shimmered up at me like a pile of yellow glitter.

"There are so many references about *Hedera* damaging walls and stone. Growing in the dark without light, becoming a menace . . . He was very focused on the havoc it would cause," Ember said as she flipped through pages.

"Is that why he planted ivy vines on the walls of the Dark

Woods? He wanted it to bring down the wall and expose it?" I wondered aloud, then sighed. "I'm going to see Cora now."

Ember handed me back my father's journal, but I shook my head. "There was something yellow, like pollen, in this journal when I found it. It made me feel strange for a while. Can you see if you notice anything like that?"

"Sure. See you tonight."

The only way I knew how to get to the South Wing was through the hallway to the lab. I realized if I didn't hurry, I would run into Dr. Ply. And that would be awkward.

I hurried past his office, imagining him inside eating his sticky morning croissant. I quickly pulled open the door to the hallway and flew down it. Once I was past the lab door, I breathed out in relief.

Jack rounded a corner into the hallway just up ahead, and my heart leaped into my throat.

When he saw me alone, his face broke into a smile.

I was so glad to see him. I smiled back and hurried forward until his expression completely changed. Jack wiped all emotion from his face as his eyes focused over my head and away from me.

Then I heard Dr. Ply's voice behind me. "Good morning, Jack."

I faltered as Jack passed me with nothing more than a cold nod. "Good morning, Dr. Ply. The transposers will be along soon," Jack said smoothly.

"Very good."

I turned and watched Jack disappear into the lab. Dr. Ply stood at the second door, watching me.

"Good Morning, sir," I said nervously.

Without a word, he opened the door and stepped inside the adjoining room. The door thudded closed behind him.

I turned back around just as the transposers came around the corner.

Flex led the group, and I pressed myself into the wall as they filed past me without a word. York's eyes briefly caught mine, but

I didn't dare acknowledge him as Anna was right behind him. Her eyes flickered past me as if I wasn't there.

I watched them file into the lab, and for the first time, I wished I could go inside too. I wanted to know what happened with York and Carl. I wanted to be near Jack.

I wondered if I would ever be allowed back.

I turned and continued down the hallway alone.

———

THE SOUTH WING WAS EMPTY.

The ballroom was quiet and still. Just as I was wondering how to find Cora, the waiter who had removed the bent spoon from Cora's hand appeared at my side.

"Cora is in the conservatory. It's out those doors and to the right. You can't miss it."

"Thanks."

I crossed the checkered marble floor and opened the terrace doors that led to the lawn. Warm air brushed across my arms like silk, and I breathed in deeply, walking along the row of windows until I saw a glass conservatory tucked into the side of the castle. Its walls were surrounded by green hedges and blossoming trees.

I pushed the glass door open and stepped into an aroma of earth and flowers. For a second, a wave of homesickness washed over me. This smelled just like my father's shop, Forest and Fern, and The Hidden Thorn in Windermere. It was like coming home.

In the middle of the room, Cora looked completely at home as she clipped white-and-pink roses at a table. She wore a beautiful blush-colored dress and her hair was up in a loose bun.

She looked up and smiled, then waved her pruning shears at me. "Come join me. Today is too gorgeous to be inside. If you get out as rarely as I think you do, you must be desperate for the outdoors."

"I am. And this place brings back memories from my childhood," I said, breathing deeply as I walked to the table.

Cora smiled and gestured to the stool next to her. I sat, feeling my tension melt away as I soaked in all the plants. A huge pot of lavender grew in the corner of the room. I wondered if Jack had gotten my bouquet from Cora.

"Do you tend to all of these?" I asked, gesturing to a shelf lined with tiny pots of topiaries.

Snip, snip, snip. Petals and leaves dropped onto the table and floor. "Most of them, yes. Although sometimes I don't have the time, and then someone else does. The topiaries are planted into the garden your room overlooks, and the roses fill most of the rooms around the castle and, of course, the South Wing." Cora pressed a white rose into her nose, inhaling deeply. "Nature has the ability to heal, which is why I surround the transposers with it. That's why I insist that rooms are full of fresh flowers and the gardens are meticulously maintained. It's not just for vanity, as the Count or Dr. Ply would accuse."

"My father would have loved it here."

"What about you?"

"I like it too, but I was never as good with plants as he was."

"You must have felt relieved when you didn't pass the Arborist test."

"No. I felt like I failed him. It's what he wanted for me."

"Was it?"

I nodded. "Except I wasn't born with his green thumb."

"Maybe he just wanted to spend time with you and didn't know how. If you had something in common, it would be easier."

"Well, he could have just told me about the castle. That would have gotten my attention."

Cora paused and looked more serious. "He was protecting you."

"From what? I'm not a Transposer or an Arborist. I truly don't even understand why Dr. Ply wants me here."

"I do."

I looked at her, shocked. "Will you tell me?"

Cora set the last pink rose in the large pot and peeled off her gardening gloves. Her emerald eyes found mine. "I've been waiting until the time was right. There is something I want to show you."

Cora brushed the leaves from her dress as she led me out the back door of the conservatory. We stepped into a narrow alley between two castle walls. It was hidden by the conservatory, which I realized was purposeful. Goosebumps prickled my arms as I stared at the wall. I couldn't form words.

Thick vines of ivy clung to the stone of the castle walls. I stared up at the waterfall of greenery, remembering a line my father had written.

If you try to remove attached Hedera roots, you may pull down bricks, or even stone walls.

"My father was studying *Hedera* before he disappeared," I choked out, brushing my hands over the leaves. "I've been looking for it, but I've only found it by the Dark Woods . . ."

Cora stopped, her hand resting on the knob of a wooden door. "He planted this." Our eyes met. "From this point forward, there can only be trust between us. Agreed?"

I was finally on the trail of my father's clues again, and it was because of Cora. I nodded.

Cora nodded back and stepped inside.

I followed, suddenly nervous about what could be behind a door so carefully hidden from the rest of the castle. We stepped into a small entryway and Cora immediately took the stairs. I followed her up and around the circular tower until I was nearly out of breath.

We finally stopped on a floor with a narrow hallway. There was one large window and a door. It was silent.

Cora turned to me, her face somber. "Ivy, I must warn you. What you are about to see will be shocking and disturbing. I must show you this if you are to fully understand what Dr. Ply is doing with the Transposers. As you know, Dr. Ply 'studies' the mind. He puts many restrictions on the transposers. They are rarely allowed to use their hands for anything besides Carving."

I nodded, my stomach turning uneasily.

"What you don't know is that Carving is only the vehicle for what really happens. Carving necessitates intense focus—that's one part of it. The other is that they spend hours every day Carving and are forbidden from any other rote activities. Since they are allowed no other stimulation, they never learn new skills or improve upon old ones. They never mentally grow beyond Carving. This literally changes the way their brains are wired and their ability to remember and retain information. The brain only stores the information it uses most, and discards data it deems *unimportant* and *useless* to their daily life."

Cora paused to see if I understood. I nodded.

"Since the Transposers are only permitted to do one task —*Carve*—over time, they will lose the ability to perform even the most basic functions that you and I take for granted, such as opening a jar, brushing your hair, feeding ourselves, and even walking."

Now I shook my head. This was harder to wrap my mind around.

"You'll understand better when you see it. That's the only reason I've brought you here."

Cora opened the door quietly and gestured me inside. I nervously stepped into a large circular room. Sunlight streamed in through the wall of windows. There were four beds, each with a chair and table beside it. White fluffy rugs covered the floor, large vases overflowed with flowers on every table, and beautiful chandeliers sparkled dots of light all over the walls.

Green vines of ivy grew up one wall, making the room feel like a living garden. My father had been here too.

But I could hardly focus on that, for on each bed laid a man.

At first, I thought they were sleeping, because the room was so still—until I saw that each man was staring at the ceiling, eyes blank, bodies motionless. Their faces were vacant; their arms were limp by their sides. I recognized one man.

Glen.

Cora walked over to the bed closest to the window where the oldest man in the room was. He was so still. I hesitated before quietly following.

Writing in a chart next to the bed was another person I recognized. Lane, the woman who had helped Glen that night in the hallway. She was dressed in light linens and her hair was pulled into a low bun. She smiled at us.

"Hello, Lane," Cora said quietly. "This is Ivy."

"It's nice to meet you."

"Hello." I tried to hide my discomfort. I wished the men would close their eyes instead of staring blankly at the ceiling. I shifted from foot to foot, wondering what was wrong with them.

"How is he today?" Cora asked Lane.

"A little tired. He hasn't spoken yet."

Cora patted the man's limp hand affectionately. "Could you give us a second, Lane?"

"Of course." Lane set down her clipboard on the table. When she left the room, Cora spoke.

"Ivy, this is Thomas."

Cora took his hand gently in hers. His thin white hair and papery skin looked pitiful in the bright, natural light. I could see every line etched deeply into his face.

I wasn't sure if he could hear me. "Um, hello."

Thomas's expression didn't waver. His glassy eyes continued looking straight up. As I watched Cora's compassion towards him, my perception suddenly shifted.

Instead of looking down at a nameless stranger, I saw a broken man. His face seemed kind; even his eyes, which had lost all their luster, looked like they had once been joyful and wise.

It was no longer uncomfortable to see him like this. It was heartbreaking. I felt crushed by a wave of incredible sadness. "What happened to him?" I whispered.

"Thomas has lost the ability to care for himself. He can't do anything on his own anymore. Standing and walking is difficult. His hands are the only part of his body that still somewhat functions. He can still grasp things, although not very well. His body is deteriorating."

Tears burned my eyes, and I shook my head, speechless. "This is terrible."

Cora nodded. "Ivy, Thomas was the very first transposer to work with Dr. Ply."

The room went still. I couldn't speak as I realized what she meant. *This* was the outcome of transposing. Or the experiments —or both. I thought about York, who was just getting started. And Carl, who was already on this path. Now I stared down at Thomas, the end result of Dr. Ply's work.

Cora's voice trembled with anger. "You see, *this* is what happens after years and years of secret experiments and work in the lab. All these men have worked hard for Dr. Ply and the Count. When they are no longer of use to the lab, when they no longer respond to Dr. Ply's monstrous experiments, they are sent to me. *Retired* is the term Dr. Ply uses—a term too pleasant for what really happens to them." Cora looked sadly around at each man. "After years of transposing, they are unable to live normally. I do as much as I can to make their lives comfortable, but as you can see, it isn't much."

I looked around the room. One man looked to be ten years younger than Thomas, and another only seemed around forty. His life was not yet half over and he would spend the rest of it lying here. Glen had finally closed his eyes, as if Cora's words were too much.

I remembered him stumbling out of the smoky room with Anna, barely able to stand. It was horrifying.

"Ivy, there was another reason I wanted you to see Thomas."

I looked back at the old man, shriveled on the bed. His eyes had closed too and I hoped he was finally sleeping. What was so special about him?

"He's York's grandfather."

THIRTY-TWO

The room spun, but I couldn't move.

York's grandfather was *Thomas.*

"Come. I promised you the truth, but I'd rather speak elsewhere."

Numbly, I followed Cora out of the room and up another set of stairs. Thoughts whirled in my head until it clicked.

York's father was Mr. Pembroke, and Mr. Pembroke's father was *Thomas.*

Mr. Pembroke had always distrusted the Count. He never wanted York to enter the Count's Woodworking Tournament or be a Carver. I remembered his angry words in the kitchen the last time I went to see York.

There are terrible, terrible things going on inside that castle.

Mr. Pembroke must have known what happened to Thomas. That was why he hated the Count. And now his only son, York, was here, just like his father. He had been right all along.

I felt sick.

The next floor was another hallway like the last: we came to one large window and a door. Cora opened it and ushered me inside.

The room we were in now looked like the room below but

with vaulted ceilings crisscrossed with wooden beams. A white chandelier hung from the rafters, and a stained glass window cast colors of light over the cream furniture.

The shelves on the far wall held dozens of pots of white orchids.

For a moment I couldn't speak. I just stared as the realization rocked through me like waves battering the shore.

Cora had put the white orchid on my bed.

Cora knew more about my father. About his work.

I pointed to the plants. "Where are they from?"

"They are what I saved from your father's collection."

I sank down on the couch. "Why?"

"Just as I brought you to see Thomas so that you would understand the dark and very real side of Dr. Ply's work, I brought you here to show you these. So you will believe me when I tell you that you can trust me, just as your father did."

I leveled my gaze at her, needing answers now. "Exactly what did he trust you with?"

Cora sank down on the couch across from me. "I know you have many questions. About your father and about what you saw in the room below us. But let me start at the beginning.

"Many years ago, before I even came to the castle, Thomas was a gardener here. The Count caught him Carving a piece of wood from a special tree of his, and he was furious until he saw that Thomas had transformed the wood into laun. That was the first time the Count realized how important a Carver was. He and Dr. Ply brought Thomas back to the castle and tested him. Transposing and the experiments broke something in him. Poor Thomas has never recovered. I was brought here to cure Thomas, but sadly, he was too far gone. I stayed, hoping to spare others from such an outcome. But then the Count began hosting his Woodworking Tournament in Windermere to find more Carvers like Thomas."

I swallowed. "And he found Carl."

Cora nodded. "Carl was just the first from Windermere."

"But my father came before that. When? And why did he choose to work here?" My voice trembled with anger. "Why couldn't he stop this from happening? Why haven't you?"

Cora took a deep breath. "We've tried, believe me. Your father began working for Dr. Ply just after your mother left. He was heartbroken and confused by how she'd disappeared. He always suspected there was something different about her. You see, your mother was able to enter the Tree Garden when he could not."

I remembered the solid wall of air that wouldn't let me inside unless I held the owl. I could imagine how frustrated my father would have been, as an Arborist, to find a place like the Tree Garden, but not be able to get inside.

But my mother could.

It must have been *she* who'd discovered the wooden owl was a key, and given it to my father.

Cora continued. "Dr. Ply discovered your father could enter the Tree Garden and paid him to deliver the laun for him. Your father agreed because he wanted to know more about your mother's abilities. He wanted to find her again. However, as he learned what Dr. Ply was really doing, he was outraged. He began searching for a way to stop him. Then he decided to stay and help me."

Cora looked out the window.

"I asked him to get a file that was locked in Dr. Ply's office, so I could understand what these 'experiments' really consisted of. I knew Dr. Ply was hiding the real extent of it, and I thought if I had evidence to hand the Count about how barbaric they were, I could convince him to put a stop to it. Your father did get the files, but Anna noticed and accused him of taking laun from the office too. That night, he disappeared."

I stared at the rows of orchids.

Cora's voice softened. "I became your benefactor. I arranged for you to live with the Taylors and kept you off Dr. Ply's radar for as long as I could. You were kept from Carving, and I hoped that you would become an Arborist. When I saw you that night in the stable, I realized that Dr. Ply had found you and brought you to the castle. He even hid you for over a month in that horrible room."

"Why? Why did Dr. Ply or the Count care about me?"

"Partly because of your father. They're still not sure what happened to him and they do not like loose ends. But also because you got into the Tree Garden. They wonder if you can do more."

A chill went through me. Dr. Ply already suspected me of having extra abilities, as I'd feared. "But I could only enter because of my mother's owl. Dr. Ply knew that."

"I think Dr. Ply also always wondered if your father really did steal some laun. They wonder if you have it without knowing it."

A realization came over me. "Is that why Mr. Mallon gave me my father's journal?"

Cora shook her head. "If they thought it was in there, they would never have given it to you. Mr. Mallon's job is to study the Carvers and identify those with unique characteristics that interact well with laun. You were of age, and I think he simply gave you the journal to make contact and learn about you. He was also watching York, because of who York's grandfather was. I believe they pulled you into the competition to ensure York joined too. They must have noticed your bond and knew if they gave you the spot, York would enter to support you. But in the Woodworking Tournament, Mr. Mallon told the Count that he thought you'd seen what happened with York's wood before anyone else did. That was all they needed to hear. Dr. Ply made up a position and brought you here too."

"How do you know all this?"

"Jack told me."

"*Jack?*"

Cora smiled. "Yes. You already know he's worked here for most of his life. He started in the stables until the Count noticed his potential and made him his prospective heir. However, Jack only just became involved in the lab. The transposers respect and like him, and Dr. Ply noticed that Jack had a more calming effect on them than Flex ever did. I told Jack everything. Now he gives me information without Dr. Ply or the Count knowing."

Something eased in me as any doubt I had about Jack melted away. I bit my lip, realizing that Jack was now in the same position my father had been in. And look what had happened to him.

"Cora, you said my father disappeared, not that he died. Is he still alive?"

Something passed across her face. "I'm sorry, Ivy. I don't have the answer to that."

A lump formed in my throat and my eyes filled with tears. I hastily wiped them away with the back of my hand. "So what now?"

Cora sighed. "Things are changing, I can feel it. I'm worried. York is an incredible transposer and is really all the Count and Dr. Ply have now. Besides Thomas, the others have never been as gifted or as strong. I worry he will burn out faster than Thomas did if we don't act soon."

"What should I do?"

"Study your father's journal. Watch and learn. When the time comes, we will all try our best to stop this once and for all."

I chewed my lip. "I don't know how much I can help now that Dr. Ply's shut me out."

"Tomorrow you are going back to the lab. I'm sure it will be unpleasant, but I suggest that you act as repentant as possible. Dr. Ply may still have use for you and give you another chance. Seize any opportunity to discover his plan, or at least warn me if you think he intends to experiment on York."

"I won't let York end up like Thomas. I want to help you like my father did."

"I knew you would," Cora said, smiling.

"There's still so much I want to know. Does York know his grandfather is here?"

"Not yet."

"Are you going to tell him?"

Cora nodded. "When the time is right. The only reason I have not shown him yet is because I didn't want to compromise his standing with Dr. Ply."

I thought back to when Dr. Ply told me about the Transposers touching laun. *Once a person touches laun, they only want it more. And once a Transposer has handled it, they become fixated. Obsessed.*

York's hands in the Tree Garden. It was my fault he turned into a Transposer.

And the light I'd seen; somehow, I was changed too. But I wasn't a Transposer, or I would have been able to transpose wood in the Tournament like York had.

"York loves being a Transposer. What if he can't stop?"

"Once York sees what transposing has done to Thomas, I think he'll love it a little less."

I thought about the dust I saw leaving Carl; the shimmering pile on the floor under his chair. "How is a Transposer broken?"

"Transposers are much more sensitive to situations than normal people because of their genetic makeup. I wish your father could explain it to you. He was fascinated by it."

"Because of my mother?" I asked.

Cora smiled. "I think that's what started your father's fascination with Stygian, and Dyadics. That was where she was from, you know."

I sat up, startled. "I didn't know that."

Cora nodded. "That was the first point of contention between your father and Dr. Ply; Dr. Ply was furious that your father believed in such things. However, the Count shared his beliefs, and would not let your father go. Your father was too smart, and he knew too much at that point."

I huffed out a breath. This was more information than I'd ever received about either of my parents, and I felt like I needed days to sift through it. Along with everything else I'd learned about the castle.

"Now it's time you return to the Top Floor," Cora said.

I stood up, knowing there was so much more I needed to ask

and tell her. But my head was too full. "Will I come back here again?"

"No. We must be very discreet now, and take care not to raise any suspicion—especially from Anna. She has been watching you very closely. No one can know what we spoke about here. If you need me, go to your room and order Turkish Delight. I will come to you."

"What's Turkish Delight?"

Cora smiled. "A special dessert from Stygian, my old city. It's delicious." The smile faded from her face. "Remember, there are eyes everywhere."

———

EMBER WAS NOT IN THE ROOM WHEN I RETURNED. I wondered where she could be; I needed to talk to her. Anxious, I checked the library, but it was empty. Everyone was probably still in the lab, but where was Ember? Before I could panic, I remembered Cora's note had said she would send for Ember after me.

I would just have to wait.

I had nowhere else to be, so I sat down with a cup of coffee and waited for someone to pass by. No one did.

I mulled over everything I'd learned. I hadn't told Cora about Ember transposing the wood in the lab. In the huge reveal about my parents, it slipped my mind.

Cora thought York was the only Transposer that could create laun—that he was in danger of suffering greatly at the hands of Dr. Ply and the Count because of it—but Ember was even more powerful than he was. Ember was in danger, but Cora couldn't protect her if she didn't know.

I jumped off the couch. I had to tell her right away.

I sat back down, knowing I couldn't rush over to the South Wing. I had to act normal. Maybe, if Ember was with Cora right now, she was telling her herself. I hoped so.

Waiting was harder than I thought it would be.

After flipping through several books without seeing the pages, I almost walked over to the stable to find Jack. I couldn't, though; I had to stay here in case Ember needed me.

Hours passed with no sign of anyone. *Where were they?*

Maybe Dr. Ply had brought Ember to the lab again . . . and she'd transposed, but this time everyone saw her. I paced the room, imagining worst-case scenarios.

By dinner, Ember still hadn't returned. I went to the ballroom alone, hoping to find someone there.

But even the dinner table was emptier than usual. I ate slowly, feeling cold and alone. Where was everyone that worked in the lab? Surely they weren't still in there? The anxious pit in my stomach doubled.

I wanted to see Jack more than anything.

But he never came.

And neither did Ember.

At this point, I would have been glad to see Anna.

After dinner, I rushed back to my room, only to find it still empty. What was going on?

I pulled out my father's journal, but I was so distracted that I kept reading the same line over and over again.

Hedera growing on a stone wall will cause serious damage and prove to be a menace . . .

I fell asleep in the chair.

Ember never came back to the room.

THIRTY-THREE

Rays of sunlight crept across my face, making the insides of my eyelids pink.

For a moment I laid still with my eyes closed. I was back in Windermere. I could smell the lavender fields outside my window and hear muffled footsteps downstairs. It was so peaceful and I wanted to savor the wonderful feeling as long as I could. I'd missed this house more than I realized.

A cold draft made me shiver and I reluctantly opened my eyes. The room tilted and changed, and I became painfully aware that I was not back in Windermere after all, but crumpled awkwardly in a chair in the Count's castle. Every happy feeling disappeared as I looked around, shivering.

The fire had burnt out sometime during the night and the room was now cold. I stretched out slowly, my neck cramped from sleeping so long at an odd angle. Windermere had been so real for a second that I could cry.

"Good morning," Ember said from across the room.

I flew out of the chair. "Where have you been!"

Ember sat on the bed, already dressed and combing her long, black hair. The comb froze mid-air and her violet eyes widened.

"I've been here all night. You were asleep when I came in and I didn't want to wake you."

"But yesterday—all afternoon I was waiting for you! You never showed up to dinner. Neither did Jack or Anna."

"Oh." Ember resumed brushing. "I was with Cora the rest of the day. I had dinner in the South Wing. Sorry to worry you. I thought you'd know where I was."

Ember didn't seem distraught or upset, so I let myself breathe easier. "I was really scared."

Ember peered at me. "Is something wrong? Did something happen?"

"No, at least I don't think so." I rubbed my forehead. "I must have been in a really deep sleep. I feel awful."

"Yeah, you were. I even dropped a book but you slept right through it."

There was a knock on the door, and I jumped.

"It's OK. I just ordered tea," Ember said, going to open the door.

The tea was delivered, but not by Vernon. I hadn't seen him since my first night on the Top Floor, when he told me about my father disappearing in the castle woods. Vernon hadn't been back since.

I had been too preoccupied to even notice.

Had Vernon been punished for sharing a secret with me? I sank into the chair, feeling another worry pile upon my shoulders.

Ember poured the tea and added cream and sugar, just the way I liked it. She handed it to me with a smile.

"What did you do with Cora yesterday?" I asked.

"I saw Thomas," she said gravely.

I nodded, relieved. "I saw him too. What happened to him is . . . just unspeakable. Did you tell Cora about the wood you transposed?"

"No. I meant to, but I didn't get a chance."

"We should tell her as soon as we can. I know she will protect you. We need to tell her that Dr. Ply calls you a *natural transposer*."

"Ok. Whoever sees her first tells her," Ember said, and I nodded. "Are you going to the lab today?"

I frowned. "I think so. It will be hard, now that I know the fate that awaits every transposer. How am I supposed to watch York and let him continue to transpose? And how can I face Dr. Ply?"

As I sat back in my chair, my elbow knocked my tea cup from its saucer. The china crashed to the floor, shattering in pieces at our feet.

"Oh, sorry! Did I get you?" I asked, leaning forward to pick up the pieces.

But Ember didn't answer.

I glanced up at her. She was staring down at the broken china with a stunned expression.

"What is it?" I asked. "What's wrong?"

Ember looked stricken and pale. She didn't even blink.

"Ember!" I nervously gave her shoulders a shake. "Talk to me!"

Ember turned toward me with the strangest look on her face.

"What is it?" I was almost scared to know.

"I remember," she said slowly. "I remember *everything*."

THIRTY-FOUR

Ember's Lost Memory

"Ember, wake up."

Ember groaned and rolled over, pulling the pillow over her head. She was so comfortable—

"Ember!"

Ember turned to the other side, grumbling. "But I just got to sleep . . ."

"Ember! I'm serious, wake up! Airlend asked to see you immediately. Ink is waiting."

Ember sighed and sat up. With her eyes still closed, she stretched and let out a jaw-splitting yawn. Heavy fabric was pushed into her hands, and she opened her eyes to see flickering candlelight illuminating Devi's worried face.

That woke her up. "OK, OK. I'm awake."

"Then *hurry*."

Ember quickly pulled off her nightgown and pushed her arms through the dark dress.

"It's still cold out. That one is best," Devi said, looking briefly out the window.

The still-dark sky looked like a glittering blanket; the stars twinkled ruby, emerald, topaz, sapphire, and diamond. Ember paused as she always did to soak up the view, knowing that soon the sun's rays would wash away the colors.

Devi cleared her throat.

"Ok, ok." Ember ran a brush through her long dark hair and looked in the mirror. "I'm ready."

"Then go!"

"Going!" Ember hurried down three flights of the winding staircase and pushed open the door outside. The morning was chilly, and she was glad for her warm dress.

Ink, Airlend's white deer, was grazing as she waited. When she saw Ember, she lifted her head gracefully and turned away into the woods.

Ember followed, but as she got into the tree line, she felt a tug to turn and see her home again without knowing why. She looked back at the white castle with its round gold doors and windows. The chimney exhaled puffs of grey smoke into the sky, as if saying goodbye. She shivered and continued after Ink.

The ground was cold and damp with dew. Trees stretched into the sky, their white velvety leaves matching the branches. The White Forest had been named for the ancient white oaks that stretched endlessly over the hills and mountains. The only color of the forest came from sage grass and tiny wildflowers that sometimes bloomed at the trees' feet.

It was quiet and peaceful as if everyone were still asleep besides her and Ink.

Soon, the forest thinned as the ground began to slope downwards. Just as the sky was changing from dusk to light blue, they arrived at Keeper's Cottage. Yellow light from the windows illuminated the outside.

Ember patted the deer's neck. "Wish me luck."

The deer blinked her black eyes and nudged Ember's side in

farewell. But she stayed near, nibbling grass as Ember pushed the door to the cottage open and walked inside.

A warm fire greeted her. The cottage was small, but the living area was cozy and light. Vases of wildflowers, white furniture made from the wood of the forest, two large chairs, a desk, and a stove filled the room. As usual, there was no staff here. Airlend was completely alone, standing in the middle of the room by the stone fireplace.

She was tall and willowy, and her white hair cascaded down her shoulders, covering her delicate dress. She turned and met Ember's violet eyes with her ice-blue ones. Instantly, the crease in her brow relaxed and she gave Ember a true, rare smile.

"Good morning." Ember yawned. "It's so early."

"I'm sorry." Airlend smiled affectionately before turning serious. "But there is much to do."

"Is everything alright?" Ember asked, hoping this wasn't about her issue with the dwarves—or rather *their* complaints against her.

"I hope it will be. Please sit. There are things I need to share."

Ember's brow wrinkled as she sat. She had never been summoned this early before. Was Airlend going to continue their last conversation? It hadn't gone so well. She watched Airlend cautiously, prepared to argue her case again.

"First, I'll make us tea."

Airlend filled a teapot with water and set it on the stove, then pulled out a jar of dried herbs and dropped them into the cups. When the teapot whistled, she poured the steaming water over the herbs.

She walked over to a table filled with rows and rows of glass vials, each filled with a different color liquid. Patiently, she picked through them until she found a small vial filled with liquid the color of glittering midnight and set it aside.

Ember had never seen Airlend use that particular vial before, and she wondered what it was for.

After a few minutes, Airlend strained the tea and then poured it into Ember's favorite blue-and gold-tea cups. She quickly stirred both cups before walking over to Ember with the tray.

"I need to tell you something very important." Airlend set the cups on a small table.

Maybe Airlend was going to apologize and say she understood Ember's decision now.

"OK." Ember picked up her cup and saucer and took a long drink. It tasted like blueberries.

Airlend kept her eyes on the fire and slowly sipped from her own cup. Besides the crackling from the burning logs, the room was silent. Ember waited patiently. She was used to long silences from Airlend and learned long ago that it was better to let Airlend talk in her own time. So, she sipped her tea as Airlend stared into the fire.

Finally, Airlend spoke. "Ember, the White Forest is in danger, and it's my fault."

Startled, Ember put her tea down. That was not what she expected Airlend to say. "That's ridiculous."

Airlend smiled, softly. "You have such faith in me. But I was not always who I am now. There was a time when I was very young. I made a mistake. One that haunts me still."

Ember stared at her, frowning. Airlend never made mistakes.

"Years ago, when I was newly charged as the Keeper, I forgot to renew the ward around the White Forest. It was only down for half of the morning, but that was all it took for an outsider to enter."

Ember drew in a sharp breath. Outsiders didn't come here. If they happened to make it up the mountain, they would wander and wander—always at the edge of the tree line, never to make it inside. The idea that someone had made it in . . .

"I was young, naive. Fresh out of my training, where I was kept isolated so I could learn all I needed to. When I became the Keeper, I was arrogant, and I thought I had everything under control. But in that brief moment, everything changed."

Airlend's voice dropped to a whisper as Ember sat frozen. She was unable to believe the weight of what Airlend was revealing—and her head was beginning to feel foggy and clouded. She yawned.

Airlend looked at her sharply. "Stay with me, Ember. I need your help. I'm sorry, but I must send you away."

Ember was alarmed, but she found it impossible to panic. A heaviness settled in her chest; her breathing was becoming slower and deeper.

"Airlend . . . what's happening to me?"

"You're falling into a deep sleep. When you wake up, you'll be somewhere new and you won't remember anything. I need you to forget who you are, just for a little while. Where you are going is dangerous, and if they knew who you were—how valuable you are—you wouldn't stand a chance. The only way it will work is if you don't remember anything. When the time is right, the darkness will lift, and you will know what to do and how to get back."

"No! Is this because—"

"It is because I need you."

Ember's eyelids grew heavier by the minute and she fought to look at Airlend. "The outsider . . . what happened to them?"

Airlend looked back into the fire. "He stayed a month," she said quietly. "We had to be sure any power from the laun was drained from him. But in that time we formed an . . . an attachment. This man was different. He was charismatic, the most driven person I'd ever met in my short life. But he was banished and my punishment for letting the ward fall was to take an oath to never see him again." Airlend's voice had dropped lower than a whisper.

Ember leaned forward dizzily, straining to hear what she would admit next.

"Except I broke that oath. I summoned him back and gave him a piece of the forest. An acorn." Airlend lowered her head for a moment as if she was ashamed.

Ember swayed back in her chair, her head heavy and aching. There were so many questions she wanted to ask, but they were slipping through her thoughts, forgotten before she could form the words.

After a moment, Airlend lifted her head, her face determined, her voice strong again. "He used my gift against me and has been depleting the White Forest ever since. The balance has been thrown dangerously off and I cannot ignore it any longer. I must right this horrible wrong before we lose this place. And only you can help me do it."

"I *can't* go now." Ember forced out the words. The fog was pushing down on her mind; she couldn't think clearly anymore. "Why me?"

"Because . . . he's your father."

Ember tried to understand, but the words slipped past her with no meaning.

"One more thing. Ember, look at me."

Ember forced herself to focus on Airlend's intense blue eyes. "You will meet a girl named Ivy Rune. Bring her back with you. It's very important. Do you understand?"

Ember's tea cup slipped to the floor, shattering. She looked at the pieces scattered . . . she should pick them up. But she couldn't stop her eyes from closing or her body from slumping slowly back into the chair.

Everything went black.

THIRTY-FIVE

Ember looked up at me, but her eyes were far away, like she was still seeing something else.

"You remember?" I asked excitedly.

She frowned just as there was a sharp knock on the door.

It swung open and Anna stepped into the room. When she saw us sitting by the fire, she looked disappointed she hadn't caught us doing something we shouldn't be.

"Ivy, Dr. Ply wants you to meet him in his office. I see you're ready to go—please head there now."

I looked down. I was still wearing the clothes I'd worn yesterday. I desperately wanted to shower and change, but I knew that Dr. Ply wouldn't wait.

I said goodbye to Ember, wishing we had more time to talk, and walked down the hallway. I smoothed my hair and dress as best I could, my dread growing the closer I got to his office.

What would he say if he learned that Ember remembered who she was? Or that—yet again—I was withholding information from him?

I twisted my hands, wondering how much longer I could keep up this charade. I reminded myself of what I now knew: My whole position here was a lie.

Dr. Ply had never trusted or needed me.

I stopped in my tracks; I'd forgotten the bag with my father's journal and the small box of dust. It was back in the room with Anna. I groaned; I couldn't go back for it now.

I knocked on the door and entered as I usually did. Except now my palms were slick, and my heart thumped uneasily as I went to stand in front of Dr. Ply's desk. I waited for him to acknowledge me.

"Good morning." I tried to make my voice sound strong—and guilt-free.

He didn't look up.

I knew he'd heard me, but minutes passed slowly as I waited, shifting awkwardly. Was this the way I would be treated from now on? If it was, it was a small price to pay compared to how he treated the Transposers.

I pressed my anger down beneath my calm mask. My father had sacrificed his life to help the Transposers. I was determined to finish what he had started.

Finally, Dr. Ply set his papers down and took a long sip of his coffee. His eyes caught mine. "Have a seat."

I hid my annoyance and disgust as I sat. This man used people, ruined them, and then cast them aside without regret. If I wasn't careful, I would be next.

Dr. Ply studied me for a moment. I kept my expression carefully blank.

"Have you enjoyed working with Cora these last few days?" He acted as if he had not dismissed me coldly; as if I hadn't been kept away from the lab as punishment.

I chose my words carefully. "Honestly, I found the South Wing a bit boring. All Cora does is decorate. I wasn't challenged at all. I missed working in the lab. Your work is much more meaningful."

Dr. Ply looked surprised. "What did you help her with?"

"Flower arrangements for the South Wing. The whole time I felt I was missing out on important things here. Yesterday, I had the afternoon free and I didn't know what to do with myself. I would have preferred to read another experiment, or to work on something important."

I wondered if I was laying it on too thick, but Dr. Ply seemed pleased. He relaxed back into his chair, folding his hands over his round stomach.

"Cora does gravitate towards socializing rather than meaningful research or work. It is good to hear that you missed serious academic study. Yesterday was quite a day in the lab, and I'm afraid you lost the opportunity for some valuable training."

It was easy to look disappointed, because I wanted to know what had happened in the lab yesterday.

Dr. Ply considered me a moment longer. "I was conflicted about welcoming you back. I wasn't sure what to make of York staring into the mirror as if he knew he was being studied. Perhaps I was too quick to assume that you somehow alerted him to it. So . . . I will choose to believe you and we can put the matter behind us."

I nodded. "I promise I had nothing to do with that."

"Fine." Dr. Ply leaned forward and placed his hands on the desk. "We will move on. As I said, yesterday was an extreme day in the lab, so Cora insisted we start this afternoon rather than this morning. I really don't have to do her bidding, you understand, but I'd rather go along with her on these little matters so I can refuse her requests when they truly affect my work. I would like you to go to the Dark Woods and track how much Ember's tree has grown before meeting me back in the lab."

"Thank you for giving me another chance. I really am committed to you and your work. I won't let you down again." The words fell out of my mouth like lead. But Dr. Ply didn't seem to notice.

He nodded solemnly at me.

I breathed out a sigh of relief as soon as I stepped into the hallway.

I made my way down the lawn to the Dark Woods, wondering

what had happened that made Cora ask for the morning off. I looked around, hoping to catch a glimpse of Jack. Maybe he would be on Loon; then at least I could see them both. But the lawn was empty.

I hurried past the manicured gardens, stone sculptures covered in green moss, and rows of elegant topiaries, wishing the day would pass quickly so I could just talk to Ember. I was dying to know what she remembered.

Finally, I reached the leafy archway of the Dark Woods.

I unlocked the door and pushed it open with a groan. I was greeted by black misshapen trees and dark twisted branches. It was still unbelievable how deformed these trees were. Their shapes seemed to serve as a sign of perverted power . . . a warning that they were trying to alter nature—and nature wasn't allowing it.

I breathed in the somber, silent air, feeling my energy drain from me and leak into the dirt, dying as everything else did here. Before my mood was entirely ruined, I hurried over to Ember's tree.

I stopped and lifted my head in awe.

The tree was *beautiful*.

It grew tall and straight as an arrow into the sky. The branches were evenly distributed around the trunk, the color a whitish grey. Leaves were already sprouting, making it look like spring had arrived in a forest forever charred by fire.

Something glinted and caught my eye.

Laying under the tree were golden dots.

I dropped to my knees and saw they were actually tiny gold acorns. They were shining as if the sun was trapped inside them. I inhaled sharply. Could they be laun?

There were about thirty scattered all around the tree's roots. I looked up into the branches but didn't see any left above. It was as if the tree had grown and shed them all at once.

I rocked back onto my knees, unsure what I should do.

They were important; I was sure of that.

Should I tell Cora first? I knew I couldn't get to the South

Wing unnoticed. She still needed to be told about Ember—that Ember had remembered who she was—and now, this.

But it was a very bad idea not to tell Dr. Ply immediately. I had just pledged myself to him (again). He would expect me to come to him. Cora had instructed me to regain his trust.

What if Dr. Ply already knew about the acorns and had sent me here as a test?

I looked back at the golden acorns. Dr. Ply wasn't expecting me back until lunch. I could try to make it to the South Wing first.

I thought about hiding all the acorns, in case anyone else came, but if it was laun, I didn't want to touch it. It would take too long to pick them all out of the grass, but I thought I should bring one to Cora.

The heavy iron key was in one pocket and I didn't want it to dent the acorn. I also didn't want to fish around for the acorn in the other pocket and risk touching it. So I used my sleeve to cover my hand as I picked the acorn up. I hoped I wouldn't run into anyone. It was obvious I was holding something.

I locked the door and hurried back to the castle, searching again for Jack or Cora, so I could hand the acorn to them. But the gardens remained empty. The whole castle felt empty lately and I wondered why.

I hurried back down the winding hallway, passing the dark and empty lab. I continued toward the South Wing, my footsteps echoing down the long hallway. My heart beat just as fast as I reached the door that led to the South Wing. I was just about to open it—

"Where are you going?"

I froze at the sound of Anna's cold voice.

I turned slowly, keeping my hand with the laun behind my back.

Flex was with Anna, watching me suspiciously. This was bad. If it had only been Anna, maybe I had a chance. Flex's towering figure and bulging arms changed the situation.

"I'm looking for Dr. Ply. I thought he said he would be in the lab, but he wasn't. I thought he went this way," I lied, my heart pounding.

Anna's eyes narrowed. "And where do you think this door goes to?"

I did my best to look confused and innocent. "Another lab?"

"Nope."

"I'll head back. All these doors look the same to me."

I took a step forward but Anna motioned to Flex, who quickly blocked me. I nervously stepped backward.

"What's in your hand?"

My fist tightened. "Nothing."

"Show me," Anna said fiercely, stepping forward.

"No. It's for Dr. Ply. I have orders not to show anyone."

Anna frowned, but then her face cleared. "Flex and I will take you to his office, so you don't get lost again."

———

THE GOLDEN ACORN SHONE UP AT ME FROM DR. PLY'S desk. Anna and Flex had been asked to wait outside.

"And you said there are *more*?" Dr. Ply's voice still sounded strange.

"Yes."

My nerves were frazzled. For over an hour, Dr. Ply had been quizzing me about the tiniest details of the acorns and Ember's tree. At first, I tried to be vague, but eventually, his questions made it impossible to leave out details without sounding like I was hiding something. I wondered why he didn't just go and see it for himself.

It was obvious now that he hadn't known about the acorns before sending me to the Dark Woods. In fact, he didn't seem like he'd ever expected something like this to happen.

"I estimated about thirty, all the same size, like they'd all dropped at once," I answered, again.

"And you took *only* this one?"

"Of course."

"And you came straight here? You told no one else?"

"Yes. I was trying to find you when Anna stopped me."

"Incredible. I must tell the Count right away. This sets every-thing into motion." Dr. Ply suddenly sprang into action and began gathering his paper. "Now, about Ember. I told you not to develop a real friendship with her. Have you? I need to know *now*."

I jumped, confused. Did he forget we talked about this earlier?

"Well, as you said, we are sharing a room. So we have gotten used to each other," I said cautiously.

"That will be changing too. I'm canceling the lab today. I need to go see the Count immediately. Tell no one about this; just go back to the Top Floor and go to dinner as usual."

I watched him frantically search his desk and throw items into his bag. He looked completely undone. What would he do if he knew that Ember had her memory back?

"What do I say if anyone asks about the lab?" I asked.

"Just say I needed more time for research. After the day we had yesterday, no one will doubt that."

"What happened yesterday?"

"Now is not the time. Go."

I stood, hesitant to leave. This felt like a mistake. I gave the golden acorn one last reluctant look. It shone up at me from the table, in a slightly bewitching way.

I turned and began walking towards the door.

"Wait," Dr. Ply called. "On second thought. Leave your key here. You will not be visiting the Dark Woods again."

I turned around slowly, panicking. I'd just given him impor-tant information and now he was taking away my key?

"I thought the Dark Woods was my responsibility?"

"*Was*. No longer will be."

He stared at me impatiently, so I walked back to the desk and took the heavy key out from my pocket. I dropped it into Dr. Ply's waiting hand. My stomach sank as it disappeared into his closed fist.

I'd messed up. I'd just lost access to the acorns for Cora.

"Many things will change now. Because of your close ties with York and Ember, I need time to rethink your involvement with the lab. I kept you isolated to avoid unpleasant situations like this. You can thank Cora for this. If she hadn't insisted on you working with her, I would not have to do this. However, what's done is done. I will of course let you know what I decide. If I think it's best for you not to continue on with me, you will be free to return to Windermere. No other position in the castle is suitable for you."

"Wait." I couldn't hide my shock. "I didn't think anyone was able to go back after they worked here?"

"Usually that is the case, but this is a very unique situation. After working for me, I don't think you would fit in any other role in the castle. Of course, I would have to take precautions for our peace of mind. Your memory would need some altering, but don't worry," Dr. Ply said, seeing my horrified expression. "It is painless and absolutely harmless. I have performed the procedure many times with splendid results. It's the *only* way you could return to Windermere."

My mouth hung open. I'd seen Dr. Ply's work firsthand with Carl. And the outcome was Thomas and Glen.

"Oh, it's really not as bad as it sounds. This way, you can return to Windermere without the worry that you might spill important details about the castle. After all, the Count would never release you otherwise. Trust me, you don't want to stay in the castle without a position. I don't believe you cared for your first room, did you? If you were demoted, not only would you be in worse quarters, but your work would be some sort of physical labor. Truly, I'm being kind, sending you back home. I'm sure you'd rather return to your previous life than be worse off than a servant for the rest of your existence. And, of course, you can take your horse with you."

I trembled. How had this gone so wrong?

"But all this is still undecided. I need to speak with the Count. It may turn out that you can stay with me after all, so don't be too worried yet. Perhaps I can find a way for you to work with York and Ember while maintaining objectivity through my experiments. Cora certainly threw a wrench in my plans for you, didn't she? Anna! Flex! Come in here!" Dr. Ply suddenly shouted as I jumped.

"I don't have to tell you not to speak of this to anyone again, do I?" Dr. Ply said, his eyes cutting back to me as the doorknob turned.

My whole body was trembling now. I couldn't stop it. "No."

Anna opened the door, and Flex was right behind her.

"Anna, please take Ivy to the Dome room to wait for me. I need to see the Count. Flex, go with them, and see that Ivy stays put."

Then Dr. Ply hurried from the room, leaving me with Anna, who smiled.

Thirty-Six

I walked between Anna and Flex, my dread growing with every step.

I tried to force the rising panic down and remain calm, but I could not see a way out of this. They were going to lock me in the Dome room while Dr. Ply and the Count decided my fate.

All I could see was Carl's face as the machine ripped life from him. I balled my fists at my side, but I couldn't stop the trembling. Dr. Ply said that machine was used for many things. What if he used it on me?

Tonight.

I wished the halls weren't so empty. No one knew where I was. No one could save me.

Anna opened the door to the Dome room and stepped back for me to walk inside.

Maybe I could surprise them and run. The South Wing was just a few steps more down the hall—I hesitated.

As if he'd read my mind, Flex took my elbow and forced me inside.

I twisted around him. "Don't do this, Anna, please! What happened to you? How can you help him ruin people?"

Anna looked at me impassively as she took a step closer. I

shrank beneath her cold, grey stare. When she finally spoke, her voice was quieter than ever before.

"This *room* happened to me. Just as it will happen to you."

My mouth dropped open as Anna turned to leave the room. She paused in the doorway. "Don't worry; after a while, it's not so bad. You won't feel anything anymore. Not even the cold."

Flex stepped out and Anna slammed the door shut behind them. The lock clicked. I was alone with the machine and the empty glass domes. Outside, Anna's voice drifted away.

Then there was only silence.

Any shred of composure I had disappeared. I ran to the door and began to pound, screaming for anyone to hear me and open it. Eventually, my fists began to hurt and go numb. My throat turned hoarse . . . and there hadn't been one sound outside. Either Flex was just as unmoved as Anna, or he'd left too.

I slid down the door and drew in a shuddering breath. The machine was on my right, and I couldn't bear to look at it. I knew if I saw the black cables, I would come completely undone.

There was such cruelty in the decision to make me wait here beside it. Dr. Ply was a monster, more heartless and more manipulative than I could have fathomed.

I stood and quickly crossed the room to be as far away from the machine as I could get. I sank onto the cold floor, pulled my knees into my chest, and dropped my head down, blocking the room from sight. I had to think. I only had so much time left, before my memories were stripped from me and I became a shell of who I once was.

Like Anna.

What had she been like before Dr. Ply altered her? Maybe she'd even been like me.

I hugged my knees tighter as a sob escaped my chest. I thought of everything I loved. Of Windermere, it's warm shops, how lovely and simple life was there. Of riding Loon through the woods, the Tree Garden, and York and I eating sweet rolls from

Wilder's Bakery. I thought of the lavender fields at the Taylors' and of Mr. Gable's enchanting shop of wood Carvings.

I remembered the night I'd met Jack in the stable, seeing him with the Count's horses, and that first glimmer of a spark lighting between us. Of the library, before we were interrupted. I would never have a chance at that moment again. Tears slipped down my face.

I wondered how everything would feel without my memories.

Would I be like Anna when this was over? Cold, emotionless, and cruel? Would I care about the things I loved anymore? Would my eyes lose their life, and become vacant, too?

I wished I could talk to my father; ask him if he had ever been in this room, why he hadn't prepared me better. I sniffed, wiping my nose with the back of my hand, as another thought struck me.

What if my father had had his memories stripped from him before he disappeared?

What if that was why he'd left? Not because he didn't care for me or his life anymore—but because he *couldn't*?

What if he had been rendered incapable of caring about anything except for one thing . . . Had only been able to focus on one thing, just like the Transposers?

What if, for him, that one thing had been plants?

Goosebumps rose on my arms.

What if my father had tried to prepare me in the only way he could?

Hedera . . . Ivy.

Me.

My chest rose and fell as I tried to wrap my head around my jumbled thoughts. My father hadn't been obsessed with a plant . . . He had been talking about *me*. *Hedera* was code.

My heart beat faster.

The day Mr. Mallon brought the journal to me . . .

All the times I'd seen the light . . . On the ruined ship. Around Cora. Surrounding the Tree Garden. On York's hands.

My father had stolen laun . . . and hidden it by grinding it down to dust like I had seen Ember do with her tea. He'd put it in the journal as pollen, something he'd always done.

Everyone just thought it was yellow pollen . . . but my chest and eyes hurt after I inhaled it. It wasn't until afterwards that I saw the light on the ship for the first time, and later, around Cora.

I'd inhaled laun, not pollen.

That's how *I* was changed.

Had my father predicted I would be brought to the castle, simply because I was his daughter? Had he tried to protect me by ensuring I touched the laun first, arming me with an extra ability? Was that the real reason behind his final journal?

My heart raced as I thought through every line he'd written; it was everything he'd meant to tell me, but couldn't say.

I had finally understood the words the way—at least, I thought—my father intended:

Ivy has lots of tricks up her sleeve . . .

Ivy is almost impossible to kill and stays green even when kept in the dark . . .

Ivy can severely damage mortared stone . . .

Ivy seeks out cracks, and uses them to enhance power and penetrate buildings . . .

If you try to remove Ivy, she will pull down bricks—or even stone walls . . .

Ivy growing on a stone wall will cause serious damage and prove to be a menace . . .

I shook as tears fell down my face.

Ivy can bring down stone . . . the stone of a castle.

I looked up and gasped.

All around the room, tiny particles of dust hovered in the air and glimmered within the glass domes on the shelves.

My legs trembled as I stood in disbelief. Somehow, it heard me, like when I'd struggled to gather Carl's dust in the box, and it clung tighter to itself, as if it had *listened* to me. As if it was trying to help.

Could it hear my thoughts?

What if there was more to my ability?

What if I could do more than *see* the light, and the dust—what if I could manipulate it?

I took a deep breath and imagined the dust gathering in the middle of the room.

Dust particles floated up from the bottom of the glass domes. One by one, the domes sparkled with glints of light, as the dust seemed to bounce off the inside of the glass, like it was trying to get out.

It *was* listening.

But I needed to move fast.

I grabbed the stool Dr. Ply used during the experiment and rushed around the room, quickly opening each glass dome to free the dust inside. As it floated out, the particles gathered themselves in the middle of the room.

When I finished opening the last dome, I turned toward the cloud of swirling, shimmering golden dust.

I looked at the crude machine sitting in the corner, knowing there was more golden dust trapped within from the countless times it had been used to drain the life out of the transposers. I imagined the dust freeing itself.

Slowly, a stream of dust began to rise from every crack of the machine. The glittering swarm joined the cloud in the center of the room.

I couldn't quite believe it. I walked closer and swept my hand gently through the gold cloud. Within it, the air felt cool and heavy.

I looked at the door and imagined the words my father had written coming to life: *Ivy growing on a stone wall will cause serious damage.*

The dust slowly moved to hover over the door. Then golden vines appeared on the stone framing the door, creeping up and spreading along each crack and fissure. It sparkled as it grew. I heard the grinding of stone and cracking around the lock of the door as the stone broke away in a cloud of dust.

My father *had* been trying to help me. He had given me the words to speak to bring down castle walls. *I* could crumble the stone.

Breathless, I ran to the door and brushed the crumbles of stone away from the wall. Now that the locking mechanism was free, the door eased open quietly.

I nearly collapsed in relief before running back over to the desk for another metal box. I found one filled with syringes and bottles and tossed them out, thinking about the dust gathering again. It streamed into the box and I closed the lid.

When I looked back out, the hallway was empty. I quickly closed the door behind me, hoping no one would jiggle it open or check to see if I was still in there. Flex probably just left for a moment, so I hurried down the hall as fast as I could.

I initially headed toward the South Wing, but stopped—Dr. Ply intended to experiment on Ember. She would lose her memories before I even knew what they were. I had to save her. Then we would both go to Cora.

I turned and ran up two flights of stairs, to a place I hadn't been in a long time, praying Flex or Anna didn't appear. I'd forgotten how cold this hallway was.

As I turned the corner, I skidded to a stop, my heart thudding in my chest.

Sebastian stood in the center of the hallway, blocking my old door.

The blood drained from my body. I was frozen, unsure if I should run or not. Would he help me or stop me? Was he *Nicholas*, my father's old friend, or Sebastian, the Count's man?

Sebastian didn't say a word as he walked toward me, his black suit swallowing up the light. His face was unreadable. I forced myself to stay still and not shrink away. My chin lifted as he came closer. As I waited for some indication of what he would do, my fist curled at my side.

He covered the distance between us but as he reached me,

Sebastian didn't stop. As he passed by me, he muttered, "Keep the owl on you. Always."

Then he disappeared around the corner. I shook as I listened to his footsteps fade down the stairs. He didn't stop me. I bolted to the door, unable to think about what that meant.

The door to my old room opened easily, and I pulled it closed behind me. I stopped in surprise. The room was empty; there were no beds anymore, and no torches hung on the back wall, either. I didn't have a moment to think about that either. I ran to the closet and opened the wall to the secret tunnel.

Running down the stone tunnel without a light, I felt for the first door that had taken me to the Top Floor so many months ago. I had been so naive then.

Finally, I found it, pulled it open, and dodged around the suit of armor. My heart felt like it was going to explode as I hurried past the suits of armor and reached the corner that opened up into the grand reception area, skidding to a stop. I peeked around it, my heart hammering in my chest. No one was there.

Before my nerve ran out, I raced past the front desk, up the stairs, and down the hallway and flew into my room, praying Anna wasn't inside.

THIRTY-SEVEN

E mber was frowning down at a note when I burst through the door.

She jumped up. "What's wrong?"

I crossed the room and threw myself under her bed, pulling the covers down to the carpet.

"What are you doing? What happened?" Ember asked.

"*Shhh.* Sit down or act normal in case Anna comes in. And if she does, say you haven't seen me since breakfast. Don't act like you know I'm gone," I ordered, peeking out.

"Alright." Ember's voice was calm as she looked around for something to do. She began building up a fire, and I heard the dry wood catch the flame and flicker to life.

"Now tell me why you're under the bed," Ember said, sitting down pretending to read a book.

I didn't speak until the warmth seeped into me and I felt stronger. "Dr. Ply locked me in the Dome room. He went to see to the Count and I escaped!"

"What!" she exclaimed, jumping up and facing the bed.

"*Sit* down."

For the first time ever, Ember glared at me, but she sat.

"You know the tree I told you about—the one that grew from your laun?"

Ember nodded.

"Today, I found golden acorns under it."

Her eyes widened.

"I took one and tried to go to Cora with it first, but Anna found me and took me to Dr. Ply. He lost it. He said that you and York were going to be used for something and he's going to send me back to Windermere, but first, he has to *erase* my memory of the castle. Then Flex and Anna locked me in the Dome room with a horrible machine he uses to *break* people."

Ember sank back in her chair. "I guess that explains why I just received a note from Dr. Ply telling me to collect my things because I'm moving to the South Wing."

"It's already starting." I rested my head in my hands. "We have to find a way to tell Cora."

"But how? Anna's watching me. I'm surprised she is not here now."

"She's probably waiting on Dr. Ply to finish with the Count. We better keep our voices down." I sighed and whispered, "What should I do? They'll discover I'm gone any moment; I can't stay here. Should we go to the stable? Take Loon and go? What about York? And the Transposers? I can't just leave now. I'm meant to help, I know it."

I looked at the metal box of dust, beside me on the carpet. Should I use it on Dr. Ply? What if I imagined the vines tangling around him and the Count . . . Then what? We could escape? But how would that solve anything?

Ember frowned. "I know what the Count wants."

My heart jumped in my chest. "That's *right*! Tell me what you remembered!"

"I'd rather tell you and Cora together. Can we go find her? I can look ahead down the hallway as you follow behind."

I remembered Cora's last words to me. "Wait. Cora said if

there was an emergency, to order rose Turkish Delight and wait in my room. She would come to me."

"Then that's what we'll do." Ember jumped up and tugged on the cord.

There was a knock at the door. My heart raced, expecting Anna to burst through the door and tear apart the room looking for me. Ember made it to the door before it opened. I heard a voice I didn't recognize, then Ember's ordering. I breathed a sigh of relief when the door shut again.

"Five minutes." Ember sat back down and stared into the fire.

I stayed under the bed, trying to breathe normally and think through our next step. First I had to find a better place to hide—maybe the tunnels.

I peeked up at Ember. Her face looked different. A light expression lingered as if her face suddenly remembered its normal expression. There was a confidence there that gave me hope. I wondered how she could know what the Count wanted. How could she know such a thing?

Another knock startled me. Ember answered it, and I hoped it would be Cora, but it was the same voice I'd heard before. The door closed and Ember returned holding a pretty silver platter piled high with rose-colored treats dusted with powdered sugar. She set it on the table.

"Do you want one?"

"No."

We waited in silence.

"How long should we wait before I find a better place to hide?" I asked nervously.

Then there was another knock. Ember and I stared at each other, realizing at the same time that it was not coming from the door.

It was coming from the full-length mirror on the wall.

Ember jumped up and went to the mirror. A sharp *tap-tap-tap* sounded again.

She felt all around the edge of the frame. "I think there's a latch." She pressed it and pulled the mirror out toward herself. It swung open slowly, revealing a large tunnel, and Cora emerged.

"Hello, Ember! I got Ivy's message." Cora swept into the room elegantly, as though she hadn't just walked out of a dusty tunnel hidden behind a mirror. "Where is she?"

"Down here!"

Cora looked around and finally located me. She suppressed a smile. "Why are you under the bed?"

"I've just escaped from Dr. Ply!"

Cora's smile disappeared. "What do you mean?"

"First we both need to get back in that tunnel!" I crawled out from under the bed and ran to the tunnel. Cora stepped inside with me, and together we swung the mirror back so that it stood just barely ajar and we could talk to Ember, who stayed in the room, ready to close the mirror if Anna burst in. I sank against the cold, stone wall in relief now that I was hidden properly.

Cora leaned against the wall and folded her arms, looking between us expectantly.

Ember nodded to me. "You go first."

I quickly caught Cora up on how Ember had changed the wood to laun, not York, and how the white tree had grown from it. Cora's brows rose as she looked at Ember, but she didn't interrupt. I told her about the golden acorns, Dr. Ply's plans to use Ember and York in an experiment, and how I was about to be sent back to Windermere with my memory altered.

When I was finished, Cora was pale with anger. "He wouldn't dare try that again! He did that with past Transposers so he could control them better, but it left them worthless. Ivy, this *will not* happen. I promise you I'll stop him." She turned to Ember. "So, you're a Transposer too. That explains the note informing me that you are moving into the South Wing. Dr. Ply doesn't waste any time. What else do I need to know?"

Ember took a deep breath. "This morning I remembered everything. My mother is Airlend Frost; she's the keeper of the White Forest. My home is in the mountains above Windermere.

My last memory was having tea with her while she explained why she was sending me here. After that, I was in the Tree Garden, where Ivy found me." Ember took a breath. "Airlend sent me here to stop the Count from ever finding the White Forest again. And to stop his poor attempt at making a forest here."

Cora looked surprised. "I know of Airlend Frost and her White Forest. The Count told me his story because he was desperate for my help. He said he'd discovered a place that exceeded this world in beauty and riches and that he'd met a woman there. He was obsessed with finding her and the forest again. I know the Dark Woods are his attempt to recreate the White Forest. In hopes of *what*, I'm still not certain. Perhaps riches, or power, or to simply gain her attention—"

"He was after the acorns all along," Ember said. "They're the only way for an outsider to get back into the White Forest, because of the wards. Without one, they can't see the Forest, even if it's right in front of them. Now that I created them here, the Count can use them to find it again."

"Why did Airlend send you? Did she know you could create laun?" I asked.

"Of course. In the White Forest, I am a Tree Healer."

I looked behind Ember at the white orchid on her bedside table. It was almost a foot taller than yesterday and tiny white buds were just beginning to form. "A what?"

"A Tree Healer. If a tree is too old, or in poor health, I can return it to its original form—laun. We then plant the laun and a new tree grows. There are strict laws about replacing laun in the White Forest. My role is to help keep that balance."

"Why would Airlend send you here if you're needed in the White Forest as a Tree Healer?"

Ember hesitated, and I had a feeling she was deciding to leave something out. "To get all the pieces of the White Forest back. All the acorns. Because the Count had one, he was able to cause this much harm to others to get more. I have to take them back with me. If I succeed, this madness with the Transposers will end."

"But the Transposers' lives will still be ruined," I said quietly.

Ember looked at us with fresh intensity. "The White Forest is the most wondrous place you can imagine. The air, the trees—everything sings with power. Just being there, you feel young and healthy, like you can do anything. Perhaps it can cure the Transposers."

A longing swept through me to see this place for myself, a longing similar to the force I felt holding the laun. Something was waiting there for me.

"You both are welcome to come with me and speak to Airlend," Ember said. "Perhaps we can figure out a way to help the Transposers?"

Ember's violet eyes were brighter than ever as she talked about her home. The veins under her arms also pulsed a dark gold. It was as if even speaking about it had strengthened her, or that Ember was somehow part of that power herself.

I took a deep breath. "I'll go. But I need to tell you both something first. I see light. I mean, I can see light around what you both do."

Cora and Ember glanced at each other, puzzled.

"I haven't told anyone this, but when others have abilities—when they perform them in front of me—I see a golden light form around them. Sometimes it's just golden light, like when York transposes and creates laun. I *see* that happen. Cora, with you it's all the colors of the rainbow, like when I saw you melt that spoon. And Ember, I can see a glow under your skin, running through your veins. It makes them look gold, not blue, like ours."

Cora raised an eyebrow. "This sounds like something a Dyadic can do."

Ember studied her arms. "My veins look gold to you? Do you see it, Cora?"

Cora walked over and looked closely at Ember. "No, I see blue."

"I think I'm able to see powers, or extra abilities," I said. "But it's not all the time. It's when something is happening. Except with you, Ember. With you, it's always there—a part of who you are, more than just something you can do."

"Most of the time, you see active power, then," Cora said.

"What does that mean?"

"It means you have a very rare gift," she said seriously.

Ember's eyes widened and something in her expression startled me. "What is it?" I asked.

"Nothing." Ember shook her head. "Nothing."

"There's more." I took a deep breath. "I was only able to escape just now because I . . . *spoke* to the dust in the experimenting room and it listened to me. It made itself into vines of ivy and helped me open the door. I was thinking of the lines in my father's journal, and the dust listened."

Cora looked between us, frowning. "Dust?"

"When Dr. Ply forced me to witness his private experiment on Carl, I saw shimmers of light leaving Carl's body as he was electrocuted. I just thought of it as dust, but I think it was part of his power, or life force. I collected it all."

"Spoke to dust?" Cora looked surprised. "Have you ever done this before?"

"Never. I didn't know I could."

"And no one else knows about this?"

Ember's eyes were still wide as she listened.

"No one."

"Good. Don't breathe another word about it. If Dr. Ply or the Count ever find out, you will never—and I mean *never*—leave this castle."

"That settles it." I turned to Ember. "We're leaving now."

Ember nodded. "We'll go to the White Forest. I know Airlend will protect you."

I looked at Cora. "Will you come with us?"

Cora nodded slowly. "Yes, I think the time has finally come. I would love to see this place full of power and help you get home, Ember. And perhaps learn how I can help the retired Transposers. Maybe Airlend Frost can help them too."

"We can't leave York here," I said.

"Of course not. Leave that to me," Cora assured me.

"Where is Jack?" I asked, realizing how long it had been since I last saw him.

Cora frowned. "A ship from Stygian arrived and he is down at the beach, helping unload and bring supplies to the castle."

My stomach dipped. "When will he be back?"

"I'll try to send word to him, but we have to leave as soon as I can pull everything together. If anyone gets a hint of our plans, we're finished. It's just a matter of time before they find you missing. I'm uneasy staying a minute longer than we need to."

"We need to gather *all* the acorns and take them with us," Ember stressed. "With even one, the Count can follow us and find the forest."

"I think they're still in the Dark Woods, but Dr. Ply took my key," I said.

"I can get us in," Cora said with a wave of her hand.

"There is also an acorn in Dr. Ply's office," I admitted. "I was trying to bring it to you, Cora, but Anna and Flex stopped me."

"We need that one too," Ember said, worry creasing her face.

Cora frowned. "That will be harder. I do wish Jack was here. Once we start this, we must be prepared to leave the castle immediately. We can't wait."

I nodded, but my heart sank at the thought of leaving without saying goodbye to Jack. Of leaving without him, period.

"We'll need to be ready for a long journey. Are you both up for this?" Cora said.

"We don't have a choice," I said.

Ember nodded.

"No, it seems we don't. This has happened faster than I anticipated," Cora said. "Very well. I will go back to the South Wing and make preparations. Ember, stay here so we don't raise any suspicions. Ivy, stay in this tunnel in case Anna or Flex notice you're gone and search the room. I'll come back for you both as soon as I can. If I don't send someone by this tunnel in three hours, assume something has happened to delay us, and Ember, go on to dinner as usual. I don't want Anna suspecting anything and alerting Dr. Ply. Pack light and thoughtfully, and leave your things in the tunnel; I don't want Anna to see anything unusual if she checks the room."

Again, we nodded somberly.

"Be careful and talk quietly. I'll see you in a few hours."

Thirty-Eight

"Stay there and I'll pack," Ember said, handing me a blanket.

The mirror closed, leaving no light in the tunnel. I sighed and wrapped the blanket around me. I couldn't believe how quickly everything had changed.

I had extra abilities.

My father had been trying to help me all along.

My mother was from Stygian. I hadn't even had a second to think about *that*.

The mirror opened again and Ember handed me my bag. "I thought you'd want this."

"Thank you!"

I opened it to find my father's journal, the bag of orchid seeds, my jewelry box, and the smaller box of dust I'd collected from Carl. I put the bigger box of dust in my bag next to my mother's owl. Why had Sebastian told me to keep it with me? Did he know I was leaving? Was he pretending to help again? I hadn't thought about the owl since I was able to get into the Tree Garden on my own. What else was it meant for?

I leaned my head back against the wall, thinking.

If everything worked out, tonight I would be far from the

castle. With York. That had been my goal all along—to get us out before anything bad happened. But I was torn.

I didn't want to leave Jack.

I closed my eyes, remembering the first time I saw him in the stable when all the Count's horses were desperate for his attention. I remembered the way his eyes twinkled when he knew Loon had come to the castle. When he'd sensed my doubt about how he felt at that first dinner, and reassured me by pressing our feet together under the table. How he'd planned his moves so carefully . . . But now I was leaving. And he would be here, continuing to lose at chess.

I wanted everything to work out, and I wanted Jack to come most of all.

The mirror opened again, and Ember set two more bags inside the tunnel.

"There. I picked out everything we'll need. There's a jacket in there for you. Going up to the mountain will be cold, but when we reach the White Forest, it's warm." She looked at my face. "How are you feeling?"

"I wish we could just leave now. The wait is making me anxious."

"I know. But we have a plan. We just have to follow it." Ember leaned against the mirror frame.

"Tell me more about your mother," I said.

"Airlend is the last Keeper of the Forest. She is respected, kind, and powerful. And I miss her."

"Does it bother you at all that she sent you here blind?" It was similar to what my father had done to me. I'd had to figure it all out on my own, just like Ember had.

Ember frowned. "Not *how* she did it, but *that* she did it." She sighed. "It's complicated."

"Are you two close?" I wondered.

"Yes. Although, we had a big disagreement before I left. Our first. So this makes it even more complicated."

There was a noise by the door. The mirror quickly swung shut, plunging me into darkness.

"Oh!" Ember said from the other side of the wall. Her voice was muffled. "You startled me!"

"What are you doing?" Anna asked.

My heart dropped and I stayed as still as I could.

"Just changing," Ember said. "Did you need something?"

"Why are you dressed for outdoors?"

I held my breath as I waited for Ember's response.

"I was going to the garden, but I don't have to if you need me," Ember lied, smoothly.

"Have you started packing to move to the South Wing?"

"Not yet."

"Good. I'll have someone else do it. Come with me."

My stomach flipped. Ember couldn't leave now; Cora wasn't back yet!

"Where?" Ember's voice sounded higher.

Anna answered, but they must have been walking out of the room by then because I couldn't make out anything she said. I stood up quietly, my heart pounding, and pressed my ear to the back of the mirror.

I heard the door to the room shut.

Then there was only silence. Panic flooded me. What were we going to do now? How were we supposed to find Ember and accomplish everything else?

I felt around the mirror for the latch, but there was only one on the other side. I couldn't get back into the room. I was stuck in the tunnel.

I heard footsteps behind me and whirled around.

"Cora?" I whispered.

"*Shhh*. Yes, it's me."

"Ember's gone! She just left with Anna!"

Cora came closer, holding a glowing lantern. She wasn't wearing her usual silk dress, but outdoor riding clothes.

"Does Anna know I'm gone? Is that why she took Ember?" I asked.

Cora's brow creased. "I don't think so. Flex is sitting outside the door, last I heard." She seemed to be thinking very quickly. "Fine. You and I will go to the Dark Woods now. It's getting dark and hopefully we won't be noticed. Are these your bags?" Cora asked, looking down. "We'll take them with us."

I picked up a bag and Cora took the other.

"One step at a time, Ivy. Let's get the acorns first, then we will find Ember."

I nodded, following her down the dark tunnel.

Every few feet, light danced on the wall from the torches, mingling with our shadows. Occasionally the tunnel split in two directions, but Cora led the way through the twists and turns without pausing.

"This tunnel goes all over the castle," she said over her shoulder. "We can get around almost everywhere undetected."

"Does it connect to other tunnels?"

Cora's voice echoed backward. "Yes, but less than a handful of people know how to navigate them."

Cora took a sharp right and the tunnel turned colder. I pulled my coat tighter.

We stopped at a door, which Cora unbolted and pushed it open. The cool night air and darkening sky greeted us as we stepped into the manicured garden.

"Careful not to be seen from the windows," Cora whispered, creeping along the edges of the tall square hedges.

My heart raced, knowing that at any moment we could be discovered and brought back to the castle. I imagined Dr. Ply strapping us to his chair and shocking us until we were broken while Anna watched calmly. I shivered and hurried through the darkness after Cora.

"I'm uneasy with all of this too," she said, seeing my face. "It's happened so fast. Our plans are rushed. And I don't want to leave the retired Transposers here. But we have no choice. And I know Lane will help them until I return."

"Did you find Jack?" I asked hopefully.

Cora's lips pressed together in a frown. "I sent word. I don't like leaving him."

That made two of us.

We stopped at the Dark Woods' door. Cora reached under the green vines and jiggled the knob, but it was locked.

I waited for her to pull out a key. When she didn't, I wondered how we were going to get in. I looked up at the tall stone wall circling the Dark Woods. I didn't think we could climb over it. We'd been standing here too long; I didn't want us to get caught. I looked back at Cora, worried.

Cora held the lock in both hands. Her brows creased as if she was concentrating intently. I looked down at her hands and saw the shimmering light appear around her. A thin line of color glimmered around her silhouette. Light shone from inside her cupped hands and a drop of silver fell to the ground.

Steel from the lock.

Cora was *melting* it, just as she had melted the spoon.

I watched, amazed, as the silver ran freely through her fingers, dropped to the ground below, and formed a pool on the grass that glittered in the moonlight.

Cora unclenched her fingers as the light faded. The entire bottom of the lock was lying on the ground, liquified. Only the top metal loop, which Cora didn't touch, was still intact and dangling from the door.

"What did you see?" Cora asked as if nothing spectacular had happened.

"Lights, every color of the rainbow . . ." I breathed, not knowing how else to describe it. I'd seen her do this before, but watching it again was incredible. "What are you doing exactly?"

"I'm considered an alchemist. In Stygian, it's the gift of altering metal." Cora wiped the silver liquid from her hand on her handkerchief. "I can change almost anything if I want to. Essentially, my power is destroying an object; I don't create, as the transposers do. I'm the opposite."

"Who else knows this about you?"

"Only two of my people in the South Wing, and the Count, who—believe it or not—*does* believe in extra abilities; the White Forest made him believe. It is Dr. Ply who wishes to erase any trace of them."

"Why does the Count allow him to ruin the Transposers?"

Cora shrugged. "I've asked that same question for many years. I think the Count's philosophy is that the end justifies the means. He wants something, and he won't let anything or anyone stand in his way. Do you see any light now?"

"No."

"But you saw it when I destroyed the lock?"

"Yes."

"See? Active power. You can see it happening. But you don't see it in me unless I am using it."

Cora pulled the rest of the lock off the door and threw it into the woods. Then she pushed dirt over the liquid silver with her foot. "Quick, help me bury this."

We gathered leaves and piled on the dirt, stomping all over the grass until all traces of the silver disappeared.

"Alright, Ivy." Cora straightened up. "Lead the way."

We walked into the stillness of the Dark Woods. The hair on my neck prickled. Being here at night was worse than in the day. It felt haunted and angry. Shapes of twisted branches cast long and strange shadows along the ground as we walked. The silence pressed down on us, weighted and heavy. At any moment, I was sure that something would reach out and snatch me.

Cora's lip turned up in distaste. "This place is absolutely horrid."

I hurried us to the lone grey tree, which was now towering over all the other mangled trees.

"Impressive." Cora studied the tree carefully. "Let's hurry. The sooner we get these acorns, the sooner we can leave."

From her inner pocket, Cora pulled out gloves and a bag to put the acorns. Under the moonlight, the acorns glimmered, and it was easy to locate all of them. We quickly gathered them and examined the branches, carefully checking to make sure none had been left behind.

"It's like the tree dropped them all at once," I said as Cora looked up into the branches to see if any were hiding up above. "Is that normal?"

"I'm not sure."

"Ok, what's next?" I asked.

Someone stepped out of the shadows. "Ivy and Cora. Fancy meeting you two here."

THIRTY-NINE

I rocked back on my heels, shocked.

Jack stood half-hidden in the shadow of a tree.

Cora let out a sigh of relief as Jack's face broke into a smile. I couldn't help it—I jumped up and ran to him. He folded me into a hug, lifting my feet off the ground. My face pressed against his chest, breathing in his scent of pine and spice. I pulled away, blushing as I remembered Cora. But when I turned, she was smiling.

"How did you know we'd be here?" Cora asked.

Jack grinned down at me, before looking back at her. "I got your message right before I received orders from Dr. Ply to leave the ship immediately and come guard this tree. Apparently, he thought someone might tamper with it tonight. I never dreamed it would be you two."

"Much has changed since this afternoon," Cora said seriously.

Jack nodded. "I gathered. What's the plan?"

I looked at Cora, wondering the same thing. But instead of panic, I felt a relief so powerful I could have floated away. Nothing had changed in our situation except that Jack was here, but somehow it made all the difference.

"I was serious when I said we're leaving," Cora answered.

"But our plans are rushed and there is much to do without being seen. Anna took Ember somewhere, and Ivy should be locked in the Dome room, so Dr. Ply or Anna will soon discover she's gone. I still need to get York. And we need horses."

"And the last acorn in Dr. Ply's office," I reminded her.

"Why were you locked in the Dome room?" Jack asked, his blue eyes wide.

"Dr. Ply is planning to send me back to Windermere without my memories of the castle."

Jack's jaw tightened. "That won't happen."

"No, it won't," Cora said. "We need all the acorns so Dr. Ply and the Count can't use them to follow us and find the White Forest."

Recognition flickered in Jack's eyes when he heard the name. "*That's* where Ember is from?"

Cora nodded. "She remembered today."

Jack snapped into action. "Here's what we'll do. I'll take Ivy with me to get the acorn in Dr. Ply's office. If we're seen, it'll make more sense for me to have her, not you. I can pretend I caught her in the Dark Woods and am returning her to Dr. Ply. You get York and get the horses ready. Tell anyone who asks that I need them to help unload supplies from the ship. No one will question that. While you're at it, gather as many supplies as you can—whatever you think we might need. Ivy and I will meet you at the stable. We both will look for Ember."

My heart beat furiously as Cora nodded.

"Wait!" I said, startled. "What about *this* tree?"

"What about it?" Jack asked.

"The Transposers we leave behind may be able to make laun out of this wood. I know they aren't as consistent as York, but it's still a risk. And if they do, then it can be planted, and more acorns could grow. We can't take that chance."

I looked up at the tall tree and wondered if we had time to try and chop it down.

"Don't worry, I've already thought of that," Cora said. "Although it's a shame to destroy something so beautiful."

She walked over to the tree and placed her hands on it, concentrating just like she did with the lock. Color shot out from all around her.

The tree creaked and groaned as a light flashed. A black streak leaked from Cora's hands and spread up the trunk like a dark plague. It grew until the entire trunk and every branch on the tree turned black, as if burned. The branches bent and drooped until the once-magnificent tree looked just as twisted and mangled as the rest.

Jack and I stared up in shock. Hearing Cora explain what she did, and seeing it happen on this scale, were two completely different experiences. I couldn't believe this tree had once been beautiful and white.

"See?" Cora looked at the charred tree, satisfied. "Destroyed."

"Remind me never to make you angry," Jack said, looking up in awe.

I looked at the mangled forest around us. "You did this to *all* of them?" I asked Cora, surprised.

Cora nodded. "I hate to destroy living things, but it was necessary."

"Is that why the Count brought you here? Because he knew you had abilities too?" I asked.

"Believe it or not, no. He sought me out because of my talent in medicinal herbs. He thought I could cure the Transposers. But that's a story for when we're safely away. We really need to go."

We quickly walked out of the Dark Woods and shut the door.

"I'll go through the gardens to the South Wing for York. Be careful. I'll see you both in the stable," Cora said. "And Ivy, remember your power, and use it ruthlessly."

I nodded. "I will."

Cora hurried away. I looked back up at Jack.

His brow lifted. "Should I be scared of you too?"

"I'll tell you on the way."

Jack smiled and took my hand. "Come on. I'm not letting you out of my sight again."

My heart pounded as his warm hand wrapped around mine. "Fine with me."

———

Together, we slipped into the castle and through the halls as silent as ghosts. Jack's hand still held mine tightly, but sometimes he squeezed it tighter.

I wondered where Anna had taken Ember. I hoped we would find her before it was too late. The longer our plan took, the more it could fall apart. I tried not to focus on all the impossible things we needed to do, and instead on Jack's steady hand around mine, but it was difficult.

My heart pounded as the echo of our footsteps traveled up ahead of us. The closer we got to Dr. Ply's office, the harder I prayed he hadn't returned yet.

Finally, Dr. Ply's office appeared at the end of the long empty hallway. Instead of heading towards it, Jack pulled me into a dark alcove. My heart thudded against my ribs. Had he heard something?

"What is it?" I whispered. My heart raced at the thought that someone had heard us.

In one smooth movement, Jack turned me around into the shadowed corner so I was caught between him and the stone wall. His face was closer than ever and his breath warmed my lips. My stomach dipped. I swallowed, my knees suddenly weak.

"Just in case this doesn't go as planned . . ." Jack murmured.

Before I could respond, his lips gently pressed against mine. My heart caught in my throat. I held my breath and tried not to ruin the moment. Jack's hand wove into my hair and pulled me closer, making every thought slip away.

He pulled away slowly, letting his lips hover just above mine.

"I should have asked . . . but I've wanted to do that for such a long tim—"

I reached up on my toes and cut off his words.

After a moment, he chuckled against my lips. "Have it your way, then . . ."

My hands wrapped around his neck, and all I could think about was how perfectly we fit together; how badly I never wanted anything to separate us again.

A moment later, we both pulled back, our noses still touching. We drew in shaky breaths and smiled at each other.

"The acorn?" Jack's brow rose.

"The acorn," I repeated, although somehow from me it sounded more like a grumble.

Jack grinned and brushed a finger across my lips, making me shiver.

"Let's get this over with. Together."

"Together," I echoed, smiling at how right it sounded.

Again, his hand found mine, and our fingers wound together tightly. Jack looked out around the corner, and I felt him shift back into a keen and calculating protector. When he looked back at me, he seemed conflicted.

"What?" I whispered.

"I'm torn between asking you to wait here and letting me go alone or bringing you with me. I can't decide which is better. If someone is in there, you'll be exposed."

I swallowed. I didn't want to be left alone, but I could see the sense in me waiting behind.

Jack shook his head. "No, you're coming. I said I'd never let you out of my sight again, and I meant it."

I exhaled in relief. "We probably shouldn't act like we like each other so much, then . . ." I said, raising our entwined hands.

Jack tilted his head; a smile tugged at his lips. "Probably not. Although it will be much harder for me than you, I think."

"I wouldn't be too sure of that."

"I'm glad to hear it." He picked me up again and kissed me

until I was breathless. When my feet found the floor as he pulled away, my head was still in the clouds. "Ready?"

I nodded as reality set back in. We had to get the acorn, get Ember, and get out. I silently repeated the thought over and over again to keep myself from pulling him back into the corner.

Jack took my elbow like he was retrieving me from my attempted escape. We walked down the silent hallway again, but this time I was aware of every inch of air that separated us.

We paused by the office and listened. All was quiet. Jack turned the knob and opened the door.

Sconces on the wall flickered with light, but the room was empty.

Jack hurried over to the cabinet and unlocked it. I waited by the door, thinking of Cora's reminder to use my power. The boxes of dust in my bag were shut, and if I needed it, the dust couldn't get out. I put my bag down and opened both metal boxes. The dust glimmered up at me. I imagined it staying put, and it did. I set them back into my bag with the tops open.

When I looked back, Jack had taken the black cloth that held the acorn out of the cabinet and was checking inside. He raised his brow and held the cloth out to me. I took the last acorn, relieved that this part had gone smoothly. I put it in my bag next to my father's journal.

"That's all we need, right?"

I nodded.

Jack reached into his pocket and took out a bone-white chess piece.

I inhaled sharply, recognizing Mr. Gable's work. "Is that the Count's? Why do you have it? Hasn't he noticed it missing?"

Jack smiled, eyeing the white knight. "It is exactly like his; I had a replica made. I've carried it with me daily as a reminder that someday I would finally be the one to say *checkmate*. I think the moment is now." He turned and set the chess piece in the cabinet where the acorn had been, locked it, and looked back at me.

"Time to find Ember."

I frowned, at a loss as to where she could be. "Anna took her."

"Cora will have checked the South Wing. Let's try the lab and Dome room."

I remembered the whirl of the machine and the black cables on Carl. An overwhelming, paralyzing fear of returning to that room overcame me. A fear that overshadowed even the discovery of my power. Jack walked around the table toward me, seeing my face fill with dread.

He took my hand and lifted it to his lips. "Be brave. This time I'll be with you."

He was right, I wasn't alone. I tried to smile, but it wobbled nervously.

"Just remember," Jack said, "everything we want is on the other side of fear."

I nodded. "OK. Let's go."

FORTY

e crept down the hallway as I repeated those words in my head.

Everything we want is on the other side of fear.

I willed my feet to move and my breath to stay even. I had the dust and Jack was with me. Together we could face anything.

As we drew closer to the Dome room, voices echoed back to us. We eased up to the corner and pressed ourselves against the wall. Anna was in the hallway.

"Is everything alright in there?"

"Fine," we heard Flex answer. "She must have worn herself out trying to break down the door."

"Good."

Jack was frowning, but I nudged him and gestured that I wanted to see. He shifted so I could peek out from under his arm.

Flex was now in a chair, guarding the door he thought I was still behind. Anna had Carl with her, and he looked worse than ever.

A grey sheen covered Carl's skin, and his shoulders slumped. He looked nothing like the proud Carl I'd seen in Windermere. I studied his sallow skin as an idea struck. I was glad I'd thought to open the box of dust.

I imagined some of the dust leaving my bag and flooding Carl with life. My breath caught as I watched the particles shimmer into the air above me and stream down the hallway toward Carl.

Jack glanced at me as if he sensed something; I kept my thoughts and eyes focused on Carl and the glittering dust.

No one knew what was happening except me.

The dust reached Carl and sank into his grey cheeks, neck, and hands . . . then it disappeared. I held my breath as I watched and waited for Carl to react.

Anna shifted. "Dr. Ply should be here shortly; when he arrives, take Carl back to the South Wing and keep an eye on things there. Jack is in the Dark Woods. I will assist Dr. Ply with Ivy."

Jack stiffened at the sound of my name, but I barely heard her. A thrill rocked through me as I watched Carl straighten slowly as if waking from a deep sleep. Color returned to his skin; his face suddenly looked fuller as a healthy pink spread through it. His eyes searched the hallway as if he could sense someone had helped him.

Jack suddenly pulled me back and cursed under his breath.

"Who's down there?" Flex called. The crash of his chair falling over sounded.

Jack looked down at me, his eyes tense. "No matter what, stay hidden. Dr. Ply can't have you."

"No—" I whispered, but it was too late.

Jack stepped out into the hall. "It's just me, Flex." His voice sounded calm and unbothered.

Fear crashed into me as I watched Jack standing alone in the hallway. I didn't know how to help him; all I had was the dust.

"What are *you* doing here?" Anna hissed. "You're supposed to be in the Dark Woods."

"I know. I saw someone creeping around and followed them back into the castle, but I lost them. Have you seen anyone?"

I could feel the tension in the air, as if they knew Jack was lying, but couldn't accuse him of it.

"Is someone with you?" Anna sounded suspicious.

"No," Jack said easily.

"Flex, check."

"There's no need for that. Either you trust me or you don't."

"I don't," Anna snapped.

Jack coughed. "*Run . . .*"

I didn't want to leave Jack, but I couldn't let them find me. I turned as quietly as I could and hurried back down the hall.

Behind me, I heard Flex shout and Anna yell Carl's name. I hesitated, nearly turning around. Was Carl helping us . . . or was he helping them?

I slowed, torn between leaving and staying. I heard Jack and Flex yelling, and then the sound of a fist hitting skin. No, I wasn't leaving Jack.

I spun around just as my head connected with something hard.

I groaned and crumbled onto the stone floor.

———

MY HEAD FELT AS IF IT WAS PACKED WITH COTTON. MY eyes struggled to open and I couldn't move. I flexed my fingers, but something tight was binding my arms and wrist. My eyes fluttered open in panic.

I was in the Dome room.

This time, I was strapped to the chair.

Dr. Ply was sitting in front of me.

My mind felt like a muddy pond; my thoughts didn't connect or make sense. I only knew I had to get out. *Now.* I struggled against the chair, but my bonds were too tight.

"I'm not sure how you got out, Ivy. But you've made it abundantly clear that you are going to be a bigger problem than I anticipated. You've left me with no choice." Dr. Ply's voice was grave.

My eyes flashed to where Anna was standing behind him. Her grey eyes stared back, detached and impassive. I sighed. Her skin reminded me of Carl's: deathly white, like looking at a corpse. She was a broken doll, devoid of feeling and empathy.

"I would like to know how you managed to break the lock," Dr. Ply asked conversationally.

As if I was not strapped to a chair against my will.

As if he was not preparing to ruin me.

"Why don't you extract the memory yourself?" I whispered, my voice thick.

Anger flashed across his face before he tamed it. "Why don't you tell me what you *really* think of my work, before you can't anymore?"

"I'll be glad to, you monster. You ruin people with work that doesn't even matter. Everything you've done has failed. You're a pathetic scientist. All you create is people with no soul, like her." My eyes cut to Anna, who looked at me without blinking.

Dr. Ply glanced at her and disregarded her immediately. "She'll be no help to you, I'm afraid."

"And Carl?"

He hesitated and folded his hands around his round middle. "What about him?"

I needed to delay him as long as I could. "He's better now. Don't you wonder how that happened?"

"I don't have to wonder. I'll see him in the lab tomorrow and examine him. And by then, you'll be back in Windermere with no memory of this."

Rage built inside of me and it helped cut through the fog. "You're a fraud. You're a sad excuse for a human. I wish my father had stopped you."

"Yes, well. *Your father* was pathetic. What did *he* ever accomplish?"

"People respected him."

Dr. Ply frowned. "Now, if you're quite finished with your childish insults, I can begin. You can thank me for that later; I've discovered it's better to get all these unpleasant thoughts and feelings out of my subject's mind before I intervene."

I fumed; anger coursed through my body. My father wasn't pathetic—he'd given me power, a power that would bring down this castle.

A power that I didn't need my hands to wield.

The dust rose from my bag and hovered above the machine as I thought about wrapping it around Dr. Ply . . . then I stopped, because what would that change? Neither he nor Anna would unbind me if I attacked them.

Anna.

I looked at her cold, emotionless face and knew what I had to do, even if it wouldn't save me.

The machine whirled to life as I sent the glimmering dust into Anna, just like I'd done for Carl. Again, it found every piece of her skin and sunk in. Light coursed through her; the whiteness of her skin turned peach. Her eyes lit up and she took in a deep breath, as if she had been drowning and was coming up for air.

A sharp sting of electricity snapped through me, tearing a scream from my throat.

Every nerve in my body jolted with pain and shock as I arched back in the chair. My mind was on fire.

The pain faded as quickly as it started. Sweet relief filled my body. I opened my eyes . . . and gasped.

Anna stood over Dr. Ply's body, crumbled on the floor.

ANNA'S EYES FILLED WITH TEARS. "ARE YOU ALRIGHT?"

I nodded, speechless. "Is he alive?"

"Just unconscious." She moved quickly to untie me from the chair. I sat up and rubbed my arms, studying her face as she worked to free my feet. I couldn't believe she was helping me.

Anna looked completely different. There was a helpfulness and a sweetness to her face that hadn't been there before. Tears continued to stream down her cheeks.

"Can you stand? I didn't give you much of the tonic; its effects should be nearly worn off by now."

I forced myself to my feet, wincing, and held my head.

"Sorry about that," Anna said sheepishly.

"You have a talent for knocking people out. Wait! Where is Jack?"

"I'll take you to him. Do you have any more of whatever it was you gave me?"

"I hope so," I said, looking into my bag, hoping all the dust wasn't gone. "Why? Do you need more?"

She shook her head as more tears fell. "Not for me. For the others."

Oh. I quickly looked inside the boxes. Dust glimmered up at me. "Yes!"

"Let's go."

We left Dr. Ply on the ground and rushed out into the hall.

"Ivy! Thank God," Jack shouted from the other end of the hall. His shirt was torn and the side of his face was scraped. The door to the lab was open behind him; I saw Flex's legs spread out on the ground like a massive felled tree. Carl stepped out from behind Jack. His posture was straight and his face was full of light, just like Anna's was now.

"Impressive," I said, smiling.

"All Carl," Jack said, rushing up to me. "I heard you scream. Are you alright?" He looked like he was going to jump between me and Anna, but his step faltered when he saw she was crying.

"I'm so sorry I told Flex to attack you," Anna sobbed. "Please forgive me."

He looked at me, shocked. "What did you *do* to her?"

I grinned, watching Carl stare at Anna in awe. "Just reminded her of who she was. Anna knocked Dr. Ply out and saved me. Now she wants to help us save the other Transposers."

"Oh. Well, thanks." Jack looked at her skeptically, like he didn't quite believe it was her.

Anna nodded. "I'll never work for Dr. Ply or the Count again."

Carl stepped closer to her. "Me either."

Jack ran a hand through his hair. "Why don't you fill me in as we go."

We hurried down the hall, and I explained everything that happened in the room and what I wanted to do next.

Jack nodded. "I'll find Cora and Ember. Carl will stay with you and Anna. Meet in the tower."

I nodded. Jack hugged me tightly before we split up.

Anna, Carl, and I hurried through the garden and into the conservatory. We raced past the plants and out the back door, into the hidden alley of vines my father had planted and beyond, to the circular tower.

I was going to finish what he'd started thanks to his faith in me and my ability to solve his clues. I finally had.

I looked back at Anna and Carl, still not quite believing they were cured. Carl hummed with energy. Anna looked remorseful and thoughtful.

After we made it up the three winding flights of stairs to the infirmary, I knocked on the door. Lane answered; when she saw Anna, a look of fury crossed her face, and she blocked the entry protectively.

"What is *she* doing here?"

"She's cured, Lane," I said, stepping forward. "So is Carl. We came to help the others."

Lane looked shocked as she took in the new Carl and Anna. Cora raced up the stairs with York and Jack behind her. Even she stopped and looked at Anna and Carl in surprise.

A smile lit up her face. "Incredible!"

"Where's Ember?" I asked, worried, looking behind her.

Cora's smile faded. "I'm not sure." She looked at Anna.

Anna shook her head. "I left her in the South Wing; if she's not there, I don't know where she went. I promise."

Cora nodded. "Do what you have to quickly, Ivy. Then we'll find Ember."

I nodded as Lane stepped aside to let me into the silent room with the men lying in their beds. I called the shimmering dust out of my bag once more and it floated overhead, stretching out in perfect lines to reach each man.

All around the room, one by one, eyes began to open.

FORTY-ONE

The Count

The Count cracked his knuckles impatiently.

Something was wrong—he could *feel* it in the air. An hour had passed since Anna had knocked on the secret door and beckoned to Dr. Ply, interrupting their planning. The doctor had yet to return.

The Count stood and walked over to the window, considering his next steps. This was the most hopeful he had been in years. Everything was finally working in his favor. He had York, who was gifted; Ember, who was a surprise; and the golden acorns, which were the key to it all.

How could anything go wrong now?

Whitecaps rolled on the deep blue sea. He turned his gaze away and upward into the mountains. Stars were just beginning to light up the sky, reminding him of the treks up the mountain in his youth. It was time to go back. Now that he had the acorns, he was sure to find the White Forest. He would order Jack to organize a trip as soon as possible.

Behind him, his door opened so quietly he shouldn't have heard it. He turned, expecting Dr. Ply to apologize for entering without knocking, but it wasn't the doctor or his staff.

It was the girl.

Ember.

She walked into the room, staring at him with violet eyes that reminded him of Velora and Sebastian and that whole forgotten island in the deep sea. She didn't appear afraid, which unnerved him for only a second. He despised her for that. For that moment, her composure reminded him of someone else.

"You are trespassing in my personal, private study. Where is Dr. Ply?"

"Obviously not with me."

"Did he send you?" the Count asked impatiently.

"No. I don't take orders from him," she responded, calmly. "Or you."

The Count inhaled sharply, taken back by her boldness. This would not stand. No one spoke to him like this. No one burst into his private library.

Her eyes swept over him, and then the room, studying the surfaces of tables and shelves as if looking for something.

"What do you want? Leave now and go back to the lab."

"No, I don't think so."

She opened her hand, revealing a short branch with shoots of green buds. She took a deep breath and he watched, speechless, as the branch grew and more branches sprouted from it. They spread like vines throughout the room. Leaves multiplied and sprouted, and acted as hands, turning over books and bottles, opening pages of books, and searching.

The Count could only watch, frozen and fascinated, as a branch made its way to him. Leaves touched his neck and shoulders and then retreated. The branches shrank down and receded back into the short branch once again in her hand.

The Count blinked.

She stared at him again. "Nothing is left."

The words made no sense, but he'd known where she was from the moment the branch began to grow.

"You're from there. The White Forest," he choked out.

She tipped her head slightly. "The place you are trying to destroy."

"No. No. Not destroy . . ."

"Then what? Why do you want to return so badly?" She tilted her head and studied him as if looking for anything worthy within him. He didn't like the scrutiny but was compelled to answer honestly.

"Because of *her*."

"Airlend."

He nodded, not trusting his voice.

"You wish her peace?"

The Count hesitated and her face changed instantly.

"When did you know where I was from?" she asked.

"Just now."

"And what do you see when you look at me?"

He studied her, cursing himself for his blindness. "Her."

"Nothing else?"

"No." The Count shook his head, angry at her question. Who was she to question him? He was the one who questioned others. "What should I see?" he bit out.

Her face was suddenly carved from stone, and he wondered what he had said to cause the change.

"You are never to return there again. Stop trying. There is nothing for you there. Only destruction. If you come back, I will destroy you myself."

He bristled at her orders and was about to respond when the branch shot out from her hand again, spiraling and twisting toward him like an arrow aiming for his heart.

The spiraling leaves and branch had sharpened into a fine point, and it stopped just inches from his chest. He looked down at the branch, which was writhing as if it wanted to complete the kill, but was being held back.

He looked away from the branch and back up at her. "It will take much more than that to intimidate me."

"Then that will be your downfall."

The branch receded back into her hand and without another word or look in his direction, she turned and left the room, shutting the door behind her.

The Count jumped up and rushed to the door, but it was locked. As was his secret door.

He was locked in.

FORTY-TWO

My head spun with everything that had happened tonight.

After the transposers awoke, there had been more tears and hugging. York had met his grandfather, Thomas, a moment I would never forget. They had the same mannerisms, and I could tell that York was more like his grandfather than anyone else in his family.

Seeing them reunite made me miss my parents so badly that my heart ached.

Another plan had to be made. Most of the transposers were from Stygian; Anna agreed to help Lane get them all to the Stygian ship tonight since we couldn't take them with us. Thomas had asked to go back to Windermere, but it was too soon for that. The Count would check there first. So Thomas agreed to go to Stygian with the others until we knew he was truly safe from the Count. Cora fluttered around everyone, looking so relieved and happy that she practically glowed as she organized everything.

After we watched the group fade into the woods toward the ship, we hurried into the stable where the horses stood ready, saddled, and full of bags.

Loon was waiting, and I flung my arms around her, relieved.

I heard gasps and looked up to see Ember rush into the stable. She was holding a small stick, and she looked around as if counting everyone.

"Ember! Where were you?" Cora asked, drawing her into a hug.

"I'm fine. Let's get far away from here," Ember said.

Cora nodded. "Let's go."

York went to help Ember with her horse. I leaned against Loon, surprised at how everything had worked out. It was unbelievable, really.

"Need help up?" Jack asked, suddenly right next to me.

I jumped, making him laugh. "Sorry!"

I smiled as he helped me mount Loon. She whinnied and stomped her feet, excited by the crisp night air and the promise of a ride. My life at the castle was over.

Relief pulsed through me. I was making it out, surrounded by the people I cared about most. York and I hadn't been ruined after all.

I felt excited—hopeful, even. The White Forest would be my biggest adventure yet.

Jack mounted his black horse next to me.

"Ready?" he asked everyone.

I glanced at Cora, who was watching me intently. Something in her expression caused the excitement to fade and my heart skipped a beat.

"What is it?" I asked, panicking that something had gone wrong, that Cora had kept something from us.

"Before we head to the White Forest, we need to make a stop," Cora said without taking her eyes from mine.

"What? No, we can't . . ." Ember protested.

Everything slowed. All I could focus on was Cora's face.

Something was about to change.

"Cora?" My voice sounded far away and my head was suddenly too light. "What stop?"

"I hope you have more dust, Ivy. Because your father *is* alive. And you're going to cure him."

FORTY-THREE

The Count

The Count paced the room, turning the encounter with the girl over and over in his mind.

Who was she that Airlend had sent her? Why had she asked if he saw something in her? What was there to see? He couldn't make sense of it. All he knew was that he was very, very angry.

He felt like a caged animal. She had kept him locked him in here the entire night. And where the devil was Dr. Ply?

The lock on his secret door clicked.

The Count turned to see Dr. Ply walk into the room. The long night had left its mark, and his head was bloodied. There was something else in his expression—defeat.

"What happened?" the Count demanded. Every nerve in his body waited to be reassured.

Dr. Ply sank into the chair, the weight of his body sounding like a bag of flour being dropped on the floor. He rubbed his head.

"They're gone. All of them," he said wearily. "Cora, Ember, York, Ivy, and Jack. Gone."

"*Gone where?*"

Dr. Ply continued in his defeated tone as if the Count had not spoken. "They took all the acorns; even the one locked in my office."

The Count seethed with anger, trembling all over.

"There is more."

The Count turned the full wrath of his eyes on the doctor and watched him shrink beneath it.

"*How could there possibly be more?*"

"Ember's tree is destroyed. I saw it myself this morning. It's now as black as the others, as if it was burned. It's utterly ruined."

The Count turned back to the window again so he would not kill the doctor in this blind rage.

"The retired Transposers are gone. Anna and Carl are missing, or else lost and hurt. Or perhaps they are gone too. I found Flex knocked out; he didn't know anything. I'm sorry."

The Count stared up into the mountains. A cloud blotted out the sun and a shadow fell over the castle. A coldness crept through him. He'd lost it all—*again*. His transposers, the acorns, and the tree.

"Every transposer is gone?"

"Yes."

"And our supply of wood?"

"Out."

The Count turned back to the doctor, trying to salvage something. This would not be the end for him. "They don't have much of a head start. I'll go after them."

"All the horses are gone. The stables are cleared out," Dr. Ply said, wincing.

All his prize horses.

"*Then get horses from Windermere.* And if you tell me one more thing is impossible, I will kill you myself."

Dr. Ply paled. "I'll send someone right away. But who will go after them? We would have sent Jack, but he is gone."

Jack's betrayal hit the Count deeply. He had trusted him as much as he had trusted the man sitting across from him. A critical mistake.

One he would never make again. A thought occurred to him.

"Are you *sure* Jack went willingly?"

Dr. Ply shook his head. "Anna saw him in the hallway with Ivy. He was also seen going into my office with her and taking the acorn hidden there."

The Count turned back toward the window, thinking.

"Perhaps Jack only went with them because he couldn't stop them. Perhaps he intends to inform us of their whereabouts. He has been with me for a long time. I can't understand why he would turn on me now that I was considering naming him my heir."

"Yes, I considered that possibility," Dr. Ply responded. "He left this in the cabinet in place of the acorn. Does it mean anything to you?"

The Count turned as Dr. Ply set a white knight on the table. Confused, the Count looked over at his black-and-white marble chessboard. It was still set up from his last game with Jack, where his white queen had checkmated Jack's black king. He'd won.

But Jack hadn't been playing chess on that board.

He had been playing in life.

Checkmate.

For a moment, the Count could not speak as brilliant white anger coursed through every vein in his body.

He walked swiftly across the room and knocked the table over; the pieces shattered as they hit the floor. Dr. Ply jumped in his seat.

The Count slowly bent and picked up the white queen. It was the only piece that did not break. He squeezed it tightly in his hand as if he could choke Airlend Frost herself. *The white queen always won.*

But he would not let her win—not like this.

The Count gripped the white queen and looked back at the tender base of the doctor's throat. He straightened as he watched the artery pulse there, nervously. His thumb stroked the queen in his hand. A proper plunge with the edge of the crown could do enough damage that the doctor would bleed out on the floor in a matter of moments . . .

What did he need him for anymore, anyway?

He had ruined everything.

He deserved to be the first to pay.

The doctor's Adam's apple bobbed as he swallowed thickly. "Alexander?"

The Count hadn't heard that name in a long time, and he never wanted to hear it again. The last time it had been spoken to him, it had come from the scarlet lips of Airlend Frost . . . he had not allowed anyone to repeat it in his presence since.

The doctor would pay for this mistake too.

Just as the Count was raising his hand, an idea seized him.

Dr. Ply cowered in his chair, his eyes darting between the Count's face and the queen his hand.

The Count's arm lowered.

Dr. Ply swallowed in relief.

The Count turned back toward the window, thinking.

"I *made* Jack. I taught him the lay of the woods. I will find his trail and go after them. You will stay here. Someone has to look after the castle."

Dr. Ply nodded quickly, sagging in relief.

"I need at least fifteen strong men—and hurry. I'll leave within the hour."

Although he was tired, Dr. Ply ran from the room.

Looking out the window, a surge of adrenaline awakened every fiber of the Count's being. He had been in this library for far too many years.

He belonged out there.

In the wild.

He would take back what they'd stolen—and he would make them *all* pay dearly for their betrayal. He studied the white queen in his hand.

First, he would let them lead him to the White Forest.

ACKNOWLEDGMENTS

This book has been a journey! It was the first book I ever wrote and it took me many years to figure out how this story wanted to be told. Everyone says don't publish your first book, but I couldn't leave this one in a drawer. Instead, I set it aside, wrote other books, took writing courses, and read nonstop to learn how to tell a better story. I'm very proud of what it's become.

To my editor, Megan McCullough, thank you for your detailed eye. To Krafigs Designs, thank you for another amazing cover! To Kim Churchill, thank you for lending your magic to the audiobook.

To my beta readers, Laura Tiffany, Raina Bray, Holly Schacht, Lauren Terry, Anika Watkins, Josh Schacht, and Aaron Petersen, thank you for your excellent feedback!

To my parents, who let me roam free. And to my dad, who noticed an important detail that is now an essential part of book three's plot, thank you!

And you, reader. Thank you for befriending Ivy and loving this world! I hope you found a place to escape and were entertained and intrigued. Books are magic and I love sharing my worlds with you!

To my family, Aaron, Kennedy, and London. Thank you for supporting me and giving me time to write. I couldn't have done it without each of you.

Lastly, thank you, God. For always watching out for me.

About the Author

Sara Knightly is a recovering nomad who lives in Boise, ID with her husband and two daughters. She spends her days dreaming up the next story idea, searching for the perfect coffee shop, and planning another trip to the Redwood Forest.

Turn The Page For More . . .

Forest Ever White

Chapter One

The moon gleamed like a giant eye, watching our group ride further away from the Count's castle.

We passed beneath the Count's forest, the dark canopy above painting us with crooked shadows. I kept Loon at a generous distance from everyone, a torrent of emotions swirling within me. We must have ridden an hour already, but I was unwilling to speak to Cora yet—to *anyone*. I was having trouble digesting the news she had sprung on me before our escape.

My father was still alive.

He hadn't died ten years ago.

You're going to cure him too.

A soft neigh sounded behind me. I turned, seeing York and Ember riding silently behind me. Even though she was on a horse, Ember looked small next to York. Her long black hair was swept behind her shoulders, and her delicate face looked pale in the moonlight, but her violet eyes shone back at me as she nodded encouragingly. Beside her, my best friend offered me a smile, but his brown eyes looked troubled.

I turned back around, appreciating the space they were giving me to process Cora's announcement. I knew they each would be beside me in an instant if I showed I needed them, but I didn't. Not yet.

I stared numbly ahead at Jack's strong silhouette and dark hair. Next to him, Cora swayed gracefully on her tall, black horse. From what I overheard, Jack was insisting we take a longer route to wherever my father was, to throw off the Count, who was surely coming after us after what we had just done. But Cora shook her head, holding firm to our path.

It wasn't lost on me that *Cora* was leading us through the woods, even though Jack was the expert.

She had made this journey many times.

I remembered the first time I met her in the castle. I had snuck out of my room and Jack found me. He'd taken me to see the Count's horses. When Cora had flown into the stable, she'd been concealed under a dark cloak. She had just returned from a long ride and made us swear not to tell anyone we'd seen her.

Now I knew she had been to see my father.

I'd trusted her and she'd lied to me. Cora had lied to me every time I'd asked her if my father was alive.

My heart burned even more than it ached.

I gripped my reins tighter as that burning anger swelled within me. Loon tensed, so I quickly let the reins go and breathed in deeply, allowing the scent of moss, leaves, and the soft glow of moonlight to soothe me. I had to calm down and think rationally. But we had been through so much tonight, and I was tired.

Fireflies began to fill the darkness with flashes of light.

The shimmering dots reminded me of the dust I had commanded in the Dome Room, where Dr. Ply broke people with magic. Only hours ago, he had locked me in there, planning to modify my memory. But I'd managed to finally solve my father's clues and escape.

My father had written clues in the last journal he'd kept, and now I knew that in his countless references to the sprawling ivy *Hedera*, he had not been talking about a plant all along, but *me*. With my father's words to guide me, I'd used my magic to commandeer the dust. It had listened. I was still amazed when I remembered how the dust had turned into shimmering vines and glowed as it climbed up the wall and crushed the stone around the lock in the Dome Room. After I escaped, I used the same dust to cure the people Dr. Ply had destroyed in his experiments: His assistant Anna; Carl, my old class-mate from Windermere; and the four other retired Transposers.

Goosebumps rose on my arms. Their healing had been amazing to behold. When the dust absorbed into their dull, life-less skin, they had been restored to their right minds and filled with a warm, living glow. Even their formerly emotionless eyes sparked with light as their life's essence was returned to them. We'd gotten them safely away on a ship to Stygian, far away from the Count and Dr. Ply.

Once we found my father, our group would head to meet Ember's mother, Airlend Frost, the Keeper of the White Forest. A land of magic and power.

A land the Count had been so desperate to find that he'd sought out people with magic for the sole purpose of stripping it away from them so he could use it for himself.

Of course the Count would follow us. If not tonight, tomorrow.

We were losing time by going to see my father first.

I swallowed. What state would he be in? Was he ruined, like the retired Transposers; laying in a bed, staring lifelessly up at the ceiling, wasting away? Or had he been left like Anna and Carl; with the ability to function, but cold and emotionless? I wasn't sure which would be worse.

You're going to cure him too.

The pit in my stomach deepened. It had been ten years since I'd last seen my father. So much had happened. I had grown and changed into a different person. Surely, he had too.

Did I even have enough dust left to cure him? Was *that* why Cora had waited to reveal this to me until now? Because now there was hope that *I* could cure my father, where there had been none before?

My anger receded like a wave. Perhaps this omission from Cora had been one of kindness.

More of Cora and Jack's whispers drifted back to me.

A swift stream cut through the path ahead of us, racing over the rocks. Instead of crossing it, Cora led her horse into it. The fast current flowed around her horse's legs.

Jack hesitated and I stopped Loon beside him. Ember and York paused next to us.

"What are you doing?" Jack asked Cora.

Cora turned in her saddle toward us, the moonlight highlighting her beautiful face. It was hard to hold on to any anger when Cora turned her warm, sympathetic gaze on mine. She seemed to understand that I was struggling. Her emerald eyes held mine before I looked away.

"We walk through the water about a mile before going west," Cora said to Jack. "This way we leave no tracks."

My eyes darted back to Cora in surprise. Surely my father had not been so nearby these past ten years?

"And where is it we're going?" Jack sounded impatient. "I can't guide us safety if you don't tell me."

"There is no time to plan another route now. When we make it to camp, we'll talk." Cora turned around and urged her horse forward.

Jack huffed out an exasperated breath. "How long do you expect the horses to walk over wet stones in the dark?"

"We're losing time."

Jack sighed as Cora splashed out of sight. Then he turned to me. "Are you alright?"

I stared at him. Tonight everything had changed between us. Just a few hours ago, he had kissed me. I had felt excited and hopeful about us. That was before I'd learned my father was alive. If Jack had kept this from me too, it would change everything.

"Did you know?" I whispered, holding his blue eyes with

mine.

Jack exhaled. "No, Ivy. I swear. I had no idea he was alive, or that Cora knew."

Relief flooded me. I couldn't take any more betrayal tonight. It helped to know that Ember, York, and Jack had been just as surprised as I was.

"It will be alright," Jack said gently. "No matter what happens, we're all in this with you."

I looked over to see York and Ember both nod solemnly. Ember smiled softly as if to say it would be alright. My eyes skipped to York, my best friend since childhood. He had known my father, known what these last ten years of my life had been like without him. A lump formed in my throat. York's presence was familiar and reassuring, but even he had changed in the castle. He looked as if he was battling his own emotions now.

York shrugged at me. "He's alive. That's good news, right?"

I twisted the reins in my hands. "Cora said he's ruined. What if I can't help him?"

"We won't know until we see him." Ember's soft voice cut through the darkness. "Until then, don't dwell on the worst."

I nodded, the tightness in my throat easing. I had spent a decade surviving in Windermere without my father. I had spent a year in the Count's castle without anyone until I'd made these friends. I wasn't alone anymore. Whatever was ahead, I could face it with them by my side.

Cora's voice floated back to us above the bubbling water. "Still coming?"

"Right behind you," Jack said. He reached out and held Loon's halter as he led our horses into the water. A moment later, York and Ember splashed in behind us.

Ember was right. I shouldn't expect the worst just yet. Knowing my father was alive was good news.

When we stopped to make camp, I planned to make Cora tell me everything.

I was done with secrets.